Published by Rogue Press.
Editing by Katie Jackson



For more information, contact author Nina Jarrett. www.ninajarrett.com

# THE HIDDEN LORD

INCONVENIENT VENTURES

BOOK TWO

NINA JARRETT

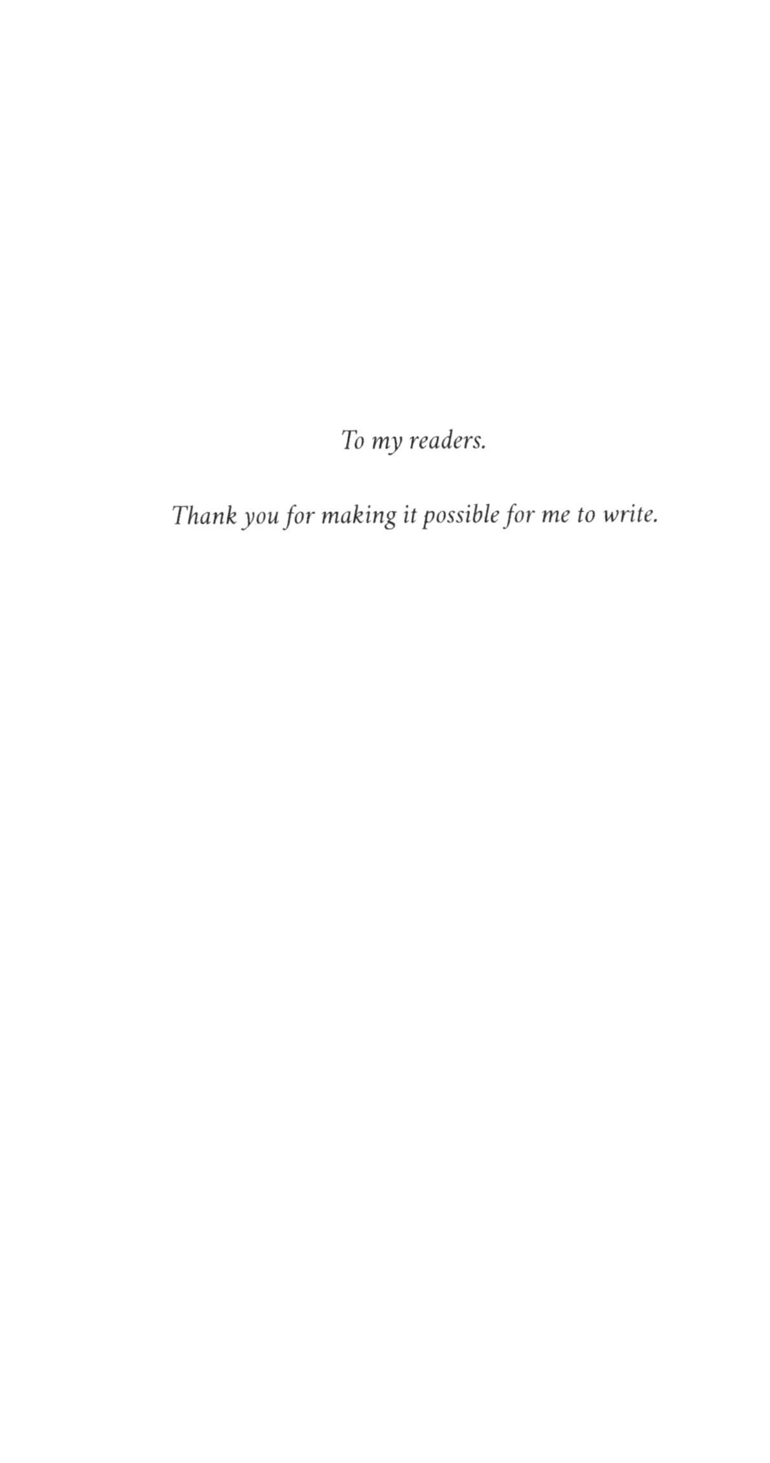

*To my readers.*

*Thank you for making it possible for me to write.*

# PROLOGUE

*"For there may no man do more than his heart will suffer him."*

**Sir Thomas Malory, *Le Morte d'Arthur***

* * *

MARCH 13, 1794, TRENWITH ABBEY

The wheels crunched to a halt on the gravel drive, and Gabriel pressed his small face to the window, watching as servants in livery emerged from the imposing stone façade of Trenwith Abbey. The house loomed before him like a fortress, all gray stone and sharp angles beneath a pewter sky that promised rain. He clutched his traveling case, a battered leather thing that had belonged to Papa, and tried to swallow the knot in his throat that had been there since the fever took them both.

Five-year-old Gabriel Strathmore stepped down from the carriage on unsteady legs, his black mourning coat too large for his thin frame, the sleeves hanging past his wrists. The March wind cut through the wool, and he shivered as he was led up the wide stone steps by a footman who did not speak to him.

The entrance hall was vast and cold, with marble floors that echoed his small footsteps and portraits of stern-faced ancestors staring down from gilt frames. Gabriel had never been to Grandfather's house before. Papa had said the old man did not care for children, and now Gabriel understood why. Everything here was hard and silent and unwelcoming.

"His lordship will see the boy in the library," announced the butler, a thin man with disapproving eyes.

Gabriel was led through corridors that stretched on forever, past closed doors and shadowy alcoves, until they reached a room lined floor to ceiling with books. A fire crackled in the grate, but it gave no warmth to the chamber. Behind a massive mahogany desk sat an elderly man with steel-gray hair and cold blue eyes. Beside the fireplace stood another man, younger though no less forbidding, with fair hair and the same sharp features. This must be Uncle James, Papa's older brother.

"So," said the viscount without preamble, not rising from his chair, "you are Charles's boy."

Gabriel nodded, his throat too tight to speak. He wished to speak, to say how he would be good and quiet and cause no trouble, but the words would not come.

"What am I to do with you?" Grandfather continued, his voice as cutting as the wintry wind outside. "Your father never possessed an ounce of sense, marrying your mother against my wishes. And now they are both dead, leaving me to clean up their muddle."

The words struck Gabriel like physical blows. Papa had been the kindest, gentlest man in the world, and Mama had sung to him every night before bed. They were not a muddle.

They were everything good and warm and safe, and now they were gone forever.

"Well?" The old man's voice sharpened. "Have you nothing to say for yourself? What am I to do with you now?"

Gabriel tried to be brave, tried to stand straight as Papa had taught him, but his lower lip began to tremble despite his best efforts. "I-I could be good, sir," he whispered. "I could be very good and quiet, and I would not be any trouble, I promise."

But even as he spoke, hot tears began to spill down his cheeks, and he could not stop them. They came in a rush, carrying with them all the grief and terror and loneliness of the past fortnight. He pressed his hands to his face, trying to muffle the sobs that shook his small frame.

"Good God," Uncle James said with disgust, turning away from the fireplace. "Look at the state of him. Carrying on like a girl."

Grandfather's expression hardened further. "Cease this display immediately," he commanded. "You are a Strathmore, boy, and Strathmores do not weep and wail like common peasants."

But Gabriel could not stop. The tears came harder now, great gulping sobs that echoed in the vast room. He wanted his mama to hold him and sing away the sadness. He wanted Papa to lift him onto his shoulders and tell him stories about brave knights. He wanted to go home to the little house with its warm kitchen and soft cushions and the smell of Mama's lavender water.

"This is intolerable," Uncle James said, his voice clipped with distaste. "The boy is clearly unfit for civilized company."

"Indeed." Grandfather rose from behind his desk, walking over to tower over Gabriel like a stern monument. "I will not have such unseemly behavior in my house. You will learn to govern yourself, or you will be sent away."

Gabriel tried to speak, tried to apologize, but he could only hiccup and sob, his small chest heaving with the force of his grief.

The viscount's mouth tightened into a hard line. "Hartwell," he called to the butler, who appeared in the doorway as if he had been waiting. "Fetch Mr. Dutton from the carriage. Tell him there has been a change of plans."

Gabriel's legs felt weak. Mr. Dutton was Grandfather's man of business. The stern, silent man who had collected him from the house where his parents had died.

"Very good, my lord."

"The boy will be taken to Oxford immediately," Grandfather commented to his oldest son, his voice devoid of warmth. "I shall tell Dutton to find a suitable tutor. Someone who can teach proper conduct and rid the child of this unseemly weakness. I will provide funds for room, board, and instruction, but I will not have such disgraceful behavior under my roof."

Gabriel felt the floor tilt beneath his feet. They were sending him away? But he had only just arrived. "Please," he managed between sobs, "I can be better. I can be quiet. Please do not send me away."

"You should have thought of that before making such a spectacle," Uncle James said coldly. "Perhaps a few years with a proper tutor will beat some sense into you."

Minutes later, Mr. Dutton appeared, nodding curtly at the viscount's instructions. He placed a firm hand on Gabriel's shoulder without speaking.

As Gabriel was led away, still crying, he heard his grandfather's voice drift from the library. "Five years old and already displaying such weakness. Thank God Charles did not live to see what manner of son he raised."

Gabriel found himself back in the cold entrance hall, his small traveling case still sitting where the footman had left it.

Mr. Dutton checked his pocket watch with the same detached efficiency he had shown throughout the dreadful journey from Gabriel's former home.

"Come along, boy," he said quietly. "The carriage is waiting."

As they stepped outside into the freezing wind, Gabriel turned back once to see his grandfather standing in the distant library window, watching their departure with the same cold expression. Uncle James stood beside him, already turning away as if Gabriel had ceased to exist the moment he left the room.

The carriage door closed with a final, condemning click, leaving Gabriel with the terrible understanding that he was truly unwanted. He pressed his face against the worn leather seat and wept for everything he had lost. His parents, his home, and now even the hope that family might provide some comfort in his sorrow.

Gabriel knew he would have to learn to bury such feelings deep, where they could not be seen. But that afternoon, as the wheels rolled away from Trenwith Abbey forever and Mr. Dutton pointedly paid him no mind, he cried himself into exhausted sleep and dreamed of his mama's gentle hands smoothing away his tears.

# CHAPTER 1

*"Ye shall see wonders and hid things."*

**Sir Thomas Malory, *Le Morte d'Arthur***

* * *

DECEMBER 20, 1821, LONDON

Miss Henrietta Bigsby reread the page for the thousandth time. Uncle Reggie was in the country, attending a house party for the holidays. Her mother, as proprietress of the preeminent stone manufactory in all of England, if not the world, was managing a large order. Her twin, Maddy, was away in Scotland with her new husband, touring his estates, and Henri was ... bored.

Her work as private secretary to Uncle Reggie, a former member of Parliament and now political advisor to Westminster, kept her active and occupied, but now that she had all this time on her hands, Henri found herself chewing on a recent remark from her mother. The words still echoed in her mind from the night of Madeline's nuptials, held right here in the walled garden where she currently sat.

*"Henri is not good at keeping secrets."*

Eleanor Bigsby had laughed, unaware she had shaken Henri to her core. Being a perfectionist in all things, it was appalling to realize she had a reputation for gossip. Hardly an admirable trait!

Which was why it had been sitting heavy on her soul while she wrestled with what to do about this hitherto unsuspected character flaw. Henri was competitive by nature, and it did not sit well that she was inferior in this regard.

Sighing, she put the book beside her on the bench and leaned her head back against the large stone urn, which was the centerpiece of the walled garden. Truly, she wished she could have discussed the matter with Maddy before her departure to Scotland, but Henri had been busy preparing Uncle Reggie for his trip to the country, and it was only after his departure that she had had time to herself.

She was dismayed by how frequently she had been mulling such an inconsequential remark, but surely, there must be some way for her to break the habit while she found herself with too little to do during the holidays?

*Bah, why can I not shake these thoughts? It has been weeks since Mama's comment! If only Maddy had not left so suddenly, then we might have discussed this.*

The scrunch of heavy footsteps on the garden path alerted her that she was being joined by at least two of the residents from the property next door. This garden was shared with the Baron of Blackwood, who resided with his family on the matching estate and who had numerous houseguests of late. She wondered if she should announce her presence when she heard the quiet thud of something heavy being placed down. On the garden bench on the other side of the urn, perhaps?

A deep and cultured voice she did not recognize broke the silence of the winter afternoon.

"What are you doing?"

The voice of an Italian gentleman responded. "This oil … it is not oil."

There was a pause, then the Italian continued. "It is tempera."

"Tempera?"

The Italian explained with a bemused tone. "Artists sometimes used this technique to hide things. Tempera is an egg-based paint. Messages. Secrets. It can be layered over oil to conceal what is beneath. But the nature of the paint, the way it dries, the way it absorbs light, it does not behave quite the same way."

"Are you saying there is something beneath this painting?"

Henri arched her brows. What fresh intrigue was this?

Then, realizing what she was about, she winced. Perhaps she did have a personality flaw. Nevertheless, she rose to her feet and hesitated again about announcing her presence.

"That is exactly what I am saying. But only parts of it. Matteo wrote to his sister to point the way to this painting. And in this painting, he left a message. When we remove the tempera, we reveal the true oil beneath."

Henri walked around the urn and realized she was looking at Lord Sebastian, the towering blond brother of the Duke of Halmesbury. Both brothers had the appearance of warriors descended from Valhalla to walk amongst mere mortals, and there could be no mistaking the family resemblance. He stood with his arms crossed, watching as a tall, lean Italian man delicately rubbed at the surface of a painting with his handkerchief, his dark brows furrowed in concentration. The afternoon light bathed the garden, filtering through the bare branches of the trees and lending an almost ethereal glow to the painting.

"See here," the Italian murmured, more to himself than to Lord Sebastian, as he swiped another careful stroke over the lower portion of the painting. "The tempera layer is fragile, prone to flaking when dry. But look beneath it, the colors are richer. Deeper. Oil paint. And I suspect something more."

Lord Sebastian exhaled sharply, glancing between his friend and the painting. "You truly believe there is a hidden message?"

"I know there is," his companion answered, his voice tinged with excitement. "The sixteenth-century masters were clever, Sebastian. They used layers like this to obscure secrets. Sometimes to mask knowledge, sometimes to conceal messages meant only for a particular viewer." He wiped again, and beneath the faded film of tempera, something more distinct began to emerge.

Lord Sebastian took a step closer, clearly curious.

Henri could not see the painting well with both men obscuring her view, so she decided it was time they noticed her presence.

"I say, what are you gentlemen up to?"

Lord Sebastian started, instinctively adjusting his stance. Beside him, his friend straightened abruptly, his fingers pausing mid-motion on the painting. Both men turned toward her.

"Lady Campbell?" Lord Sebastian queried, recovering first, his voice tinged with wariness.

Henri grinned. "Ah, no. I fear you have mistaken me for my twin."

She stepped forward, hands tucked into the folds of her stylish spencer.

"Miss Henrietta Bigsby, at your service. I live next door. We share this garden with the Scotts."

Lord Sebastian exchanged a look with his friend, whose expression was still one of cautious surprise. But then his friend shrugged, apparently willing to share his enigmatic finding with her.

Henri stepped forward and tilted her head, her gaze drifting over the painting. "My, what a beautiful piece. But I suspect you two are more interested in what is beneath the surface, are you not?" She leaned down to examine the section the Italian had been rubbing with his handkerchief. "Whatever could you be looking for?"

She observed the flicker of mistrust that returned to the gentleman's face, a look she knew well as Uncle Reggie's private secretary. Gentlemen visiting his townhouse were often startled to find a lady managing his political correspondence, but Henri had learned their ways. A lady's wit and beauty, she found, could disarm even the most skeptical man.

Her face lit with a radiant smile, a charming dimple appearing on her right cheek. His gaze softened, captivated by the sparkle of her amber eyes beneath delicate lashes. His mouth parted slightly, as if he were dazed by her warmth.

Beyond his friend's shoulder, the duke's brother arched a fair eyebrow in quiet rebuke at her subtle arts, unmoved by her allure. But Henri had heard he was courting Lady Harriet Slight, the *ton*'s celebrated auburn widow, whose beauty far outshone her own. It mattered little. It was his companion who was her focus.

"Signor Lorenzo di Bianchi," he said, offering a courtly bow, his misgivings fading under her charm. Henri took her duties with Uncle Reggie seriously, navigating the skepticism of men unaccustomed to a lady in political circles with grace.

"Lorenzo di Bianchi," she repeated, savoring the musical

flow of his name. "How perfectly romantic. And you must be Lord Sebastian?" She dropped a curtsy in response to Lord Sebastian's brief bow before turning back to his friend. "And this painting. Is it yours?"

"*Si*, in a manner of speaking," Signor di Bianchi replied, his voice revealing his fervor for the subject at hand. "It was a creation of my ancestor, Matteo di Bianchi. A master painter of the Renaissance who studied under the great Leonardo himself."

Henri's eyes widened with genuine interest. "A student of da Vinci? How extraordinary! Uncle Reggie—my great-uncle, Mr. Reginald Wells—would be absolutely fascinated. He has quite a passion for art."

At the mention of Wells, Lord Sebastian straightened. Henri caught it immediately.

"You know of him?" she asked, tilting her head.

"Mr. Wells is known in certain circles," Lord Sebastian told his friend. "A man of considerable political influence."

"Indeed he is," Henri agreed, her smile never wavering. "And I am his private secretary. I handle his correspondence, manage his appointments, and keep his secrets." She paused meaningfully, concealing the slight pinch of guilt at her shameless maneuvering. Lorenzo di Bianchi had a secret, which meant she now had an opportunity to prove her mother wrong. She could seal her lips, and she had kept Uncle Reggie's secrets when it truly mattered. Although she had a feeling that sometimes he wished for her to spread certain news to the other secretaries. His own maneuverings. "All of them."

Her guilt sharpened at the untruth.

The Italian's face was a picture of discomfort and propriety warring. "Miss Bigsby, this matter … it is not exactly …"

"A proper subject for a lady's ears?" Henri finished

sweetly. "Gentlemen, I assure you, working for Uncle Reggie has exposed me to far more scandalous secrets than whatever mystery you are uncovering in that painting. I handle correspondence between ministers who despise each other, arrange meetings that must never appear in any official record, and manage information that could topple governments if mishandled."

It was mostly true, but Uncle Reggie kept the truly sensitive matters to himself. Because he, too, thought she was a gossip? She took a step closer, invigorated with determination.

"I can see you have reservations about trusting me, but I give you my word as a lady that I am entirely capable of discretion when the situation demands it. And frankly, gentlemen, I believe you need my help."

"Your help?" Lord Sebastian inquired, his eyebrow arching again.

Henri moved closer to examine the painting, her gaze studying the ethereal figure emerging from what appeared to be misty water. "Well, for one thing, I can tell you that this is clearly the Lady of the Lake, Nimue, though some call her Viviane. See how the artist has positioned her hands? She is offering hidden knowledge to the viewer, just as she offered Excalibur to Arthur. But notice the expression in her eyes? There is a sadness there, a foreknowledge of betrayal. Most artists paint her as purely benevolent, but your ancestor understood the deeper mythology."

She pointed to subtle details in the background. "Those are not simply decorative elements. That is the Isle of Avalon in the distance, and if I am not mistaken, those symbols along the water's edge are ancient Celtic writing. Your Matteo was not just painting a pretty lady. He was enciphering the entire Arthurian cycle into a single image."

Both men stared at her with newfound respect. Signor di Bianchi's mouth had fallen slightly open.

"Most remarkable," he breathed. "I confess, Miss Bigsby, while I can recognize the artistic techniques, the symbolic positioning, the use of background elements to convey meaning … I lack the specific knowledge to interpret what they represent. My expertise lies in Renaissance art methods and family history, but Arthurian legend …" He shook his head admiringly. "And I fear Lord Sebastian knows even less than I do about such matters."

"Guilty as charged," Lord Sebastian admitted with a rueful smile. "I can appreciate the artistry, but the deeper meaning is quite beyond me."

"Uncle Reggie's interests outside of his work lie in Arthurian lore," Henri said confidently, pleased by their reaction. "It is a hobby for him, but more than that, I have connections throughout London's political and scholarly circles. If your mystery involves old manuscripts, rare books, or historical research, I likely know someone who can assist you." She paused. "Please," she finally said, her voice growing more earnest. "I find myself with time on my hands for the first time in years, and I confess I am quite intrigued by what you are doing. Allow me to prove myself useful."

Signor di Bianchi studied her face intently, then glanced at Lord Sebastian, who gave an almost imperceptible nod.

"Very well," he said slowly. "But, Miss Bigsby, if I am to share this with you, I must have your solemn oath that you will speak of this to no one. Not your uncle, not your mother, not even your twin sister, without my express permission. What I am about to tell you could put my family's legacy at risk if knowledge of it falls into the wrong hands. At least … it might. We have tried to be discreet."

Henri felt a thrill of excitement mixed with trepidation. Here was exactly the sort of challenge she had been hoping for. An opportunity to prove that she could indeed be trusted with important secrets. Mama's offhand remark about her inability to keep confidences had stung more than she cared to admit, but now she had a chance to demonstrate that she was capable of discretion when it truly mattered.

"You have my word, Signor di Bianchi," she replied. "I swear on my honor that I will keep your confidence."

"Then I will trust you," Signor di Bianchi said, his tone warming. "Your perspective would indeed be valuable." He paused, seeming to choose his words. "You see, I have reason to believe my ancestor left clues hidden in his artwork. Clues that could lead to other lost paintings of great importance to my family's legacy."

Henri moved closer, genuinely intrigued now. "And you think this painting contains such a clue?"

"I am certain of it." He resumed his careful work with the handkerchief, and Henri could see that letters were becoming visible beneath the tempera. "Matteo wrote to his sister about this painting specifically, claiming it held secrets that would … how did he put it … guide the worthy to greater treasures."

As more tempera flaked away, distinct letters emerged in the lower corner of the canvas. Henri squinted at them, her mind immediately cataloging the shapes.

"TWESROHYEERTLPEEVITEHST," she read aloud, then frowned. "That cannot be right. It's gibberish."

"Perhaps it is coded," Lord Sebastian suggested. "Or in another language?"

Henri studied the letters, unconsciously chewing her lower lip as she did when puzzling over Uncle Reggie's more complex correspondence. The men watched her as she muttered the letters under her breath, rearranging them mentally.

"Wait," she said suddenly, lighting up as she thought of a

fresh angle to explore. "What if it is an anagram? Uncle Reggie is quite devoted to puzzles of that sort. He is always working out riddles from old manuscripts." Her voice grew more excited. "Let me see … TWESROHY-EERTLPEEVITEHST … rearranged could be … THE TOWER … No, that leaves too many letters … THE TOWER … RHYSE … no …"

She fell silent, lips moving soundlessly as she worked through combinations. Then clarity hit.

"THE TWELVE SORTS!" she exclaimed, then shook her head. "No, that is not quite right either." She tried again. "THE TOWER … TWELVE … TOWERS … TWELVE …"

"What are you thinking?" Signor di Bianchi asked, clearly fascinated by her process.

"Uncle Reggie has made quite a study of Arthurian legend," Henri explained, still working through the letters. "He is particularly interested in the various accounts of the Round Table and … oh!" Her eyes went wide. "THE TWELVE PEERS! No, wait …" She counted on her fingers. "THE TWELVE WORTHY … THE TWELVE … oh, bother. What's the exact phrasing Uncle Reggie uses?"

She closed her eyes to access her memory. "He is always quoting from that treasured Caxton edition he owns … something about Arthur's knights being the twelve most worthy … the twelve worthiest … THE TWELVE WORTHIEST PEERS!"

Signor di Bianchi and Lord Sebastian stared at her in amazement as she opened her eyes triumphantly.

"THE TWELVE WORTHIEST PEERS," she repeated, counting out the letters on her fingers. "That's exactly the right number of letters!"

"Incredible," the Italian breathed. "But what could it mean?"

"It is from Malory," Henri explained, her excitement

growing. "The Twelve Worthiest Peers are mentioned in *Le Morte d'Arthur* as the greatest knights of the Round Table. Uncle Reggie has a beautiful Caxton early edition. He has made extensive notes and claims Caxton's version, despite being printed rather than handwritten, preserves certain details that later editions omit."

She hesitated as she noticed both men were staring at her with an intensity that made her suddenly self-conscious.

"What is it?" she asked.

"The Twelve Worthiest Peers," Signor di Bianchi murmured, moving around to examine the back of the painting. "Sebastian, help me turn this over."

Together, they lifted the painting and rotated it so Henri could see the wooden backing. The panel construction was clearly visible. Twelve individual wooden segments fitted together in a geometric pattern.

"Twelve panels," Signor di Bianchi breathed, running his fingers along the joints. "Matteo was trained by da Vinci himself. The master was famous for his mechanical devices, hidden compartments, sliding panels ..." His voice grew more excited. "If Matteo learned these techniques and if he wanted to hide something ..."

Henri watched, fascinated, as he began pressing gently along the edges of each panel. "You think each panel corresponds to one of the knights?"

"It is precisely the sort of puzzle Matteo would create," Signor di Bianchi said, his fingers playing over the surface in examination. "Renaissance artists often built secret mechanisms into their work. Not just for hiding things, but as a demonstration of their engineering skills learned from masters like Leonardo."

There was a soft click as he pressed a particular sequence along the third and seventh panels. A small section shifted slightly.

"Ah! Here we are," he exclaimed, extracting an aged parchment from the hidden compartment. "Matteo was indeed his master's pupil." The last was said with a smug pride as he unfolded the page with reverence, his hands steady despite his obvious excitement. "A sketch! And look … there are numbers and letters marked below the drawing. But if this anagram refers to Malory's work …"

Henri peered at the parchment sketch. "They could be a cipher," she suggested. "Uncle Reggie has shown me several examples from medieval manuscripts. Often they correspond to specific passages or chapters."

"You think these numbers might reference locations in *Le Morte d'Arthur*?" Lord Sebastian asked, looking over Signor di Bianchi's shoulder at the sketch.

"It is entirely possible," Henri replied. "Uncle Reggie would know for certain. His Caxton edition is quite comprehensive, and he's made extensive notes on all the various symbolic references and—"

She stopped suddenly, realizing what Lord Sebastian was suggesting.

"You want me to involve Uncle Reggie in this," she said slowly, the disappointment keen that she was not enough. But no matter, she would prove she could help in her own right.

"Could you?" the Italian asked, hope evident in his voice. "Miss Bigsby, if your uncle's Caxton edition could help decipher this sketch, it might lead me to paintings that have been lost for centuries. My family's entire legacy depends on recovering Matteo's work."

Henri felt a flutter of genuine excitement. Here was a mystery worthy of her attention, a secret that mattered to someone, and an opportunity to prove she could be trusted with important information. It was exactly what she had been hoping for.

"Uncle Reggie is still away in the country for the holidays," she said thoughtfully. "But I have access to his books. Perhaps we can examine his Caxton edition and see if these cipher marks correspond to anything meaningful."

"We would be most grateful," Lord Sebastian replied warmly.

"There is one condition," Henri added, brimming with mischief. "I insist on being included in whatever adventure this leads to. I refuse to simply facilitate access to Uncle Reggie's library and then be dismissed like a proper young lady who has done her duty."

Signor di Bianchi laughed, the sound rich and delighted. "Miss Bigsby, something tells me dismissing you would be quite impossible."

"Indeed it would," Henri agreed cheerfully. "Now then, shall we wrap this painting and visit Uncle Reggie's townhouse? I believe we have a mystery to solve, and I find myself most eager to begin."

"Indeed, but I think for propriety's sake we shall follow you in one of the baron's vehicles," Lord Sebastian responded. "I assume you have some sort of chaperon arrangement for your work with Mr. Wells."

Henri nodded. "I have a lady's maid who accompanies me."

While the men lifted the painting, Henri felt a thrill of anticipation. For the first time in weeks, she had a genuinely interesting task to occupy her mind. And, perhaps, if she was very careful with Lorenzo di Bianchi's secrets, she might prove to herself and her mother that she could indeed be trusted with matters of discretion.

The winter afternoon was growing cold, but Henri felt wonderfully warm as they made their way back toward their neighboring houses, a true adventure about to begin.

* * *

OXFORD, EARLIER THAT DAY

The key turned easily in the lock, just as Horace had promised it would in his final letter. Lord Gabriel Strathmore, the Viscount of Trenwith, stepped across the threshold of the narrow townhouse on Holywell Street, his boots echoing hollowly in the empty entrance hall. The familiar scent of old books, pipe tobacco, and lavender sachets should have been comforting, but instead, it squeezed his heart. A reminder of what had been stolen from him through a single violent event.

*"My dear boy,"* Horace had written in that last correspondence, *"should anything happen to me, you must know that I have left the house to you. It is not much, but it has been a sanctuary for learning, and I can think of no one better suited to preserve that legacy. There are matters we must discuss when next you visit ..."*

But there would be no next visit. No more discussions about Arthurian symbolism over evening tea. No more pedantic corrections of Gabriel's Latin pronunciation, delivered with that wry smile that had been the closest thing to familial affection Gabriel had known since his parents' death.

Horace Pelham was dead, murdered during what the local constabulary had dismissed as a break-in gone wrong. The old man had been struck down in his own study, his attacker leaving him unconscious on the floor where he never regained consciousness. Horace had been buried before Gabriel could even reach English shores.

Gabriel moved through the narrow corridor toward the study, his jaw clenched against the surge of emotions threatening to break through his carefully maintained composure. Anger, grief, and a hollow ache warred within his chest. He had learned long ago to master such feelings, to lock them away where they could not be seen or used against him. A lesson taught by a grandfather who had found a five-year-old's tears unseemly, and reinforced by years of military service where sentiment was a luxury no officer could afford. His diplomatic work had only served to strengthen his stoic nature while increasing his sense of isolation.

The study door stood ajar, and Gabriel pushed it open with steady fingers despite the turmoil within. The room was in disarray—books scattered across the floor, papers strewn about, desk drawers hanging open like accusatory mouths. This was no random theft. Someone had been searching for something specific.

Gabriel pulled Horace's final letter from his coat pocket, reading again the passage that had haunted him during the journey back from the Continent.

*A most peculiar young woman visited me yesterday. Miss Metcalfe, she called herself. Well-schooled in Arthurian legend, though far too young to have gained such knowledge through proper study.*

*She inquired about borrowing my first edition of Le Morte d'Arthur, the one recently gifted to me by an appreciative patron to further my studies.*

*I informed her that while it is indeed a first edition, it differs markedly from Sir Thomas's original script in Middle English. The printed version, I explained, cannot capture the nuances of the handwritten text.*

*She became quite agitated at this news and warned me that Regis Aeterni, a name I confess means nothing to me, might not understand my point of view about the book. Most disturbing, she suggested that a sect of this Regis Aeterni, the Dominus, can be violent when thwarted.*

*I fear I may have stumbled into matters far more dangerous than academic scholarship.*

Gabriel moved to the bookshelf where Horace had proudly displayed the Caxton edition. It was missing, just as Gabriel had suspected it would be. His fingers traced the empty space where the volume had rested, his mouth forming a grim line.

*Regis Aeterni.* Eternal King. The name meant nothing to Gabriel either, but the implications were clear enough. Someone had wanted that book badly enough to kill for it.

He continued his orderly search of the study, looking for any clue Horace might have left behind, any indication of who this mysterious Miss Metcalfe might be or what *Regis Aeterni* represented. But the searchers had been thorough. Whatever secrets Horace had uncovered about that first edition had died with him.

Gabriel had his men attempting to uncover information about this secretive society or find this Miss Metcalfe involved in Arthurian studies, but her name was common up north, and no one of Horace's acquaintance had heard mention of *Regis Aeterni*. The only clue he could find in Horace's home was what was not there. The missing book was the only confirmation of his suspicion that Horace had encountered this diabolical *Dominus* Miss Metcalfe had spoken of.

A surge of rage rose, white-hot and consuming. The only man who had ever shown him genuine affection, if a rather distracted and forgetful sort, and who had filled the role of father when his own family had cast him aside. For him to be murdered by strangers over a book … The injustice of it threatened to overwhelm Gabriel's careful control.

He turned sharply and strode from the study, through the corridor, and out into the December afternoon. The cold air struck his face like a slap, but it did not cool the fury burning within him. Without conscious thought, he drew back his boot and sent a loose cobblestone skittering across the narrow lane with vicious force.

The stone struck the opposite wall with a sharp crack, and Gabriel immediately felt a wash of shame at his loss of control. He drew a steadying breath and straightened his shoulders. Horace was dead, and no amount of rage would bring him back. The proper course of action would be to return to London, meet with his secretary Samuel Tyne, and prepare for the diplomatic mission to Calais that required his immediate attention. The Crown's business could not wait for personal grief.

But even important work could wait for the still living creatures depending on the old man's care.

He turned back toward the house, remembering suddenly the soft mewing he had heard earlier but dismissed in his distracted agitation. Horace's cats, Tacitus and Pliny, named after the Roman philosophers he so admired. Gabriel found them huddled together in the kitchen, a large tabby and a smaller gray, both thin and clearly distressed by their master's prolonged absence.

"Hello, old fellows," Gabriel said quietly, extending his hand. Tacitus, the braver of the two, approached cautiously and allowed Gabriel to scratch behind his ears. "You have been waiting for him to come home, haven't you?"

The cats had been Horace's constant companions, often curled in his lap while he worked or perched on his desk watching him write. Gabriel could not simply leave them to fend for themselves or rely on the cleaning woman to take care of them.

He moved to the larder and found some dried fish, which he set out along with fresh water from the kitchen pump. While the cats ate hungrily, Gabriel considered his options. His London townhouse was no place for pets. Too formal, too cold, and he was away too frequently on Crown business.

But Trenwith Abbey, his country seat, had competent staff and grounds where the creatures could live comfortably.

"Mrs. Hartwell will look after you properly," he told them, thinking of his capable housekeeper at Trenwith Abbey. "But first, you are coming with me to London. Horace would want you to be safe."

It took some coaxing and a bit more dried fish, but Gabriel managed to settle both cats into the lidded basket Horace had fashioned for them. They mewed plaintively but seemed to sense his intent was kind. He gathered what remained of their food and a small blanket that smelled of Horace, then carried the basket to his waiting carriage.

"To London," he instructed his driver, settling the basket gently on the seat beside him. "And mind the roads. We have precious cargo."

Tacitus poked his nose through the wicker slats and meowed softly. For the first time since reading news of Horace's death, Gabriel felt something ease in his chest.

But the thought of returning to his empty townhouse, of sitting across from Samuel discussing travel arrangements and coded dispatches while the hollow ache in his chest threatened to consume him, was suddenly unbearable. He needed … something. Some connection to life and cheer that might penetrate the cold isolation that had become his constant companion.

An image rose unbidden in his mind. Amber eyes bright with intelligence, honey-brown hair catching the afternoon light, a dimpled smile that could coax conversation from the most reluctant politician. Miss Henrietta Bigsby, private secretary to Reginald Wells and one of the most vivacious women of Gabriel's acquaintance. She was on the shelf as she closed in on thirty years of age, which confounded Gabriel. Were the men of the British Isles imbecilic to leave such a woman shelved? It was incomprehensible.

He had first encountered her two years ago when Crown business had required him to consult with Wells on a delicate matter of French intelligence. Gabriel had expected to meet with Wells's clerk, some dried-up scholarly gentleman, perhaps, or a younger man learning the political trade. Instead, he had been introduced to Miss Bigsby, who had demonstrated a grasp of parliamentary procedure and European politics that would have impressed a seasoned diplomat.

Their subsequent meetings had been professionally cordial but personally … challenging. Miss Bigsby had a way of looking at Gabriel as though she could see past his carefully constructed mask to something more interesting beneath. She asked questions that made him think, offered observations that surprised him, and treated him with a fondness that had nothing to do with his title or his usefulness to her employer. The fact that he sometimes took advantage of the lady's loose lips to learn the secrets of Parliament pained him.

Despite his shameful manipulations, Gabriel had found himself looking forward to those meetings with an anticipation that was disconcerting. Miss Bigsby represented hope. Hope of a genuine connection with another human being, hope of something beyond the cold duty that had defined his life. Something beyond a forgetful tutor obsessed with his books. And hope was a distraction he could ill afford.

Yet as they trundled along the narrow Oxford lane where his beloved tutor had drawn his last breath, Gabriel found himself craving exactly that sort of distraction. Wells and Horace had maintained a correspondence over the years, bonding over their shared interest in Arthurian legend. The political man's townhouse had always felt warm and welcoming during Gabriel's visits, a stark contrast to the formal emptiness of his own residence.

It was nearly Christmastide, and Wells might well be away from Town. The journey could prove a complete waste of time. But perhaps fortune would favor him with their company. A brief visit to that bustling household might provide the human connection he needed to banish this overwhelming melancholy.

And perhaps, though Gabriel hardly dared acknowledge the thought, he might catch a glimpse of amber eyes and a dimpled smile that never failed to remind him that there was still joy to be found in the world.

Gabriel pulled out his pocket watch and calculated the journey time back to London. If they detoured a little, he could reach Wells's townhouse by late afternoon. Samuel would simply have to wait until tomorrow to discuss the Calais arrangements.

For once in his meticulously ordered life, Gabriel Strathmore was going to allow himself the luxury of hope.

As the carriage trundled away from where Horace Pelham had lived and died, Gabriel tried to release his dark thoughts by anticipating his arrival at the one place where he might find a moment's peace from the ghosts that haunted him.

# CHAPTER 2

*"For all men may not have all things, after their desire."*

**Sir Thomas Malory, *Le Morte d'Arthur***

* * *

The midafternoon was winter pale, and Henri could see her breath forming small clouds as she stood at the front window of Uncle Reggie's townhouse. The narrow street near Parliament was moderately busy despite the December chill, though many of the political set had already departed London for their country estates to celebrate Christmas. The weak sunlight struggled through the overcast sky, casting everything in shades of gray and silver while she awaited the Blackwood carriage after they had agreed the gentlemen should delay their arrival for the sake of propriety. Fortunately, this street was well-accustomed to lengthy meetings and not the customary fifteen minutes of polite society calls.

A familiar clatter of wheels announced the arrival of their

carriage, its deep black lacquer gleaming despite the muted light. Henri watched as the vehicle drew to a halt before the townhouse, steam rising from the horses' nostrils while they stamped their feet against the cold. The coachman, wrapped in a heavy greatcoat, adjusted his position as Lord Sebastian emerged first, his tall frame elegant even in the simple act of stepping down. Then the Italian alighted with that barely contained thrum of energy she had observed in the garden. Even from this distance, she could see the intensity in his bearing, the way he moved with purpose rather than leisure.

*Why does he remind me of a bumblebee?* All humming energy and restless purpose, as if stillness were foreign to him?

"Miss Henri." Miss Dulwich's voice carried a note of gentle reproof from behind her. "You should not be gawking out the window like a housemaid. It is unseemly."

Henri turned from the window with a rueful smile. Miss Dulwich had served as her lady's maid and unofficial companion and chaperon for the better part of two years. A compact woman of thirty with brown hair always neatly coiled beneath a mobcap, she carried herself with the timid efficiency of someone who knew her place in the household order.

"I was merely observing the arrival of Uncle Reggie's guests," Henri said with mock dignity. "Surely, there is nothing improper in being prepared to receive them?"

Henri could see the worry in Miss Dulwich's brown eyes, though she maintained her properly respectful expression. "Indeed, miss. Though I suspect your interest has less to do with proper household management and more to do with a certain handsome foreign gentleman."

Heat rose in Henri's cheeks at the unjust rebuke, there being only one gentleman who turned her head, and she had not encountered him in some time. But before she could form a suitable retort, the brass door knocker sounded with crisp authority. Henri smoothed her hands over her morning dress and nodded to Miss Dulwich.

"Shall we?"

The butler, Thompkins, was already moving to answer the door with his usual dignified efficiency. Henri positioned herself in the entrance hall, close enough to greet the visitors properly but far enough to maintain decorum. The cold December air swept in as the door opened, carrying with it the scents of frost and coal smoke.

"Lord Sebastian. Signor di Bianchi." Henri offered a welcoming smile as the two men stepped inside with their greatcoats buttoned up against the elements. "How good of you to come."

Lord Sebastian removed his hat and offered a polite bow. "Miss Bigsby. Thank you for arranging this meeting."

But it was the Italian who captured Henri's attention. His dark eyes burned in juxtaposition to his polite exterior, and when he took her gloved hand in greeting, she could feel the barely restrained energy radiating from him.

"Miss Bigsby," he said, his accented voice fond despite the formal words. "I cannot express how grateful I am for your assistance. The opportunity to examine your uncle's Caxton edition ... it may be the key."

Henri smiled broadly. Finding something useful to do after Uncle Reggie's prolonged absence? It was as if heaven itself was favoring her!

"I have prepared everything in Uncle Reggie's library," she said, leading them through the narrow corridor lined with shelves stuffed with political treatises and parliamentary papers. "Though I confess I am somewhat anxious about whether we shall find what you seek."

Miss Dulwich fell into step behind them, her presence a comforting reminder of etiquette even as Henri's pulse quickened with anticipation.

The library was her great-uncle's pride and joy, a cozy room lined floor to ceiling with books, warmed by a cheerful fire that Thompkins had laid earlier. The precious Caxton edition of *Le Morte d'Arthur* lay open on the reading table, its aged pages yellowed but still clearly legible. Mirrors had been arranged to reflect adequate light without endangering the ancient text with the use of oil lamps or candles.

"Magnificent," Signor di Bianchi breathed, moving immediately toward the book. His reverence was evident as he approached the table, hands clasped behind his back as though afraid he might inadvertently damage something precious.

Henri watched as he withdrew the sketch they had discovered hidden in the painting's panels, unfolding it with infinite care beside the open Caxton edition. The parchment looked small and fragile in the dim light, its coded letters and numbers mysterious as hieroglyphs.

"Now then," Henri said, settling into the chair beside him while Lord Sebastian positioned himself where he could observe their work. Miss Dulwich claimed a seat near the fire, producing her needlework with the pragmatic efficiency of a lady's maid who knew how to remain usefully occupied while properly invisible.

"Shall we begin with the first sequence? What appears to be K-12-7?"

Signor di Bianchi's finger traced the letters on the sketch. "This twelve … it refers to a knight, perhaps?"

Henri delicately turned the pages of the Caxton edition to a section describing the fellowship of the Round Table, her finger running down the list of names as they appeared in that passage. "If *K* stands for knight, then twelve might indicate the twelfth named in this telling—"

"Sir Gareth," Lord Sebastian read over her shoulder,

comparing the sketch to the page. "But then … what of the seven?"

For the next two hours, they worked with growing frustration, attempting every method they could devise. Henri wondered if the numbers might refer to book and chapter divisions, to particular verses, or to lines within a speech. They tried using the knights' names as keys for various ciphers, read passages backward, and sought patterns in the letters themselves.

Surely, this ancestor did not intend his clue to be impossible to solve?

The Italian grew agitated as each attempt failed. Henri could see the tension in his shoulders, the way his hands moved restlessly when he was not actively writing or pointing. There was something almost desperate in his determination, as though this quest represented far more than mere curiosity about a family legacy.

*What demons drive a man to search so relentlessly for answers about the past?*

"Perhaps," Henri ventured after their latest attempt yielded nothing but gibberish, "the code requires a different key entirely. The Twelve Worthiest Peers might be the starting point, but not the solution itself."

Signor di Bianchi ran his hands through his dark hair. "You may be correct, Miss Bigsby. But what other key could Matteo have intended? He pointed to this book specifically for the clue, no?"

As the room grew tense with disappointment, Henri sat back with a huff of defeat. "I am sorry. I had hoped Uncle Reggie's book would provide the answer you seek."

Signor di Bianchi looked up at her then, and she saw a flash of vulnerability beneath his determined exterior. "The fault, it is not yours, Miss Bigsby. Perhaps I have been too eager, too hopeful that the solution would be so simple."

As the clock chimed four, both gentlemen began to gather their things with obvious reluctance. Lord Sebastian assisted in cautiously folding the sketch, while Henri returned the Caxton edition to its proper place on the shelf.

"We are grateful for your efforts," Lord Sebastian said as they prepared to depart. "Though the afternoon has not yielded the results we hoped for."

Signor di Bianchi bowed politely as they said their farewells. "If you discover any other approach we might try, please, do not hesitate to send word. This mystery, it has consumed my thoughts for many years."

Henri assured him she would and saw them to the door, Miss Dulwich dutifully accompanying her. As their carriage disappeared into the December afternoon, she felt a peculiar mixture of dashed hopes and resolve. She had failed to help with the Italian's mystery, but the failure only made her more eager to prove herself capable.

The remainder of the afternoon passed in routine correspondence. She had arranged to receive Uncle Reggie's political associates in his absence, managing the daily business that could not wait for his return from the country. Two secretaries called on behalf of their employers— one seeking clarification on a parliamentary vote scheduled for the new year, another requiring Uncle Reggie's opinion on a proposed trade measure.

Henri handled both matters with efficiency, her mind only half-focused on the familiar work. The other half continued to puzzle over the mysterious sketch.

She was addressing a letter to the secretary of a prominent MP when Thompkins appeared in the doorway.

"Miss Bigsby, Lord Trenwith has called. He asks if he might have a word."

Her quill stilled above the page. Lord Gabriel Strathmore.

She felt that familiar flutter of awareness that always accompanied his visits.

"Of course. Show him to the drawing room. I shall be along directly."

Henri set aside her correspondence and checked her appearance in the small mirror above Uncle Reggie's desk. Her morning dress was still fresh, her honey-brown hair neatly arranged despite the afternoon's work. She pinched her cheeks to bring color to them and smoothed her skirts before making her way to the drawing room.

The viscount stood before the fireplace, one hand resting on the mantelpiece as he stared into the flames. He had removed his greatcoat and gloves, and his sandy brown hair was slightly mussed from his now-absent hat. There was something in his posture. A tension she rarely observed in his usually friendly demeanor. He had the appearance of a man carrying the weight of the world on those admittedly impressive shoulders.

"Lord Trenwith," she said, stepping into the room. "What a pleasant surprise."

He turned at her voice, and Henri was struck by the darkness in his hazel eyes. There was none of his usual easy charm, none of the subtle flirtation that typically colored their interactions. Instead, he seemed almost ... haunted.

*What shadows are chasing you today, my mysterious lord?*

"Miss Bigsby." His voice was warmer than his expression. "I trust I am not intruding? I was passing by and thought I might call to offer season's greetings to your household."

Henri tilted her head, studying him with growing concern.

"That is very kind of you," she said. "Though I fear Uncle Reggie is still in the country for the holidays. He is not expected to return until after Twelfth Night."

Something flickered across the viscount's features. Disappointment? Relief? Henri could not be certain, but she had the distinct impression that his reaction was not entirely genuine.

"Ah. Of course. I should have realized he would be away from Town during the holidays." Lord Trenwith moved away from the fireplace, some unnamed tension filling the room in a way that was uncharacteristic. "Perhaps I might impose upon your hospitality for a cup of tea? The afternoon is rather cold, and I find myself reluctant to return immediately to business."

Henri gestured toward the comfortable chairs arranged near the fire. "Certainly. Miss Dulwich, would you be so good as to ring for tea?"

As they settled themselves, Henri covertly studied Lord Trenwith's profile. He seemed different this afternoon. Less controlled, more vulnerable somehow. There was a tightness to his jaw that spoke of strain, and she noticed the way his hands rested with studied casualness on the chair arms, as though he were consciously preventing them from betraying some inner agitation.

"I trust your Christmas preparations are proceeding well?" she ventured, pouring tea when a servant entered with the tea service.

Lord Trenwith's smile appeared forced. "As well as can be expected," he replied, accepting the delicate china cup with hands that were, Henri noticed, perfectly steady despite whatever was troubling him. "Though I confess the season holds little charm for me. Too much solitude, perhaps."

Henri felt a pang of sympathy. She had always sensed a certain loneliness about Lord Trenwith, though he carried it with such dignity that it was easy to overlook. Rather like a well-dressed ghost haunting the drawing rooms of their political circles.

"Surely you have invitations? A man of your standing must be much sought after for Christmas festivities."

The viscount's smile was brief and did not reach his eyes. "Invitations, yes. Inclination, rather less so."

They spoke of inconsequential matters for perhaps twenty minutes— the weather, the thin Christmas social season in Town, mutual acquaintances who had departed for their country estates. But Henri remained aware of that underlying tension in Lord Trenwith's manner, of him performing the role of charming visitor rather than simply being himself.

When the lord finally consulted his pocket watch and rose to take his leave, Henri found herself reluctant to let him go. There was something almost fragile about him this afternoon, despite his impressive height and commanding presence.

"I fear I must not impose further on your afternoon," he said, though Henri detected a note of reluctance in his voice as well. "I have … obligations that require my attention. Cats that need settling, business to attend to before departing Town."

"Cats?" Henri asked, surprised by this unexpected domestic detail.

His expression softened for the first time that afternoon. "A recent acquisition. Two rather elderly felines who have found themselves in need of a new home." His voice held a tenderness that was at odds with his earlier reserve.

"How fortunate that they found their way to you," Henri said gently. "I hope they shall be comfortable in their new circumstances."

"As do I." The viscount moved toward the door, then paused, looking back at her with an expression she could not quite interpret. "Miss Bigsby, if you should ever find yourself in need of assistance, you know you have only to send word."

The offer was made casually, but Henri heard something deeper beneath the words. A genuine concern that pleased her even as it puzzled her.

"That is very kind of you, Lord Trenwith. The same stands in return, of course."

He smiled then, a real smile that briefly banished the shadows from his handsome face. "Thank you. That means more than you know."

After he departed, Henri remained in the drawing room, staring thoughtfully at the dying fire while Miss Dulwich removed the tea things. The viscount had always been an enigma, but this afternoon's visit had revealed new depths to that mystery. She found herself wondering what had driven him to Uncle Reggie's door on this cold December afternoon, what burden he carried that cast such shadows in his usually confident demeanor.

She had heard the stories, of course. How he had unexpectedly inherited his title when both his grandfather and uncle had died within months of each other several years ago, and as a newly titled lord, he had left military service to work in diplomacy. It was said he had been raised by tutors rather than family, that he had served with distinction in some capacity during the war, though the details remained vague. But Lord Trenwith himself never spoke of his past, deflecting personal questions with such skill that one hardly noticed until he had already long departed the room.

Henri shook her head and returned to Uncle Reggie's study to finish her correspondence. Lord Gabriel Strathmore was undeniably attractive, intelligent, and emanated a fundamental decency that appealed to her. But he was also a lord, while she was merely a commoner, Uncle Reggie's political connections notwithstanding. More importantly, marriage would mean the end of her independence, the career she had built as Uncle Reggie's private secretary, the intellectual stimulation that made her life meaningful. She had seen too many women lose themselves in marriage, their own ambitions and capabilities subsumed into their husband's world. Henri had no intention of following that path, no matter how compelling the gentleman might be or how much Maddy's departure had left her out of sorts. Not that such a high-ranking peer would ever pay her serious attentions.

With determined effort, she turned her mind back to the letter she had been writing before Lord Trenwith's arrival. But as she dipped her quill in ink, her thoughts drifted back to Signor di Bianchi's mysterious sketch. Somewhere in that collection of letters and numbers lay the key to a centuries-old puzzle. Henri was certain of it.

She had sworn to keep his family's secret, but there was nothing preventing her from continuing to work on the problem in private. Uncle Reggie's library contained far more than just the Caxton edition. Perhaps tomorrow she would begin a more systematic investigation of Arthurian texts, looking for patterns or references that might illuminate the code.

Henri smiled to herself as she sealed the completed letter. She had found herself not one challenge but two—unraveling Matteo di Bianchi's centuries-old mystery and understanding the enigmatic Lord Trenwith who had appeared at her door like a lost soul seeking sanctuary.

Both promised to be far more engaging than her usual correspondence with members of Parliament.

As Henri rose to extinguish the lamps, she caught sight of her reflection in the darkened window. Her amber eyes held a spark of excitement that had been missing for weeks. Whatever lay ahead, she had the distinct feeling that her quiet winter in London was about to become considerably more interesting.

# CHAPTER 3

*"For many be called, but few be chosen."*

**Sir Thomas Malory, *Le Morte d'Arthur***

* * *

JANUARY 22, 1822

The bitter January wind cut across the Calais harbor like a blade, carrying with it the salt-tinged promise of snow. Gabriel stood on the narrow balcony of his rented lodgings, his hands braced against the iron railing as he watched the sun sink toward the gray waters of the Channel. The dying light painted the harbor in shades of amber and rust, a beauty that felt almost mocking given his current circumstances.

*Three weeks in this godforsaken port.*

Gabriel would not be in this wretched backwater if the King had not asked it as a personal favor. But any member of the peerage knew that when the monarch requested a favor, it ceased to be a request and became a pleasantly worded command. He should be in London, learning the truth about what had happened to Horace Pelham, pursuing the bastards who had murdered the only constant presence of his childhood. Instead, he was trapped in this endless circus of diplomacy, watching French bureaucrats shuffle papers while English agents rotted in secret prisons.

*Three weeks of this tedium, circling like vultures fearful of setting down.*

But today, they had finally reached an agreement, and the crucial document was on its way to Paris to be authorized. Despite his frustration, Gabriel knew he needed to maintain his patience. Men were relying on him. Loyal English operatives who had been captured years earlier during the chaos of Napoleon's final campaigns. After multiple failed negotiations, when diplomatic relations had crumbled like week-old bread, Gabriel had been specifically requested by none other than the Marquis Étienne de Beaumont. The newly appointed lead negotiator for the Bourbon monarchy had insisted that only Gabriel could represent English interests in these delicate talks.

*And God help me, I actually respect the cunning French bastard.*

He and Étienne had first encountered each other in the aftermath of Waterloo, opponents across numerous negotiating tables, circling each other like wary wolves. Yet somehow, despite their opposing allegiances, they had discovered common ground. Similar in age and interests, both ruthless in pursuit of what they believed right, both sharing a mutual abhorrence for the needless bloodshed of war.

Their acquaintance stretched back even further than their professional dealings. Étienne had spent a year under Horace's tutelage when his family fled Napoleon's France as royalists in exile. Gabriel remembered the arrogant French boy who had disrupted the quiet rhythm of Horace's household, bringing Continental sophistication and fierce political debates to their scholarly sanctuary.

A mutual trust, fragile as spun glass but genuine nonetheless, had grown between them as they successfully penned agreements on behalf of their respective governments. As much as one could trust an opposing representative, Gabriel had come to rely on Étienne's word. These negotiations were too important to abandon, no matter how much he longed to pursue Horace's killers.

Yet Gabriel had endured weeks of the French government's maddening devotion to procedure. The Bourbon monarchy operated with a bureaucratic precision that would make a church deacon weep with envy. Every document required three signatures, every decision filtered through endless committees, and every meeting scheduled with ritualistic formality that bordered on the theatrical. The negotiations could only be conducted during prescribed hours, in designated rooms, with proper witnesses present and the correct seals affixed to every piece of correspondence. All of which was laughable because outside of those meetings, he had to pretend to be Monsieur Grantham, a merchant from Britain, as they continued their secret negotiations. But this was the meeting point between London and Paris, and Calais was a city of secrets.

*By God, they move slower than a funeral procession in a blizzard.*

Gabriel was a man of action, accustomed to decisive moments and swift resolutions. This endless minuet of diplomatic niceties tested his patience like Chinese water torture. When he had expressed his frustration to Étienne just two days prior, the marquis had merely shrugged with that particular Gallic resignation that suggested centuries of experience with governmental inertia.

*"My friend, you must understand the Bourbon court survived revolution and exile by clinging to order like a drowning man clings to driftwood,"* Étienne had said, gesturing with his coffee cup.

*"Protocol is not merely preference. It is survival itself. We have learned that chaos leads to the guillotine."*

His dark eyes had held a trace of sympathy. *"But I assure you, we have made more progress in these weeks than the previous negotiating teams achieved in as many years."*

That progress, however, came with an unspoken understanding that had been delivered with the casual tone of a man discussing the weather.

*"Any deviation from proper procedure, any appearance of disrespect for our methods—it would be viewed not merely as poor diplomacy, but as a personal affront to the Crown itself. Such things cannot be overlooked, Gabriel. Not by me, not by anyone. The King's ministers would have my head, and rightly so."*

The warning had been clear. Étienne had staked his considerable reputation on these negotiations. A breach of protocol would not merely end their talks. It would destroy the marquis's standing at court and delay the release of loyal agents.

Duty before personal desires. Always.

But that knowledge did not ease the restless energy that consumed him. Gabriel turned from the balcony and made his way back into the cramped study that served as his temporary office, the weight of unfinished business pressing down upon him like lead.

His secretary, Mr. Samuel Tyne, stood beside the desk, sorting through a modest pile of correspondence with his usual meticulous efficiency. A man of forty years, thin and scholarly, with prematurely gray hair and the perpetually ink-stained fingers of his profession. He had served Gabriel faithfully for three years, managing the tedious details of his diplomatic work with unflappable competence.

"Any word from London regarding the book?" Gabriel asked without preamble, settling into the chair behind his desk.

Tyne looked up from the letters, his pale eyes brightening slightly. "Indeed, my lord. A rather promising development, I believe." He withdrew a leather-bound catalog from the stack of mail. "The latest auction catalog from Leigh and Sotheby's has arrived. Sir Alpheus Danbury is liquidating a portion of his library to fund what his agent describes as an acquisition of singular importance."

Gabriel accepted the catalog, noting the weight of the fine paper beneath his fingers. Sir Alpheus Danbury was renowned among collectors for both the veracity and rarity of his manuscripts. If he was selling, it meant the old man had found something extraordinary.

"The negotiations?" Tyne inquired delicately. "I trust they continue to progress favorably?"

Gabriel's smile was grim. "The agreement was reached this afternoon and dispatched to Paris. I am hopeful it will receive swift authorization."

"Very good, my lord. Will there be anything else this evening?"

Gabriel waved him away with a distracted gesture, already turning his attention to the auction catalog. He waited until Tyne's footsteps had faded down the corridor before opening the leather binding.

*What would you make of this, old friend?*

The irony was bitter as wine left too long in the cask. Gabriel no longer possessed any genuine interest in Arthurian lore. Not without Horace to share discoveries with, to debate interpretations, to bring the ancient legends to life with his passionate scholarship. Yet here he was, searching for clues among medieval tomes like some treasure-hunting antiquarian.

He leafed through the catalog, scanning the descriptions. Danbury's collection was indeed impressive—illustrated books of biblical themes, philosophical treatises, chronicles of the Crusades. But it was near the end of the listings that Gabriel found what had drawn his attention.

> *Lot 127: Caxton's Le Morte D'Arthur, First Edition, 1485. Fine condition, lacking only the final leaf. Provenance: Library of the Earl of Westmorland.*

Gabriel's pulse quickened. Finally! A possibility of getting his hands on a copy of the book Horace had been brutally killed for. But it was the next entry that made his nerves tingle with intuition.

> *Lot 128: The Hoole Book of Kyng Arthur and of His Noble Knyghtes of the Rounde Table. Manuscript. Attributed to Sir Thomas Malory. Vellum. Late 15th century. Written in the author's hand in Middle English, with unique variant readings not found in printed editions. An extraordinary survival from the medieval period, offering insights into Malory's original conception of the Arthurian legends. Provenance unknown. Estimate: £2,000–£3,000.*

Gabriel exhaled in excitement, the thrill of the hunt reawakening as he thought back to Horace's final letter in which he had written that the Caxton first edition was not the original work. Horace had informed his visitor Miss Metcalfe about it and had stated that an original manuscript written by Malory himself would be markedly different from the published version. If Danbury was selling the original edition, Gabriel needed to see it for himself.

*By Jupiter! This is fate itself.*

He stared at the entry until the words burned themselves into his vision. Every instinct he possessed, instincts that had saved his life countless times in the chaos of battle, screamed that this was connected to Horace's murder. A manuscript of Malory's work, with unknown provenance, appearing for sale just weeks after his tutor had been killed for his interest in Arthurian texts and their connection to the mysterious *Regis Aeterni* was far too opportune to ignore.

*I must see that manuscript. Whatever the cost.*

Gabriel's hands trembled slightly as he turned to the front of the catalog to check the auction date. January 28, 1822. Six days hence. The sale would be held at Danbury's estate rather than the usual auction rooms, doubtless a concession to the old man's standing and the prestigious reputation of his library.

For a long moment, Gabriel sat frozen, his mind racing through the implications. The timing was catastrophically inconvenient. The French negotiations were almost complete, requiring his constant presence. The marquis had staked his reputation on Gabriel's involvement. To abandon the talks now would be viewed as the gravest betrayal, a breach of protocol that could destroy not only their current agreement but likely any possibility of future cooperation in regard to the release of the British agents.

This was the fourth attempt to reach terms over the past year, and with Gabriel and Étienne's unique relationship, progress was being made for the first time. It was the very reason that he had been commanded to take the lead on this vital opportunity to sort the matter.

*Men's lives hang in the balance. English agents who have waited years for freedom.*

But as Gabriel stared at the catalog entry, he saw not the diplomatic consequences but Horace's cluttered study with its books scattered like fallen leaves, drawers ransacked, the life's work of a gentle scholar destroyed by ruthless hands. If this manuscript held answers about *Regis Aeterni*, about the forces that had killed the only father he had ever known, could he let the opportunity slip away for the sake of politics?

*Forgive me, Étienne. Forgive me, you brave souls rotting in French prisons.*

His decision crystallized in his mind. He would leave for London when the Bourbon government closed for business on Thursday afternoon. He would see that manuscript, learn its secrets, pursue whatever trail it might reveal. The French would never know he had left Calais in the middle of the night, as long as he returned by Sunday night with no one aware of his absence.

*Horace deserves justice.*

Gabriel reached for his pen and began to write out a schedule that would see him to Danbury's estate and back with no one the wiser. It could be done, with careful planning and determination. Then he drafted a letter to Captain Joubert to inform him of his plans. *The Silhouette* had slipped him in and out of England in his guise as Monsieur Grantham several times over the years, and it would be an integral piece of his hidden return to English soil.

As he wrote, Gabriel allowed himself a moment of bitter amusement. He had spent years learning to navigate the treacherous waters of diplomacy, to balance competing interests with delicate precision. Yet here he was, risking everything on the chance that a medieval manuscript might hold answers to a modern murder.

*Horace would appreciate the irony. Trust a dead tutor to lead me into the greatest gamble of my life.*

The wind rattled the windows as Gabriel sealed the letter, and somewhere in the distance, a church bell tolled the hour. The moment negotiations closed on Thursday, the Bourbon court following the strictest hours as the good bureaucracy it was, Gabriel would have three days to reach Danbury's estate and return before government hours resumed. London and back. Three days to uncover the truth about *Regis Aeterni* and the forces that had stolen Horace from him.

*God help me, I pray the weather will be in my favor.*

* * *

THE LONGCASE CLOCK in Uncle Reggie's study chimed, each note reverberating through the silent townhouse like the tolling of a funeral bell. Henri slumped deeper into the leather chair behind her uncle's mahogany desk, staring at the pile of correspondence that had accumulated during his extended absence. Letters from minor MPs seeking clarification on procedural matters, dinner invitations requesting Uncle Reggie's sharp wit to enliven the tediously dull, and endless appeals for meetings—none of these could she grant on his behalf.

*When did my life become so wretchedly mundane?*

She picked up the next letter, something about drainage improvements in a Derbyshire constituency, and immediately set it aside again. The words seemed to swim before her eyes, rendered meaningless by the crushing weight of her boredom. This was not the vital correspondence that usually crossed Uncle Reggie's desk, the kind that shaped policy and influenced the direction of government. These were the dregs, the letters that normally waited weeks for attention while more pressing matters took precedence.

*And here I am, reduced to answering drainage inquiries like some provincial clerk.*

Henri rose from the chair and moved restlessly to the window, pressing her forehead against the cold glass. The street beyond was nearly deserted, most of London's political elite still gone for the holiday season to their country estates. The very cobblestones seemed to mock her with their emptiness, a physical manifestation of the intellectual void that had consumed her life these past weeks.

She missed Madeline desperately. Her twin had married their neighbor, Simon Scott, now Lord Campbell, just two months ago and had departed immediately for Scotland to tour his estates. Henri had been genuinely happy for her sister, who had found both love and adventure in her unlikely match with the half-Scottish nobleman. But Madeline's absence left a hollow ache that no amount of political correspondence could fill.

*At least one of us escaped the tedium of spinsterhood.*

Uncle Reggie's continued absence only deepened her melancholy. In all the years Henri had worked as his private secretary, he had never left London for such an extended period. Even during parliamentary recesses, he remained in Town, hosting dinners for visiting dignitaries, consulting with ministers on forthcoming legislation, and maintaining the vast network of contacts that made him one of the most influential men in Westminster despite holding no official title.

*But now ... nothing. As if he has simply vanished from the political world entirely.*

The King's coronation had been the pinnacle of Henri's professional life. Weeks of frantic preparation, delicate negotiations, and crisis management had required every ounce of her intelligence and diplomatic skill. She had thrived on the chaos, the sense that she was helping to orchestrate events of genuine historical importance. The memory of those exhilarating weeks last summer only made her current circumstances more unbearable by comparison.

*Perhaps Uncle Reggie is planning to retire.*

The thought worried her deeply. She had noticed signs of weariness in him following the coronation, a subtle withdrawal from the political machinations that had once energized him. At seventy-three, he had earned the right to rest. But where would that leave her? What purpose would her life hold without the intellectual challenges that had defined her identity for the past decade?

She would soon be nine and twenty, firmly on the shelf and in need of a new role if Uncle Reggie did announce his retirement. She supposed it was inevitable, but she had never taken the time to consider it. She could work with Maddy and their mother at Bigsby's, but stone manufactory did not stir her blood in the least.

*I cannot bear the thought of becoming one of those purposeless spinsters who fill their days with embroidery and gossip.*

Henri turned from the window and surveyed the familiar study with new eyes—the walls lined with political treatises and parliamentary papers, the desk where she had drafted letters that influenced the course of legislation, the comfortable chairs where cabinet ministers had confided their concerns and sought Uncle Reggie's counsel. Would it all disappear when he retired? Would she find herself relegated to managing household accounts and supervising the servants?

*There must be something worthwhile I can accomplish while he is away.*

Her gaze fell upon a stack of catalogs and circulars that had accumulated in his absence. Publishers' announcements, auction house listings, invitations to lectures at the Royal Society—the sort of material that usually received cursory attention when more pressing matters demanded their time. Perhaps she could sort through them, identify anything that might interest him upon his return.

Henri settled back into the chair and began working through the pile. Most of it was exceedingly dull, as she had expected— advertisements for improving agricultural implements, announcements of new novels that Uncle Reggie would never have time to read, notices of parliamentary papers available for purchase. But near the bottom of the stack, she found a leather-bound catalog from Leigh and Sotheby's that made her pause.

Henri opened the catalog with mild curiosity, expecting to find the usual assortment of classical texts and historical documents that serious collectors favored. The early listings confirmed her expectations with decorated books of biblical psalms, chronicles of the Crusades, and philosophical treatises in Latin and Greek. But as she turned the pages, one entry caught her attention as her mouth dropped open in startled realization.

*Lot 128: The Hoole Book of Kyng Arthur and of His Noble Knyghtes of the Rounde Table. Manuscript. Attributed to Sir Thomas Malory. Vellum. Late 15th century. Written in the author's hand in Middle English, with unique variant readings not found in printed editions. An extraordinary survival from the medieval period, offering insights into Malory's original conception of the Arthurian legends. Provenance unknown. Estimate: £2,000–£3,000.*

Henri stared at the description, her heart beginning to race with sudden excitement. The author's hand. In Middle English. Not a copy, but Malory's original manuscript!

She thought immediately of the sketch, of the coded

letters and numbers that had defied all their attempts at interpretation using Uncle Reggie's Caxton edition. What if they had been using the wrong key entirely? What if the code could only be unlocked using Malory's original words, written in the medieval English that predated Caxton's printed version? When Matteo di Bianchi had drawn that sketch three hundred years ago, there would have been more of Malory's original works available.

Henri checked the auction date listed on the catalog's cover. January 28, 1822. Six days hence. Her mind began calculating rapidly. If she wanted to examine the manuscript before it disappeared into some private collector's library, she would need to act quickly. But Sir Alpheus Danbury was notoriously reclusive, unlikely to welcome unexpected visitors during the busy period preceding such an important sale. Friday the 25th would be the fitting day for a social call. Close enough to the auction that the household would be preparing, but not so close as to be intrusive.

Henri closed the catalog and rose from the chair, her earlier lethargy completely forgotten. For the first time in weeks, she had discovered something that demanded her immediate attention, a puzzle worthy of her intelligence and skills. The prospect of solving Signor di Bianchi's mystery, of proving that she could be trusted with important secrets, filled her with an energy she had not felt since the coronation.

*I must speak with Signor di Bianchi immediately.*

Henri quickly collected her pelisse and gloves, donning them as she called for her carriage to be sent to the front. She needed to return home at once to arrange a meeting. She made the journey back to her family's estate with Miss Dulwich, her mind racing with the implications of her discovery.

Once home, Henri slipped out through the shared garden that connected her family's property with the neighboring estate. The January air was bitter, making her shiver despite the thick wool of her pelisse as she hurried along the gravel path, her thoughts focused entirely on the opportunity at hand. If the Malory manuscript unlocked Matteo's code, it could change everything for Signor di Bianchi.

She spotted him through the windows of the baron's library, bent over a book with his characteristic concentration. Henri picked up a handful of small stones and tossed them gently against the glass, a signal she and her sister had used as children to summon Simon out when discreet communication was necessary. The Italian looked up, startled, then moved to exit the terrace doors and peer down at her from the terrace balustrade.

"Miss Bigsby? What brings you out in such weather?"

"I must speak with you urgently," Henri called softly, glancing around to ensure they were not observed. "Can you meet me by the walled garden?"

He nodded and disappeared inside. Henri hurried to the shared garden, where the large stone urn that had served as a landmark during their first meeting stood sentinel among the bare rosebushes and the Roman gods casting long shadows in silent observation. Within minutes, Signor di Bianchi emerged through the gateway, wrapped in a heavy greatcoat against the cold.

"You seem excited," he observed, his dark eyes studying her flushed face with curiosity. "Has something happened?"

"I believe I have found the key to your ancestor's puzzle," Henri said without preamble, withdrawing the auction catalog from beneath her pelisse. "Look at this. Lot 128."

He accepted the catalog and read the description she indicated, his expression growing animated as he absorbed the implications. When he looked up, his eyes held the same intensity she had observed before their failed attempt to decipher the sketch.

"*Madonna mia*," he breathed. "This could be exactly what we need. But how can we examine it? The auction is only six days away."

"Sir Alpheus Danbury is an acquaintance of Uncle Reggie's," Henri explained, her words tumbling out in her excitement. "I could call upon him under the pretense of expressing Uncle's interest in the collection. Friday would be the ideal day. Saturday will be insensitive, but Friday is early enough to avoid the final preparations for the auction."

The Italian's brow furrowed with concern. "But would he allow you to examine such a valuable manuscript? And more importantly, would he permit you to test our theory using the sketch?"

Henri felt a flutter of nervousness as she considered the delicacy of her request. "That brings me to a question I must ask of you. I need to take the sketch with me."

"*Che cosa?*" His voice sharpened with alarm. "Miss Bigsby, that sketch is irreplaceable. If something were to happen to it …"

"Nothing will happen to it," Henri assured him, though she understood his reluctance. "But consider the alternative. This may be our only opportunity to see the Hoole manuscript before it vanishes into some private collection. If we wait until after the auction, we may never have another chance."

"But surely I could accompany you? If we explained the situation to Sir Alpheus …"

Henri shook her head firmly. "Sir Alpheus is extremely particular about his visitors. He is elderly, set in his ways, and has very specific ideas about proper social conduct. An unexpected visit from a stranger would likely result in our being turned away without so much as a glimpse of his library."

She paused, choosing her next words carefully. "Furthermore, I must be frank with you. Sir Alpheus belongs to a generation that holds certain ... traditional views about foreigners. Your Italian heritage, however distinguished, might unfortunately work against us in securing his cooperation."

His jaw tightened slightly, but it was clear that he understood the unfortunate reality of English social prejudices. "And you believe he would be more receptive to you?"

"I know he would," Henri said with confidence. "Uncle Reggie has mentioned me routinely in his correspondence with Sir Alpheus over the years, and the old man has always liked me. He knows I can be trusted with valuable documents, and my connection to Westminster politics would give me credibility that a stranger could not claim."

The gentleman stood silent for a long moment, clearly wrestling with the decision. Henri could see the internal struggle playing out across his features, his desperate desire to solve the mystery warring with his reluctance to entrust the precious sketch to someone else's care.

"The risk ..." he began.

"Is worth taking," Henri finished firmly. "Signor di Bianchi, this manuscript may be the key to everything your ancestor intended. If we let this opportunity pass, we may never learn the truth about Matteo's message."

The wind picked up, sending dried leaves skittering across the gravel path between them. Henri pulled her pelisse closer against the cold but maintained her steady gaze on his face. She could see the moment when his resolve crumbled, when hope overcame caution.

"Very well," he said finally, his tone heavy with reluctance. "But you must promise me—"

"I swear to you on my honor that I will guard it with my life," Henri interrupted, ringing with sincerity. "The sketch will not leave my sight from the moment you give it to me until I return it safely to your hands."

Signor di Bianchi nodded slowly, putting the catalog under his arm, then fished out a notebook to show her the folded parchment within its pages. As he placed the notebook in Henri's gloved hands, she felt the weight of his trust and the magnitude of the responsibility she was accepting.

"Friday morning," she said, securing the notebook in her reticule. "I will call upon Sir Alpheus and examine the Malory manuscript. If fortune favors us, we shall finally unlock the secret that Matteo di Bianchi left for us to discover."

*And perhaps prove to myself that I am capable of achieving discretion.*

As Henri made her way back into her home, she felt the familiar thrill of anticipation that had been missing for so many weeks. Friday could not come soon enough.

*The dim light, barely revealed against the stone walls of the Bodleian Library's basement archive, cast long shadows between the towering stacks of manuscripts and forgotten volumes. Alaric Devayne sat hunched over a wooden table scarred by decades of scholarly use, the auction catalog spread before him like a map to buried treasure. He had been poring over it for weeks, waiting for the right time to act. And now that time was approaching and his anticipation was climbing.*

*His hollow cheeks and sunken eyes bore the telltale marks of too many years reading in poorly lit rooms, his angular features made sharper by the meager light. Despite the clerk's clothing he wore, serviceable brown wool and a simple waistcoat, his boots were of military grade, a remnant from his days as a field interrogator in Napoleon's campaigns.*

Lot 128: The Hoole Book of Kyng Arthur and of His Noble Knyghtes of the Rounde Table.

*Devayne's gloved fingers traced the entry. He always wore gloves now. He had done so since strangling that French officer with his bare hands outside Toulouse. Some habits, once learned, became permanent fixtures of a man's character.*

Provenance unknown.

*A smile played at the corners of his thin lips. Unknown to the fools at Leigh and Sotheby's, perhaps. Unknown to the collectors who would bid blindly at auction. But not unknown to him. He had learned the true power that lay hidden within Malory's stories.*

*Power was not inherited. It was taken. The ideology of the Dominus burned in his chest like a sacred flame. Too long had the world been governed by those who claimed authority through accident of birth. Too long had true knowledge been hoarded by the weak and the unworthy. Those who understood the old ways knew that power belonged to those with the will to seize it.*

*Devayne pushed back from the table and moved deeper into the archives, his footsteps silent on the stone floor. Years of military training had taught him to move without sound, and old habits served him well in his current profession. The other library assistants thought him merely obsessive, a harmless clerk lost in dusty tomes and ancient languages.*

*They had no idea what he truly sought.*

*He paused before a particular shelf, running his finger along the spines of volumes that few scholars ever requested. Hidden among the theological treatises and philosophical commentaries were texts that held secrets most men would never comprehend.*

*Records of power that transcended the petty squabbling of kings and parliaments.*

*January 28th. Six days until the auction. But Devayne had no intention of bidding alongside wealthy collectors and scholarly dilettantes. The manuscript would be his long before the auctioneer's hammer fell.*

*Friday.*

*Wage collection day. He would collect what the library owed him and then disappear from Oxford. After years of shuffling through these dusty archives, it was time to move on to greater things. There would be no return to this place of servitude once he possessed what he sought.*

*Sir Alpheus Danbury's household would be busy with preparations for the sale. A house full of servants focused on cataloging and arranging would hardly notice one more shadow moving through the corridors. The old man's staff would be tasked with keeping the collection secure during the public viewing days. Friday would find the estate more vulnerable.*

*The manuscript would provide both the knowledge and the means to leave this life behind forever. No more bowing to head librarians. No more cataloging the scribblings of dead monks. Real power awaited.*

*A sound from the upper floors made him look up. Footsteps overhead, distant murmurs. The library would close soon, and he would have to wait until tomorrow to continue his research. But that was acceptable. He was a patient man when patience served his purposes.*

*Devayne closed the catalog and tucked it beneath a stack of legitimate research materials. To any casual observer, he was simply another library assistant, working late on some obscure scholarly project. The perfect camouflage for a man with decidedly unscholarly intentions.*

*As he gathered his things and prepared to leave, Devayne allowed himself one final look at the auction catalog Lot 128. Soon, the manuscript would be his, and with it, the power it contained. Power that was not inherited but taken by those strong enough to reach for it.*

*In the dim light of the Bodleian's depths, Alaric Devayne smiled the cold smile of a predator who had finally scented his prey.*

# CHAPTER 4

*"And yet it must be done, for it is the best way."*

**Sir Thomas Malory, *Le Morte d'Arthur***

* * *

JANUARY 25, 1822

Friday morning arrived with the sort of crisp winter clarity that made even the most mundane errands seem charged with possibility. Henri adjusted her gloves as the carriage wheels found their rhythm on the London streets, her mood bright with anticipation. Today was perfect. Danbury would be home, receiving visitors before the Monday auction, and she would finally examine that mysterious manuscript.

Yet beneath her excitement lay a persistent flutter of anxiety. What if the manuscript revealed nothing useful? What if Signor di Bianchi's sketch was merely the fantasy of an artist's imagination rather than a genuine clue? What if she had got his hopes up only to disappoint him again?

Henri pushed these doubts aside, focusing instead on the thrill of the chase. This was precisely the sort of adventure that made her blood sing, the kind of intellectual puzzle that had drawn her to Uncle Reggie's political work in the first place. Here was mystery, intrigue, and the tantalizing possibility of uncovering secrets that had lain hidden for centuries.

The journey from her family estate on the outskirts of London proved longer than Henri had anticipated. Despite the footwarmers tucked beneath their feet and the heavy woolen traveling rugs draped across their laps, the January cold seeped relentlessly through the carriage walls. Henri's breath misted in the frigid air, and she found herself grateful for the thick cloak that enveloped her from throat to ankles. The windows had frosted over within the first mile, creating intricate patterns of ice that obscured the winter landscape beyond.

The carriage lurched and swayed over rutted country roads that had yet to benefit from proper maintenance, each bump and jolt making her stomach lurch. The iron-rimmed wheels clattered loudly against the frozen ground, occasionally striking stones that sent sharp vibrations through the vehicle's frame. Henri steadied herself against the worn velvet squabs, their rich burgundy fabric slightly damp from the cold. The smell of leather, lacquer, and wool filled her nostrils.

Outside, the winter countryside rolled past in muted shades of brown and gray. Bare trees etched grim patterns against the pale sky, their branches heavy with frost that reflected the weak sunlight like scattered diamonds. Occasionally, Henri caught glimpses through the clearer portions of the windows—a farmhouse with smoke curling from its chimney, a flock of sheep huddled against a stone wall, a frozen pond reflecting the colorless sky.

"Miss Bigsby," Miss Dulwich ventured from her corner of the bench, her hands folded primly in her lap beneath her traveling rug, her voice slightly muffled by the woolen scarf wrapped around her throat, "perhaps you might explain why you requested I bring along that particular volume?"

Henri could see the moral struggle playing out across her companion's features. Miss Dulwich was a woman of impeccable propriety, and Henri's erratic behavior clearly troubled her deeply. Yet loyalty to Henri's family and perhaps a grudging fondness for Henri herself kept her from demanding to be returned home immediately.

Henri glanced at the shabby book resting beside her, a tattered copy of *The Pilgrim's Progress* she had purchased for a few shillings from a street vendor. "All will become clear presently, Miss Dulwich. Trust me."

The chaperon's expression suggested that trust was precisely what she found most alarming about this expedition, her normally composed features pinched with cold and growing concern. "Miss Bigsby, I must express my reservations about this entire undertaking. Your behavior of late has been … most irregular."

"Irregular times call for irregular measures," Henri replied cheerfully, then lifted the book and, with great deliberation, began tearing pages from it. The paper crackled in the cold air, each tear unnaturally loud in the confined space. Miss Dulwich's gasp of horror created a visible puff of condensation. Another particularly violent bump sent both women swaying against their seats, and Henri had to grip the book more firmly to prevent it from sliding to the floor.

"Miss Bigsby! What on earth—"

"I am creating evidence," Henri replied serenely, applying

her teeth to the leather binding with the dedication of a determined terrier. The taste was rather unpleasant. Bitter and dusty, with an undertone of old glue and something indefinably animal. But the effect was exactly what she required. The cold had made the leather harder, requiring more effort to create convincing tooth marks. She persevered, imagining herself as one of Sir Alpheus's overeager hounds. "One must commit fully to one's role, you understand."

"Evidence of what?" Miss Dulwich pressed, her voice climbing toward hysteria, each word accompanied by its own small cloud of vapor. "And why must you ... oh, dear heavens, why must you chew it?"

"Canine literary preferences." Henri examined her handiwork with the critical eye of an artist, then gnawed another section for good measure, the sound unnaturally loud in the enclosed space. "Sir Alpheus's hounds have notoriously expensive taste in literature. I am merely providing proof of their latest transgression."

Miss Dulwich stared in fascination and terror as Henri continued her rigorous destruction, the carriage's constant motion adding an element of chaos to the proceedings. The vehicle swayed as they rounded a corner, and several torn pages fluttered briefly before settling again on the floor like fallen leaves.

"Are you quite certain you have not taken leave of your senses? This deception ... surely it cannot be necessary?"

"I have never been more certain of anything in my life." Henri piled the torn pages about the bench, tucking several pieces into Miss Dulwich's reticule for later deployment. The paper felt crisp and fragile in the cold, crackling softly as she moved it. "This adventure shall prove definitively that I can keep a secret. Mama will be so proud when I tell her—" She paused mid-gnaw, struck by the fundamental contradiction in her reasoning. "Which, of course, I cannot do, as it is a secret."

The irony was rather delicious … and disappointing.

Miss Dulwich leaned forward slightly, her moral distress evident in every line of her posture. "Miss Bigsby, I feel compelled to ask what drives you to such lengths?"

Henri considered the question seriously, pausing in her destruction to meet her chaperon's worried gaze. "Have you ever felt, Miss Dulwich, that your life was like a drawing room? Perfectly arranged, utterly predictable, and completely stifling? I have spent years managing Uncle Reggie's correspondence, attending the proper social functions, saying the proper things to the proper people. But this …" She gestured with a half-gnawed piece of leather. "This is real. This is discovery. This is the chance to uncover something that …" Henri stopped, gathering her thoughts. "There is logic behind the madness."

"At what cost?" Miss Dulwich asked quietly.

"At whatever cost is necessary," Henri replied, surprising herself with the conviction in her voice.

As the wheels transitioned from country lanes to the better-maintained roads approaching Danbury's estate, the ride became marginally smoother, though no warmer. The landscape began to change, winter-bare hedgerows giving way to more manicured parkland, and Henri felt her pulse quicken with anticipation. She explained Miss Dulwich's crucial role in the deception, her words visible in the frigid air.

Miss Dulwich regarded the chewed leather with evident distaste, holding the pieces gingerly even through her gloves. Her face had gone quite pale, whether from cold or moral anguish, Henri could not tell. "And what if we are discovered in this deception? What if Sir Alpheus realizes what we have done?"

"Then we shall claim it was all a dreadful misunderstanding," Henri replied with more confidence than she felt, pulling her traveling rug more tightly around herself as another blast of cold air found its way through a gap in the door. "But we shall not be discovered, because you are going to be absolutely brilliant at this. I have complete faith in your abilities."

The praise brought a faint flush to Miss Dulwich's cheeks, and Henri could see her wavering between propriety and loyalty. "I hope there is good reason to do this."

"The best," Henri replied. "A friend requires my help."

Miss Dulwich was quiet for a long moment, her breath creating small clouds in the frigid air as she considered. Finally, she straightened her shoulders with the resolve of a woman stepping onto a battlefield. "Very well, Miss Bigsby. I shall do as you ask. But I pray we do not live to regret this day's work."

"Regret," Henri said with a smile that was equal parts confidence and mischief, "is for people who never take chances."

Eventually, Sir Alpheus Danbury's estate rose before them like something from a Gothic novel, all towering chimneys and ivy-covered walls. Henri practically bounced with the excitement she was containing as they approached the imposing front entrance.

The butler who answered their knock was precisely the sort of austere figure one expected at such an establishment—tall, dignified, and possessed of the particular arrogance that suggested he considered most visitors beneath his notice.

Henri presented her card with her most winning smile. "Miss Henrietta Bigsby to see Sir Alpheus, if you please. I am here on behalf of my uncle, Mr. Reginald Wells, regarding Monday's auction."

The butler's expression shifted almost imperceptibly from dismissive to calculating. Uncle Reggie's name carried considerable weight in important circles. "If you would be so kind as to wait in the morning room, Miss Bigsby, I shall inquire whether Sir Alpheus is receiving."

The morning room proved to be a testament to Sir Alpheus's eccentric tastes. Oriental vases competed for space with medieval tapestries, while classical busts gazed from every available surface. Henri had barely settled herself when rapid footsteps echoed in the corridor.

"Miss Bigsby!" Danbury greeted her with the sort of enthusiasm reserved for unexpected windfalls. His thin, elderly frame practically vibrated with delight, and despite his eighty-two years, his eyes sparkled with the fervor of a much younger collector. "What an unexpected pleasure. I trust your esteemed uncle is well?"

"Indeed, Sir Alpheus. Uncle Reggie speaks of you with the greatest affection." Henri deployed her most charming smile. "He mentioned you might be parting with some treasures at Monday's auction, and I confess myself consumed with curiosity about your Arthurian manuscript."

An expression of pleased appraisal settled across Danbury's features. "Ah, you share your uncle's appreciation for the finer things. Come, come. Though I must warn you, the library light is rather poor at this time of the year. One must be exceedingly careful with such precious items."

The library was a marvel of organized chaos. Books climbed toward the ceiling in magnificent towers, and lavender was everywhere—tied in bunches from the ladder rails, tucked in porcelain jars atop the shelving brackets, and arranged in shallow blue-and-white bowls where one might expect inkstands. The dried blooms served the practical purpose of repelling moths that might otherwise feast upon precious bindings.

"The manuscript you inquire about is quite extraordinary," Danbury continued, producing a leather-bound treasure with reverent gloved hands. "An original work in Sir Thomas Malory's own hand, written in Middle English. Your uncle would appreciate the historical significance immensely."

"How magnificent!" Henri exclaimed, her enthusiasm only half-feigned. She nudged Miss Dulwich, who had gone rather pale and appeared to be questioning every decision that had led to this moment.

Danbury beamed at her appreciation. "Few young ladies possess such discernment. You must handle it with the utmost—"

"Sir Alpheus!" Miss Dulwich's voice rang out with surprising if shrill authority. "I believe I have discovered something most distressing in your hall." She pointed dramatically toward the corridor. "Pieces of gnawed leather. And there are more scattered about. Your hounds appear to have got into your library!"

The effect was instantaneous. Danbury's face went ashen, then flushed crimson. "Impossible! The library is strictly forbidden to those beasts!" He rushed toward the door, then spun back in horror. "Which book? Dear God, which book have they destroyed?"

"I cannot say, sir, but you had best investigate immediately," Miss Dulwich replied with admirable gravity. "Perhaps if I might assist you in tracking the trail? I fear there may be more damage than what I initially observed."

"Yes, yes! Your keen eye might spot what I miss in my distress!" Danbury seized upon the offer with desperate gratitude, and Miss Dulwich shepherded him toward the corridor, leading him away from the library and leaving Henri blessedly alone. Her lady's maid had several more bits of evidence to sow as she searched the manor with the baronet.

The moment his footsteps faded, Henri pulled Signor di Bianchi's sketch from her reticule and spread it beside the manuscript. Her heart hammered against her ribs as she studied the cryptic codes, searching for patterns, connections, anything that might—

"Hurry," she whispered urgently to herself, bent over the ancient pages. "There must be an answer here, some key that makes sense of it all." The yellowed parchment mocked her haste, demanding the careful study of a scholar rather than the hurried examination of an intruder operating on borrowed time.

The scent of old leather and parchment filled her nostrils as she bent closer to the text, her eyes darting between the pages and the mysterious symbols on Signor di Bianchi's sketch. Each minute felt like an eternity, and the silence of the library pressed against her ears. The sound of Sir Alpheus's alarm had grown more distant, but she knew it was only a matter of time before he exhausted the planted evidence and returned to his precious books.

Henri forced herself to focus on a series of intertwined letters that seemed to match a portion of the sketch. Her finger traced the delicate brushstrokes, noting how different this was from Uncle Reggie's Caxton edition. This was the original Middle English, unaltered by the printer's modern sensibilities. The archaic spellings and authentic medieval script held the key to understanding the cryptic markings before her. The connection was there, she could feel it, but the meaning remained frustratingly elusive.

"Step away from that book, miss."

The voice was soft, cultured, and absolutely terrifying. Henri gingerly closed the sketch between the pages of the manuscript, grasping it close, then spun to find a tall, angular man standing in the doorway, a flintlock pointed directly at her heart. His sallow skin and dark-rimmed eyes gave him the appearance of a scholar who had spent far too many years squinting at illegible writings in poorly lit rooms.

"Who are you? What do you want?" Henri's words emerged steadier than she felt, though her mind raced with confusion. How had this stranger appeared in Sir Alpheus's library? Why was he threatening her?

"Someone who has been watching your activities with great interest." His smile was thin and cold. "Hand over the manuscript, if you please. Along with that rather interesting sketch you seem so eager to examine."

"I do not know what you mean," Henri replied. "This is Sir Alpheus's library, and I am his invited guest. You have no right to be here."

"Rights are for those with power, miss," he replied coldly, never wavering in his aim. "I have both the means and the motive to take what I require. You, I fear, have neither. Now, hand over Malory's manuscript and the sketch."

Henri clutched it closer to her bosom, her mind racing through possibilities, none of which seemed likely to result in her continued good health. "I am afraid I cannot do that. You see, I am rather fond of my continued existence, but these possessions are not mine to give."

"How unfortunate," the man replied, his finger moving toward the trigger. "I was rather hoping you would prove more reasonable."

* * *

Gabriel left his carriage concealed among the trees beyond Danbury's estate and approached the manor on foot. He had retrieved the vehicle from a discreet inn near Sandgate Cove where it waited for occasions such as this, when his work required him to travel incognito through England. Dressed as a common coachman, he would attract no notice.

The manuscript within these walls might hold the key to understanding the forces that had killed Horace. Gabriel could not return to Calais empty-handed, not when captive English agents depended upon the success of his negotiations.

Avoiding the manor's occupants, he found the library along the northern wall, where tall French doors opened onto a stone terrace. Through the glass, Gabriel could see the reflecting mirrors and towering shelves that marked Danbury's famous collection.

Movement inside made him freeze. A woman stood pressed against the far wall, while a man loomed before her with something glinting in his raised hand.

Gabriel tested the door handle. Locked, but the aged mechanism yielded to his blade worked between frame and wood. The voices within became clear as he eased inside and shut the door to prevent a draught from alerting the weapon-wielding fiend of his presence.

"Rights are for those with power, miss," came a cultured voice. "I have both the means and the motive to take what I require. You, I fear, have neither. Now, hand over Malory's manuscript and the sketch."

"I am afraid I cannot do that," the woman replied with remarkable composure, her voice striking a chord of memory which he could not place. "You see, I am rather fond of my continued existence, but these possessions are not mine to give."

Gabriel saw the man's finger move toward the trigger of his flintlock and moved without conscious thought. Three strides carried him across the library as the man spun toward him, eyes widening. Gabriel seized the would-be killer by the throat, his grip finding precise pressure points, while forcing the pistol-wielding arm down. As he rendered his opponent unconscious, the pistol discharged harmlessly into the floor.

Only then did Gabriel turn to face the woman he had rescued.

"Lord Trenwith?"

Gabriel's heart plummeted in his chest. It was Miss Bigsby. Impudent, charming, and a terrible gossip. In fact, he had spent many an hour chatting nonchalantly with Reginald Wells's private secretary in the pursuit of information about the denizens of Parliament, which was how he had grown to know and like her. If anyone was sure to reveal his presence in London—who knew all the key players of their political circles and would have word back to Calais or even Paris of his midnight jaunt, thus ruining his negotiations to free the men held in France—Miss Bigsby would be the one to achieve it.

She was even more beautiful than he remembered, though he tried to push that treacherous thought aside. Her honey-brown hair framed her heart-shaped face. Her amber eyes, those remarkable eyes that seemed to catch and hold every nuance of light, were wide with shock. Gabriel was tempted to lean in and press a kiss to her lush rosebud mouth. To settle her nerves, he told himself. Not because he had always thought Wells's secretary was the most fascinating woman of his acquaintance.

Steeling himself for the unwelcome declaration he had to make, a flash of dread rushed through him at the thought of lovely Miss Bigsby bursting into an unholy rage when he said the words out loud. But there was no time for hesitation or diplomacy. A servant or Danbury himself could happen on them at any moment. He had to choose between ruining a young woman and the continued imprisonment of good men who had helped end the war so many years earlier. It was reputation over life and death, and he knew there was no decision to reach.

"I am afraid you will have to come with me."

Her expression turned from gratitude to confusion in an instant. "What—"

Before she could finish the question, Gabriel pulled her toward him and hauled her slight form under his arm to walk swiftly toward one of the library doors leading onto the terrace. At first she was docile, likely stunned, but then she began to wriggle in an effort to get free. He ignored the protests falling from her spellbinding lips—she would soon realize she had no say in the matter—but he was terrified of hurting her delicate frame, so he swung her up and shifted his position to clasp her in both arms against his chest, her arms tethered to her sides by his own, her feet dangling just below his knees. And he nearly groaned aloud at the unexpected pleasure of feeling the soft swells of her full breasts pressed to his own hard planes, plumped up around the edges of the manuscript she clutched. A stirring in his buckskins announced he indeed was only getting harder.

Belatedly recollecting the villain who had attacked her, forgotten in the surprise of her presence, he turned to find the library empty. The scoundrel must have awoken and scampered away, along with his flintlock. It was an amateur mistake, further evidence of the detrimental effect Miss Bigsby had on his focus, and there was naught he could do about it without revealing his presence in England. Too many lives hung in the balance, and he had already gambled with those lives. At least he did not recognize the other man, which meant the other man likely did not recognize him. But had he heard Miss Bigsby calling out his title? It all depended on when the scoundrel had come to.

Gabriel carried Miss Bigsby through the terrace doors and across the frost-covered grounds. The cold bit through his rough coachman's clothing as he made his way toward the woods where his carriage waited concealed among the winter-bare trees. He had always been attracted to Miss

Bigsby, though he had never allowed himself to acknowledge it fully. There was something about her quick wit, her genuine warmth, her fearless pursuit of whatever captured her interest that called to parts of him he had long thought dead. During their conversations in London drawing rooms, he had found himself lingering longer than necessary, savoring the way her eyes lit up when she spoke of a subject that excited her, the musical quality of her laughter, the graceful gestures of her hands as she emphasized a point. This was why he avoided her for weeks or months at a time. She was a weakness he could ill afford.

"This is kidnapping!" she declared, her amber eyes flashing. "You cannot simply—"

"I can and I must," Gabriel replied grimly as he reached the hidden coach. "Miss Bigsby, you are in considerably more danger than you know. That man was prepared to kill you for what you carry."

Gabriel deposited Miss Bigsby onto the carriage seat and immediately set about securing both her and the precious items she carried. He carefully extracted the manuscript and sketch from her grasp, wrapping them in oiled cloth from beneath the driver's seat before placing them in a secured compartment designed for sensitive documents. Thankfully, her excellent English manners made her slow to react to this unprecedented violation of her person. But, even as his conscience flayed him, Gabriel could not deny the fierce satisfaction that coursed through him. She was his to protect now, whether she wanted it or not. His to shield from whatever forces had brought armed men hunting manuscripts and sketches. His to—

"What are you doing?" Miss Bigsby demanded, her voice sharp with alarm as she realized his intentions.

"Ensuring you do not flee the moment my back is turned," Gabriel replied resolutely, producing silk cords from the carriage's hidden compartments. These preparations had served him well during his more secretive work, though he had never imagined using them on an innocent woman.

"You cannot mean to—" Miss Bigsby began, but Gabriel was already securing her wrists with practiced efficiency, though he took care to ensure the bonds were firm without being painful.

"I am sorry, Miss Bigsby," he said quietly as he produced a clean linen handkerchief. "But I cannot risk you crying out and drawing attention as we depart."

Miss Bigsby's eyes flashed with fury and betrayal as Gabriel gently but firmly secured the gag. He checked that she could breathe easily before stepping back to cover her carefully with a thick blanket to ward off the cold.

"I shall remove these restraints once we are safely away from this place," Gabriel promised, though he could see the accusation in her amber eyes. "You have my word."

The vehicle rocked as Gabriel took his place on the driver's box and guided them away from Danbury's estate, the sound of wheels on frozen ground marking their departure into an uncertain future.

The agents imprisoned in France had been kept from their families for years. They might never get another chance at freedom if Gabriel's absence from Calais became known. But thinking about Miss Bigsby, Gabriel knew there was only one solution that could preserve her honor and his mission's secrecy.

If he had to endure the hardship of his choice to come to England during the negotiations, if he had to make the ultimate sacrifice he had spent years avoiding, then so be it. Marriage it would be. A union would shield Miss Bigsby's reputation and ensure her continued security, even if it meant the end of the meticulously controlled existence Gabriel had built as insurance against further loss.

The thought of binding himself to another person, of opening himself to the kind of devastating grief he had felt when his parents died and when Horace was murdered, filled Gabriel with a cold dread. But what choice did he have? He could not leave her to talk about his presence, but because he had taken her, he could not abandon Miss Bigsby to face the consequences of vanishing. He would have to find a way to suppress his emotions and do his duty.

# CHAPTER 5

*"Alas, that ever I should be alive to be a traitor unto the most noble king that ever was."*

**Sir Thomas Malory, *Le Morte d'Arthur***

* * *

The blanket Lord Trenwith had placed over her provided little comfort against the bitter cold seeping through the carriage walls. Henri sat bound in the gloom of the curtained interior, her wrists secured behind her back with silk cords that refused to yield no matter how she twisted and pulled. The gag in her mouth made every breath feel labored, and panic clawed at her chest as the full enormity of her situation settled upon her.

This was Lord Gabriel Strathmore. Viscount Trenwith. A man she had known for some time through Uncle Reggie's political circles, someone she had thought honorable despite his reputation for being somewhat aloof. How could she have read his character so completely wrong?

And yet, for all the outrageous nature of her situation, Henri found herself strangely unafraid of him. He had, after all, rescued her from that terrifying man with the pistol. Whatever his motives for this kidnapping, she could not forget the way he had moved to save her, the careful control he had demonstrated in subduing her attacker without permanent harm. There had been something almost protective in the way he had wrapped the manuscript and sketch, in how gently he had secured her bonds to avoid causing pain. Even his promise to set her free suggested this was not the act of a madman but of someone operating under constraints she did not yet understand.

"I shall explain everything when I can," he had promised before they departed Danbury's estate. "This is the best solution for both of us, Miss Bigsby."

The best solution? Henri worked frantically at her bonds, trying to find some weakness in the knots, but Lord Trenwith had clearly known what he was about. The silk was smooth and strong, giving her no purchase to work herself free.

Her reputation was ruined. Utterly and completely destroyed. A young unmarried woman traveling alone with a man, bound and gagged in his carriage like some sort of criminal? When this became known, and it would become known, she would be finished in society. Her position with Uncle Reggie would be forfeit. Her family would be scandalized. Everything she had worked to build for herself would crumble to ash.

The carriage lurched over a particularly deep rut, and Henri had to bite down on the gag to keep from crying out as she was thrown against the hard seat. Lord Trenwith had removed anything from the interior that might serve as a weapon—the brass fittings, the small tools kept for emergencies, even the metal clasps and buckles that might be used to fray rope. He was ruthless in ensuring her captivity, which made his betrayal all the more shocking.

What could possibly drive a viscount to kidnap Reginald Wells's secretary? She tried to think of reasons, turning over their previous conversations in her mind, searching for some clue she had missed. He had always been charming in their interactions, if somewhat distant. She had thought him merely reserved, perhaps even a bit lonely beneath that aristocratic coolness. Clearly, she had been a fool.

The carriage slowed, and Henri heard voices outside. Lord Trenwith was speaking to what sounded like an ostler about changing horses. She tried to make noise, to bang against the walls with her feet, but the sounds were muffled and pathetic. No one would hear her over the bustle of a coaching inn, and even if they did, they would likely assume it was merely luggage shifting about.

This was exactly why she had never married, Henri thought bitterly as the fresh horses were hitched and they resumed their journey. The very idea of being at the mercy of a man, of having no control over her own fate, had always appalled her. She valued her independence, her career with Uncle Reggie, the satisfaction of being useful and needed for her mind rather than merely ornamental. No husband would allow her to continue such work. Most would consider it unseemly for their wives to be so involved in political matters.

Unfortunately, she had never foreseen being kidnapped and, therefore, had no plan for such a contingency. All her careful arrangements for maintaining her independence were useless when faced with superior physical strength that left women vulnerable to men's whims.

The weather began to worsen as the afternoon wore on. Henri could hear the wind picking up outside and see snowflakes settling on the carriage windows. Their progress slowed to a crawl, and eventually, they stopped altogether. She heard Lord Trenwith speaking to someone, another traveler perhaps or a local, who had warned him about road conditions ahead.

The door opened, bringing a blast of frigid air that made Henri shiver violently beneath her inadequate blanket. Lord Trenwith climbed inside, stamping snow from his boots and pulling off his gloves with stiff fingers.

"Miss Bigsby," he said quietly, settling onto the opposite seat. "I have brought you some food from the last inn. You must be hungry."

He produced a wrapped bundle and gently removed her gag, though he made no move to untie her hands. Henri worked her jaw, wincing at the stiffness, before fixing him with the most withering glare she could manage.

"How dare you," she said, hoarse from hours of enforced silence. "How dare you treat me like some common criminal? I demand you release me immediately and return me to Sir Alpheus's estate."

"I cannot do that," Lord Trenwith replied, unwrapping what appeared to be bread and cheese. "The roads ahead are impassable in this weather. We shall have to wait here until the storm passes."

"That is not what I meant, and you know it," Henri snapped. "I demand an explanation for this outrageous behavior. What could possibly justify kidnapping me?"

Lord Trenwith was quiet for a long moment, studying her face in the dim light filtering through the snow-covered windows. "There are forces at work that you do not understand, Miss Bigsby. Your safety, and the safety of others, depends upon your discretion."

"My safety?" Henri laughed bitterly. "You are the one threatening my safety! My reputation is destroyed, my position ruined. What safety is there in that?"

"Your reputation can be protected," he said quietly, "or restored, at least." He leaned forward and released her bindings, tenderly caressing her wrists with his thumbs to ease the accumulated stiffness as if with genuine concern for her well-being.

Henri stared at him, trying to read the meaning behind his cryptic words. "How?"

But Lord Trenwith had already shifted back, moving to peer out the window at the swirling snow. "Eat," he said, placing the food within her reach. "We may be here for some time."

Henri wanted to refuse, to throw his food back in his face, but hunger and cold were making her weak. She ate awkwardly, all the while studying her captor's profile and trying to understand what had transformed the reserved but courteous gentleman she knew into this mysterious figure.

Lord Trenwith mumbled about seeing to his cattle before producing thick woolen horse rugs and leaving the carriage briefly. He returned without the rugs and took up the seat across from her once more.

Hours passed. The storm showed no signs of abating, and the temperature inside the carriage continued to drop. Henri found herself shivering uncontrollably, her teeth chattering so violently she could barely speak.

"This is intolerable," Lord Trenwith muttered, watching her struggle against the cold. "We shall both perish if this continues."

To Henri's shock, he moved to sit beside her on the narrow seat, removed his greatcoat, and pulled the greatcoat and blanket around both of them, drawing her against his side. She stiffened, every propriety screaming against such intimacy, but the warmth radiating from his body was too tempting to resist.

"Miss Bigsby." His breath stirred the hair at her temple. "I know this seems unconscionable, but it is a matter of survival. We must share heat or risk freezing."

Henri wanted to protest, to maintain her dignity and her anger, but she was so cold and so tired that she found herself relaxing against him despite her better judgment. He was solid and warm, his arm around her shoulders providing a sense of security that her rational mind knew was false but that her body craved nonetheless.

"I still do not understand," she whispered, muffled against his coat. "Why are you doing this to me?"

"Sleep, Miss Bigsby," he replied, his voice gentler than it had been all day. "Perhaps things will be clearer in the morning."

Henri closed her eyes, knowing she should resist this treacherous comfort but finding herself unable to do so. She was dismayed to discover how much she enjoyed his proximity, the steady rhythm of his breathing, the way his hand moved soothingly against her arm. Even stranded and helpless, even furious and frightened, some traitorous part of her felt safer in his arms than she had since this nightmare began.

She fell asleep pressed against Lord Trenwith's side, miserable and cold and thoroughly confused, but more comfortable than she had been in hours. And if she dreamed of kind hazel eyes and gentle hands, of a different version of this journey where she was not a captive but a willing companion, she told herself it was merely the delirium brought on by cold and exhaustion.

Nothing more.

* * *

JANUARY 26, 1822

Gabriel sat in the darkness of the storm-bound carriage, holding Miss Bigsby's sleeping form against his side, and found himself wrestling with thoughts he could barely comprehend. She had asked for an explanation, had demanded to know why he was subjecting her to this ordeal, and he wished desperately that he could tell her what was happening. But even if he was not bound by oath, how could he explain what he himself could scarcely believe?

He was cursing himself for the decision to bring her with him, though it was far too late to reconsider his actions now. The shock of recognizing her in that library had clouded his judgment completely. His primary concern had been the negotiations. If Miss Bigsby returned to London with tales of encountering Viscount Trenwith under mysterious circumstances, examining stolen manuscripts and subduing armed men, word would reach Paris within days. Étienne would realize Gabriel had abandoned his post, and loyal English agents would pay the price.

That singular focus on preserving his mission's secrecy had led him to make a catastrophic error. In truth, he had only delayed the inevitable. It was certain that Étienne would learn of his betrayal when word of Miss Bigsby's disappearance reached the proper circles, and she resurfaced as his bride. His French counterpart was no fool and would piece together the sequence of events, realizing that Gabriel had abandoned the negotiations at their most crucial point to pursue personal matters.

And to make things worse, in his panic over Miss Bigsby's presence, he had allowed that villain to escape. The man who might have provided answers about Horace's murder, who could have led Gabriel to the heart of whatever conspiracy had taken his beloved tutor's life, had slipped away while

Gabriel grappled with the impossible situation her recognition had created.

He could have solved everything in that moment. Captured the assassin, forced him to reveal his masters, perhaps even uncovered the truth about *Regis Aeterni* that Horace had died for. Instead, he had been so consumed with containing the crisis that he had let the greatest lead in his investigation vanish into the winter afternoon.

While it was true that leaving Miss Bigsby at Danbury's estate might have exposed her to further risk from whatever forces had sent that armed man, Gabriel could no longer lie to himself about his motives. A more troubling concern whispered that perhaps, despite all his warnings to himself to remain aloof, he had chosen this course because some traitorous part of him had desired it.

Had he truly rescued Miss Bigsby, or had he simply used the threat to her as an excuse to claim what he had secretly wanted for two years? He was afraid that rather than being decisive, he had merely been rash. A rashness that may have been brought on by his desire for Miss Bigsby, compromising his usually precise mind.

The thought made Gabriel's stomach twist with self-loathing. He had prided himself on his control, on his ability to keep his emotions contained, yet here he sat with the most dangerous woman in London pressed against his chest, her soft breathing stirring something fierce and protective in his soul.

And he admitted to himself that in his swift action to safeguard the agents and preserve the delicate balance of their exchange, Gabriel feared he might have made everything infinitely worse.

Men would suffer for his weakness. Their families would continue to endure separation because Gabriel had been unable to resist the pull of personal justice and, subsequently, if he was being honest with himself, personal desire.

Despite the cold seeping through the carriage walls, despite the gravity of their situation, Gabriel found himself enjoying the simple act of holding Miss Bigsby more than he cared to admit. She fit against him perfectly, her slight frame tucked beneath his arm as if she belonged there. The scent of lavender that clung to her hair, the way her hand had unconsciously curled against his chest in sleep. It was torment and bliss combined.

Gabriel allowed himself to imagine, just for a moment, what it might be like to wake up to Miss Bigsby every morning. To see those remarkable amber eyes open with affection instead of accusation, to have the right to hold her without the weight of kidnapping and coercion between them. To be the man she turned to for comfort rather than the one she needed protection from.

The fantasy was so vivid, so achingly appealing, that Gabriel had to force himself to quell such sentiments before they overwhelmed what remained of his rational mind. He had no right to such dreams, no claim to the woman in his arms. She would hate him for this, and rightly so. When the truth came out, and it would come out, she would see him for exactly what he was—a man who had used his strength to claim what he had not earned honestly.

As exhaustion finally claimed him, Gabriel fell into a troubled sleep filled with dark, fractured dreams. He found himself standing once again in his grandfather's study, five years old and tear-stained, reaching out for comfort that would never come.

*"Weakness,"* the old viscount's sermon echoed as if he were standing in a great hall. *"Unseemly emotion from a Strathmore. You will learn to control yourself, boy, or you will bring shame upon this family."*

The scene twisted and shifted, and suddenly, it was Miss Bigsby standing before him, her amber eyes filled with the same cold contempt that had marked his grandfather's features. But where the old man had merely been disgusted by a child's tears, Miss Bigsby's scorn cut far deeper.

*"Is this what you call strength?"* she asked mockingly. *"Kidnapping defenseless women because you cannot face your own failures? You are not a hero, Lord Trenwith. You are a coward who takes what he wants and calls it duty."*

Gabriel jerked awake in the gray pre-dawn light, his heart racing and cold sweat dampening his brow despite the chill. The nightmare's echo lingered, her condemning words ringing in his ears even as he looked down to find her still sleeping peacefully against his shoulder, her face soft and unguarded in slumber.

The contrast between his fears and the reality of her trust —because she must trust him on some level to sleep so peacefully in his arms—left Gabriel shaken. Perhaps his dreams were merely his conscience finally asserting itself, forcing him to confront the possibility that his actions, however well-intentioned, were fundamentally selfish.

He had told himself he was protecting her, protecting his mission, protecting the imprisoned agents whose freedom depended upon his success. But as Gabriel watched the first pale light of dawn filter through the snow-covered windows, he could no longer avoid the truth that terrified him most. Mayhap, he had chosen this path not just out of duty, but because he could not bear the thought of letting Miss Bigsby slip away from him again.

And for that weakness, they would both pay a price he was only beginning to understand.

## CHAPTER 6

*"Sir, wit you well I will never consent to be taken, while my life lasteth."*

**Sir Thomas Malory, *Le Morte d'Arthur***

* * *

Around midmorning, Henri was startled awake by a sudden brightness flooding the carriage interior. She blinked against the unexpected glare, realizing that the sun had finally emerged from behind the storm clouds. The transformation was remarkable. What had been a world of gray and white only hours before was now dazzling with sunlight reflecting off the snow-covered landscape.

Lord Trenwith stirred beside her, extricating himself from their shared blanket and the greatcoat. Henri felt the immediate loss of his warmth and found herself oddly bereft as he moved away from her. The cold air rushed in to fill the space he had occupied, making her shiver despite the sun's brightness.

"I shall investigate the road," he murmured, reaching for the door handle. "The storm appears to have passed."

Henri watched him step down, his boots crunching in the snow as he walked ahead to assess their situation. She flexed her freed wrists, grateful for the temporary reprieve from the silk cords that had bound her during their earlier travel. Her shoulders still ached from the hours she had spent restrained, but at least she could move her arms freely while they sheltered from the storm. Henri took the opportunity to comb her hair out with her fingers and straighten her wrinkled carriage dress before opening the door and jumping down. She scooped up snow with her bare hands and used it to rinse out her mouth and dab her face clean before hurriedly pulling her gloves back on.

All the while, the viscount was examining the road, occasionally kicking at the snow to gauge its depth. The sight was strangely domestic, a gentleman checking travel conditions, yet Henri could not shake the fantastical knowledge that she was his prisoner, helpless like some character from a Gothic novel.

When Lord Trenwith returned, he pulled out another bundle of food procured from their last stop. Henri's stomach clenched with hunger at the sight of bread and cheese, only sharpened by the cold, but she found herself reluctant to accept anything from her captor.

"The snow is not very deep," he announced as he settled back onto the bench seat, crumpled and unshaven, but nevertheless still an infuriatingly handsome man. She dared not think what a fright she must be in comparison. "Perhaps two or three inches at most. We can leave in a couple of hours once the sun has had time to soften the worst of it."

"Leave for where?" Henri demanded. "Lord Trenwith, I insist you tell me where you are taking me."

He looked at her for a long moment, and Henri thought

she saw regret flicker across his features. But when he spoke, his voice was as controlled as ever.

"Somewhere safe, Miss Bigsby. That is all I can tell you for now."

"Safe?" Henri's voice rose despite her efforts to maintain composure. "You call this safe? I was bound like a criminal, transported against my will to heaven knows where, and you speak of safety?"

"Your current discomfort is temporary," Lord Trenwith replied, unwrapping the food. "There are matters that require my immediate attention."

Henri stared at him, trying to read the truth in his blank expression. "What matters? Lord Trenwith, I insist you tell me what this is about."

"I cannot explain yet …" He paused, seeming to choose his words with great care. "Miss Bigsby, I will tell you what you need to know."

"Then why not take me to Uncle Reggie? Or to the authorities? Why this … this kidnapping?"

Lord Trenwith was quiet for so long that Henri began to think he would not answer at all. When he finally spoke, his words were measured.

"There are considerations that must be taken into account. Larger matters that affect more lives than just your own."

The enigmatic response only fueled Henri's frustration. "I am not a child, my lord. I work in political circles. I understand that there are often complex situations that require discretion. But surely I deserve some explanation for why my life has been turned upside down."

"You deserve a great deal more than you are currently receiving," Lord Trenwith said quietly, and there was sympathy in his tone that made Henri soften with unwanted affinity. "But explanations must wait."

Henri wanted to press him further, but the futility of her situation was becoming clear. Lord Trenwith was not going to reveal his plans, no matter how reasonably she argued or how desperately she pleaded. She was entirely at his mercy, a realization that filled her with equal parts rage and an uncomfortable flutter of something that might have been anticipation.

When they were finally ready to depart, Lord Trenwith produced the silk cords and handkerchief with obvious reluctance.

"I am sorry, Miss Bigsby," he said, and Henri thought his regret might actually be genuine. "But I cannot risk you attempting to flee or attract attention as we travel."

"You cannot mean to keep me bound for the entire journey," Henri protested, even as she allowed him to secure her wrists once again. His touch was gentle but firm, and she found herself disturbingly aware of the touch of his fingers as they brushed against her skin.

"Only until we reach safety," he replied, and Henri noticed that he avoided her eyes as he spoke. "I give you my word that these restraints are temporary."

The gag followed, and Henri submitted to it with as much dignity as she could manage. There was something deeply unsettling about the intimate nature of his ministrations, the way he ensured the silk did not pull at her hair, how he checked that she could breathe comfortably around the obstruction. It was the consideration of a man who cared about her welfare, yet who was willing to override her every protest and desire. She supposed she ought to struggle, ought to attempt to make a run for it, but then she would not learn what he was up to. Strangely, they were cooperating with each other as she wondered if she had been afflicted with madness.

The journey resumed with agonizing slowness. The

melting snow had turned the roads into quagmired channels of mud and slush that sucked at the wheels and made every mile a struggle. Henri found herself thrown about despite Lord Trenwith's careful driving, and more than once, she feared they might become completely mired.

As the hours passed, Henri tried desperately to determine their direction and destination. The sun provided some guidance, but the winding country lanes made it difficult to maintain any sense of their heading. She thought they might be traveling generally southeast, but beyond that, Henri could only guess at their ultimate goal.

With time to think, Henri's thoughts raced back and forth to the events of the past day. What had her assailant been doing at Danbury's estate? The madman who had threatened her with the pistol had been there for the same manuscript as she. Had Lord Trenwith also been after the same manuscript? He certainly had made a point of bringing it along. Did she need to be worried about him? Did the scoundrel know who she was?

There were no answers, just more and more questions.

The countryside altered almost imperceptibly as the carriage rolled on. The gentle rise and fall of the land began to ease, the vistas opening wider beneath a sky brushed with pale light. Through the narrow vents, a fresher quality crept into the air. Cooler, sharper, with some elusive tang that she could not place. Henri drew in another breath, a faint unease curling in her chest without any clear reason why.

As night began to fall, Henri's worst fears were confirmed. The sound reached her ears gradually at first. A rhythmic rushing that she initially mistook for wind through trees. But as they drew closer, the sound became unmistakable. The crash of waves against shore.

Fear struck her like a physical blow. The sharp cries of gulls wheeled overhead, mingling with the wind that salted her lips. Beneath it came the ceaseless rush and hiss of water over shingle. Lord Trenwith was taking her to the coast. He meant to see her carried across the Channel. He was removing her from England entirely.

Henri began to struggle against her bonds with renewed desperation, throwing herself against the walls in an attempt to signal distress to anyone who might hear. But the silk cords held fast, and her muffled cries were lost in the sound of wind and waves.

The carriage finally stopped, and Henri heard Lord Trenwith speaking to someone in low, urgent tones. Through the window, she could make out the dark bulk of a sailboat riding at anchor in a small secluded cove. Lanterns flickered aboard, casting pale, shifting light that gleamed on the restless water, and she saw figures moving about in hurried preparation. The wind howled through the narrow channel of rocks, bringing with it the roar of distant surf.

After Lord Trenwith opened the door, she watched him retrieve the manuscript and sketch from the hidden compartment and place them in a large pocket of his greatcoat. Then he reached for her. Henri fought him with every ounce of strength she possessed. She kicked and twisted, trying to make herself as difficult to manage as possible, but his superior strength made her efforts futile. He lifted her bodily from the carriage, pressing her close to his chest, the wind whipping around them in icy gusts that rattled the door on its hinges and stung her eyes with salt spray.

"Miss Bigsby, please," he shouted over the shrieking wind. "I know this seems frightening, but you must trust me. I will not allow any harm to come to you."

Henri's response was a renewed struggle that nearly sent them both tumbling onto the slick, uneven ground. His arms tightened around her, the muscles in his shoulders bunching as he fought to maintain his footing on the slippery shingle, wet with spray and treacherous with hidden rocks. She caught a glimpse of a weathered man leading their carriage and horses away into the darkness, the animals' breath steaming in the cold night air, presumably to return both vehicle and team to whatever inn or stable Lord Trenwith had arranged. The efficiency of the operation suggested it had all been planned in advance.

As they neared the edge of the cove, Henri heard a voice raised in anger. A stocky man with graying hair and wind-beaten features stood in a small boat that bobbed and bumped against the rocks, gesticulating furiously and shouting in rapid French.

"*What are you doing?*" the captain demanded, cutting sharply across the wind. "*You told me nothing about a woman!*"

Lord Trenwith replied in French, his tone calm but unyielding. Henri caught enough of the exchange to understand that the captain was furious about her presence and the delay it had caused.

"*We are late,*" the captain snapped in French. "*The tide is already turning. We should have left an hour ago.*"

"*Then we must leave now,*" the viscount called back firmly, shifting her weight in his arms. Henri twisted violently, trying to break free, but he merely tightened his hold with grim determination.

Without waiting for further argument, he stepped into the freezing shallows, icy water swirling around his boots and soaking the hem of his coat. Salt spray lashed them both in punishing gusts, and Henri gasped as freezing droplets struck her face and neck to send a convulsive shiver down her spine.

She realized abruptly that Lord Trenwith must be just as cold. She felt the tremor that rippled through his body where it pressed against hers, his coat already heavy and sodden with seawater, the wind tearing at his hair and clothes without mercy. Yet he did not hesitate. He did not slow. His grip was secure, even protective, and his jaw was set in a hard, determined line as he trudged forward against the pull of the waves.

He splashed through the water to the waiting small boat, shifting her higher in his arms to keep her dry.

"*Captain Joubert, I apologize for the delay,*" he called evenly over Henri's head, as calmly as if he were discussing the weather rather than restraining a furious woman while raising his voice in the damp flurry of turbulent air. "*Circumstances required ... flexibility.*"

Captain Joubert muttered something uncomplimentary in French about being discovered, but he finally gestured for them to board, shaking his head in irritation. Lord Trenwith did not wait for further argument. He shifted her in his arms and stepped into the swaying boat, placing her firmly onto one of the narrow benches before settling down beside her, boots dripping and coat heavy with seawater. Silently, without meeting her eyes, he removed the gag from her mouth and the cords from her wrists.

They pushed off immediately, oars biting into the black water with harsh, rhythmic splashes. Salt spray stung her face, and she wrapped her aching arms around herself, shivering violently in her cloak, which was miraculously mostly dry due to his efforts to keep her above the splash of the waves. Lord Trenwith sat close beside her, his breathing harsh with effort, water streaming from his lower half to pool around his sodden boots in the bottom of the boat.

When they reached the sloop's side, crewmen hauled them aboard with hurried, rough efficiency. Henri stumbled as the deck pitched underfoot, her shoes slipping on the wet planks. Lord Trenwith's grip on her arm steadied her just long enough for him to steer her toward the companionway.

Captain Joubert barked orders behind them, clearly eager to be underway.

Lord Trenwith guided her below into a small dimly lit cabin, the lantern swaying wildly on its hook with each heave of the ship. He urged her onto a narrow bunk and immediately the oilskin bundle from his overcoat pocket. She watched in frozen silence as he carefully unwrapped the manuscript and sketch to check them, his fingers steady as he rewrapped them despite the pitch and roll of the vessel. He stowed them securely in what appeared to be a waterproof chest, snapping it shut with decisive finality.

Without pausing, he began to peel off his drenched coat, the fabric making a wet, sucking sound as he forced it from his arms. Henri blinked, startled, then quickly turned her face away, her cheeks burning with mortification as she realized he was shedding his soaked garments. But not before she caught a glimpse of broad shoulders, rippling muscles, and a sandy brown dusting of curling hair over his powerful chest, which caused an unexpected stirring of curiosity. She heard the thud of boots hitting the deck and the rustle of linen and wool as he changed.

Henri kept her gaze fixed firmly on the bulkhead, despite her impulse to glance back, watching instead the long shadows cast by the flickering lamplight across the cramped cabin. Heat prickled in her ears despite the chill that clung to her shivering form, and she wrapped her arms tighter around herself, determined not to turn and look. This might be the closest she had ever been to a naked man, but she would resist the urge to peek if it killed her. Behind her, she heard the sound of dry clothes being pulled on with brisk, impatient motions.

At last, he spoke from just behind her shoulder, rough but steadier. "You may turn around now, Miss Bigsby. I am decent."

Henri barely nodded in response, having become wretchedly seasick from the listing of the boat. The bile rose in her tight throat, made worse by the dryness from having been gagged for so long and thus preventing her from voiding her stomach properly. She began to choke, panic flooding through her as she struggled to breathe around her body's rebellion.

Lord Trenwith was beside her instantly. "Easy," he murmured, supporting her as she leaned over a basin he had somehow procured. "Let it come, Miss Bigsby. Fighting it will only make you feel worse."

Henri was too miserable to appreciate the irony of receiving comfort from her captor. She retched violently into the basin, her body shaking with the force of her illness, and found herself grateful for Lord Trenwith's steady presence. His hand rubbed soothing circles on her back, and he held her hair away from her face with surprising tenderness.

"I am sorry," he said quietly as her stomach finally began to settle. "I had hoped we might make a calmer crossing."

Henri wiped her mouth with the cloth he offered, trying to muster the energy for renewed anger. But exhaustion and illness had drained her reserves, and she found herself slumping against him despite her best intentions.

"Where are you taking me?" she whispered, barely audible over the sound of waves against the hull.

Lord Trenwith's arms came around her, drawing her more securely against his chest. She felt his lips brush against her hair, the touch so fleeting she might have imagined it.

"To France," he admitted quietly. "But only temporarily, Miss Bigsby. I promise you will return to England soon."

"France?" Henri tried to pull away, but her weakened state made resistance impossible. "Lord Trenwith, you cannot mean to … This is lunacy. Why France?"

"Because it is the only place where certain matters can be

resolved," he replied, his breath warm against her ear. "You will be safe while I complete what I came to do."

Henri wanted to demand more answers, to rail against his high-handed treatment of her, but another wave of nausea swept over her. She found herself clinging to Lord Trenwith's coat, using his solid presence as an anchor against the relentless motion.

"Breathe slowly," he murmured, low and rumbling. "Focus on something steady. The sound of my voice, perhaps."

Despite everything—the kidnapping, the restraints, the terrifying ride to an unknown destination—Henri found his presence oddly comforting. There was something infinitely reassuring about his calm competence, the way he anticipated her needs before she was even aware of them herself.

"I do not understand any of this," she whispered against his shoulder.

"I know." His hand moved to stroke her hair, the gesture tender. "And I am sorrier for that than you can possibly know. But I swear to you, Miss Bigsby, upon my honor as a gentleman, that no harm will come to you while you are in my care."

Henri closed her eyes, allowing herself to sink into the unexpected comfort of his embrace. She could feel the vessel pitching and rolling as it fought its way through rough seas, but wrapped in Lord Trenwith's arms, she felt oddly secure.

It made no sense. He had kidnapped her, transported her against her will, and was now taking her to a foreign country for reasons he refused to explain. By all rights, she should be terrified of him, should be fighting with every breath to escape his hold.

Instead, she found herself thinking of the way he had rescued her from that armed man in Sir Alpheus's library. The careful consideration he had shown even while binding her wrists. The gentle way he tended to her illness, as if her comfort mattered to him despite the circumstances.

Lord Trenwith was many things. High-handed, secretive, infuriatingly controlled. But Henri knew that he was not, at heart, a villain. Which only made her situation more confusing.

As the ship carried them through the storm-tossed Channel toward France, Henri allowed herself to rest in the arms of the man who had turned her life upside down. Tomorrow, she would demand answers. Tomorrow, she would find a way to assert some control over her fate.

Tonight, seasick and exhausted and more confused than she had ever been in her life, she simply held on and tried to trust in Lord Trenwith's promise that he would see her safely home.

*Alaric Devayne was a victim of his own obsessions. He slept poorly, ate too little, and attacked his interests with such fervor that it verged on a madness, a disease of the soul for which he would have been well-advised to take a long and brisk constitutional to pay his surroundings some mind.*

*Obsession was why, from a rocky outcropping above the cove, he watched the dark vessel slip away into the storm-lashed night. The wind whipped his coat around him as he strained his eyes to follow the ship's lanterns until they disappeared entirely into the churning darkness of the Channel.*

*He had followed them from Danbury's estate, keeping well back on the muddy roads until the storm had forced him to seek shelter at a wayside inn. Rather than reveal himself to the other travelers, he had bedded down in the stables with his horse, wrapped in his greatcoat and listening to the wind howl through the night. When dawn broke clear, he had ridden as hard as he dared to pick up their trail again, eventually finding the wheel ruts in the softening snow. The pursuit had been arduous, but his determination had been rewarded when he had spotted their vehicle making its way down the steep path to this secluded cove.*

*What he had witnessed from his hidden vantage left him deeply unsettled. The woman had clearly been struggling against the man, fighting him with desperate energy as he carried her aboard the vessel. Her hands had appeared to be bound, though the darkness and distance made it difficult to be certain.*

*Alaric frowned, trying to piece together what he had observed. The man had rescued the woman from his attack in the library yet now appeared to be taking her against her will. Why save her only to kidnap her? The manuscript was valuable, certainly, but why take the woman from England altogether? There had to be more at stake, some larger game being played that he could not yet comprehend.*

*The proximity to Dover gave him hope. If they were using this cove for their crossing, they might well return the same way. Smugglers were creatures of habit, preferring routes they knew to be safe from the revenue officers.*

*Alaric made his decision quickly. He would ride to Dover and establish himself near the docks, watching for any sign of their return. A few coins in the right hands would secure him information about unusual arrivals. Perhaps he could even find a local boy to keep watch on this particular cove, someone who knew the tides and could alert him to any nighttime activity.*

*The manuscript was still within his reach, but now his curiosity extended far beyond the ancient text. Whatever the man was truly after, whatever had driven him to such desperate measures, Alaric intended to discover it.*

*He had no choice but to be patient. But patience, he reflected grimly as he made his way back to his horse, had always been one of his particular strengths.*

# CHAPTER 7

*"Wit you well, I will never be your wife."*

**Sir Thomas Malory, *Le Morte d'Arthur***

* * *

JANUARY 27, 1822

Miss Bigsby had demanded answers with what little strength remained to her, but the combination of fear, exhaustion, and the vessel's relentless motion had soon overwhelmed her weakened constitution. She had collapsed into an uneasy sleep against Gabriel's shoulder, her breathing finally settling into a more regular rhythm as her body surrendered to its need for rest.

Gabriel held her steady for what felt like hours, doing what he could to provide her fragile peace. Gradually, he became aware that the ship's violent pitching had begun to ease somewhat. The storm was still raging, but the worst of it seemed to be passing, and the vessel no longer felt as though it might tear itself apart with each wave.

When he was certain Miss Bigsby was deeply asleep, Gabriel extracted himself from beneath her, settling her as comfortably as possible on the narrow bunk with his coat wrapped around her for warmth. She stirred slightly but did not wake, and he waited several more minutes before quietly making his way above deck.

The wind still howled across the deck, and spray stung his face as he emerged from the cabin. The captain was at his post near the wheel, shouting orders to his crew as they worked to keep the ship on course.

*"She is finally at rest?"* André called out when he spotted Gabriel, his guttural French almost carried away by the brisk wind, but his weathered face was no longer etched with the desperate concentration required during the height of the storm.

Gabriel nodded, moving closer so they could speak without shouting. *"The seasickness exhausted her completely. I have never seen anyone so ill."*

André studied Gabriel's face in the dim light from the ship's lanterns, likely noting the tension around his eyes, the careful way he moved as if his entire body ached with strain. *"You look like a man carrying the weight of the world, my friend. This is not like you."*

*"I feel terrible for what I have done to her,"* Gabriel admitted, the words coming more easily in French, as if the foreign language provided some distance from the magnitude of his actions. Or, mayhap, the fact that he saw the captain so infrequently made him unusually loquacious as he confessed his worries to the older man. *"She is an innocent woman, André. She did nothing to deserve this. But my mission left me without choice. There are lives hanging in the balance."*

*"Ah, but you forget something important,"* the captain declared, leaning forward with the intensity Gabriel had come to know well over their years of working together. He showed admirable restraint in accepting Miss Bigsby's presence without needing any justification. But the captain possessed a healthy dose of Gallic pragmatism. *"You are a good man, Gabriel. A man of honor. You will find a way to make this right."*

*"How can I possibly make this right? I have ruined her reputation, destroyed her independence, forced her into a situation where marriage to me is her only option to salvage anything of her former life."*

André was quiet for a long moment, considering. *"Then you must take extraordinary measures to make it up to her."*

They continued their discussion for several minutes, but then the boat began to rock more violently.

*"I should return to her."* Gabriel sighed, glancing back toward the cabin. *"She should not wake alone in a strange place."*

*"Go,"* André replied with understanding. *"But think on what I have said."*

Gabriel made his way back below deck, moving carefully in the still-rough seas. He slipped quietly into the cabin, where Miss Bigsby remained deeply asleep. Her determined little chin was slack in exhaustion, her normally creamy skin clammy from the ordeal of seasickness, yet even in this vulnerable state, she was achingly beautiful. He settled down beside her, watching over her as the ship continued its journey through the night.

This was unprecedented for him. In all his years of diplomatic work, of careful negotiations and calculated risks, he had never allowed personal considerations to complicate his missions. He had trained himself to remain detached, professional, focused solely on the task at hand.

But Miss Henrietta Bigsby had always been his weakness.

From the moment he had first met her in her uncle's drawing room two years ago, she had fascinated him in ways he had not believed possible. Her sharp wit, her bubbly personality that could light up even the most tedious political gathering, the sheer courage and skill it took for her to hold a man's position in the hostile environment of Westminster politics. She navigated the pompous members of Parliament with a grace and intelligence that left Gabriel in awe.

He had never made any advances toward her, had never allowed himself to hope for more than their professional interactions and the occasional social pleasantries. The phantasy of Miss Bigsby had been safer than risking the devastating reality of her rejection. A woman of her caliber, her independence and strength, would hardly be interested in a man who lived half his life in shadows, who disappeared for weeks at a time on Crown business he could never discuss.

But now she had no choice. The scandal of her disappearance, the ruin to her reputation, meant that marriage to him was her only path to salvaging anything of her former life. The thought should have brought him satisfaction, but instead it filled him with a gnawing dread and guilt so profound it threatened to choke him.

*"There will still be questions when we return to England."* Gabriel recollected his admission from his discussion above deck. *"People will wonder why she vanished, where she has been. The gossips will have a field day regardless of what explanation we provide."*

*"Then you must give them a story they can accept,"* André had replied pragmatically. *"A romantic elopement, perhaps. A secret courtship that culminated in an impulsive flight to France for a hasty wedding."*

Gabriel had almost laughed at the bitter irony. *"If only it were that simple."*

*"It can be, if you make it so. But you must be prepared to be the kind of husband she deserves. A man with fortitude, who can defend her against the worst of the scandal and gossip. You must also be willing to give her space to breathe, to not overwhelm her with your own needs and fears."*

Gabriel knew André was right, but the prospect terrified him. How could he maintain the careful distance required to avoid frightening Miss Bigsby away when every instinct demanded he hold her close, protect her from a world that would judge her harshly for circumstances beyond her control? How could he be the stoic, reliable husband she would need when her very presence threatened to undo the iron control he had spent years perfecting?

The truth was that a rejection from Miss Bigsby now, when she was his wife in all but name, might very well kill the last embers of his heart. He had survived the deaths of his parents, the cold indifference of his grandfather, years of isolation and dangerous work, by locking away what remained of his heart. But Miss Bigsby had slipped past his defenses without his even realizing it, and now she held the power to destroy him completely.

*"I have never been in this situation before,"* Gabriel had eventually confessed. He certainly was being garrulous, but perhaps he was simply missing his tutor. *"I do not make lasting connections with women as a rule. It is safer that way, cleaner. But Miss Bigsby is different. She has always been different."*

André had smiled, the expression transforming his weathered features. *"Then perhaps this is not the disaster you believe it to be. Perhaps this is simply fate forcing your hand, giving you what you have always wanted but were too afraid to pursue."*

Gabriel returned to the moment. Even unconscious, Miss

Bigsby seemed to trust him on some fundamental level, and that trust was both a gift and a terrible responsibility.

*I pray André is right. For both our sakes.*

The ship lurched violently, and she stirred against him, a small sound of distress escaping her lips. Gabriel's arms tightened around her, and he found himself making a silent vow. Whatever the cost, whatever sacrifices were required, he would find a way to make this right. Miss Bigsby deserved his complete devotion to her happiness and well-being.

Even if it meant finding the strength to be the stoic, reliable husband she would need, while keeping his own desperate need for her hidden lest he frighten her away completely.

* * *

THE FIRST THING Henri noticed as consciousness returned was the absence of the ship's violent motion. The relentless pitching and rolling that had made her so wretchedly ill had ceased, replaced by a gentle rocking that suggested they were anchored in calmer waters. Dim gray light filtered through the small cabin window, and she could hear the distant calls of seabirds overhead.

"Miss Bigsby." Lord Trenwith's voice was quiet, careful not to startle her. "We have arrived."

Henri sat up slowly, her body protesting after the night's ordeal. Through the porthole, she could see a rocky coastline bathed in the soft golden light of dawn. The water here was a different color than the storm-tossed Channel they had crossed, a calmer blue-green that spoke of shallower depths and sheltered harbors.

"Where are we?" she asked, though she suspected she already knew the answer.

"Near Blériot-Plage," Lord Trenwith replied, moving to gather the wrapped manuscript and sketch. "We are in France, Miss Bigsby."

France. The reality of it made her swallow in dismay. She was no longer in England, no longer under the protection of English laws or social conventions. She was completely at the mercy of a man whose motives remained utterly mysterious to her.

"What happens now?" Henri's voice emerged steadier than she felt.

Lord Trenwith paused in his preparations, and for a moment, she caught a glimpse of something like uncertainty in his hazel eyes. "Now I must ask for your cooperation. There are men's lives at stake, Miss Bigsby. Important matters that require discretion. I need you to come ashore quietly, without drawing attention to our arrival."

Henri studied his face, noting the lines of strain around his eyes, the tension in his jaw that spoke of trouble. Whatever had driven him to this desperate course, whatever these mysterious matters were, they clearly weighed heavily upon him.

"Men's lives," she repeated slowly. "What men? What lives hang in the balance that could possibly justify kidnapping me?"

"I cannot explain fully, not yet," Lord Trenwith replied, his voice heavy with what sounded like genuine regret. "I am not permitted to speak of certain matters at present. But I give you my word that everything I have done has been necessary. Please, Miss Bigsby. I am asking for your trust."

Henri wanted to refuse, to demand answers, to rail against the impossible situation he had placed her in. But something in his expression stopped her. Beneath the aristocratic composure, beneath the careful control he maintained, she could see genuine worry. This was not the face of a man acting from callous disregard, but of someone caught in circumstances as terrible as her own.

Against her better judgment, against every instinct that screamed she should resist, Henri found herself nodding. "Very well. But I want answers, Lord Trenwith. Real answers, not cryptic hints about matters I cannot understand."

Relief flickered across his features. "You have my word that explanations will come as soon as I am able to give them."

The landing proved trickier than Henri had anticipated. The ship's boat was small and unstable, forcing her to accept Lord Trenwith's steadying hand as they navigated the short distance to the rocky shore. The dawn air was crisp and cold, carrying with it the unfamiliar scents of French coastal vegetation and the lingering salt of the Channel crossing.

Henri kept her word, remaining silent as they made their way up a narrow path from the cove. But her mind raced with questions and fears. What manner of business required such secrecy? What forces were at work that could drive a viscount to such desperate measures?

Her confusion only deepened when they reached the top of the path and found a carriage waiting, driven by a familiar figure dressed in the nondescript livery of a coachman.

"Mr. Tyne?" Henri stared in shock at Lord Trenwith's secretary. Even in the plain brown coat and simple breeches of his disguise, she recognized the thin, scholarly man she had encountered perhaps twice in Uncle Reggie's drawing room during political consultations.

Mr. Tyne's pale eyes went wide with recognition and what appeared to be horror. "Miss Bigsby?" His voice climbed toward panic. "My lord, what have you done?"

"Tyne." Lord Trenwith's warning brooked no argument.

"We will discuss this later. For now, please assist Miss Bigsby into the carriage."

The secretary's hands shook as he helped Henri into the vehicle, his face pale with shock. "My lord, surely this cannot be necessary. There must be another way to—"

"Samuel." The single word cut through his protests with finality. "Drive us to Calais. Immediately."

The carriage soon lurched into motion, and Henri found herself alone with Lord Trenwith once again, thinking about Mr. Tyne's reaction to her presence. If his own secretary was shocked by her presence, if the man who presumably knew Lord Trenwith's business better than anyone was horrified by what he had done, what did that say about the justification for this kidnapping?

The interior of the carriage was dim, lit only by the pale morning light filtering through small windows. Lord Trenwith sat across from her, the bundled manuscript and sketch clutched under one arm. She considered demanding their return, but she had very nearly given her life for them and needed to make sense of her circumstances before she broached that battle. Henri studied his profile, noting details she had missed in the chaos of the past day.

He looked exhausted. Dark smudges shadowed his eyes, and there was a haggard quality to his lean features that spoke of sleepless nights and burdens too heavy to bear. His usually immaculate appearance was disheveled, his clothing wrinkled from their journey, his thick hair mussed from the sea air.

They rode in silence. Henri found herself oddly reluctant to break it, perhaps sensing that words, once spoken, would change everything between them irrevocably. But as the French countryside rolled past outside their windows, as the reality of her situation settled more fully upon her, she knew she could no longer remain silent.

"You owe me an explanation," she said quietly.

Lord Trenwith's eyes remained closed, but she saw his jaw clench almost imperceptibly. "Yes," he agreed. "I do."

But he offered nothing more, and Henri's patience finally snapped. "Then provide one! What possible justification could you have for treating me this way? For destroying my reputation, my position, my entire life?"

Eventually, he raised his lids to stare at her in the dim interior of the carriage. Henri was again struck by the notion that he had the look of a man who had not rested in some time.

"Miss Bigsby. I wish …" he began, then stopped, seeming to struggle with words that would not come. "I wish to assure you … I will do what is necessary."

"What is necessary?" Henri demanded, sharp with frustration and growing alarm.

He did not respond immediately, considering her with an odd expression that she could not interpret. When he finally spoke, his words struck her like a thunderbolt.

"Wed, Miss Bigsby. Considering the ruin you face, I understand it is my duty to wed you."

Henri's breath caught in her throat. She had been thinking of her own safety since she had woken up this morning, while a million thoughts about why Lord Trenwith was acting in such a bizarre manner collided about in her mind like so much dust in a windstorm. She had tried to suppress her worries about her reputation since opening her eyes to find herself across the Channel, but now all the consequences came rushing in like a chilly winter wind when someone opened the door.

*I am ruined!*

Her work with Uncle Reggie was likely done for. And what about how this would affect the rest of her family? Her mother's clients at Bigsby's Stone Manufactory? It was all too much to consider, so she focused on the one issue she could control.

"Absolutely not!"

The words burst from her with more vehemence than she had intended, but Henri felt no inclination to moderate her tone. Marriage to Lord Trenwith? The very idea was preposterous. She barely knew the man, despite their acquaintance through Uncle Reggie. More importantly, she had spent years guarding her independence, building a life where she answered to no one but herself.

"Miss Bigsby, please consider—"

"Consider what?" Henri interrupted, growling with indignation. "Consider wedding a man who kidnaps women? Consider binding myself legally to someone who clearly has no regard for consent or propriety? Consider destroying what remains of my autonomy to solve a problem you created?"

Lord Trenwith winced. "Your reputation—"

"My reputation is already destroyed," Henri said flatly. "Whether I marry you or not, the damage is done. At least if I refuse, I retain some measure of dignity."

"There may be ways to mitigate the scandal," he began, but Henri could see the uncertainty in his eyes. He knew as well as she did that there was no coming back from this.

"By becoming your wife? By surrendering my independence, my career, my very self to become Lady Trenwith?" Henri shook her head firmly. "I think not."

Something flickered across Lord Trenwith's features. Hurt, perhaps, or disappointment. But it was gone so quickly that Henri might have imagined it.

"You may change your mind when you have had time to consider your options," he said quietly.

"I will not change my mind," Henri replied with absolute certainty. "I have seen too many women lose themselves in marriage, become mere extensions of their husbands. I will not follow that path, regardless of the circumstances."

Lord Trenwith fell silent then, turning to stare out the window at the passing French countryside. But Henri could see the tension in his shoulders, the way his hands clenched and unclenched in his lap. Whatever response he had expected from his proposal, her flat refusal had clearly affected him more than he cared to show.

"Tell me why," Henri said suddenly. "Tell me why you did this to me. What could possibly justify such actions?"

For a moment, she thought he might actually answer. Vulnerability flickered in his expression, a crack in the careful composure he maintained. She caught a glimpse of something raw and desperate beneath the surface, making her chest tighten with unexpected sympathy.

But then the mask slipped back into place, and Lord Trenwith's face became unreadable once more.

"I am not permitted," he said simply. "Not yet. But soon."

"Cannot or will not?" Henri pressed, sensing that she had been close to breaking through his defenses.

"Does it matter?" He sounded weary, defeated. "The result is the same."

Henri studied his profile, noting the way he held himself rigidly upright despite his obvious exhaustion. His stillness reminded her of a wounded animal, dangerous but suffering. Part of her—a foolish, tender part that she tried to suppress—wanted to reach out to him, to offer comfort.

But she hardened her heart against such weakness. This man had kidnapped her, destroyed her life, and now proposed marriage as if it were some sort of solution rather than yet another violation of her autonomy. Whatever pain he might be suffering, whatever noble motives he might claim, there could be no justification for what he had done to her.

"You are right," Henri said coldly. "It does not matter. What matters is that you have taken my choices away from me. You have decided what is best for my life without consulting me, without considering what I might want. And now you expect me to be grateful for your offer of marriage?"

Lord Trenwith's hands tightened, the only sign he was striving for composure. "I expect nothing," he said quietly. "I merely offer what protection I can."

"Protection?" Henri laughed bitterly. "You speak of protection while holding me captive in a foreign country. You speak of duty while destroying my reputation. Your logic is rather twisted, my lord."

He said no words in response, but Henri saw him flinch as if she had struck him. Good. She wanted him to feel some measure of the anguish he had caused her. She wanted him to understand that his actions had consequences, that she was not some chess piece to be moved about at his convenience.

The carriage rolled on through the French countryside, carrying them toward whatever fate awaited in Calais. Henri turned to stare out her own window, watching unfamiliar landscapes pass by and trying to plan her next move. Marriage to Lord Trenwith was unthinkable, but she would need to find some way to return to England, some way to salvage what remained of her life.

She could not be weak. She could not allow herself to be swayed by momentary glimpses of vulnerability in her captor's eyes. Whatever game Lord Trenwith was playing, whatever his ultimate goals, Henri would find a way to reclaim her freedom.

Even if it meant hardening her heart against every instinct that whispered she might be missing something important about the man sitting across from her in stony silence. Which would be easier if she had not relied on his tender care when she had found herself so ill during the tumultuous sea journey.

*And do not forget he rescued you from a madman.*

Henri suppressed what would have been a telltale groan of dismay as her thoughts warred within her cranium, driving her to the brink of her own special kind of madness.

# CHAPTER 8

*"Ye did me great untruth, and there was no cause why ye should do so."*

**Sir Thomas Malory, *Le Morte d'Arthur***

* * *

The carriage drew to a halt behind a tall, narrow house of weathered gray stone that blended seamlessly with the overcast French sky. Henri peered through the window at the nondescript building, noting how it appeared deliberately unremarkable. No coat of arms adorned the walls; no elaborate ironwork decorated the windows. It was the sort of place chosen to not attract attention.

Lord Trenwith stepped down first, then turned to assist her from the carriage. For a moment, Henri considered crying out, drawing attention from any passersby who might witness her plight. But as she glanced around the narrow lane, she realized how futile such an attempt would be. They were clearly in some sort of service alley, hidden from the main thoroughfares. More importantly, she was now in France, where English law held no sway and her cries for help would likely be met with blank stares or, worse, indifference.

As Lord Trenwith's hand touched hers to help her down, Henri found herself reluctantly remembering his proposal of marriage. Whatever his motives for kidnapping her, however ill-advised his methods, he had offered her his name and title. A man intent on true harm would hardly make such an offer. The thought brought her little comfort, but it did suggest that her immediate safety was not in jeopardy.

She would have to wait this out. Bide her time, gather information, and look for an opportunity to escape or negotiate her freedom when the timing was right.

Mr. Tyne led them through a plain wooden door into what was clearly the servants' entrance of the house. The narrow corridor beyond was dimly lit and smelled of cooking fires and lye soap. Henri caught glimpses of a kitchen to one side, where she could hear the quiet bustle of domestic activity, but Mr. Tyne hurried them quickly past and up a narrow staircase.

"Miss Bigsby," Mr. Tyne said as they climbed, his speech tight with barely suppressed anxiety. "Welcome to *La Maison Grise*. I must ask you to understand that these arrangements are … temporary. Accommodation has not been prepared for you, but everything necessary will be provided for your comfort."

*The Gray House, indeed.*

Henri said nothing, saving her breath for the steep climb, only noting minutes later that Lord Trenwith had left them. The staircase went on forever, winding upward through the heart of the house until they reached what must have been the very top floor. Mr. Tyne opened the door to a small spartanly furnished room tucked beneath the eaves.

"I regret the modest nature of the quarters," Mr. Tyne continued, clearly uncomfortable with his role as her gaoler. "A maid will be along shortly to assist you and provide you with a meal. I trust you will find everything ... adequate."

Henri stepped into the room and heard the unmistakable sound of the key turning in the lock behind her. She was well and truly trapped now, locked in an attic room in a foreign country with no hope of immediate rescue.

Her thoughts threatened to drown her as they flittered to her family. Miss Dulwich would have informed her mother what she had been doing at Danbury's. Mama might even think to speak with Signor di Bianchi, whom Henri's lady's maid would recall from her attendance during their examination of Uncle Reggie's Caxton edition. Eleanor Bigsby, being an intelligent woman, would likely guess Henri had been taken unwillingly because she had no mode of transport to leave the estate and no reason to run off. But beyond that, Miss Dulwich would have no knowledge to point to where Henri might be. Nay, no rescue could come from that quarter. It was up to Lord Trenwith to see to his urgent business and then release her as he had promised he would. In the meanwhile, she could not contemplate her family's distress without feeling overwhelmed by anguish, so she put the thoughts aside until the time came to deal with it.

The space was small but clean, furnished with a narrow bed, a washstand, a little table, and a single chair positioned near the window. The walls were bare except for a simple crucifix hanging above the bed, and the floor was covered with worn wooden planks. There was a bit of a chill, but being on the upper floor, some heat must be rising from below to ward off the worst of the cold. It was the sort of room that might house a servant or perhaps a governess, functional but devoid of any comfort or personality.

Henri moved to the window, hoping to gain some sense of her location. The glass was old and slightly warped, but it provided a view of the city spread out below. From her high vantage, she could see the distinctive outline of a harbor in the distance, with tall masts rising like a forest of bare trees against the gray sky.

It had to be the Calais harbor. She cursed herself for not paying closer attention during their journey, for not asking Lord Trenwith directly where he was taking her. But then again, would he have answered honestly?

The harbor view told her she was in a major port city, which meant there would be ships traveling back to England regularly. If she could find a way to escape this room, if she could reach the docks and find passage … Henri pushed the thought away. Such plans were premature until she better understood her situation.

She turned her attention to the room itself, examining every surface for potential weaknesses. The door was solid oak with heavy iron hinges that showed no signs of looseness. The window was too small to climb through, even if she could somehow survive the four-story drop to the alley below. The walls were thick stone, offering no hope of breaking through to adjacent rooms.

Henri sank into the single chair, feeling the weight of her situation settle upon her like a heavy cloak. She was well and truly trapped, dependent upon Lord Trenwith's mercy and whatever mysterious business had brought them to France.

A soft knock at the door interrupted her brooding. The key turned, and a woman entered carrying a wooden tray. She was perhaps thirty years of age, with dark hair neatly braided beneath a simple cap and the sort of pale complexion that spoke of long hours spent indoors. Her brown dress was plain but well-maintained, marking her clearly as a servant in this household.

*"Bonsoir, mademoiselle,"* the maid said quietly, keeping her eyes downcast as she set the tray on the small table near the window. *"Je reviendrai bientôt avec des couvertures et des affaires de toilette."*

Henri's French was sufficient to understand that the woman would return shortly with blankets and washing things, but when she tried to engage her in conversation, the maid simply shook her head and hurried toward the door.

*"Excusez-moi,"* Henri called after her. *"Comment vous appelez-vous?"*

The woman paused, glancing back with obvious reluctance. Then she was gone, the door closing firmly behind her and the key turning once more in the lock.

Henri lifted the cloth covering the tray and found simple but substantial fare. Fresh bread, still warm from the oven, a portion of beef bouillon, and a small pot of butter accompanied by a cup of wine. The aroma rising from the food made her stomach clench with sudden, sharp hunger.

Only then did Henri fully realize how exhausted she was. The past two days had been a whirlwind of fear, confusion, and physical ordeal—the threatening villain, the kidnapping, the terrifying carriage ride, the storm-tossed Channel crossing and wretched seasickness, and now this imprisonment in a foreign country. Her body ached in places she had not known could ache, and her mind felt sluggish with fatigue.

Moreover, now that the worst of the seasickness had passed, she found herself genuinely ravenous. She could not remember when she had last eaten a proper meal, and the simple food before her looked more appealing than the finest feast.

Henri ate with enthusiasm. The bouillon was hearty and

well-seasoned, the bread fresh and satisfying. As she ate, she found her spirits lifting slightly. Whatever Lord Trenwith's ultimate plans, whatever strange game was being played out around her, at least she was being treated with basic consideration.

As she finished the last of the bread, Henri heard the maid's footsteps on the stairs once more. True to her word, the maid returned with an armload of clean blankets and a pitcher of steaming water for washing.

"*Merci,*" Henri said as the maid efficiently arranged the blankets on the narrow bed. "*Can you tell me where we are?*" she inquired in her passable French.

But the other woman merely shook her head again, her expression stiff as she completed her tasks and departed without another word.

Alone once more, Henri considered her options. The warm water beckoned invitingly, and the clean blankets promised the first comfortable rest she would enjoy since this nightmare began. Her practical side whispered that she would need all her strength for whatever trials lay ahead.

*Rest now, gather my resources, and face tomorrow's challenges with a clearer head.*

Henri moved to the washstand and began the process of making herself presentable once more. As she cleaned away the grime and salt spray of their journey, she caught sight of her reflection in the small mirror above the basin. Her honey-brown hair was disheveled, her amber eyes shadowed with fatigue, and her traveling dress was hopelessly wrinkled from their adventures.

But she was alive. She was unharmed. And despite the impossible circumstances that had brought her here, Henri found herself clinging to a stubborn spark of hope.

Tomorrow would bring new challenges, new opportunities. Today, she would rest and prepare herself for whatever Lord Trenwith's mysterious business might reveal.

* * *

GABRIEL MADE his way down the narrow corridor to the small study that served as his office in *La Maison Grise*, his footsteps echoing hollowly in the cramped space. Behind him, he could hear Mr. Tyne's agitated breathing as his secretary struggled to keep pace, clearly working himself into a state of moral indignation that Gabriel had no desire to endure.

The study was spartanly furnished, containing only a simple desk, two chairs, and a small bookshelf that held the essential documents required for Gabriel's work in Calais. He moved immediately to the desk and began unwrapping the precious cargo they had retrieved from Danbury's estate, his hands working to secure the ancient vellum from any damage. The lunatic with the pistol had been there for the same reason as him—to claim the manuscript. Did that mean the scoundrel was part of this *Dominus* who might have killed Horace? If he had not been so distracted by Miss Bigsby's presence, he might have secured him as a prisoner so he could question the man. But it was far too late for regrets. He would simply need to study the manuscript and see if it pointed to the reason for Horace's murder.

But, first, he reluctantly informed the panicking Tyne why he had brought Miss Bigsby back with him. Fortunately, his secretary had not seen her trussed up because she had agreed to cooperate on French soil.

"My lord," Mr. Tyne began, "I must express my grave concerns about what has transpired. This situation has become completely untenable."

Gabriel did not reply, focusing instead on examining the

manuscript for any signs of damage from their harrowing journey. The pages appeared intact, though he noticed several spots where the binding had loosened slightly. With infinite care, he shifted it back into order, his movements deliberate and reverent.

"Do you comprehend the magnitude of what you have done?" Mr. Tyne continued, beginning to pace the small confines of the room like a caged animal. "Miss Bigsby is not some unknown provincial miss whose disappearance might go unnoticed. Her great-uncle is Reginald Wells, one of the most influential men in Westminster! And her mother, good Lord, her mother holds a royal warrant and personally services the King's architectural whimsies. The woman built stone gewgaws for half the royal residences!"

Gabriel's hands stilled for a moment as he processed this information. He had known Miss Bigsby came from a politically connected family, but he had not fully appreciated the extent of their influence in both governmental and commercial circles.

"My lord, are you listening to me?" Mr. Tyne's voice climbed toward hysteria. "When word of Miss Bigsby's disappearance reaches London, and it will reach London, there will be investigations. Questions will be asked. People will remember seeing you in the vicinity of Danbury's estate. This entire farce is going to wind up with both of us hanging from the end of a rope!"

Gabriel finally looked up from the manuscript, his gaze cold and steady. "No one saw me, Mr. Tyne." Not wholly true. There was the scoundrel who had intended to shoot her. "Are you quite finished with your cataloging of potential disasters?"

The secretary flinched at the icy tone. "My lord, I merely wish to point out that you have dragged me into this mingle-mangle of unprecedented proportions. I committed to assist with diplomatic correspondence, not to aid in kidnapping young ladies of prominent families."

"And yet here you are," Gabriel replied quietly, returning his attention to the manuscript. "Perhaps you should have given more thought to the nature of my work before accepting the position."

Mr. Tyne's mouth opened and closed several times, as if he were struggling to find words adequate to express his outrage. "My lord, with all due respect, this goes far beyond the usual discretions required in diplomatic service. Miss Bigsby's family will have half of Parliament searching for her within the week. What possible explanation could we offer that would satisfy such inquiry?"

Gabriel lifted the sketch that Miss Bigsby had been clutching so desperately, studying the intricate drawing and coded symbols that had somehow led to this impossible situation. The delicate parchment was fragile in his hands, yet it represented something that might finally provide answers about Horace's murder.

What did any of this have to do with his beloved tutor's death? The manuscript, the sketch, the mysterious forces that had sent that armed man to Danbury's library. There had to be connections he was missing, patterns that would emerge if he could just find the right perspective.

"My lord?" There was a note of desperate pleading. "Surely, you must see that this course of action is fraught with peril. There must be some way to extricate ourselves from this situation before irreparable damage is done."

Gabriel set the sketch aside and fixed his secretary with a look that had quelled more experienced diplomats than the nervous man before him. "The situation is what it is, Tyne. We shall deal with the consequences as they arise."

"But Miss Bigsby's refusal of your proposal—"

"Is a temporary setback," Gabriel interrupted with a finality that brooked no argument. "Nothing more."

Mr. Tyne stared at him with a mixture of horror and fascination. "My lord, you cannot seriously intend to … That is, surely, you do not mean to force the young lady into marriage against her expressed wishes?"

Gabriel was quiet for a long moment, his gaze drifting back to the sketch. Miss Bigsby rose unbidden in his mind. Those remarkable amber eyes flashing with indignation, her determined little chin set in stubborn refusal, the way she had looked at him as if he were a stranger rather than the man who had risked everything to save her from the wrong end of a musket ball.

"Request that a meal be brought to my room," Gabriel said finally, rising from the desk with movements that betrayed none of the turmoil roiling within him. "I require rest before tomorrow's meetings."

"My lord, we cannot simply ignore—"

"Good day, Tyne."

Gabriel walked past his secretary without another word, leaving the man standing in the study with his mouth agape. He made his way up the narrow staircase to the small chamber that served as his private quarters, his head swimming from lack of sleep and the crushing implications of everything that had transpired.

Marriage to Henrietta Bigsby. The very thought sent conflicting waves of anticipation and dread coursing through him. He had dreamed of such a possibility for two years, had fantasized about what it might be like to claim the right to hold her, to wake up beside her each morning, to be the man she turned to for comfort and companionship.

But not like this. Never like this.

The reality of her rejection hit him with renewed force as he closed the door to his chamber and leaned against it, finally allowing his carefully maintained composure to crack. She had refused him. Absolutely and without hesitation, as if the very idea of marriage to him was repugnant.

Gabriel had enjoyed liaisons with women in his past, so he should have taken Miss Bigsby's rejection in his stride. He knew women desired him, so it was juvenile to feel so hurt. So unworthy.

But no matter how much he tried to stow his emotions, she simply brought out the worst in him. She made him feel things when he had not permitted such mawkish sentimentality since arriving as a boy at Horace's home nearly thirty years earlier.

Now he had more emotions than he could count.

Resentment that she had not acknowledged that without his timely arrival she could have been shot through the heart by that lunatic at Danbury's home.

Dejection because he had finally made his offer only to be soundly rebuked.

Anger at the gods of fate for putting him in this predicament.

Shame that maybe his decision to kidnap her might not have been altruistic at all, but rather an enactment of his suppressed desires.

Heartbreak because—

*Am I cataloging emotions I am not meant to have?*

But chastising himself did not ease the ache of her rejection, no matter how much he willed it so. Until, eventually, drawing a deep breath to calm the turmoil, he resolved she would marry him before they left Calais. He would find a way to persuade her. He wished he could simply tell her how much he wanted this. Wanted her.

But history had taught him that revealing one's emotions only led to trouble. Deuce it, having emotions in the first place was a damned terrible burden to shoulder. They must be squashed with ruthless determination lest they fester and destroy a man. Loneliness was the best weapon to contain unbridled feelings. He simply needed some distance from the delectable Miss Bigsby, some time to himself, and astute logic would be restored.

Gabriel moved to the narrow window that overlooked the harbor, watching the distant shadows of ships bobbing at anchor under the morning's bleak light. Somewhere back in England lay the answers he sought, the connections between Horace's murder and the mysterious manuscript that had brought him to this impossible crossroads. The attempt to murder Miss Bigsby for the very manuscript and sketch that now lay on his desk proved he had found the right threads to unravel to solve the violence committed against his tutor. Given his conversation with Miss Bigsby earlier, it was going to take some persuasion to convince her to disclose her role in this mystery.

Tomorrow, he would meet with Étienne, would focus on the vital work of securing the release of English agents who had spent years in French captivity. Today, he would rest and prepare himself for the challenges ahead.

And somehow, he would find a way to convince Miss Bigsby that marriage to him was not the disaster she believed it to be.

Even if it meant ruthlessly burying needs that he had spent a lifetime learning to suppress.

# CHAPTER 9

*"For love is free; and will not be commanded."*

**Sir Thomas Malory, *Le Morte d'Arthur***

* * *

Henri stirred from sleep as the church bells chimed the evening hour, their deep bronze tones drifting through her small window to pull her from the first restful slumber she had enjoyed since this ordeal began. Sunlight no longer filtered through the glass, replaced instead by the soft glow of lamplight from the street below, and the room was cooler than when she had gone to bed. She had slept through most of the day, and her body felt considerably restored from the trials of their Channel crossing.

A soft knock at the door announced someone's return. The maid entered with her customary downcast eyes, carrying a pitcher of steaming water and fresh linens.

*"Bonsoir, mademoiselle,"* she murmured as she set about

preparing the washstand. *"Monsieur Grantham demande votre présence pour le dîner."*

Henri sat up slowly, her mind still foggy from sleep. "Monsieur Grantham? Dinner?" The name meant nothing to her, though the servant's tone suggested this person held considerable authority in the household.

*"Oui, mademoiselle. Il vous attend en bas."* After the maid informed her that the mysterious Grantham was waiting downstairs, she fell silent as she moved about the small room, laying out the washing things with practiced skill. Despite Henri's attempts to engage her in conversation, the maid remained stubbornly uncommunicative, responding only with nods or brief phrases in French.

As the maid helped her wash and arranged her hair into a more presentable style, Henri's mind raced with possibilities. This mysterious Monsieur Grantham might be the person in charge of her captivity, perhaps someone with the authority to arrange her return to England. Cooperation seemed the wisest course, though Henri remained uncertain what she would do if an opportunity for escape presented itself.

She possessed a small purse with enough funds for modest travel expenses, money she had brought for her intended day trip to Hertfordshire to visit Sir Alpheus. But certainly not enough to secure passage back to England, particularly if she found herself stranded in a foreign port without assistance.

If this truly was Calais, as she suspected from her view of the harbor, there would be a British consulate somewhere in the city. Perhaps she could make her way there and throw herself upon the mercy of His Majesty's representatives. The thought provided some small comfort as the maid finished her ministrations and departed, once again turning the key in the lock.

Henri had barely settled herself back into the single chair

when footsteps sounded on the stairs outside. The key turned, and she heard a soft knock before the door unlatched and opened to reveal Lord Trenwith himself.

Her breath caught in her throat. Gone was the rumpled gentleman who had carried her aboard the ship in his rough coachman's attire. Instead, he stood before her dressed in understated evening wear, a simple dark coat and plain waistcoat that suggested a man of modest means rather than a peer of the realm. The transformation was so complete that had she encountered him on the street, she might have taken him for a minor merchant or perhaps a clerk in some respectable firm.

"Miss Bigsby," he said quietly, offering a small bow. "I trust you are feeling better after your rest."

"Lord Trenwith." Henri rose from her chair, studying his altered appearance with curious eyes. "Though I suspect I should be addressing you as Monsieur Grantham?"

Something flickered across his features, surprise perhaps, or approval at her quick deduction. "You are quite observant. Yes, while we are in France, that name serves my purposes better."

"And what purposes might those be?" Henri asked, but the viscount merely gestured toward the door.

"Perhaps we might continue this conversation over dinner? I believe you will find the fare more substantial than what you were served earlier."

Henri had little choice but to follow him from the room and down the narrow stairs.

The dining room proved to be a small but comfortable chamber on the ground floor, furnished with a simple table and chairs that matched the house's deliberately unremarkable character. Candles provided cheering light, and the aroma of well-prepared food made Henri's mouth water with renewed hunger.

The meal that followed was indeed substantial—hearty French fare that included a rich soup, roasted chicken with herbs, fresh bread, and a selection of local cheeses. Henri found herself eating with more enthusiasm than she had felt in days, the simple pleasure of good food helping to restore both her strength and her spirits.

The viscount proved to be an attentive host, ensuring her wine glass remained filled and inquiring politely about her comfort. Yet beneath his courteous manner, Henri sensed the same controlled tension she had observed during their carriage journey. He was watching her carefully, as if gauging her reactions.

They spoke of inconsequential matters at first. The weather, the quality of the food, the general bustle of port cities. But as the meal progressed and Henri's patience wore thin, she finally set down her fork and fixed him with a direct stare.

"What is this all about?" she demanded, her shoulders squaring with renewed determination. "I have been patient, Lord Trenwith, but I require answers. What are we doing in France? Why have you brought me here against my will? And who, precisely, is Monsieur Grantham?"

He was quiet for a long moment, his hazel eyes studying her face as if memorizing every detail. When he finally spoke, his words carried a weariness that aged him beyond his years.

"I am engaged in a sensitive negotiation," he said slowly, each word chosen with obvious care but more communicative than he had been in the past three days. Clearly, he was more relaxed now that they had reached their destination. "My presence in England had to remain absolutely secret. Any knowledge of my departure from France could have catastrophic consequences."

Henri leaned forward, sensing that she was finally

approaching the truth behind her kidnapping. "What sort of negotiation? With whom?"

"I cannot reveal those details," he replied, and Henri saw genuine regret in his expression. "It is a matter of life and death, Miss Bigsby. More than that, I am not permitted to say."

"Life and death," Henri repeated, her mind racing through the implications. "Whose life? Whose death?"

"I cannot say."

The pieces began falling into place in Henri's mind. A secret negotiation in a French port city. Lord Trenwith's mysterious comings and goings, his careful avoidance of any details about his diplomatic work. Perhaps English agents imprisoned abroad?

"You are negotiating for the release of prisoners on behalf of the Crown," she stated. It was not a question.

His slight shrug neither confirmed nor rejected her deduction, but Henri felt some of her anger begin to ebb, replaced by a grudging understanding of the forces that had led to her predicament. If his lordship truly was working to free imprisoned Englishmen, if lives truly hung in the balance, then perhaps his erratic actions made some sort of sense. She supposed she should be grateful that he had arrived at Danbury's library when he had, or she might even now be buried in the cold, hard ground while her family wept over her premature demise. She tried not to let this soften her resolve as she considered this alternate circumstance, but it was difficult to resist.

"But why kidnap me?" she pressed. "Surely, there were other ways to handle whatever crisis my presence at Danbury's estate created."

"Perhaps," the viscount admitted. "But I was not permitted the luxury of careful consideration. The situation required immediate action."

"And now?" Henri asked. "How long must I remain your prisoner while these negotiations continue?"

Lord Trenwith was quiet for another long moment, his fingers turning his wine glass slowly on the table. "Perhaps in a few days I will be in a position to tell you a little more," he said finally. "For now, I can only ask for your patience."

Henri's temper, which had been simmering throughout their conversation, finally boiled over. She pushed back from the table and shot to her feet, her chair scraping loudly against the wooden floor.

"Patience?" she demanded, beginning to pace the small confines of the dining room with quick, agitated steps. "You speak of patience while holding me captive in a foreign country? You expect me to sit quietly while you conduct your mysterious business, giving me no indication of when I might expect to return home?"

She spun to face him, her hands gesticulating wildly as days of frustration poured out in a torrent of words. "I have been kidnapped, bound, transported across the Channel against my will, and locked in an attic like some common criminal. My reputation is destroyed, my position lost, my family undoubtedly worried sick. And you ask for patience?"

He remained seated, watching her outburst with the sort of calm attention one might give to a force of nature. His very stillness only inflamed Henri's anger further.

"You speak of honor and duty," she continued, her voice rising with each word. "But where is the honor in treating me like a possession to be moved about at your convenience? Where is the duty in destroying an innocent woman's life to serve your political machinations?"

She stopped directly in front of his chair, blazing with righteous indignation. "I may be merely a secretary, Lord Trenwith, but I am not a fool. I understand the complexities of diplomatic work, the need for discretion and secrecy. But I am also a human being, with rights and desires of my own. Rights that you have trampled upon without a moment's consideration."

He set down his wine glass and looked up at her, his expression unreadable. "Are you quite finished, Miss Bigsby?"

"No, I am not finished!" Henri snapped, resuming her agitated pacing. "I am far from finished. You have turned my entire world upside down, and I deserve better than cryptic hints and requests for patience. I deserve the truth, the whole truth, about why my life has been sacrificed to your political necessities."

She whirled to face him again, her chest heaving with the force of her emotions. "And I deserve the courtesy of being treated as an intelligent adult capable of understanding complex situations, rather than a child to be managed with pretty lies and false promises."

Lord Trenwith rose slowly from his chair, his movement deliberate and controlled. When he spoke, it was quiet but carried an undertone of steel that made Henri take an involuntary step backward.

"You are quite right, Miss Bigsby," he said. "You deserve a great deal more than you have received. But unfortunately, what we deserve and what circumstances permit are rarely the same thing."

Henri stared at him, surprised by his calm acknowledgment of her grievances. She had expected argument, justification, perhaps even anger in return. Instead, she found herself facing a man who was as trapped as she was herself.

The silence stretched between them, heavy with unspoken truths and impossible choices. Henri's anger began to ebb again, replaced by a bone-deep weariness that matched the exhaustion she saw in the viscount's eyes.

"How long?" she asked quietly. "How long must this continue?"

"I cannot say," he replied with obvious regret. "But I give you my word that it will end as soon as it is possible. And when it does, I will do everything in my power to make amends for what you have suffered."

Henri sank back into her chair, suddenly feeling every hour of the past few days weighing upon her shoulders. She was trapped in a situation beyond her control, dependent upon the word of a man whose motives she could only partially understand.

But at least now she had some glimpse of the larger forces at work. If the viscount truly was negotiating for the freedom of imprisoned Englishmen, if lives truly hung in the balance, then perhaps her sacrifice served some greater purpose.

However, she was finally getting the chance to vent her ire, and he would damn well listen until she was done.

* * *

GABRIEL REMAINED SEATED as Miss Bigsby jumped to her feet once more and resumed her impassioned tirade, watching her pace the small dining room with the sort of focused attention he usually reserved for diplomatic negotiations. But this was no ordinary negotiation, and Miss Bigsby was certainly no ordinary opponent.

She moved with such grace even in her anger, her hands gesticulating expressively as she cataloged his transgressions with devastating precision. The firelight caught the honey-brown highlights in her hair, and her cheeks were flushed with the force of her emotions. Gabriel found himself thinking that he had never seen her look more beautiful than she did in this moment, blazing with righteous indignation.

As he watched her animated figure, Gabriel's mind drifted to considerations of the past few years. His life had felt adrift since unexpectedly inheriting his title and consequently losing his more immersive place in the military, disconnected from any sense of real purpose beyond his diplomatic duties. The endless negotiations, the careful balancing of competing interests, the isolation that came with his clandestine work—it had all begun to feel hollow, meaningless.

But sitting here, watching the young lady's passionate defense of her rights and dignity, Gabriel found himself thinking that marrying her might not be such a terrible thing after all, despite his aversion to allowing someone so close to him. Perhaps he could make some changes to his life. Perhaps he could inform the Crown that he was no longer available for these covert assignments. Perhaps he could take Miss Bigsby to his country seat at Trenwith Abbey and properly assume his duties as a viscount with an accomplished bride at his side who could help him properly represent the people who relied on the title there.

The prospect sounded oddly pleasant. More than pleasant, if he was being honest with himself. The only obstacle to such an appealing future was that Miss Bigsby would have to agree to wed him.

Her tirade rose to a crescendo as she delivered her final accusations, then she stopped directly next to his chair, breathing hard from the exertion of her speech.

"What do you have to say to that, Lord Trenwith?" she demanded, her chin lifted in challenge.

Gabriel considered her for a long moment, taking in the determined set of her jaw, the way she held herself with such dignity despite everything she had endured. Then he slowly rose to his feet, gazing down into her face with a renewal of interest that he made no attempt to hide.

"Gabriel," he said quietly.

"What?" Miss Bigsby blinked, clearly not expecting such a response.

"If we are to wed, you should call me by my given name. Gabriel."

She shook her head firmly. "We are not to wed, Lord Trenwith."

"Gabriel," he repeated with gentle insistence.

She firmed her jaw, delivering her words with great deliberation. "We are not to wed, Lord Trenwith."

Gabriel smiled then. He was beginning to understand something important about Miss Henrietta Bigsby. She was not a woman who could be bullied or cajoled into submission. She would have to be persuaded, and persuasion was something Gabriel had considerable experience with.

A woman like her, possessing such courage and passion, such a sense of adventure ... It must take an iron will to keep the fires of desire banked. A spinster, on the shelf—what would happen if those fires were lit?

Gabriel felt his loins begin to thrum in approval as he considered how he could convince her to accept his offer of marriage. And how much he would enjoy that act of persuasion. This was the one occasion in which his personal wishes and his duty deliciously coincided.

"I find I like the challenge, Miss Bigsby," Gabriel said, his tone carrying a warmth that had been absent during their earlier conversations. "You have always had a knack for engaging my senses, for making me feel more alive and connected with the world."

She stared at him, clearly taken aback by this unexpected turn in their conversation. "Lord Trenwith, I hardly think—"

"Gabriel," he corrected gently, then gestured toward the door. "But perhaps we should continue this discussion another time. You have had a long day, and I suspect you would benefit from more rest."

Gabriel offered his arm, and after a moment's hesitation, she accepted it. They made their way back up the narrow staircase in relative silence, though Gabriel was acutely aware of her presence beside him. The scent of lavender that clung to her hair, the warmth of her hand resting lightly on his sleeve, the rustle of her skirts as they climbed.

When they reached her door, Gabriel turned to face her, noting how the lamplight from the corridor cast soft shadows across her features.

"Good night, Miss Bigsby. I trust you will sleep well."

She opened her mouth as if to speak, perhaps to deliver another lecture about his high-handed behavior or to demand more answers about their situation. But before she could declare whatever protest was forming, Gabriel stepped closer and gently cupped her face in his hands.

"Gabriel," he murmured, his thumbs brushing lightly across her cheekbones. "My name is Gabriel."

Then he leaned down and pressed his lips to hers, the kiss soft but unmistakably purposeful. Miss Bigsby went very still in his arms, her intake of breath sharp with surprise. But she did not pull away, and Gabriel allowed himself to savor the feel of her mouth, the way she melted against him despite her obvious shock.

When he finally lifted his head, her eyes were wide with confusion. Gabriel smiled and took a step back, executing a small bow.

"Good night, Miss Bigsby. Sweet dreams."

He waited until she had entered her room and closed the door behind her, then locked it before making his way back down the corridor. Tomorrow would bring new challenges, new opportunities to convince her that marriage to him was not the disaster she believed it to be.

But tonight, Gabriel found himself looking forward to the campaign ahead with more enthusiasm than he had felt for anything in years. Henrietta Bigsby was proving to be the most intriguing and worthwhile challenge of his entire diplomatic career.

And like his other negotiations, this was one he had every intention of winning.

* * *

To her dismay, Henri opened like a flower to the sun, their kiss deepening as his large hands came up to clasp her waist. But then they were gliding upward, and she felt his fingers brushing the under swell of her breasts. Everything was white-hot heat as hitherto unsuspected passion burst out of her like a tidal wave sweeping over the shore.

She barely comprehended he was speaking before the door was shut, followed by a decisive click announcing it was locked.

Henri stood frozen for several heartbeats, her hand pressed to her lips, still feeling Gabriel's mouth against hers. Her heart hammered against her ribs, and she felt oddly breathless, as if she had been running rather than simply kissed by a man she should despise.

When she finally turned back to her chamber, Henri stopped short in amazement. The sparse attic room had been transformed during her absence at dinner. A plush rug now covered the rough wooden planks, and a comfortable upholstered chair had been positioned near the window. Two gowns hung from pegs beside the casement, their fabric fine enough to suggest they had been carefully selected rather than hastily procured.

Novels were stacked invitingly on the small table, and cheerful curtains now covered the window, blocking the view of the harbor but making the space feel more like a proper bedchamber than a prison cell. A tray on the table held a crystal jug, glasses, and a plate of biscuits that smelled of butter and sugar.

Henri moved slowly through the transformed space, touching each new addition with wondering fingers. Someone had taken considerable care to make her comfortable, to provide not just the necessities but small luxuries that might ease the tedium of captivity. Gabriel's doing, undoubtedly.

*Blast it! It is Lord Trenwith, not Gabriel!*

She sank into the new chair, her mind still reeling from the kiss they had shared. Henri raised her hand to her lips again, remembering the taste of him, the way his mouth had moved against hers with such confident expertise. She had been kissed before, of course. Several gentlemen had attempted to court her over the years, and she was not so naïve as to be completely inexperienced in such matters.

But nothing had prepared her for the intensity of her response to his lordship's touch. The way her entire body had come alive under his hands, the heat that had pooled low in her belly, the shocking desire for him to continue his exploration. It was as if some dormant part of herself had suddenly awakened, demanding things she had never allowed herself to want.

Henri shook her head firmly, trying to dispel such dangerous thoughts. She was being manipulated, clearly. Gabriel had recognized her physical response and was attempting to use it against her, to weaken her resolve through seduction rather than force. It was a clever strategy, she had to admit. Far more pleasant than the restraints and gags he had employed during their journey.

But she would not be swayed by a few stolen kisses and some comfortable furnishings. Marriage to Gabri—*no*—Lord

Trenwith would mean the end of her independence, the surrender of everything she had worked to build for herself. She had seen too many intelligent women lose themselves in matrimony, their own ambitions and capabilities subsumed into their husband's world.

Henri had always been determined to remain her own woman, to answer to no one but herself. The scandals awaiting her in England might make that more difficult, but they did not make it impossible. There were options available to a woman of her education and connections. Perhaps Uncle Reggie could arrange a position with one of his political allies. Or perhaps she could escape the scandal by leaving Britain altogether.

The prospect held little appeal compared to her former life, but it was preferable to surrendering her autonomy entirely.

Henri rose from the chair and moved to examine the gowns that had been provided. They were beautiful garments, well-made and fashionable, though she wondered how Gabriel had managed to procure them so quickly. The thought that he might have had women's clothing readily available for such purposes was distinctly unsettling.

She selected one of the novels from the table and settled back into the comfortable chair, determined to distract herself from troubling thoughts about his motives and methods. But as she tried to focus on the printed words, her mind kept drifting back to the kiss, to the unexpected passion that had flared between them.

What was his game? Was this elaborate courtship genuine, or merely another form of coercion designed to secure her compliance? And more troubling still, why did part of her hope it might be real?

Henri closed the book with a frustrated sigh and prepared for bed, changing into the clean nightgown that had been laid out for her. As she settled beneath the soft blankets that had replaced the rough coverings that had warmed her earlier, she found herself wondering what Gabriel had done with Signor di Bianchi's sketch.

Her neighbor's quest seemed like something from another lifetime now, a simple mystery that had inadvertently drawn her into this complex web of politics and passion. She hoped Signor di Bianchi was not too worried about the sketch's disappearance, though she suspected he would be frantic with concern by now. She dared not think of her family's state of mind lest she burst into tears.

As sleep began to claim her, Henri's last conscious thought was of Gabriel's hands on her waist, the gentle brush of his fingers against her breasts, and the way he had whispered her name like a caress. Tomorrow, she would need to steel herself against such persuasions, to remember that her freedom was worth more than any temporary pleasure he might offer.

But tonight, in the comfortable darkness of her transformed prison, Henri allowed herself to remember the taste of his kiss and wonder what it might be like to surrender to the passion he had awakened within her.

# CHAPTER 10

*"For needs must I go with thee, or else I am shamed."*

**Sir Thomas Malory, *Le Morte d'Arthur***

* * *

JANUARY 28, 1822

Henri stirred from sleep to the sound of church bells echoing across the rooftops, their bronze voices announcing that Monday morning had arrived. In the pale light filtering through her new curtains, the events of the previous evening seemed almost dreamlike—the kiss, the transformed room, the unexpected comfort of Gabriel's arms around her. She touched her lips reflexively, still able to taste the memory of his mouth against hers.

The sound of quiet movement in the room drew her attention to the maid, who was arranging fresh linens on the washstand with her characteristic efficiency. The maid's dark hair was neatly braided beneath her cap, and she moved about her duties with the sort of invisibility that marked an experienced servant.

*"Bonjour,"* Henri said, sitting up in the comfortable bed and pushing her hair back from her face. Her body ached from the travel, and she supposed she mayhap should try to escape, but she did not feel under immediate threat and needed to recover.

The maid glanced up briefly, offering a small nod of acknowledgment before returning to her work. *"Bonjour, mademoiselle."*

Henri had been attempting to engage the woman in conversation since her arrival, with limited success. But this morning, perhaps emboldened by the previous evening's revelations about Gabriel's work, she decided to try a different approach.

"You know," Henri said conversationally as she swung her legs out of bed, "it would be much easier for both of us if I knew how to address you properly. When I need your attention, I mean. It seems rather inefficient to simply call out '*excusez-moi*' every time I require assistance."

To her surprise, the maid paused in her work, considering this practical argument. The woman clearly understood English. *"Je m'appelle Lisette, mademoiselle."*

"Lisette," Henri repeated with a wide smile. "What a lovely name. And please, you may call me Miss Bigsby, or Henri if you prefer. There's no need for such formality when we are sharing such close quarters."

The maid's expression softened slightly at Henri's friendly tone, though she remained reserved. *"Oui, mademoiselle ... Miss Bigsby."*

It was progress, however small. Henri allowed Lisette to assist her with washing and dressing, selecting one of the new gowns that had appeared in her room. The fabric was a soft blue wool that complemented her coloring, and the fit was surprisingly accurate considering Gabriel could not have had her measurements.

*Deuce it, Henri. It is Lord Trenwith!*

As Lisette finished arranging Henri's hair into a simple but elegant style, footsteps sounded on the staircase outside. A soft knock followed, and Henri called for the visitor to enter.

To her surprise, it was Mr. Tyne who appeared in the doorway, looking slightly uncomfortable but resolute. His thin frame was impeccably dressed despite their unconventional situation, and his pale eyes held a mixture of duty and genuine concern. He carried a tray of food that looked to be enough for both of them, and Lisette left them alone together.

"Miss Bigsby," he said with a slight bow. "I trust you slept well?"

"As well as can be expected," Henri replied, studying his face for any hint of his purpose. "To what do I owe the pleasure of your company, Mr. Tyne?"

The secretary cleared his throat delicately. "Lord Trenwith … that is, Monsieur Grantham instructed me to keep you company this morning. He felt you might appreciate some conversation while he attends to his business affairs."

Henri gestured to the comfortable chair that had been added to her accommodations. "Please, do sit down. I confess I would welcome the company, though I suspect your employer has additional motives beyond my entertainment."

Mr. Tyne seated himself in the chair, his posture primly formal despite Henri's welcome. "His lordship is concerned for your comfort and well-being, Miss Bigsby. These are … unusual circumstances for all of us."

"Indeed they are," Henri agreed, taking a seat on the edge

of the bed since there was only one chair. "Tell me, Mr. Tyne, how long have you been in Lord Trenwith's employ?"

"Nearly seven years now," the secretary replied, relaxing slightly as Henri guided the conversation toward safer topics. "I began working for his lordship shortly after he inherited the title."

They spoke of general matters for some time—the bustle of Calais as a port city, the differences between French and English customs, the weather that had been perpetually gray and damp. Mr. Tyne proved to be a more engaging conversationalist than Henri had expected, possessing a dry wit and keen observations about their surroundings.

But as the morning progressed and Henri's patience wore thin, she finally set aside pretense and fixed him with a direct stare.

"Mr. Tyne, I appreciate your efforts to distract me, but I must know what is happening. How long am I to remain here? What is Lord Trenwith's business in Calais? And when might I expect to return to England?"

The secretary's pale face grew even paler, and he shifted uncomfortably in his chair. "Miss Bigsby, I fear that is not my place to say. Such matters are well above my station, and his lordship has not seen fit to confide the details of his work to me."

"But surely you must have some indication of his plans?" Henri pressed. "You cannot tell me that you serve as his secretary without knowing anything of his business."

Mr. Tyne was quiet for a long moment, clearly struggling with conflicting loyalties. "I can tell you that Lord Trenwith is a man of honor, Miss Bigsby. Whatever his methods that brought us here, I am certain he will find a way to mitigate any damage to your reputation."

Henri felt her heart sink at this confirmation of what she already knew. "My reputation. Yes, I suppose it is quite thoroughly destroyed by now. And Sir Alpheus must be quite beside himself over the missing manuscript."

"Has his lordship … that is, has he spoken to you about possible solutions to your situation?" Mr. Tyne asked delicately.

Henri looked up sharply, studying the secretary's expression. "He has proposed marriage, if that is what you're asking."

Relief flooded Mr. Tyne's features, but it seemed like a performance to her mind. "Thank heavens. I confess, Miss Bigsby, I have been quite beside myself with worry about you. His lordship's proposal does provide a path forward that would preserve your standing in society."

"And I have refused him," Henri said flatly.

"I beg your pardon?"

Mr. Tyne blinked at her as if she had announced her intention to sprout wings and fly to the moon, but she had the impression he might be pretending. Did Mr. Tyne already know about her refusal? Was this yet another tactic of persuasion, pretending he did not know in order to raise it in conversation? Had Gabr—*Faugh! Lord Trenwith*—instructed him?

"I said I have refused his offer of marriage," Henri repeated with more force. "I will not be coerced into matrimony."

"But … Miss Bigsby …" Mr. Tyne stammered. "Surely, you understand the gravity of your situation? An unmarried woman, traveling unchaperoned with a gentleman, remaining in his company for days … The scandal will be enormous."

"I am quite aware of the scandal," Henri replied with more composure than she felt. "But I fail to see how binding myself legally to the man who created this situation improves my circumstances."

Mr. Tyne leaned forward in his chair, his expression earnest. "Miss Bigsby, you must understand, reputation is a fire. It burns fast. But Lord Trenwith will burn with it to shield you. His lordship is not offering marriage out of mere duty or obligation. He genuinely wishes to protect you from the consequences of … of this unfortunate situation. Raising your station to that of a peeress would mitigate much of the damage."

"Unfortunate situation?" Henri's voice rose slightly. "Mr. Tyne, I was kidnapped. Bound and gagged like a common criminal. Transported to a foreign country against my wishes. Lord Trenwith created this situation through his own actions, and now you suggest I should be grateful for his offer to resolve it through marriage?"

The secretary flinched at her blunt assessment but did not retreat from his position. "I understand your anger, Miss Bigsby. Truly, I do. But surely you can see that his lordship's proposal offers the best possible outcome?"

"The best outcome would have been not kidnapping me in the first place," Henri retorted. "But since Lord Trenwith seems incapable of properly explaining why such drastic action was necessary, how can I possibly allow such a man to control my future? If he cannot trust me with the truth about his motives, how can I trust him with my life?"

Mr. Tyne was quiet for several minutes, and Henri could see him wrestling with some internal conflict. When he finally spoke, his voice carried a conviction that surprised her.

"Miss Bigsby, I have worked for Lord Trenwith for many years, and I will tell you this. He is the most honorable man I have ever had the privilege to serve. Yes, he is intensely private. Yes, even after all these years in his employ, I cannot claim to have a good sense of what my master is thinking most of the time. But his loyalty and honor are beyond reproach."

Henri studied the secretary's earnest face, noting the genuine conviction in his pale eyes. "You truly believe that, don't you?"

"I do," Mr. Tyne replied without hesitation. "I may not understand his methods, Miss Bigsby, but I am certain there was a good reason he elected to behave in such a … dastardly fashion. Lord Trenwith is not a man who acts without attention to the greater good."

"Then why will he not explain his reasons to me?" Henri demanded. "If his motives are so noble, why all the secrecy and evasion?"

Mr. Tyne hesitated, then reached some internal decision. "He may not trust you, perhaps not even me, with the full details of his work. But you can certainly trust him, Miss Bigsby. Open his heart, and I am sure you will find it as bottomless as the Atlantic Ocean. Monsieur Grantham would lay down his life for you."

Henri tilted her head, studying the secretary's expression. "Yes, I keep hearing about Monsieur Grantham."

He winced visibly. "Lord Trenwith uses that name when he is engaged in sensitive matters. I fear I cannot say more than that without betraying his confidence."

"Sensitive matters," Henri repeated slowly. "Diplomatic work, I assume? Intelligence, too, I presume? Something that requires him to maintain a false identity while in France?"

The secretary's uncomfortable silence was answer enough.

Henri rose from the bed and moved to the window, gazing out at the harbor view where ships bobbed at anchor in the gray water, their masts creating a forest of vertical lines against the overcast sky. Somewhere among those vessels might be her passage back to England, if she could find a way to reach them. But, if she did so, would she imperil the men Gabriel would not talk about?

"Mr. Tyne," she said without turning from the window, "I appreciate your loyalty to your employer. Truly, I do. But you must understand my position. I am being asked to marry a man who refuses to explain why he destroyed my life, who conducts his business under false names, who apparently considers kidnapping an acceptable solution to his problems. Would you advise your own sister to accept such a proposal?"

When she turned back to face him, Mr. Tyne looked deeply troubled. "Miss Bigsby, I … that is … the circumstances are highly unusual …"

"Indeed they are," Henri agreed. "And until Lord Trenwith sees fit to treat me as an intelligent adult capable of understanding those circumstances, I see no reason to consider his proposal seriously."

She returned to her seat on the bed, noting how Mr. Tyne's distress increased with every word she spoke. "I do not doubt that you believe in your employer's essential goodness, Mr. Tyne. But belief is not the same as knowledge, and I require rather more substantial evidence before entrusting my future to a man I barely know."

"But Miss Bigsby," the secretary began desperately, "your reputation—"

"Will survive or it will not," Henri interrupted with more confidence than she felt. "But I will not surrender my independence to preserve it. There are other options available to a woman of education and determination."

Mr. Tyne stared at her with obvious dismay, clearly unprepared for such stubborn resistance to what he saw as the obvious solution to her predicament. Henri almost felt sorry for him. He was clearly a good man caught in an impossible situation, trying to serve both his employer's interests and his own sense of moral obligation.

"Is there anything I can say to convince you to reconsider?" he asked finally.

Henri considered the question seriously. "Lord Trenwith could start by treating me as an equal rather than a problem to be managed. He could explain his work, his reasons for bringing me here, his plans for resolving this situation. He could demonstrate that he sees me as a partner rather than a possession."

"And if he were to do those things?" Mr. Tyne pressed.

Henri met his gaze steadily. "Then I would consider his proposal on its merits rather than dismissing it out of hand. But until that happens, Mr. Tyne, I'm afraid your employer will have to find another way to solve the problem he has created."

The secretary slumped back in his chair, looking defeated. Henri commiserated, caught as he was between his loyalty to Gabriel and his obvious distress at her situation. But she would not be swayed by pity or guilt. Her future was too important to sacrifice on the altar of someone else's convenience, no matter how honorable their intentions might be.

Outside, the church bells began to toll the noon hour. Henri wondered what Gabriel was doing at this moment, whether he was conducting his mysterious negotiations or plotting his next attempt to convince her to accept his proposal.

Whatever his plans, she would be ready for them. She had made her position clear to Mr. Tyne, and to Gabriel himself. Now it remained to be seen whether Lord Trenwith was capable of the honesty and trust that any real partnership would require.

Henri suspected she would not have long to wait for her answer.

* * *

GABRIEL EMERGED from his morning meeting with Étienne feeling both elated and cautiously optimistic. Word had arrived from Paris that the King's counsel was reviewing their negotiated treaty with favorable attention. Étienne expected the approved documents to be returned within a couple of days. Maybe as soon as tomorrow.

After weeks of delicate negotiations, they were finally approaching the conclusion. The agreement that would secure the release of the English agents was tantalizingly close to completion. Soon Gabriel would be free to return to England and address the more personal matters that had complicated his life so dramatically. The mystery of the manuscript needed to be resolved, and he needed to learn what Miss Bigsby's involvement was once he could secure some spirit of cooperation with her. Her situation weighed heavily on his thoughts.

The afternoon hours passed quickly as Gabriel focused his attention on Miss Bigsby's sketch and the manuscript pages he had been working on. With the negotiations essentially complete and only the formality of royal approval remaining, he could dedicate his full attention to unraveling the mystery that had led him to Danbury's estate.

Gabriel applied his considerable analytical skills to the coded symbols. His training in cryptography, honed through years of diplomatic work, served him well as he began to identify patterns and relationships between the sketch and the manuscript text.

By midafternoon, he had made significant progress. The sketch was indeed a map, as he had suspected, with the coded symbols corresponding to Malory's original work. More importantly, he had managed to work out what appeared to be the solution to the first clue.

Gabriel sat back in his chair, studying his work with satisfaction. The connection between the sketch and Horace's murder was still unclear, but at least now he had concrete progress to discuss with her. Perhaps sharing this discovery would help rebuild some of the trust he had so carelessly damaged.

He called for Mr. Tyne and instructed him to bring Miss Bigsby down for tea. It was time to attempt a more civilized approach to their relationship, to see if he could salvage something from the wreckage of the past few days.

When Miss Bigsby appeared in the doorway of the small sitting room where Gabriel had arranged for tea and scones to be served, he was struck once again by her natural elegance. The blue gown she wore complemented her coloring beautifully, and someone, presumably Lisette, had arranged her honey-brown hair in a style that was both practical and becoming. Despite everything she had endured, she carried herself with a dignity that commanded respect.

"Miss Bigsby." Gabriel rose as she entered, offering a slight bow. "Thank you for joining me. I thought perhaps we might enjoy a more pleasant afternoon than our previous encounters have provided."

Her expression remained composed as she took the seat he indicated, though Gabriel noticed how she positioned herself to maintain maximum distance between them. "Lord Trenwith. Or should I say Monsieur Grantham? I confess I am no longer certain which identity you prefer."

"Gabriel will suffice," he replied, pouring tea. "I had hoped we might move beyond such formalities."

"Formalities seem to be all we have left," she rebuked coolly, accepting the delicate china cup he offered along with a scone smothered in jam. "Given that you refuse to share anything of substance about your work or your motives." She kept her eyes firmly locked on his as she took a dainty bite of her scone.

Gabriel felt his jaw tighten at her pointed reference to his continued secrecy, and at the way her tongue darted out to lick jam from her lips, but he forced himself to maintain his composure. "There are matters I cannot discuss freely, as I have explained. But perhaps we might find other topics of mutual interest."

"Such as my continued captivity?" she inquired with deceptive sweetness. "How much longer do you intend to keep me here, Lord Trenwith? Surely, your mysterious business must be nearing completion." She sipped her tea while still holding his gaze in challenge.

Gabriel set down his own cup with careful precision. "Miss Bigsby, you must understand that your situation is more complex than simple captivity. There are considerations—"

"Yes, you keep mentioning these mysterious considerations," she interrupted, her amber eyes flashing with irritation. "But you never seem inclined to explain what they might be. Instead, you speak in riddles and expect me to accept your word that everything you have done has been necessary."

Gabriel studied her face, noting the stubborn set of her jaw and the fire in her gaze. This was not the Henrietta Bigsby he remembered from their previous encounters—the charming, vivacious woman who had made his visits to Wells's townhouse so memorable. This Miss Bigsby was guarded, suspicious, and clearly angry. He had created this version of her through his own actions, and the knowledge sat heavily on his conscience.

"Very well," Gabriel said finally. "If you must know, part

of my reluctance to release you immediately stems from your … reputation for indiscretion."

Her cup rattled against its saucer as she set it down sharply. "I beg your pardon?"

"It is well-known that you cannot keep a secret," Gabriel continued, though he regretted the words even as he spoke them. "Your tendency to share information, however innocently, could compromise sensitive matters that affect more lives than just your own."

The color drained from her face, and Gabriel saw genuine hurt flicker across her features before anger replaced it. "I see. So in addition to being your prisoner, I am also your burden, a gossip too irresponsible to be trusted with important matters."

Gabriel realized immediately that he had made a terrible mistake. Her pain sliced him like a dagger when he saw how his words had wounded her. "Miss Bigsby, that is not what I meant—"

"Is it not?" She was muted. Anguished. "You have made your opinion of my character quite clear, Lord Trenwith. I am a woman who cannot be trusted, who must be managed and controlled for the greater good."

Gabriel reached across the small table, intending to take her hand. "Please, allow me to explain—"

Miss Bigsby pulled back as if his touch burned. "Oh, I think you have explained quite enough," she replied, rising from her chair with swift, angry movements. "Now perhaps you would be so good as to explain something else. That sketch I was carrying when you … rescued me from Sir Alpheus's library. What have you done with it?"

Gabriel hesitated, recognizing the shift in her demeanor. She was no longer the hurt woman seeking understanding. Rather, she had become harder, more calculating. "I have been studying it. Making some progress, actually, in deciphering its meaning."

"How fascinating," she declared with false brightness. "And did it occur to you to include me in this investigation? Or am I too much of a gossip to be trusted with such important work?"

The bitterness in her voice made Gabriel wince. He had wanted to share his discoveries with her, but now she was throwing his own words back at him with devastating accuracy. "Miss Bigsby, please. If you could tell me about the sketch—"

"No, you have made your position clear. I cannot keep secrets, so I cannot be trusted with information. Very well. But if that is your view of my character, then surely you can understand why I might be reluctant to share any information with you. Why I feel compelled to prove you wrong!"

Gabriel felt his temper begin to rise at her stubborn refusal to listen to reason. "This is childish, Miss Bigsby. The sketch may hold important clues that affect both our futures."

"Then perhaps you should have thought of that before insulting my integrity," she replied with icy composure. "If you believe I am incapable of discretion, then surely, my knowledge of that sketch's origins would be of little value to you."

Gabriel recognized the trap she had set for him, and he had to admire her tactical skill even as it frustrated him beyond measure. She was using his own words against him with the precision of a seasoned diplomat. This was not the charming, slightly scattered woman he had thought he knew. This was someone far more formidable.

"You are being deliberately difficult," Gabriel said, his own composure beginning to fray.

"I am being consistent," she corrected. "You have told me I

cannot be trusted. Therefore, it would be irresponsible of me to cooperate or share sensitive information with someone who might use it improperly."

Gabriel found himself in the unusual position of being outmaneuvered in a negotiation, and he did not care for the experience. This version of her—cold, calculating, and entirely justified in her anger—was not one he knew how to handle. He was accustomed to the vivacious woman who had always seemed pleased to welcome him at her uncle's home. This stranger wearing Miss Bigsby's face was proving to be a far more challenging opponent than he had anticipated.

"Very well," Gabriel said, forcing himself to remain calm. "Perhaps we might set aside the matter of the sketch for now and discuss more immediate concerns. Such as your future."

"My future?" Her eyebrows rose in mock surprise. "How kind of you to consult me on the matter. I was beginning to think you intended to make all my decisions for me."

Gabriel pressed on despite her resistance to his opinions. "Miss Bigsby, whether you wish to acknowledge it or not, your reputation has been severely compromised by these events. Marriage to me remains the most practical solution to your difficulties."

"And I have already declined your generous offer," she replied with cutting politeness. "Perhaps it is time you accepted that answer as final."

"I cannot do that," Gabriel said firmly. "You do not fully understand the consequences of the scandal that awaits you in England. There are alternatives we might consider. Perhaps a period abroad while the worst of the gossip dies down. Mr. Wells has connections worldwide. You could start fresh in the Americas, where such matters carry less weight."

She stared at him for a long moment, her expression unreadable. "You would prefer to exile me to another continent rather than accept my refusal of your proposal?"

"I would prefer to see you safe and respected," Gabriel replied. "If marriage to me is truly so distasteful, then yes, I would arrange for you to begin a new life elsewhere rather than watch you destroyed by gossip and scandal."

"How noble of you," she replied dryly. "But I fear you have misunderstood something fundamental about my character, Lord Trenwith. I love my work. I love the intellectual challenge, the sense of purpose, the ability to contribute meaningfully to important matters. Marriage, to you or anyone else, would end all of that. As would starting fresh in the Americas."

He felt a flicker of hope and his resolve firmed. Marriage to him would be Miss Bigsby's closest match to what she desired. "I would not say that. As my wife, you could serve as my political hostess, just as you have done for your uncle. Your skills and connections would be invaluable in that role."

She shook her head firmly. "As your wife, I would be your appendage. Any influence I possessed would be derivative, dependent entirely upon your goodwill and approval. That is not the same as independence, Lord Trenwith, no matter how you might dress it up."

Gabriel studied the set of that stubborn mouth and realized she was going to stand firm against his proposal, and as much as he wanted to point out that her influence as her great-uncle's secretary was just as derivative, mayhap even more so than as his viscountess, he knew it was not the right tactic. The more he pushed in this direction, the more she resisted.

Miss Bigsby did not fully comprehend the censure that a young woman was exposed to by scandal. Her position with Reginald Wells was already lost. No man of his standing, no matter his loyalty to his great-niece, could employ a woman whose reputation had been so thoroughly compromised. Her entire family would be tarred with the brush of controversy.

Her mother might lose clients over it, to a point that Bigsby's Stone Manufactory could face serious trouble.

He had seen what the taint of disgrace could do. He had seen what a loss of reputation could do to an intelligent and sensitive woman such as the delightful Miss Bigsby, and he would not allow the light in her riveting amber eyes to be extinguished. Leaving her to the ravages of gossip was not an option, so he racked his brain for ideas of how to persuade this unusual opponent who refused to see sense.

But as the silence between them extended, he saw her eyes flutter down to his mouth, before dropping to his chest to caress along his shoulders. It was a sign of weakness, a chink in her obstinacy. She was aware of him as a man, which made her nervous. Susceptible. And she had definitely responded to his kiss the night before.

A knowing smile spread across his lips as he rose from his chair and moved around the small table toward her. If she would not willingly agree to their vows, he would make it impossible for her to walk away. It was ruthless, but necessary, because Gabriel would never leave the vibrant Miss Bigsby to feel the brunt of society's censure, which would kill the spark of liveliness in those fascinating eyes.

This wedding was the best method to prevent it. The two of them might have other plans, but they would have to find a way to reconcile themselves to a partnership. Meanwhile, there was no reason why they could not enjoy the benefits of such an arrangement.

He tugged her into his embrace before she could protest. His mouth closed over hers as a startled squeal was soon smothered and she yielded to his kiss.

He skimmed his tongue over the seam of her lips, coaxing her to allow him access, and when she finally relinquished, their tongues tangled together in a symphony of strawberry preserves and elegant tea.

Gabriel felt her resistance crumble as passion flared between them, just as it had the night before. Whatever her rational mind might argue, her body responded to his touch with an honesty that could not be feigned. This was his path forward. Not through argument or logic, but through the undeniable attraction that sparked between them whenever they touched.

Gabriel deepened the kiss, his tongue exploring the sweet recesses of her mouth as her resolve melted away entirely. A soft moan escaped her throat, the sound vibrating against his lips and sending fire racing through his veins. Her hands, which had been pressed against his chest in token resistance, now clutched at his waistcoat as she pressed herself closer to his warmth. Gabriel's own hands roamed from her waist to trace the curve of her spine, then higher to tangle in the silken strands of her hair. He could feel the rapid flutter of her pulse beneath his fingertips where they rested against her throat, could taste the lingering sweetness of strawberry on her tongue. When she arched against him with another breathless sigh, Gabriel knew with triumphant certainty that her body had betrayed every rational argument her mind might make.

When he finally lifted his head, Miss Bigsby's breathing was unsteady and her eyes were wide with confusion and desire. Gabriel smiled with satisfaction, knowing he had found the key to winning this particular negotiation.

"Think about it, Miss Bigsby," he murmured against her ear. "Think about what we could have together."

He released her then, stepping back with the confidence of a man who had just gained a significant advantage. She might refuse his proposal with her words, but her body told a very different story. And Gabriel intended to use every weapon at his disposal to ensure she made the right choice.

After all, this was simply another form of diplomacy. And he had never lost a negotiation yet.

# CHAPTER 11

*"For love is not to be won by force, but by gentleness and truth."*

**Sir Thomas Malory, *Le Morte d'Arthur***

* * *

Henri found herself in a strange state of bewilderment as Mr. Tyne escorted her back to the attic after that extraordinary tea. Her lips still tingled from Gabriel's kiss, and she could not seem to banish the memory of his hands tangled in her hair, the warmth of his mouth moving against hers with such devastating skill.

"Miss Bigsby," Mr. Tyne said as he opened her door to allow her in, "his lordship has requested that you prepare for dinner this evening. Lisette will assist you with … appropriate attire."

Henri blinked, struggling to focus on his words when her mind kept drifting back to the sensation of Gabriel's tongue exploring her mouth. "Dinner?"

"Yes, miss. A more formal affair, I believe." Mr. Tyne's

pale cheeks held a slight flush, as if he were embarrassed by whatever preparations had been made. "I shall return shortly to collect you."

The key turned in the lock behind her, and Henri leaned against the closed door with a smile still playing about her lips. But it evaporated like steam into the air when she realized what had happened. Lord Trenwith had distracted her completely. The dratted man had not answered a single question during their entire encounter, and she knew no more about his work or his plans than she had before. He was so damn adept at keeping his secrets to himself!

"Fool," she muttered to herself, moving to stand before the small mirror above her washstand. Her reflection showed flushed cheeks and slightly swollen lips. Clear evidence of her shameful surrender to his advances. "You let him manipulate you with a few kisses, like some green girl with her first beau."

Henri gave herself a stern mental lecture as she paced the small confines of her chamber. She had spent years building her independence, creating a life where she answered to no one but herself. She would not throw all of that away simply because Gabriel Strathmore possessed the ability to make her knees weak with a single touch of his lips.

Marriage meant surrender. It meant becoming someone's property, losing her independence, her very self. She had seen it happen to countless intelligent women who had allowed themselves to be swayed by passion or romantic sentiment. Henri would not join their ranks, no matter how skillfully Gabriel might kiss her.

She was still lecturing herself when Mr. Tyne returned with Lisette, unlocking her door with obvious purpose.

"Miss Bigsby," Mr. Tyne said, "his lordship has arranged for you to prepare properly for this evening. We shall escort you to more suitable quarters."

Henri followed them down the narrow staircase to a bedchamber on the second floor that was far more elegant than her attic room. To her amazement, a copper bathtub had already been filled with steaming water, and Lisette was arranging things about the room. On the bed lay the most beautiful gown Henri had ever seen—a creation of deep emerald silk that shimmered in the lamplight.

"I shall wait outside your door to … to provide you p-privacy," Mr. Tyne continued, averting his gaze, then he retreated to the corridor, closing the door firmly behind him as Lisette began her preparations.

"Where on earth did Monsieur Grantham acquire such things?" Henri asked the maid, reaching out to touch the exquisite fabric. "Surely, he did not have evening gowns simply lying about in anticipation of kidnapping women."

Lisette's English was likely too limited to answer such a complex question, but she smiled and began unlacing Henri's day dress with efficient movements.

The bath that followed was a revelation. Henri could not remember the last time she had enjoyed such luxury. Water hot enough to steam, French-milled soap that smelled of lavender and roses, soft towels that felt like silk against her skin. As she soaked in the perfumed water, she found herself wondering once again about Gabriel's mysterious resources.

When Lisette helped her into the emerald gown, Henri gasped at her reflection in the large mirror. The dress fit as though it had been made for her, the bodice modest but flattering, the silk falling in elegant lines that emphasized her figure without being improper. Henri wondered if it was Mr. Tyne who was a wizard of arranging such things, although her journey from Danbury's had certainly proven that Lord Trenwith was a resourceful man in his own right.

Lisette had somehow produced delicate combs for her hair, arranging the honey-brown strands in an elaborate style that made Henri look like someone she barely recognized.

*"Très belle, mademoiselle,"* Lisette murmured with obvious satisfaction as she made final adjustments to Henri's appearance.

Henri studied herself in the mirror, hardly able to believe the transformation. She looked like a lady preparing for a grand ball, not a prisoner being held against her will in a distant port city. The realization was both thrilling and deeply disconcerting.

When Gabriel arrived to escort her to dinner, Henri's breath caught in her throat. Gone was the understated merchant persona of Monsieur Grantham. Instead, he stood towering before her dressed in fine evening wear that left no doubt about his true station. Impeccably tailored black coat, pristine white linen, and a waistcoat that probably cost more than most people earned in a year. He looked every inch the wealthy viscount he was, commanding and elegant and utterly devastating to her hard-won composure.

"Miss Bigsby," he said, offering a bow that was both respectful and somehow intimate. "You are absolutely radiant."

Henri felt heat rise in her cheeks at the genuine admiration. "Lord Trenwith. You seem to have undergone quite a transformation yourself."

Gabriel smiled, offering his arm. "Shall we?"

The dining room had been transformed as completely as Henri herself. What had been a simple chamber last evening was now set with gleaming silver, delicate china, and crystal that caught the candlelight like captured stars. The meal that followed was a feast worthy of any London mansion, with multiple courses of expertly prepared French cuisine and wines that spoke of careful cellaring.

Throughout dinner, Gabriel was charming in a way that

made Henri's defenses crumble despite her best efforts to maintain them. He spoke of books they both enjoyed, shared amusing anecdotes about his travels, and listened to her opinions with the sort of genuine attention that was all too rare in her experience with gentlemen.

But it was the moments of vulnerability she glimpsed beneath his polished exterior that truly unsettled her. The way his smile sometimes faltered when he thought she was not looking. The careful way he chose his words, as if each one mattered tremendously. The intensity with which he watched her, as though memorizing every expression that crossed her face.

As the evening progressed, Henri began to comprehend something that shook her to her core. This elaborate seduction—the gown, the dinner, the careful attention to every detail—was not simply about convincing her to accept his proposal. There was a desperate quality to Gabriel's efforts that suggested far more was at stake than mere convenience or duty.

And thus, Henri came to the startling realization that perhaps this evening was not about whether she needed him, but rather about him needing her.

The thought should have given her satisfaction, should have provided her with ammunition to use against his manipulations. Instead, it filled her with an unexpected tenderness that threatened to undo all her carefully constructed arguments against marriage. More than anything, her work with Uncle Reggie had always been the most rewarding when she had accomplished something that only she could have done. And, perhaps, accepting the role of Gabriel's wife and political hostess would not be such a hardship after all if the viscount desired it so fervently.

When Gabriel rose from the table and offered his arm, Henri found herself accepting it without thought. He escorted her back to the elegant bedchamber where she had prepared for dinner, and it was there, in the privacy of the candlelit room, that he drew her into his arms.

Henri was lost in a sea of desire, heady with the knowledge that Lord Trenwith genuinely yearned to make her his wife. His mouth found hers with the same skill and passion as before, but now Henri could taste something new in his kiss. A vulnerability that made her heart race and her resolve crumble like sand castles before the tide. Lord Gabriel Strathmore, the controlled and enigmatic viscount, needed her in ways that went far beyond simple physical craving or social convenience.

And Henri was beginning to suspect that she might need him as well, despite every rational argument her mind could marshal against such perilous sentiment. As his hands traced the silk of her gown and his lips moved against hers with desperate hunger, Henri found herself wondering if perhaps there were some risks worth taking after all.

Even if it meant surrendering the independence she had fought so hard for.

* * *

GABRIEL HAD INTENDED this evening to be a calculated seduction, a ruthless bid to secure Henri's agreement to marriage through passion rather than logic. But as he held her in his arms, felt her responding to his kisses with such sweet abandon, he found it difficult to remember that this was supposed to be mere strategy.

The taste of her lips, the soft sighs that escaped her throat, the way she pressed herself against him with such trusting surrender—none of it felt manipulative. Instead, Gabriel lost himself in the perfection of Miss Bigsby's responses to his touch. There had been a softening in her attitude, a shift for which he did not have an explanation, but he was grateful. So very, very grateful.

"You are beautiful," he murmured against her throat, his hands moving to the fastenings of her emerald gown. "So beautiful."

She trembled beneath his touch, but not with fear. Gabriel could see the desire darkening her amber eyes, could feel the rapid flutter of her pulse beneath his lips as he pressed kisses to the delicate skin of her neck. When she did not protest, when instead she arched toward him with a soft moan, Gabriel felt the last of his deliberate control slip away entirely.

He worked the intricate fastenings of her gown with careful fingers, each small button and hidden hook demanding patience he struggled to maintain. The silk was of the finest quality, requiring delicate handling even as his body burned with need. When the dress finally loosened and pooled at her feet like liquid emerald, Gabriel's breath caught at the sight of her in her stays and chemise.

The candlelight played across her pale skin, casting golden shadows that emphasized the gentle curve of her waist, the swell of her breasts above the top edge of her undergarments. Gabriel reached for the laces of her stays with reverent hands, his fingers fumbling slightly with the complex arrangement of ribbon and whalebone along with his overwhelming desire for the treasure he was holding.

As her stays fell away, leaving her clad only in thin cotton and silk stockings, Gabriel felt his mouth go dry. The chemise was nearly transparent in the candlelight, revealing the dusky circles of her nipples, the flare of her hips, the shadow between her thighs that made his body throb with want.

"You are magnificent," Gabriel breathed, his hands skimming over the soft cotton that was all that remained between them. "More beautiful than any woman has a right to be."

Her breath hitched as he gathered the hem in his hands, lifting the chemise slowly over her head. The garment whispered as it fell to the floor, leaving her standing before him in nothing but her silk stockings and the flush of desire that painted her skin rose-gold in the lamplight.

Gabriel took his time removing his own clothes, noting how her eyes followed his movements with innocent fascination. When he stood naked before her, he saw her gaze travel over his chest, down the flat plane of his stomach, to the evidence of his arousal that jutted proudly from the nest of dark hair.

"Do not be afraid," Gabriel murmured, seeing the slight widening of her eyes at the sight of his manhood. "I will be gentle with you, Miss Bigsby. I give you my word."

He lifted her and carried her to the bed, laying her down against the soft white linens with the sort of care one might show a priceless work of art. The contrast of her honey-brown hair spread across the pillow, her creamy skin against the pristine sheets, was enough to make Gabriel's hands tremble with anticipation.

But he forced himself to go slowly, to savor every moment of this extraordinary experience. She was a gift he had never expected to receive, and he would not rush through the unwrapping.

Gabriel started at her feet, his hands gentle as he rolled down her silk stockings one at a time. He pressed kisses to her delicate ankles as he revealed them, marveling at the softness of her skin, the way she gasped and writhed beneath his ministrations.

"Gabriel," she breathed, his name a prayer on her lips that made his heart race and his cock throb.

He kissed his way up her calves, pausing to lavish attention on the sensitive skin behind her knees. Her hands clutched at the bedsheets, her back arching as he continued his slow exploration of her body. The scent of her arousal, sweet and musky, filled his nostrils and made his mouth water with the desire to taste her.

"Trust me," Gabriel murmured against her inner thigh, his hands gentle but insistent as they urged her legs apart. "I will take care of you, Miss Bigsby. I promise."

Gabriel had been with women before, but never with a virgin, never with someone who responded to his touch with such innocent passion. Every gasp and sigh was genuine, every movement of her body beneath his hands a revelation that made his blood burn hotter.

When his mouth found the sweet core of her, she cried out in shock and pleasure, her hands flying to tangle in his hair. Gabriel gentled her with soft words and softer touches, using his tongue and lips to bring her to the edge of release before drawing back, teaching her body the rhythm of desire.

"Please," she gasped, her hips lifting toward his mouth in unconscious invitation. "Gabriel, please, I need ..."

"I know what you need," Gabriel murmured against her heated flesh, his voice rough with desire.

He brought her to climax with his mouth, watching in awe as pleasure transformed her face, as her body convulsed beneath his ministrations. The sight of her lost in passion, the taste of her release on his tongue, nearly undid his control entirely.

When her breathing had steadied somewhat, Gabriel moved up her body, pressing kisses to her stomach, her ribs, the valley between her breasts. Her nipples were pink and tight with arousal, and Gabriel could not resist taking each one into his mouth in turn, using his tongue and teeth to draw soft moans from her throat.

"Are you ready for me?" Gabriel asked, positioning

himself between her thighs. His manhood pressed against her entrance, slick with her arousal but still formidably large against her small opening.

She nodded, her eyes wide but pleading as she looked up at him. "Yes," she whispered. "Yes, Gabriel. Please."

Gabriel entered her slowly, fighting every instinct that demanded he bury himself to the hilt in her welcoming heat. Her body resisted at first, unused to such invasion, and Gabriel felt the moment when her maidenhead gave way, saw the flicker of pain that crossed her features.

"Breathe," Gabriel murmured, holding himself still within her. "The worst is over, I promise. Just breathe."

Her body gradually relaxed around his, accepting his presence as Gabriel began to move with careful, measured strokes. The tight heat of her surrounding him was almost more than he could bear, but the wonder in her eyes as pleasure began to replace discomfort made every moment of restraint worthwhile.

"Is this … is it always like this?" she breathed in amazement as Gabriel moved within her.

"No," he replied honestly, straining to maintain control. "This is extraordinary, Miss Bigsby. *You* are extraordinary."

What followed was unlike anything Gabriel had ever experienced. This was not the practiced coupling he had known with other women, calculated to bring mutual pleasure and nothing more. This was deeper, more profound. A joining of not just bodies but souls that left Gabriel shaken and transformed.

She moved beneath him with increasing confidence, her initial hesitation giving way to passion that matched his own. Gabriel found himself drowning in her responses, in the way she called his name, in the perfect fit of their bodies together. The sound of skin against skin, the soft cries of pleasure that escaped her lips, the scent of their joined bodies. All of it combined to create an experience that transcended mere physical pleasure, and he was very much afraid it was going to be difficult to suppress his feelings as he had done in the past.

When release finally claimed them both, her climax triggering his own in a rush of sensation that left him gasping, Gabriel collapsed against her with a groan of satisfaction that came from the very depths of his being. For long moments they lay entwined, breathing hard, hearts racing in perfect synchronization.

Gabriel knew he should move, should withdraw from her body now that they were sated. Miss Bigsby was inexperienced, a maiden who would likely experience some soreness from their coupling. But he found himself strangely reluctant to break the connection between them, to end this perfect moment of intimacy.

She shifted beneath him, her amber eyes fluttering open to look up at him with such rapturous satisfaction that Gabriel felt his breath catch. Her smooth thighs bracketed his hips, and the soft globes of her perky breasts were pressed against the hard planes of his chest. Gabriel found himself in lavender-scented heaven when, to his surprise and dismay, he felt his softening cock already beginning to stir back to life within her tight heat. It was unprecedented for his body to demand a second helping so soon, but the sight of her flushed cheeks and kiss-swollen lips was proving irresistible.

"I apologize, Miss Bigsby," Gabriel murmured, capturing one of her hands and raising it above her head, which caused her magnificent breasts to arch upward enticingly. "But I am afraid we are not yet done."

He leaned down to capture her plump lips yet again, thinking with wonder that being married to her might not be such a penance after all. In fact, as she responded to his renewed passion with eager enthusiasm, Gabriel began to suspect that marriage to this remarkable woman might be the greatest blessing of his entire life.

The calculated seduction had become far more—genuine feeling that threatened to transform him completely. And as he lost himself once more in her sweet responses, he found he no longer cared about strategy or manipulation.

All that mattered was this woman in his arms, and the hope that she might come to care for him as deeply as he was beginning to care for her.

* * *

HENRI LAY beneath Gabriel's weight, her body still trembling from the extraordinary sensations he had introduced her to. She felt changed, transformed in ways she could never have imagined when she had awakened that morning. The ache between her thighs was a strange mixture of soreness and satisfaction, a physical reminder of what had transpired between them.

Henri was nearly thirty years old, so she had overheard a thing or two about carnal relations in a well-attended place like Westminster. The wives of politicians were not always as discreet as they might be when they thought themselves among friends, and Henri had gleaned enough information over the years to understand the basic mechanics of what occurred between husband and wife. Yet she was surprised to feel Gabriel's appendage swelling and lengthening inside her, growing firm and insistent once more.

Her mouth fell open with the realization that it was hardening again, his body preparing to take her a second time, just as his mouth claimed her lips in a deep and drugging kiss. The sensation was startling and terribly erotic. She could feel him growing within her, stretching her anew, making her breath catch with the unexpected indulgence of it as her pleasure mounted again.

Henri pulled away from his kiss for just an instant, just long enough to meet his eyes and whisper the words that had been hovering on her lips since they had entered the bedchamber. "Henrietta," she said breathlessly. "Henri to my family."

Gabriel's eyes darkened, as though her permission to use her given name meant far more to him than simple courtesy. "Henri," he murmured, testing her name on his lips like a prayer. "My beautiful Henri."

This time, their joining was different. Where before Gabriel had been careful, gentle, mindful of her inexperience, now there was a new urgency between them. Henri found herself responding with equal fervor, her body already knowing his rhythm, already craving the pleasure he could bring her.

She marveled at the way her body knew what to do without instruction, how her hips rose to meet his thrusts, how her legs wrapped around his waist to draw him deeper. The sounds that escaped her throat were foreign to her own ears and seemed to drive Gabriel to greater heights of passion.

"You feel so perfect," Gabriel groaned against her throat, his voice rough with desire. "So tight, so warm. I cannot get enough of you."

Henri felt a surge of feminine pride at his words, at the evidence of how thoroughly she affected him. This powerful, controlled man was losing himself in her, and the knowledge filled her with a heady sense of her own power.

Gabriel's movements became more urgent, more demanding, and Henri found herself swept along in the tide of sensation. Her hands roamed over the broad expanse of his back, feeling the play of muscles beneath his skin, the slight dampness of perspiration that spoke to his exertion.

When Gabriel shifted his angle slightly, Henri cried out in shock and pleasure as he found a spot within her that made stars dance behind her eyelids. He understood her reaction immediately, repeating the movement until Henri was writhing beneath him, her hands clutching at his shoulders as sensation built to an unbearable peak.

"Let go," Gabriel commanded, hoarse with need. "Let me see you fall apart again, Henri. Let me watch you come undone."

The words pushed Henri over the edge, and she found herself convulsing around him, her body clenching rhythmically as waves of pleasure crashed over her. The intensity of it was even greater than before, leaving her gasping and shaking in Gabriel's arms.

Gabriel's own release followed moments later. He growled deep in his throat, tossing his head back in ecstasy, and Henri was amazed, smugly proud, that she could solicit such primal responses in a man so aloof and controlled. To see him lose that careful composure, to know that she was the cause of his abandon, filled her with a satisfaction that went far beyond the physical pleasure they had shared.

Then he collapsed his long, hard body over hers, catching himself on his elbows so he would not crush her with his weight. His face pressed into the side of her neck in an oddly affectionate gesture that made Henri's heart clench with unexpected tenderness.

For long moments they lay like that, breathing hard, hearts thumping in unison. Henri found herself thinking about what Mr. Tyne had told her earlier. Gabriel was intensely private, how even his closest associates struggled to understand what he was thinking. Despite his stoic exterior,

Gabriel did hold her in high regard. He wished to forge a closer connection.

The aggravating man needed her. Henri recalled that glimpse of raw thirst she had seen lurking in his eyes. The realization made her spirits soar as she understood better how to make this new path palatable. Perhaps marriage to Gabriel would not mean the loss of her independence so much as the gaining of a purpose she had never considered. It was up to her to draw him out, to help make him whole.

"Gabriel," Henri whispered, her fingers combing through his sandy hair as he nuzzled against her throat. "Are you well?"

He lifted his head to look down at her, and Henri was startled by the vulnerability she saw in his hazel eyes. Gone was the careful mask he usually wore, replaced by naked honesty that made her breath catch.

"More than well," Gabriel replied quietly. "Henri, I … what we just shared …" He seemed to struggle with words, as though the emotions coursing through him were too complex to express easily.

Henri looked up into his eyes, seeing the hope and fear warring there, understanding suddenly that this proud, controlled man was laying his heart bare before her. Even as he fought for his self-control, the knowledge that she held such power over him, that she could bring him joy or devastation, was both thrilling and terrifying.

As she lay beneath him, their bodies still joined, feeling the steady beat of his heart against her chest, Henri found her acceptance of her new path. After all, what challenge could be more worthy of her intelligence and determination than unlocking the mysteries of Gabriel Strathmore's guarded heart?

* * *

Gabriel helped Henri clean herself, his hands gentle with a dampened cloth from the basin. The intimacy of the act, tending to her in this tender way, felt more vulnerable somehow than what they had just shared. He was acutely aware of every soft sound she made, every flutter of her lashes as she watched him minister to her.

When he finished, Gabriel found himself at a loss. The desperate need to secure her agreement pressed against his chest like a physical weight. He had shown her passion, pleasure, the promise of what their marriage could hold. But would it be enough? The uncertainty clawed at him, making him feel more exposed than he had ever been in a negotiation. Never had the stakes been so personal, so vital to his very existence.

He climbed back into the bed beside her, his movements careful and controlled despite the chaos in his mind. Gabriel pulled the coverlet over them both, then hesitated, unsure whether to reach for her or maintain a respectful distance. The moment stretched between them, heavy with unspoken words and the weight of decisions yet to be made.

Henri settled the matter by turning toward him, her soft body seeking his. Gabriel's arms came around her instinctively, drawing her close against his chest. The simple trust in her gesture made his throat tight with emotion he barely recognized.

"Gabriel," Henri whispered against his shoulder, soft but clear in the quiet room. "I will marry you."

The words washed over him, stealing his breath entirely. Gabriel went rigid, certain he had misheard, that his desperate mind was conjuring the very words he most longed to hear. But Henri lifted her head to meet his gaze, and the steady determination in her eyes confirmed what she had said.

Joy. Pure, overwhelming, and utterly foreign. It crashed

over him in waves which he did his best to hide. Gabriel had known satisfaction, triumph, even contentment, but this feeling was different. It filled every corner of his being, bright and warm and so intense it was almost painful. For a moment, he could not speak, could not breathe, could only stare at her in wonder.

"You … you truly mean it?" The question escaped him before he could stop it, revealing the depth of his uncertainty. "This is not some stratagem to make me lower my guard so you might escape?"

Henri's lips curved in a wry smile. "As you so astutely pointed out, I have never been good at keeping secrets. I am honest to a fault, and it would be nigh impossible for me to pretend such a thing convincingly." Her expression grew more serious. "And I keep my promises, Gabriel. When I give my word, it means something."

Gabriel searched her face, looking for any sign of deception, any hint that this was merely a clever maneuver. But all he saw was Henri—brilliant, fierce, beautiful Henri—staring back at him with an acceptance that made his heart race.

Unable to contain himself any longer, Gabriel pulled her fully into his arms, burying his face in the fragrant locks of her hair. He breathed her in deeply, this woman who had agreed to be his wife, who had just given him everything he had scarcely dared to hope for. The sweetness of her filled his senses. The subtle scent of her skin, the feel of her body pressed against his, the steady rhythm of her breathing.

"Henri," he murmured against her temple, her name a prayer on his lips. "My Henri."

She nestled closer to him, her hand resting over his heart as though she could feel the way it thundered in his chest. Gabriel tightened his hold on her, as if she might disappear if he loosened his grip even slightly.

Sleep should have come easily after such emotional and

physical exertion, but Gabriel found himself caught in a restless half-doze. The moment his eyes closed, the dreams began. Memories of his grandfather's cold rejection, the disgust in those pale blue eyes when Gabriel had grieved as a boy. *"Five years old and already displaying such weakness,"* the old man's harsh criticisms echoed in his mind.

He jolted awake with a gasp, his heart pounding, only to find Henri still warm and solid in his arms. The relief was immediate and overwhelming. She was here, she had chosen him, she had promised. Gabriel buried his face in her hair, breathing in her scent like a talisman against the ghosts that plagued him.

But each time he drifted off again, the dreams returned. His grandfather's cutting disgust, the certainty that he was fundamentally unworthy of love, that anyone who claimed to care for him was either lying or would inevitably leave when they discovered his true nature. He would wake with a start, his arms automatically tightening around Henri to reassure himself that she was still there, that this was not some elaborate dream destined to crumble like everything else he had ever dared to want.

Each time he surfaced from the tormented sleep, the joy of her acceptance would wash over him anew, followed quickly by a fierce protectiveness and the paralyzing fear that, somehow, he would lose her too.

Gabriel held her through the night, his body finally finding rest even as his heart remained full to bursting with this new, precious happiness that Henri had given him, along with the creeping dread that he would lose her if he misstepped.

# CHAPTER 12

*"The heart that holdeth love in silence suffereth a thousandfold."*

**Sir Thomas Malory, *Le Morte d'Arthur***

* * *

JANUARY 29, 1822

The morning sun streamed through the tall windows of the council chamber as Gabriel and Étienne set their hands to the treaty. The ceremony was brief but momentous. Weeks of careful negotiation reduced to ink upon vellum and sealed with the firm clasp of hands between two men who, though they had stood for opposing nations, had found a measure of mutual respect.

"*Mon ami*," Étienne said as they shook hands, his dark eyes filled with genuine satisfaction. "I cannot express my gratitude for your involvement in these talks. Without your persistence and diplomatic skill, I fear we would still be arguing over the wording of the first paragraph."

Gabriel felt a surge of relief so profound it was almost dizzying. He could finally leave Calais. "The pleasure was entirely mine, Marquis. These men have waited far too long for their freedom."

"Indeed. I have already sent word to the prison authorities," Étienne assured him, straightening the stack of signed documents with characteristic precision. "The prisoners will be handed over to your consulate by evening. You may inform your government that the matter is concluded to everyone's satisfaction."

Gabriel nodded, maintaining his professional composure even as his heart began to race with different concerns entirely. The negotiations were finished. The agents would be free within hours. Which meant he was also free to attend to the more pressing matter of securing their marriage license and ensuring that Henri remained safely by his side.

"If you will excuse me," Gabriel said, already moving toward the door. "I have some urgent personal business to attend to before the prisoners arrive."

Étienne inclined his head graciously. "Of course. Until this evening, then."

Gabriel made his way through the consulate corridors with swift purpose, his mind already turning back to the practical matters of arranging his wedding. But beneath his efficient planning, a cold dread had begun to settle in his chest like winter fog.

He had revealed too much last night. In the aftermath of their passionate joining, when Henri had whispered her acceptance of his proposal, he had allowed himself to show the depth of his need, his desperate longing for her presence in his life. The memory of his own vulnerability made him cringe inwardly. What manner of man allowed a woman to see such unseemly emotion? What manner of husband would he prove to be if he could not control these feelings that overwhelmed his careful composure whenever she was near?

*She agreed last night, but that was in the heat of the moment,* Gabriel thought as he strode through the streets toward the offices where marriage licenses were procured. *Now that she has had time to reflect, to consider what manner of man I truly am …*

The terrible possibility that Henri might have reconsidered her acceptance grew with each step. She was intelligent, perceptive, capable of seeing through any pretense to the raw need he had displayed so shamelessly. Perhaps she had realized that accepting his proposal would mean binding herself to a man who clearly struggled with his emotions.

Gabriel felt exactly like that five-year-old boy standing in his grandfather's library, having ruined his only chance at belonging to a family because he could not contain his weakness. Just as his boyhood tears had disgusted the old man into sending him away, perhaps his emotional display had shown Henri exactly what kind of man she would be marrying. One who could not maintain the proper reserve expected of a gentleman.

*I revealed too much. I let her see how much I need her, and now she will realize what a poor bargain she has struck.*

By the time Gabriel reached *La Maison Grise,* his anxiety had crystallized into near certainty that Henri would greet him with news of her changed mind. Or Tyne would reveal she was missing, that she had escaped.

He paused at the door, steeling himself for the crushing disappointment that seemed inevitable. Perhaps she would be kind about it, offer some gentle excuse about reconsidering the hasty nature of their arrangement. Or perhaps she would be honest about his unsuitability as a husband, the way his emotions overcame his better judgment whenever she was near.

Gabriel opened the door and found Henri in the small sitting room, dressed in the blue gown that complemented her coloring so beautifully. She looked up as he entered, and for a heart-stopping moment, he searched her expression for any sign of regret or withdrawal.

Unable to contain himself, Gabriel crossed the room in swift strides and pulled her into his arms, claiming her lips in a kiss that was both desperate and grateful. She was still here. She had not fled after he had left their bedchamber this morning, had not informed him that she had reconsidered. It was so overwhelming that for a moment he could barely think beyond the warmth of her body against his.

"The negotiations are concluded," Gabriel said against her hair, his voice rough with emotion he was already trying to suppress. "We can be married on Wednesday."

Henri smiled up at him, but Gabriel was already pulling back, mentally rebuilding the walls that had crumbled so completely the night before. He had shown her too much already. From this moment forward, he must be the reserved, controlled husband she deserved. Not the desperate, emotional man who had laid his heart bare in a moment of weakness.

As he settled into a more somber and distant demeanor, Gabriel told himself it was for the best. Henri needed a husband who could protect and provide for her, not one who would burden her with the intensity of feelings he clearly could not manage properly. He would give her everything she required, but he would not make the mistake of revealing the depths of his need again.

She deserved better than a man who behaved like a sniveling babe, clutching affection that might be snatched away at any moment.

* * *

Henri had been sitting quietly in the small parlor, attempting to read one of Gabriel's books, when Lisette burst through the door with an energy that was startling in its intensity. The French woman's entire demeanor had shifted overnight. Where before she had been respectful but reserved, she had practically glowed with excitement.

"*Mademoiselle!*" Lisette had exclaimed, her hands clasped together as if in prayer. "Oh, but this is *magnifique*! You are to marry Monsieur Grantham!"

Henri had blinked in surprise at the sudden flood of enthusiasm. "Yes, we are to be wed."

"Ah, *mais non*, you do not understand," Lisette had interrupted, settling into the chair across from Henri. "Monsieur Grantham, 'e is … 'ow you say … *très bon homme*. A very good man, *oui*?"

The way Lisette spoke the words suggested depths of meaning that Henri had yet to grasp. "What do you mean?"

Lisette's eyes had glistened with tears. "My *frère* … brother, Jean-Claude, 'e was in very big trouble, some years ago. Ze authorities, zey say he was smuggler. But it was not true." She had paused, dropping to a reverent whisper. "Monsieur Grantham, 'e save Jean-Claude from certain arrest."

Henri had felt her heart skip. This had been the first real glimpse she had been given into Gabriel's character beyond his composed exterior. "How did he—"

"'E use 'is connections, 'is influence," Lisette had continued, her words growing livelier with emotion. "But more than that, 'e do it to 'elp a man 'e barely know, just because it was right. Jean-Claude, 'e would 'ave gone to prison, but Monsieur Grantham … 'e find a way."

The revelation had left Henri speechless. It was evidence of the man she had sensed beneath Gabriel's reserve.

Someone capable of great courage and compassion, even if he was determined to hide these qualities from her. And it certainly shed light on Lisette's willingness to turn a blind eye to Henri's captivity.

"*Monsieur* is so private, *oui*?" Lisette had said with a knowing look. "Too much alone, that one. 'E need a wife to care for 'im, to bring ze love into 'is life. You, I think, you be very good for 'im."

Before Henri could respond, Lisette had left the room, but not before giving Henri a meaningful smile that suggested she understood far more about their situation than anyone had given her credit for.

The door opened suddenly, and Gabriel strode into the room with swift purpose. Before Henri could even greet him properly, he crossed to her and pulled her into his arms, claiming her lips in a kiss that was both aggressive and gentle. The intensity of it left her breathless and slightly bewildered.

"The negotiations are concluded," Gabriel said against her hair, his voice rough with emotion. "We can be married on Wednesday."

Henri smiled up at him, pleased by this news, but almost immediately she noticed him pulling back, his expression becoming more reserved. The warmth that had been in his eyes moments before retreated behind his usual careful control.

When Henri seized the opportunity to ask about his work —"What exactly were these negotiations about?"—she watched his expression close off with disappointing swiftness.

"Diplomatic matters," Gabriel replied with his customary evasion, settling into a more somber demeanor. And just like that, he had withdrawn behind the curtain again, as though the kiss had never happened, and Henri was confronted by a stranger once more.

Her spirits sank. Even after everything they had shared, after her agreement to marry him, he was still determined to keep her at arm's length. She found herself recalling Mr. Tyne's advice about patience, about the need to coax Gabriel out of his deep privacy. Clearly, it would take more time than she had hoped.

"Would you join me in the study?" Gabriel asked, apparently oblivious to her disappointment. "I have something to show you regarding the sketch you were carrying."

Henri's curiosity overcame her frustration, and she followed him to the small room he had been using as an office. The desk was blanketed with papers covered in his neat handwriting, and she could see the sketch laid out alongside copious notes.

"I have decided to tell you about my mission," Henri said, settling into the chair across from his desk. If he would not volunteer information about himself, perhaps sharing her own secrets would encourage reciprocity. "I was at Danbury's on behalf of Signor Lorenzo di Bianchi, an art historian who has been researching Arthurian legends. We believed the Malory manuscript might contain clues to his ancestor who went missing here in England."

Gabriel nodded slowly. "And the sketch?"

"It was hidden in a family painting. Signor di Bianchi suspected it was a map of some kind, but neither of us could decipher it."

Gabriel's expression grew animated as he turned the sketch toward her. "Indeed I have. Look here, these letters and numbers below the drawing. I used the manuscript text to decipher them, and they all point to one location."

Henri leaned forward eagerly to study the markings he indicated. "You managed to break the code?"

"The manuscript provided the key," Gabriel explained, gesturing to his pages of notes. "Once I understood the pattern, the letters and numbers revealed a clear reference."

The sketch showed a veiled knight with a sword in his hand, standing before a pillared arch that was shrouded in swirling smoke. At the knight's feet, a serpent coiled around what appeared to be fragments of a shattered crown.

"The imagery follows classic Arthurian symbolism," Gabriel explained, pointing to the various elements. "The knight represents the quest for truth. His face is hidden because the seeker must prove worthy before the revelation. The serpent coiled at his feet signifies treachery and betrayal. The forces that brought down Arthur's kingdom."

Henri studied the dark fragments strewn around the serpent. "And the shattered crown?"

"Arthur's broken realm," Gabriel replied solemnly. "In the legends, Arthur's crown was shattered when Camelot was destroyed. The fragments represent the lost kingdom. Dispersed and hidden, waiting to be restored when the rightful heir returns."

Then he pointed to the code written beneath the drawing.

"These letters and numbers. See here, K-12-7, and here, R-15-3, and scattered throughout are more sequences like G-8-11 and S-4-9."

Gabriel opened the Malory manuscript to demonstrate his method. "The letters and numbers correspond to specific words in Malory's text," he explained, his finger moving between the sketch and the manuscript pages. "Each coded sequence tells you exactly which word to extract."

He showed Henri his method. "The Winchester copy is not set out in numbered chapters. Each new passage begins with a large titled line. Here the code uses the first letter of that heading. K marks a passage that begins 'King Arthur,' and

R marks one that begins 'Round Table.' So K-12-7 means the twelfth such passage, seventh word. R-15-3 is the fifteenth 'Round Table' passage, third word. If we gather each word in the order set out on the sketch, the hidden message appears."

Henri watched as Gabriel demonstrated, finding each word in the manuscript according to the cipher.

"The brilliance is in its simplicity. Anyone with access to this specific manuscript can solve it, but without the key text, the numbers are meaningless."

"You are brilliant."

His cheeks reddened, the only indication he had heard her, as he continued. "When I extracted each word according to the cipher, they formed this clear directive." He showed Henri the phrase he had assembled.

She squinted at his sprawling handwriting, reading it out loud. "Where armies fell and smoke rose, truth lies in ash and stone. Seek the chapel that never was."

Gabriel gestured toward the sketch. "At first, I thought the curl of smoke a fanciful embellishment. But look closely. The line rises in a long, even sweep, narrowing to a fine point, just like the solitary hill of Roseberry Topping. Even the shading suggests the soft wreath of morning mist that clings to its slopes, giving it the look of a pale crown adrift in the clouds. And here, the stones set in this pattern. Not random, but radiating outward like the petals of a rose." Gabriel's eyes lit up as he explained the final connection. "The artist is not merely drawing. He is enciphering. Stones for the rose, the smoke for the hill. I was stationed near there once. It rises alone above the plain, unmistakable against the sky. The villagers call it the Rose of Smoke for the way the mist enfolds it at dawn. My tutor spoke of it with reverence and claimed Arthur fought battles in its shadow. I dismissed it as another fireside tale until now. This sketch is no coincidence. It directs us to a particular ruin, what the clue names 'the chapel that never was.'"

Henri wondered about the tutor. His tone made her think that the man was no longer part of this mortal coil, but she did not know what to say. How to ask. Gabriel was so private about his thoughts.

He looked up at her with obvious satisfaction. "There are ancient ruins near Roseberry Topping, believed by some to have once been a chapel where Arthur's sword was blessed. But according to the deciphered message, there is something more. A chapel that perhaps contains the next piece of the puzzle."

Henri stared at the elegant cipher work spread before them, amazed by the complexity hidden within what had appeared to be a simple medieval drawing. Gabriel's analytical skills had transformed seemingly random symbolic elements into a precise map, revealing layers of meaning that connected Renaissance artistry to ancient Arthurian legend.

"This is incredible."

Gabriel nodded. "After we are wed, we shall return to England and investigate properly."

Henri felt emboldened by his enthusiasm to press for more information. "Gabriel, what were you doing at Danbury's that morning? What is your interest in the Malory manuscript?"

But immediately, she watched his expression grow guarded again.

"I am helping you assist Signor di Bianchi," he responded carefully. "Is that not sufficient?"

The disappointment was immediate. Here she had taken such a tremendous leap of faith, agreeing to marry a man she barely knew, and he still would not trust her with even the most basic information about his behavior. She would have to endeavor to be patient, but it was not a trait she was known for.

"Of course," Henri said quietly, though her tone undoubtedly betrayed her feelings.

Gabriel must have sensed her resentment but made no move to address it directly. Instead, he changed the subject with characteristic efficiency. "I have taken the liberty of arranging for a letter to be delivered to your family on Wednesday evening, informing them of our arrival some time on Thursday."

Henri stared at him. "You have already arranged this? Without consulting me about what the letter should say?"

"I thought it best to handle the matter promptly," Gabriel replied, his tone suggesting he saw nothing amiss with his autocratic decision. "Your mother and great-uncle will need time to adjust to the news."

The casual way he had made such personal decisions on her behalf was both dismaying and illuminating. This was apparently how Gabriel approached all matters. With careful planning and complete control, but without any thought to consulting those affected by his choices.

Henri was beginning to understand just how private and self-contained her future husband truly was. The question that haunted her was whether she would ever be able to breach those carefully constructed walls, or whether she would spend her marriage forever on the outside, looking in. She had no wish to be treated as … as … well, she did not wish to be treated as his private secretary!

No, she would not be relegated to the role that Mr. Tyne held. She would find a way to be Gabriel's wife and partner as he had intimated. With time, he was going to learn that she would not be assigned to the role of subordinate.

* * *

GABRIEL NOTICED the subtle shift in Henri's demeanor immediately. The way her shoulders tensed slightly when he mentioned the letter to her family; the careful neutrality that crept into her expression when he evaded her questions. She was withdrawing from him again, and the familiar panic began to claw at his chest.

He had shown her the deciphered sketch, shared his expertise, allowed her glimpses of his work. Yet still she remained disappointed by him. The fear that she might reconsider their arrangement, that she might find him wanting as a husband before they had even spoken their vows, made his chest tighten.

Gabriel rose from behind his desk, moving around to where she sat studying the papers. "Henri," he said quietly, gruffer than he intended.

She looked up at him, those amber eyes angry and bright in a way that terrified him more than any armed opponent ever had. Without allowing himself to think, Gabriel reached for her, drawing her up from the chair and into his arms. If words failed him, if he could not give her what it was she was seeking, perhaps he could remind her of the physical connection that blazed between them.

"Gabriel, what are you—" Henri began, but her protest was cut short as his mouth claimed hers in a kiss that was hungry, desperate, and utterly consuming.

Gabriel lifted her easily, settling her on the edge of his desk among the scattered papers. His hands roamed over her curves with growing urgency, reacquainting himself with every line and hollow of her body. When Henri responded with equal fervor, her fingers tugging at his shirt to run them up his bared skin, Gabriel felt some of the terrible tension in his chest begin to ease.

"I need you," he murmured against her throat, the words escaping before he could stop them. "Henri, I need …"

But he could not finish the thought, could not reveal the depth of longing that threatened to overwhelm him. Instead, he showed her with his hands and mouth, with the reverent way he worshipped her body through her clothes, grateful that women did not wear small pants as his hand slid up her leg to the juncture of her thighs where he discovered she was slick and ready for him, and then he was even more gratified when a guttural moan escaped her lips. He continued to caress her folds, circling the pearl at the center of her pleasure.

Their joining was fierce and urgent, Henri clinging to his shoulders as Gabriel moved within her with increasing intensity. The study chair creaked under their combined weight when he pulled her into his lap, her skirts bunched and billowing around them as she learned to move with him, to take her own pleasure as much as she gave it.

Gabriel was amazed anew by how completely Henri surrendered to the passion between them. There was no artifice in her responses, no calculation in the way she cried out his name when he found that perfect rhythm that drove them both toward completion. She was utterly genuine, utterly present, and the knowledge that she was his filled him with a fierce possessiveness.

When Henri collapsed against his chest, breathing hard, Gabriel held her close and marveled at the transformation her presence wrought in him. With her in his arms, he felt substantial, real in a way he had never experienced before. For so many years, he had felt like a ghost moving through life, observing from the edges, never quite connecting to the world around him. But Henri anchored him, made him feel like a man with a beating heart rather than a hollow shell going through the motions of existence.

The loneliest recesses of his soul, places he had thought permanently sealed off from human connection, warmed in her presence. She reached parts of him that he had forgotten existed, brought light to corners of his soul that had been shrouded in darkness for decades.

But even as Gabriel savored this revelation, he knew he must guard it. Such intense emotions, such reliance on another person's presence, were precisely the kind of weakness that had cost him his grandfather's acceptance all those years ago. Henri deserved a husband who could provide for her and accompany her through society with strength and composure. She did not need to be burdened with the knowledge of how completely she had captured his heart, how thoroughly she was becoming essential to his very sense of self.

Gabriel pressed his lips to Henri's hair, breathing in her scent, and resolved to keep these harmful sentiments locked away. He would adore her with his body, provide for her with his resources, and shield her from the world with his position. But he would not overwhelm her with emotions that even he did not fully understand.

It was enough that she remained in his arms. It had to be enough.

# CHAPTER 13

*"Me repenteth of this marriage, for I fear we did not wisely."*

**Sir Thomas Malory, *Le Morte d'Arthur***

* * *

JANUARY 30, 1822

Henri stood in the stark, utilitarian office of the British consulate, her hands trembling slightly as she smoothed the fabric of her wedding gown. The same traveling dress she had worn when Gabriel first kissed her seemed woefully inadequate for such a momentous occasion. Around her, the mundane business of diplomacy carried on in hushed tones, clerks shuffling papers and officials conducting the ordinary affairs of government with no regard for the life-altering ceremony about to take place.

It was early enough that the office remained relatively quiet, lending an air of secrecy rather than celebration to their nuptials. Henri could not help but contrast this dismal affair with the romantic wedding Madeline had enjoyed just months earlier. Her twin had been married at night in the garden shared with Simon's kin, surrounded by family and friends, with fragrant hothouse flowers decorating the ornate urn and lanterns illuminating the faces of loved ones. The celestial garden had seemed the perfect setting for Psyche and Eros to unite in matrimony, with Uncle Reggie and Mama beaming with joy as Reverend Stone performed the ceremony under the light of the silver moon.

Here, there were no flowers, no family, no joyful tears. Only Lisette standing as witness beside a consulate staffer Henri had never met, both looking as somber as if they were attending a funeral rather than a wedding. The contrast brought home to Henri just how disparate she and Gabriel truly were, how little she knew of the man she was about to marry, and how utterly soulless their vows would be. Perhaps she would have felt better if Mr. Tyne had been present, but he had already left for England to make arrangements for their arrival.

Gabriel stood beside her in his coat and buckskins, his expression composed but distant. Even now, at their wedding, he seemed to be holding himself apart from her, as if this were merely another negotiation to be concluded rather than the joining of two lives. Henri searched his face for some sign of affection, some indication that this moment held meaning for him beyond securing her silence and cooperation, but found only that familiar mask of careful control.

The consulate's chaplain began reading the marriage service in a monotonous voice, as if he had performed such duties countless times before and without particular interest in the couple before him. Henri tried to concentrate on the solemn words, on the gravity of the vows she was taking, but her thoughts kept straying to how utterly alone she felt in this stark, official room. No mother to dab at her eyes with a handkerchief, no Uncle Reggie to offer a steadying arm, no twin sister to share her hopes and fears.

When Gabriel spoke his vows, steady and sure, Henri detected no emotion in the formal words. She wondered if he felt anything at all beyond relief that his problem was being solved efficiently. When her turn came, Henri's voice nearly caught on the promises to love and honor, knowing how one-sided such devotion might prove to be.

The ring Gabriel slipped onto her finger was beautiful but unfamiliar. It felt heavy and foreign on her hand, a tangible reminder of how quickly her life had changed and how little control she had over her own fate.

When the official pronounced them husband and wife, Gabriel's kiss was brief and chaste, more duty than desire. Henri felt a sharp pang of disappointment at the missed opportunity for connection, for some acknowledgment that they were embarking on a shared journey rather than simply concluding a transaction.

The harbor teemed with noise and motion as they made their way toward the sleek cutter that would carry them across the Channel to Dover. Dockhands shouted over the cries of gulls, and the scent of salt and tar lingered thick in the air. Lisette accompanied them, forming a small party that resembled a diplomatic delegation more than a honeymoon. Henri watched as Gabriel supervised the loading of their trunks, his instructions brisk, his gaze rarely still. He moved with quiet urgency, as though every minute on French soil was one too many. She sensed … not fear, precisely, but a driving need to be away.

During the crossing, Henri was compelled to retreat to the windward side of the deck more than once, the gentle sway of the calm sea still enough to unsettle her stomach. The brisk air and bright skies made it bearable, though she found herself gripping the rail with white-knuckled determination. Gabriel was attentive, fetching a blanket when she turned pale, pressing a lemon-drenched cloth into her hand with a murmured suggestion to breathe it in. But he remained otherwise aloof. His courtesy never faltered, but his thoughts were clearly elsewhere.

Henri watched him standing at the rail, her nausea subsiding just enough for curiosity to take hold. She studied his expression as he gazed toward the distant white cliffs, his brow furrowed in thought. His claim that he merely wished to assist her in helping Signor di Bianchi was implausible. There was too much precision in the way he deciphered the symbols, too much ease with Arthurian lore. No gentlemanly impulse could account for such focused interest, or such knowledge. It was becoming plain that Gabriel had a personal stake in the cipher's secrets, one he had yet to disclose.

When they reached Dover, they were met by the viscount's official carriages, complete with the Trenwith coat of arms and matched horses that spoke to Gabriel's elevated status. Henri realized she was now Lady Trenwith, a viscountess, though the title felt as foreign as her wedding ring. As they settled into the luxurious conveyance for the journey to their inn, Henri ventured to ask about their ultimate destination.

"We will rest tonight and then make for London in the morning," Gabriel informed her, consulting his pocket watch with the same precision he applied to everything else. "Roseberry Topping is quite remote, so it will take time to reach it and make inquiries about the local ruins."

"Gabriel," Henri asked carefully, "why are you truly so interested in the sketch? This seems far beyond what would be required to assist Signor di Bianchi with his research."

Gabriel's expression grew guarded immediately. "We

should solve this mystery together. Once we have found what the cipher reveals, we can go to Trenwith Abbey."

Henri's disappointment deepened. Even married to her, even having shared the most intimate moments between a man and woman, Gabriel remained as closed off as ever. Instead of the gradual revelation of his inner self that she had hoped marriage might bring, he seemed determined to maintain the same careful distance that had characterized their relationship from the beginning.

That night at the inn, when Gabriel reached for her with the same passion that had marked their previous encounters, Henri could not shake the feeling that he was using their marital relations to distract her from the emotional intimacy she craved. His touch was skillful, his attention to her pleasure complete, but beneath the passion, she sensed the same desperate quality she had noticed before, as if he were trying to forge a connection through physical means alone while keeping his heart inaccessible.

As she lay in Gabriel's arms afterward, Henri wondered what it would take to truly reach the man she had married. She had gambled everything on the belief that she could unlock his heart, but with each passing day, she began to fear that Gabriel Strathmore might be determined to remain an unsolvable mystery even to his own wife.

* * *

*Alaric Devayne pulled his collar higher against the bitter wind that swept across Dover's busy harbor, his hollow cheeks already reddened by days of exposure to the elements. From his position near the customs house, he had an unobstructed view of every vessel that approached the docks, and he had been maintaining this vigil for nearly a week.*

*His obsessive nature, which had always been both his greatest strength and his most dangerous weakness, had driven him to this point of nearly manic vigilance. He slept poorly in the cramped room he had taken at a dockside inn, ate little beyond the bread and weak beer that kept him functional, and attacked his surveillance with such fervor that the local longshoremen had begun to whisper about the strange, gaunt man who never left his post.*

*The coins he had promised among the harbor's more observant residents had already borne fruit. A sharp-eyed boy named Tommy, whose father worked loading cargo, had approached him just that morning with news of a wealthy couple on the deck of a cutter sailing in with the afternoon mist.*

*Alaric's pulse quickened as he spotted the vessel in question. Moving closer while maintaining his mask as just another clerk waiting for arrivals, Alaric positioned himself where he could observe the disembarkation without drawing attention. Years of intelligence work during Napoleon's campaigns had taught him the art of becoming invisible in plain sight, and he employed those skills now.*

*When the gangplank was lowered, Alaric felt a surge of vindication as he recognized the sandy brown hair of the man who emerged first. The same controlled bearing, the same careful way of moving that suggested both authority and the ability to violence. But it was the woman who followed that truly confirmed his suspicions.*

*She was no longer bound, no longer struggling, but Alaric could see even from a distance that her circumstances had changed dramatically. The way she moved, the deferential manner in which the French maid treated her, all suggested that she was no longer a captive.*

*His eyes narrowed as he noticed the way the man offered his arm, the subtle intimacy of their positioning as they waited for their luggage to be unloaded. When he caught a glimpse of what appeared to be a wedding ring glinting on her finger, Alaric exhaled in understanding.*

*Marriage. The perfect solution to the problem of a kidnapped woman who could ruin a man's reputation.*

*The arrival of ornate carriages bearing aristocratic arms confirmed what Alaric had already deduced about the man's elevated status. He watched the party settle into the luxurious conveyance.*

*When the carriage began to move, Alaric was ready. He had already arranged for a horse to be saddled and waiting at a nearby stable, and within minutes, he was following at a discreet distance. His military experience had taught him how to track without being detected, and the busy Dover roads provided ample cover for his pursuit. But, mayhap, he should just follow them to learn what they were about?*

*The inn where they stopped was exactly the sort of establishment that would cater to wealthy travelers, with private dining rooms and accommodations for those who preferred to avoid public scrutiny. Alaric secured a room at a smaller inn across the street, positioning himself where he could observe their movements while planning his next approach.*

*As night fell, Alaric sat at his window, studying the layout of the inn where his quarry had taken refuge. It was his hope that the manuscript and sketch were close now, probably secured in the man's traveling case or perhaps even carried on the woman's person. He had come too far and waited too long to abandon his pursuit now.*

*The woman was clearly no longer an unwilling participant in whatever scheme was unfolding, which might make his task easier. He would need to separate her from her protector, create an opportunity to retrieve what he sought without alerting the authorities to his presence.*

*Alaric checked his pocket watch, noting the late hour. Soon, the inn would grow quiet, the staff would retire, and the guests would settle into sleep. That would be when opportunities presented themselves to men willing to take calculated risks.*

*His gloved fingers drummed against the windowsill as he considered his options. The woman had had that sketch at Danbury's, had been clutching it defiantly when he demanded its surrender.*

*Alaric smiled grimly in the darkness. Tomorrow would bring new possibilities, and he would be ready to seize whatever chance presented itself. The quest that had consumed his thoughts for months was finally within reach, and nothing would deter him from claiming what he had pursued across the country and through the depths of winter.*

*The game was far from over.*

# CHAPTER 14

*"I found ye kind, and therefore ye may trust me; and now I trust not to be deceived."*

**Sir Thomas Malory, *Le Morte d'Arthur***

* * *

JANUARY 31, 1822

The carriage rolled smoothly along the well-maintained road toward London, the four matched horses maintaining a steady pace. Inside the luxurious compartment, Gabriel found himself experiencing an emotion so unfamiliar that it took him several minutes to identify it as contentment.

He was married. To Henri. The reality of it still seemed impossible, like something from a dream he might wake from at any moment. Yet there she sat next to him. Lady Trenwith. His wife.

Gabriel turned his attention to the countryside rolling past the window, the winter landscape dotted with bare trees and frost-covered fields that would eventually give way to the bustle of London. But the scenery held little interest for him. His awareness kept returning to the woman who shared his carriage, to the subtle scent of lavender that seemed to follow her everywhere, to the way she absently worried her lower lip when lost in thought.

Almost without conscious decision, Gabriel reached across the space between them and gently clasped Henri's gloved hand in his. She looked up with surprise, her fascinating eyes widening at the unexpected gesture, but after a moment of hesitation, she allowed her fingers to relax in his grasp.

The simple contact sent a warmth through Gabriel that had nothing to do with passion and everything to do with connection. He found himself marveling at how natural it felt to have her there, how the restless energy that usually consumed him during travel seemed to quiet in her presence. For the first time in years, he was not planning three moves ahead, not calculating diplomatic advantages or anticipating potential threats. He was simply present in this moment, content to hold his wife's hand and watch the English countryside pass by their window.

As the miles rolled beneath their wheels, Gabriel began to contemplate the changes that marriage would necessarily bring to his carefully ordered existence. The dangerous diplomatic missions that had defined his adult life would have to end. A married man, particularly one with a wife as intelligent and politically astute as Henri, could not simply disappear for weeks at a time on mysterious government business. The very secrecy that had armored him in his work would become a barrier in his marriage.

The thought should have troubled him. For years, his

diplomatic career had been his primary source of purpose, the work that gave meaning to his existence beyond the mere management of his inherited estates. Yet as he watched Henri's profile, noting the way she studied the passing landscape, Gabriel found himself surprisingly at peace with the prospect of change.

Perhaps it was time to take up his political responsibilities more earnestly. As Viscount of Trenwith, he held a seat in the House of Lords that he had largely neglected in favor of his more clandestine duties. With Henri's sharp political mind to assist him, he could imagine engaging more directly with the great questions of their time rather than operating from the shadows.

His estates, too, may have suffered from his inattention. Gabriel realized he knew shamefully little about the tenants and properties that provided his income, having been content to leave such matters to competent stewards while he pursued more immediately pressing concerns. A settled life would allow him to become the sort of landlord his position demanded, to take genuine responsibility for the people who depended on his land and leadership for their livelihoods.

Gabriel's thumb traced gentle circles over Henri's knuckles, and he found himself imagining a future that had been impossible just weeks ago. A life shared with someone who understood the complexities of political maneuvering, who could hold her own in drawing rooms and parlors where policy was made over tea and careful conversation. A partner rather than merely a wife.

The very thought of allowing himself such connection, such vulnerability, should have terrified him. Gabriel had spent decades building walls around his heart, constructing elaborate defenses against the kind of emotional dependence that had brought him such pain as a child. Yet Henri's presence bypassed those vigilantly erected barriers without even trying.

Still, old habits die hard. Even as Gabriel contemplated this potential transformation, he maintained his characteristic reserve. He squeezed Henri's hand gently but said nothing of the thoughts occupying his mind. He smiled when she caught his eye but offered no explanation for his unusually demonstrative mood.

The boy who had learned too early that emotional displays led to rejection remained deeply ingrained in the man. Gabriel might be slowly coming to terms with his changed circumstances, might even be allowing himself to imagine a future built around genuine connection rather than careful isolation, but he would not rush headlong into such hazardous territory.

For now, it was enough to hold his wife's hand and feel, for perhaps the first time since his parents had departed this world, that he was exactly where he belonged. The rest would come in time, if he could find the courage to let it.

* * *

As THEIR CARRIAGE rolled through the familiar streets of London, Henri felt her pulse quicken with anticipation and anxiety in equal measure. The city was bustling with its usual energy, but she could think only of the questions that had been building during their journey. Now, with Gabriel's brief moment of openness past, she decided to make another attempt.

"Gabriel," Henri began carefully, "you were remarkably adept at deciphering that sketch. It suggests considerable experience with such puzzles. What truly brought you to Danbury's that morning?"

Gabriel's expression grew guarded immediately, the

warmth that had characterized his demeanor during their quiet moments fading behind his familiar mask of control. "As I mentioned, we should focus on solving the mystery together. Once we understand what the sketch reveals, perhaps there will be more to discuss."

Henri felt her heart sink at yet another deflection. Even the simple intimacy of holding hands was insufficient to bridge the gulf between them when it came to matters Gabriel deemed too sensitive to share.

When their carriage finally drew up before the elegant Bigsby townhouse, Henri could see familiar faces at the windows. Her mother's imposing figure was silhouetted in the front drawing room, and Henri braced herself for what she knew would be a thorough interrogation.

Eleanor Bigsby met them at the door with her characteristic efficiency, though Henri detected relief in her mother's sharp eyes as she embraced her daughter. Mama was a formidable woman of six feet who had built an empire of artificial stone while raising twin daughters alone, and she had not achieved such success by avoiding difficult conversations.

"Henrietta," her mother said, holding her at arm's length to study her face. "You look well, though I confess I have been quite concerned about your continued absence." Her gaze shifted to Gabriel with polite but unmistakable scrutiny. "Lord Trenwith, I presume? Your message was rather … brief."

Gabriel stepped forward with a bow that was both respectful and commanding. "Mrs. Bigsby, I am honored to finally make your acquaintance. I regret the irregular nature of our correspondence."

Mama's expression remained impartial as she ushered them into the drawing room without the customary curtsy due a viscount. "Indeed. Perhaps you would care to explain those circumstances more fully? Henri's uncle and I have been quite at a loss to understand her sudden departure from London, more so since the rather cryptic nature of your communication."

Henri watched Gabriel navigate her mother's pointed questions with the same charm she had observed him use with officials and innkeepers. He spoke of an urgent matter requiring Henri's expertise, of the necessity for immediate travel, of his deep respect for her abilities and his commitment to her safety and reputation. All perfectly reasonable explanations that somehow managed to reveal absolutely nothing of substance.

"I am afraid I must tell you," Mama continued, her tone growing more serious, "that Signor di Bianchi has been quite distraught about Henri's disappearance. He and the young gentlemen from next door have been searching for her across the countryside, trying to trace where she went after visiting Sir Alpheus. The poor man feels responsible for her vanishing, for he was the one who had left her alone to examine that manuscript. Miss Dulwich was not able to tell us very much beyond your scheme to view it, the sound of a pistol discharging, and they found your bonnet on the table, so they feared you had not left on your own determination …" Mama broke off, her jaw tightening and clearly unwilling to relive her distress.

Henri felt a pang of guilt at the thought of Lorenzo di Bianchi's distress, not to mention what her mother and great-uncle had gone through. "He does not know we are married?"

"Married?" Mama's voice rose slightly, the first crack in her composure. "When exactly did this marriage take place?"

"Yesterday morning, in Calais," Henri replied. "We were wed at the consulate there."

Mama was quiet for a long moment, clearly processing

this information and its implications. "I see. And this was … a planned elopement?"

Gabriel stepped in smoothly. "The circumstances required immediate action, Mrs. Bigsby. I assure you that my intentions toward your daughter have been entirely honorable from the beginning."

Henri flushed at the recollection of their lovemaking, a fact which did not escape Mama's watchful gaze. Fortunately, the sound of the front door opening interrupted any further interrogation, and Henri heard the familiar sound of Uncle Reggie calling out to the butler. Within moments, her great-uncle appeared in the doorway, his usually amiable expression clouded with concern. Tall with stooped shoulders, in his early seventies, Reginald Wells was a welcome sight after the travails of the past week.

"Henri, my dear!" Uncle Reggie embraced her, his relief evident. "When I learned of your disappearance, I returned from the country immediately. With no word of your whereabouts … well, I feared the worst." He turned to Gabriel with a brief bow. "Lord Trenwith. What brings you into this affair?"

Gabriel rose and extended his hand. "Mr. Wells, a pleasure to see you again. I am afraid the circumstances have been rather extraordinary."

"You two are acquainted?" Eleanor asked, her eyebrows rising with interest.

"Indeed," Uncle Reggie replied, settling into his favorite chair. "Lord Trenwith and I have had occasion to correspond on various parliamentary matters. His diplomatic work has been quite valuable to the Foreign Office." He studied Gabriel's face with the shrewd attention of a seasoned politician. "Though I must say, I was surprised to learn of your involvement in my niece's sudden disappearance."

Henri immediately launched into her account, her natural

inclination to share taking over, only hurried along by her nerves regarding this awkward encounter. "Oh, Uncle Reggie, it was the most terrifying experience! I was in Sir Alpheus's library examining the Malory manuscript when this dreadful man appeared with a pistol. He demanded I hand over the book and was clearly prepared to use violence to get it!"

Mama's face went pale, and Henri felt terrible to impart such terrifying news when her own twin had been poisoned just months earlier. Fortunately, Maddy had had Lady Trafford at hand who was a gifted healer, or else Henri would be a twin no longer.

"A pistol? Henrietta!"

"Yes, Mama, and he was absolutely menacing about it," Henri continued, gesticulating as she spoke. "He wanted the manuscript and Signor di Bianchi's sketch, but then Gabriel appeared through the terrace doors like a hero from a novel and seized the man by the throat!"

Gabriel inclined his head politely. "I was fortunate to arrive when I did."

"Fortunate!" Henri exclaimed. "Uncle Reggie, you should have seen him. One moment this villain was threatening to shoot me, and the next Gabriel had rendered him completely unconscious. It was quite the most impressive thing I have ever witnessed."

"By George," Uncle Reggie breathed, his customary composure momentarily shaken. "You mean to say there was an actual attempt on your life?"

"Oh yes, absolutely," Henri said earnestly. "The scoundrel was clearly prepared to kill for what I was carrying. And then, of course, there was the matter of my reputation being quite thoroughly compromised by the whole affair."

Gabriel nodded gravely. "Given the circumstances, and

the likelihood that this individual might have accomplices, I felt it necessary to remove Henri from immediate danger."

Eleanor's sharp eyes moved between Gabriel and Henri. "And this danger required taking her out of the country?"

Gabriel's jaw tightened slightly. "The man's identity and motives were unknown to me at the time. I could not be certain that leaving Henri in England would guarantee her continued safety. My primary concern was ensuring she remained out of harm's way until I could better assess the threat."

Uncle Reggie leaned forward in his chair. "This manuscript must have considerable value to provoke such violence. What exactly was Henri examining that would inspire murder?"

Henri glanced at Gabriel, uncertain how much he wanted revealed. "It was the Malory manuscript. Sir Thomas Malory's original work on King Arthur. Signor di Bianchi believed it might contain clues to his ancestor's lost artwork."

"Ah, the art historian," Uncle Reggie nodded. "Yes, he's been quite beside himself with worry. Called on me twice, and I understand from Lord Blackwood next door that Signor di Bianchi and the Scott brothers have been searching for information about your whereabouts."

Her mother's expression had grown increasingly grave during this exchange. "Let me understand this correctly. You are telling me that my daughter was threatened with violence, possibly death, over some medieval manuscript? And your solution was to take her to France and marry her?"

The bluntness of the question hung in the air like a challenge. Henri watched Gabriel's face, seeing the careful calculation behind his eyes as he formulated his response.

"Mrs. Bigsby," Gabriel said finally, "I will not pretend that this is ideal. But I found myself in an impossible situation. Henri had been compromised by events that could endanger her life. Subsequently, she had been in my company, unchaperoned, for an extended period. Her reputation was at risk, and her safety remained uncertain."

Uncle Reggie's tone was sharp. "And so marriage became the most practical solution to multiple problems."

"Uncle Reggie!" Henri protested, though she recognized the pragmatism in his assessment.

"My dear," Uncle Reggie said gently, "I am not criticizing Lord Trenwith's decision. In fact, from a purely practical standpoint, it was rather elegant. He protected your reputation, ensured your safety, and solved the immediate crisis. Though I confess I am curious about the longer-term implications."

Eleanor was studying Gabriel with the keen attention she usually reserved for difficult business negotiations. "And what of this criminal individual? Has he been apprehended?"

Gabriel's expression grew guarded. "The matter is … ongoing. I have reason to believe the threat may not be entirely resolved."

"Which is why," Henri interjected, with sudden understanding of what he was about, "we are not staying in London. Gabriel insists we must travel to Yorkshire to follow the clues in the manuscript so we might learn who attacked me at Danbury's."

Uncle Reggie's eyebrows rose. "Yorkshire? What is in Yorkshire?"

"Roseberry Topping," Henri replied. "It appears to point to ruins there. Gabriel has solved part of the mystery."

"How fascinating," Uncle Reggie mused. "And you are certain this is not simply an elaborate treasure hunt that has put my niece in unnecessary danger?"

Gabriel grew firm. "Mr. Wells, I give you my word that I would not expose my wife to any risk I deemed avoidable. However, given what we have uncovered, I believe completing this investigation may be the surest way to resolve the threat permanently."

Mama was quiet for a long moment, clearly weighing everything she had heard. "And you believe Henri will be safer traveling with you than remaining in London with us?"

"I do," Gabriel replied without hesitation. "She will be more difficult to find. Moreover, her expertise may be crucial to solving this puzzle. She has already proven invaluable to the investigation."

Henri felt a flutter of pride at his words, even as she remained frustrated by how much he was still withholding. She could see her mother and uncle exchanging meaningful looks, conducting some sort of silent communication that spoke to decades of shared family responsibility.

"Very well," Eleanor said finally. "Though I insist on a proper wedding breakfast before you depart. The staff can prepare something suitable for tomorrow morning. Henri's friends and family should have an opportunity to acknowledge this union properly, even if the ceremony itself was … unconventional."

Gabriel inclined his head graciously. "That is most generous, Mrs. Bigsby. Though I am afraid we cannot delay our departure long."

"A single morning," Eleanor said firmly, "is hardly an unreasonable request for a mother who has just learned of her daughter's marriage under such extraordinary circumstances. Regrettably, Signor di Bianchi is presently beyond our reach. He would be grateful to know Henri is alive and well."

Gabriel was silent for several seconds. "May we make it a wedding dinner?"

Henri wished to object. She had hoped to speak with Signor di Bianchi and return the sketch as she had promised, but she held her tongue, uncertain who would win the quiet standoff.

Her mother exhaled sharply, before conceding. "Very well."

As the conversation continued, Henri found herself observing a fascinating dynamic between Gabriel and her mother. Eleanor Bigsby had built her empire through shrewd observation and calculated decision-making, and Henri could see her applying those same skills to assess her new son-in-law. For his part, Gabriel seemed to recognize a kindred spirit in Eleanor's businesslike approach, responding to her directness with respectful deflection.

It was almost like watching two generals negotiate a treaty, each measuring the other's strengths while maintaining perfect civility. Eleanor's questions were pointed but fair, probing Gabriel's character and intentions with the same determined intensity she used to evaluate potential business allies. Gabriel, in turn, appeared to appreciate her straightforward manner, offering more substantive answers to her inquiries than he had to Uncle Reggie's more diplomatically phrased concerns. Yet he still kept many details to himself, and Henri felt it would be disloyal to reveal anything he was not willing to disclose himself.

"You understand," Eleanor said at one point, fixing Gabriel with her penetrating stare, "that Henrietta is not merely my daughter, but a vital part of our family dealings. Her safety and well-being are not matters I take lightly."

"I would expect nothing less from a woman of your accomplishments, Mrs. Bigsby," Gabriel replied with sincerity. "Your daughter's welfare is now my primary responsibility, and I do not accept such duties carelessly. Her experience as Mr. Wells's private secretary will be invaluable as my viscountess."

Henri watched this exchange with growing fascination,

realizing that Gabriel was responding to her mother's business acumen in a way that was almost deferential. Many of high society disdained a woman in trade, especially such a successful one. But here were two people who understood power and responsibility, who recognized in each other the kind of careful calculation required to succeed in their respective worlds.

As they parted to prepare for dinner, Henri noticed subtle signs that her mother was reaching a conclusion about Gabriel's character. The slight relaxation in Eleanor's posture, the way her questions shifted from interrogation to genuine interest, the occasional nod of approval when Gabriel demonstrated particular insight or consideration.

"Very well," Eleanor said finally, and Henri could hear a decision had been made. "I can see that Henrietta has chosen well, even if the circumstances were unconventional. You clearly understand the value of what you have gained, Lord Trenwith, and I trust you will act accordingly."

Gabriel inclined his head gravely. "You have my word, Mrs. Bigsby."

Eleanor's sharp eyes softened slightly as she looked at her daughter. "And you, my dear, seem content with your choice, despite the dramatic nature of your courtship."

"I am, Mama," Henri said, though she wondered if Gabriel would ever allow her the same kind of direct assessment her mother had just conducted.

As the conversation drew to a close and arrangements were made for their overnight stay, Henri could not shake the feeling that she was watching her husband retreat further into the safety of his public identity. Each question from her family seemed to reinforce his instinct to maintain careful distance, and she began to despair that the tentative connection they had shared during their journey might never return.

* * *

Later that evening, as Henri prepared for bed in the chamber that had been hers since childhood, Gabriel found himself standing at the window, staring out at the London streets while his mind churned with an anxiety he had not experienced in years.

The dinner with Henri's family had gone well by any objective measure. He had successfully navigated their questions, earned Eleanor Bigsby's grudging approval, and maintained the diplomatic cloak that had served him so well throughout his career. Yet beneath his composed exterior, Gabriel felt as though the walls were closing in around him.

It was the way they had all looked at him expectantly, waiting for him to explain himself, to justify his actions, to become part of their family dynamic. Uncle Reggie's questioning glances, Eleanor's shrewd assessments, even Henri's eager chatter about their adventures, all combined to create a suffocating sense of being surrounded, examined, judged.

*Family.*

The word itself made Gabriel's chest tighten with old fears. These people were his family now, by marriage if not by blood, and the weight of their expectations pressed down on him like a physical force. They wanted to know him, to understand him, to draw him into their warm circle of shared affection and mutual concern.

The memory rose unbidden of standing in his grandfather's library, five years old and desperate for acceptance, only to be found wanting and shipped away like an unwanted burden. The parallel was uncomfortably clear in his mind, even though he recognized the irrationality of the comparison.

"Gabriel?" Henri's voice was soft, questioning. "Are you quite well? You have seemed rather distant since we arrived."

Gabriel turned to face her, noting how lovely she looked in her nightgown, her honey-brown hair loose around her shoulders. Any other night, he would have crossed the room and taken her in his arms, losing himself in the passion that blazed between them. Tonight, however, he felt trapped by invisible chains of memory and expectation, and even her presence did not bring peace.

"We must leave at dawn," he said abruptly, settling into the armchair by the window rather than approaching the bed.

Henri's expression grew puzzled, then disappointed. "Dawn? Gabriel, surely we can spare a day or two. I hoped to wait for Signor di Bianchi to return so I could give him back his sketch and tell him what we have learned. He's been so worried about my disappearance, and he deserves to know that his ancestor's mystery is being solved."

"Impossible," Gabriel replied, harsher than he intended. "We've delayed too long already. Every moment we remain here increases the risk that we will be followed or intercepted."

"But, Gabriel—"

"The matter is not open for discussion," Gabriel cut her off, his tone taking on the commanding quality he used with subordinates in diplomatic settings. "You will be ready to depart at dawn. That is final."

Henri recoiled as if he had struck her, her amber eyes wide with hurt and confusion. "I … yes, my lord," she said quietly, the formal address creating a gulf between them that Gabriel immediately regretted but felt powerless to bridge.

Gabriel watched as Henri climbed into bed, turning her face away from him toward the wall. The rigid set of her shoulders spoke to her wounded feelings, but Gabriel found himself unable to cross the room and offer comfort. The very intimacy that had become so natural between them now felt risky, threatening to expose vulnerabilities he could not afford to reveal.

Instead, Gabriel remained in his chair, staring out at the darkened city while his wife fell into what he hoped was sleep rather than the silent tears he suspected. The familiar weight of isolation settled around him like an old coat, providing armor at the cost of affinity.

When exhaustion finally claimed him in the small hours of the morning, Gabriel's sleep was plagued by dreams that had haunted him for decades. He stood once again in his grandfather's library, reaching out desperately for acceptance that would never come.

*"Five years old and already displaying such weakness."* The old viscount's reproach echoed with cold disdain. *"Thank God Charles did not live to see what manner of son he raised."*

The sensation of choking grief returned, the inability to hold back the sobs overwhelming his senses, but then the dream shifted, and suddenly, Gabriel was reading the letter that had shattered his world years later. The formal script of Horace's solicitor, cold and impersonal, delivered devastating news that had made Gabriel's heart stop.

> *It is with the deepest regret that I must inform you of the death of Mr. Horace Pelham. The authorities have determined that Mr. Pelham was murdered during what appears to have been a robbery of his study. His papers and books were ransacked, though no items of obvious value seem to have been taken. Funeral arrangements have been made in accordance with his wishes—*

Gabriel jolted awake with a gasp, his heart racing and cold sweat dampening his brow. The memory of receiving that crushing letter was as sharp as ever, the clinical language doing nothing to soften the brutal reality that the only person who had ever truly cared for him was gone, murdered by unknown hands.

The pale light of dawn was already creeping through the windows, signaling that their departure time had arrived. Gabriel rose quietly, dressing mechanically while his mind struggled to rebuild the walls that his dreams had so thoroughly demolished.

Today, they would begin the journey to Yorkshire, following clues that might lead him closer to understanding Horace's death and the forces that had destroyed the old man. But as Gabriel prepared to wake his wife and continue their investigation, he could not shake the fear that he was walking deeper into a trap of his own making. Perhaps he should not have taken Henri from that library, which he was now convinced had not been driven by necessity but rather a moment of weakness on his part.

# CHAPTER 15

*"Wit you well, my heart was never so heavy as it is now."*

**Sir Thomas Malory, *Le Morte d'Arthur***

* * *

FEBRUARY 1, 1822

Henri descended to the breakfast room and found Gabriel breaking his fast. His trunk stood by the door, and she could hear activity in the mews as their carriage was being prepared. The efficiency of it all only served to remind her of how completely he had dismissed her wishes the night before.

"Good morning," Gabriel said politely as Henri took her seat at the table. "I trust you slept well?"

Henri's response was a pointed silence as she reached for the tea service with more force than necessary. She was still furious about his high-handed treatment, and she had no intention of making this morning pleasant for him.

"I have made arrangements for your Miss Dulwich to travel to Trenwith Abbey," Gabriel offered, apparently hoping to fill the uncomfortable quiet. "The staff will see to her needs until we arrive."

Henri nodded curtly but said nothing, applying herself to her toast with grim determination. Miss Dulwich had wept with relief when they had encountered each other in her bedchamber the afternoon before, and she was happy the other woman would be joining her at her new home. She had told her to find Lisette directly upon her arrival at the Abbey. But if Gabriel wanted conversation, he could work for it.

"The carriage will be ready within the hour," Gabriel continued. "I thought we might make good time if we leave promptly."

Another nod. Another bite of toast. Another moment of silence that she hoped was making Gabriel as uncomfortable as his behavior had made her.

The atmosphere was so tense that Henri could practically feel Gabriel's discomfort radiating from the opposite seat. Good. Perhaps now he would understand how it felt to be dismissed and ignored.

Finally setting off, she kept her gaze fixed determinedly on the passing countryside, though she was acutely aware of Gabriel's attempts to engage her in conversation. His comments about the weather and their travel time were met with either silence or the briefest possible responses.

"Henri," Gabriel said finally, his composure clearly strained. "Surely, we can discuss whatever is troubling you."

"Can we?" Henri asked without turning from the window, sharp with sarcasm. "Or will you simply issue more commands about what I may and may not do?"

"I was perhaps … overly firm in my insistence that we depart quickly," Gabriel admitted.

"Overly firm," Henri repeated, finally turning to face him with indignation. "Is that what you call treating me like a child to be ordered about rather than your wife?"

Gabriel moved to sit beside her, gently lifting her chin so that she was forced to meet his gaze. The touch was tender, but Henri was not ready to be soothed by physical gestures.

"What is truly wrong?" he asked quietly.

Henri's composure cracked, and suddenly, words poured out of her in a torrent of frustrated accusation. "You are lying to me, Gabriel! About your involvement with the manuscript, about your interest in the sketch, about everything that truly matters. You rescued me from that horrible man, you married me, you have shared my bed, yet you still treat me like a stranger who cannot be trusted with the truth."

Gabriel was quiet for a long moment, his expression thoughtful as he seemed to weigh her words. Henri waited, hoping that her honesty might finally prompt some reciprocal openness from her husband.

"You are right," he said finally. "I am … unaccustomed to sharing my personal matters with anyone. The nature of my work has required a certain discretion that has become second nature."

She did not think it was just his work that made him secretive, recalling the vulnerability glinting in his eyes the night he had … she swallowed … deflowered her.

"But I am not anyone, Gabriel," Henri said, softening slightly. "I am your wife."

"Yes," Gabriel agreed, though Henri could see him struggling with some internal battle. "You are."

He was quiet again, and Henri could practically see him building walls even as she watched. When he spoke again, he had taken on that careful, diplomatic tone that she was beginning to recognize as his way of revealing nothing while appearing to be forthcoming.

"Perhaps we ought to solve this mystery together," Gabriel said slowly. "Truly together, as partners. And once we understand what the sketch actually reveals, I will have had time to accustom myself to this new situation. Then, mayhap, I will tell you more about why I was at Danbury's that morning."

Henri felt a mixture of hope and frustration at his words. It was something, certainly more than the complete secrecy she had been receiving, but it was still so much less than what she wanted. Still, she recognized that pushing for more now would likely cause him to retreat entirely.

"I would like that very much," Henri responded. "Being partners, I mean."

Gabriel's smile was small but appeared genuine. "Then partners we shall be, Lady Trenwith."

As they continued their journey north, Henri found herself cautiously optimistic. It was not the complete honesty she craved, and Gabriel was still clearly keeping the most important truths locked away, but it was a beginning. Perhaps if she proved herself as a partner in solving this mystery, he might eventually trust her with whatever secrets he was so determined to protect.

* * *

As Gabriel watched Henri eating the simple fare provided by the coaching inn, he found himself studying his wife with a combination of admiration and bewilderment. Even after their tense morning and the emotional confrontation in the carriage, she had greeted the innkeeper's wife with genuine warmth, inquiring after the woman's health and complimenting the cleanliness of the establishment. It was a natural grace that Gabriel envied, this ability to connect with strangers as easily as breathing.

He, meanwhile, had directed the necessary business of changing horses and arranging their meal with his usual efficiency, but he was painfully aware of the distance he created between himself and everyone around him. Even with Henri, the woman who shared his bed and bore his name, Gabriel felt as though he were living behind a wall of glass, able to see and be seen but somehow unable to truly touch or be touched.

*What kind of husband am I going to be?*

The question had been nagging at him since their wedding, but it pressed with particular urgency now as he watched Henri laugh at what the serving girl had said. After so many years of deliberate isolation, of keeping his deepest thoughts and feelings locked away from even his closest associates, Gabriel was beginning to wonder if he had lost the ability to form genuine connections altogether.

Henri deserved better than a husband who could only offer her the controlled mask he presented to the world. She deserved someone who could match her heart, who could engage with her brilliant mind not just as a diplomatic partner but as a true companion. The problem was that Gabriel had no idea how to become that man. It had been so much easier when he conversed with her before, at her uncle's home, and he had known they would never move past that point. Never make love, marry, or live together.

His experience with intimacy was painfully limited. The women in his past had been brief diversions. Connections that served a purpose but asked nothing of his true self. Henri was something else entirely, a force of nature who had crashed into his carefully ordered existence and left him questioning everything he thought he knew about himself.

Or, if he was being honest with himself, perhaps it was he that was the force of nature, practically throwing her over his shoulder to make off like some sort of brutish barbarian. Not his finest day, to be certain.

Yet even as Gabriel acknowledged his own limitations, he found himself genuinely wanting to bridge the gap between them. Henri's passionate defense of her right to know the truth, her frustration with his secretiveness, had stirred something in him that he had thought long dead. For the first time in years, Gabriel found himself caring more about another person's opinion of him than about maintaining his protective barriers.

Perhaps that was the beginning of hope. Perhaps wanting to change was the first step toward actually accomplishing it.

As they returned to the turnpike and settled into the steady rhythm of travel, Gabriel reached into the leather portfolio where he had been keeping the sketch safe from damage. The delicate parchment unfolded carefully in his hands, revealing once again the intricate details that had proven so revealing when deciphered.

Gabriel studied the drawing, his mind turning over the puzzle that had consumed so much of his attention. The knight standing before the smoke-shrouded arch, the serpent coiled around fragments of a shattered crown, the coded letters and numbers that had revealed their hidden message when matched against the Malory manuscript. It was undeniably brilliant work, the creation of someone who understood both artistry and cryptography in equal measure.

But what did any of it have to do with Horace's murder?

Gabriel's mentor had been an avid scholar, a man whose greatest passion was the pursuit of knowledge for its own sake. Horace had possessed one of the finest minds in Oxford, had corresponded with antiquarians across Europe, and had devoted his life to understanding the historical

Arthur behind the legends. Yet his study had been ransacked, his papers scattered, his books examined and discarded by hands that had clearly been searching for something specific. Something worth killing for.

What would they find in Roseberry Topping?

The connection between a Renaissance artistic puzzle and the murder of a modern scholar remained frustratingly elusive, but Gabriel's instincts told him the link was there. Too many coincidences, too many threads leading back to Arthurian manuscripts and hidden knowledge for it all to be mere chance.

"You look troubled," Henri observed. "Are you having second thoughts about our destination?"

Gabriel looked up to find Henri watching him with a quizzical gaze that saw far more than he was comfortable revealing. "Not second thoughts, exactly. More … questions about what we might find there."

"You mentioned that you were posted near Roseberry Topping once," Henri prodded carefully. "Was that recently?"

"Many years ago," Gabriel replied, grateful for a topic he could discuss without revealing too much. "I was stationed near there. The hill is quite distinctive, impossible to mistake once you've seen it."

Henri leaned forward slightly, her curiosity evident. "What did the locals tell you about it? The sketch mentioned legends, and you said your tutor spoke of Arthur fighting there."

Gabriel found himself relaxing slightly as he recalled his time in that wild, beautiful country. "The people of the region have long memories and rich traditions. They speak of ancient battles fought on the moors, of kings and warriors who sleep beneath the hills waiting to return when England has need of them. Roseberry Topping itself has always been considered a place of power, somewhere the old gods walked before Christianity came to Britain."

"And Arthur? What did they say about Arthur?"

"That he made his final stand somewhere in those hills," Gabriel said slowly, remembering conversations with local shepherds and farmers who spoke of such things as matter-of-fact history rather than mere legend. "Some claim his sword lies buried there still, others that his body rests in a cave that appears only when the conditions are precisely right. The usual blend of folklore and wishful thinking. But" —he hesitated, not wishing to mislead her about what they might find in Yorkshire—"you hear much the same in Wales and throughout the West Country, especially Cornwall."

Henri was quiet for a moment, studying the sketch with new interest. "You know much about Arthurian lore?"

Gabriel met her gaze, seeing in her expression the same mixture of excitement and apprehension that he felt himself. "Yes," he admitted. "I do." He knew she was fishing for more, but Gabriel was not yet willing to discuss Horace's death.

As the carriage carried them steadily north toward Yorkshire and whatever answers awaited them at Roseberry Topping, Gabriel found himself cautiously optimistic about more than just solving the mystery. Perhaps Henri was right to insist on being his partner in this investigation. Perhaps sharing this burden, working together toward a common goal, might indeed be the beginning of the kind of marriage she deserved and he had tentatively begun to imagine. A paradise glimpsed through a veil of mist if he could only find the path that would lead him there.

# CHAPTER 16

*"For herein may be found things which never shall be known nor understood but by him that shall achieve this adventure."*

**Sir Thomas Malory, *Le Morte d'Arthur***

* * *

FEBRUARY 3, 1822

Henri pulled her cloak tighter against the bitter wind that swept across the Yorkshire moors as their carriage finally crested the hill that revealed Roseberry Topping in all its stark majesty. The distinctive conical peak rose from the surrounding landscape like something from another world, its slopes shrouded in gray mist that clung to the ancient stones with supernatural persistence.

The weather had grown increasingly hostile as they traveled north, and now a combination of sleet and snow made the already perilous moorland paths nearly impassable.

Henri could see why Gabriel had insisted on leaving at dawn once more, despite her exhaustion from another night of restless sleep.

"There," Gabriel said, pointing toward the peculiar hill that dominated the horizon. "Roseberry Topping. Just as I remembered it."

Henri studied the imposing peak, trying to reconcile its wild beauty with the enciphered message they had discovered in the sketch. "It certainly looks like a place where legends might be born," she admitted.

The inn where they had stopped was a rough but welcoming establishment that clearly catered to travelers hardy enough to venture into this remote corner of Yorkshire during winter. The innkeeper, a stout man with weathered hands and sharp eyes, greeted them with the careful courtesy reserved for obviously wealthy guests.

Henri watched with growing fascination as Gabriel engaged the man in conversation about the local area. For someone who was so secretive about his own affairs, Gabriel was remarkably skilled at drawing information from others. He spoke to the innkeeper with the same focused attention he might have given a foreign minister, making the man feel as though his knowledge of local history and folklore was the most important thing in the world.

"Ruins, ye say?" the innkeeper muttered, scratching at the stubble along his weathered chin. "Aye, there's no shortage o' crumblin' stone round these parts. Folk tend not to pay 'em much heed. Just old ghosts and sheep now. But there's one feller knows every toppled wall an' moss-covered foundation from here to Guisborough Moor. Walks the moors like he was born o' the heather."

"And where might we find this expert?" Gabriel asked with just the right degree of interested deference.

Henri found herself studying Gabriel's face as he spoke,

noting the way his entire posture shifted when he was working to extract information. The same charming smile, the same disarming manner, the same ability to make his target feel uniquely valued and understood. A cold dread began to mount in her belly as she wondered if everything between them as man and wife was simply an extension of this same practiced seduction.

What if Gabriel's interest in her was merely the application of skills honed through years of manipulation? What if she was merely another source to be cultivated, another person to be charmed into providing what he needed? The thought made her stomach clench with a sick certainty that she had been played for a fool by a master of the art.

But then she remembered Mr. Tyne's words about Gabriel's character, his insistence that despite his secretive nature, Gabriel was fundamentally loyal to those he claimed as his own. The secretary had seen something in Gabriel that went beyond mere political tact, something that suggested genuine feeling beneath the careful mask. And she had caught a glimpse of the vulnerability he hid behind polished manners. Henri clung to that memory as Gabriel continued his conversation with the innkeeper, eventually securing directions to find the local authority on ancient ruins.

The man they found was unlike anyone Henri had ever encountered. Ancient beyond measure, with wild white hair and clothes that suggested he spent more time wandering the moors than dwelling indoors, he possessed eyes that held the sharp intelligence of someone who had spent decades observing the world around him.

"Aye, I know every stone and shadow on these moors," the old man said, rough as wind through heather. "Been walking these hills since I were no taller than a shepherd's crook. Me father did the same, and his father before him.

Many generations, watching the old places sink back into the soil, like they're trying to forget they ever stood."

Gabriel leaned forward with genuine interest. "We are particularly interested in anything connected to medieval construction, perhaps a chapel or religious site."

The old man's eyes lit up with the pleasure of someone who rarely found such an attentive audience.

"A chapel, is it? Aye, there's talk of one. East o' the Topping, near a little rise folk pass without thinkin'. Naught much to see these days. Just a scatter of stones and what might've been an altar once. Most walk by without knowin' what they're lookin' at."

Henri felt her pulse quicken. "What do you know about its history?"

"Well now, that's a tale worth the telling," the old man said, shifting on his stool like he meant to stay a while. "Local talk goes, it were some medieval noble behind it centuries since. High-born, full o' ambition, not half so much sense. Thought he'd raise a chapel where the old gods once walked. Folk say he meant to sanctify the ground, wipe out the old ways proper."

He paused.

"But the work stopped sudden-like. Walls never got past waist-height. No one knows quite why. Some say sickness, others say the men just up and left. But most reckon the land would have none of it."

Gabriel's expression had grown intent. "Do you know why the construction ceased?"

"Who can say?" the old man mused, rubbing his gloved hands together. "Might've been lack o' funds, might've been politics. Or maybe the laborers just got nervous and decided they wanted no part of building on cursed ground." He gave a slow nod, as if the tale sat heavy on old memory. "My grand-parents used to call it the Fallen Chapel, though now and then you'd hear it called the Ash House on account o' all the gray stone scattered about like the bones of some great fire long gone cold."

Henri exchanged a meaningful look with Gabriel. The description matched perfectly with the deciphered clue about seeking the chapel that never was.

"Could you direct us to this place?" Gabriel asked.

"Aye," the old man replied with a gap-toothed grin.

The site, when they finally reached it after a grueling trek across the frozen moor, the wind howling in their ears, was almost exactly as the old man's description had promised. A roughly circular clearing where mossy stones jutted unevenly from the frost-bitten earth, with what might once have been foundation walls lying half-buried beneath centuries of windblown heather and creeping bracken.

At the center of the ruins stood a crude stone altar, worn nearly smooth by time and storm, rimmed now with a thin crust of ice. A rim of sleet clung to the lower stones, making the footing unstable. Even in daylight, the place held a strange hush, the kind that came not from peace but from abandonment. A forgotten place, left to the mercy of the elements and the myths that surrounded it.

Gabriel scanned the ruins with the same deep scrutiny he had applied to the sketch. He moved gingerly, boots crunching over brittle frost as he walked the perimeter, eyes flicking from stone to stone with the wary concentration of a man who expected more than time to lie hidden here. Henri remained near what had once been the entrance, her breath rising in white puffs as she watched him test the altar's edge, stoop to examine markings, pause to trace half-buried shapes with gloved fingers.

"I am going to take a closer look beneath," Gabriel called loudly enough to carry through the whistling wind. "Some of the foundation stones may conceal a cavity."

Henri's heart clenched. The stones were slick with melt-water, and a wrong step could send him sprawling … or worse. "Be careful," she said, drawing her cloak tighter against a sudden gust that cut through wool and bone alike.

A gust of sleet rattled across the clearing, needling her face. Her boots slipped slightly on the uneven ground as she took a cautious step closer to the chapel. She watched Gabriel brace himself as he crouched beside the great altar.

She knew better than to interrupt, but still that quiet fear stirred inside her. Would he tell her what he found? Or would he bury the truth beneath his habitual secrecy?

Mr. Tyne's assurance came back to her—*"He keeps faith with those he claims as his own."* She had to believe that meant her.

A cry split the stillness. Just a sharp exclamation, quickly swallowed. Henri's stomach twisted.

"Gabriel?"

No reply.

Then, at last, his head rose above the stones, his expression tight but composed.

"I think I have found carvings on the altar," he said, his words nearly lost in the wind.

Henri stepped forward through the biting cold, heart pounding. Thankfully, after stopping in London, she had proper half-boots on her feet to navigate the icy terrain.

Gabriel emerged from behind the altar, his face flushed with cold but his eyes bright with discovery. The wind had whipped his dark hair across his forehead, and Henri could see that despite the bitter conditions, he was energized by whatever he had found among the ancient stones.

"Henri," he called, beckoning to her with careful urgency. "I need you here. But watch your step! The stones are treacherous with this ice."

Henri made her way painstakingly across the frozen

ground, each step requiring careful placement to avoid the patches of black ice that had formed in the shadows of the tumbled stones. The wind cut through her cloak with vicious intensity, making her eyes water and her fingers ache even within her gloves. Gabriel extended his hand to steady her while Henri considered his leather Hessians with envy.

"What did you find?" she asked breathlessly.

Gabriel led her to the crude altar at the center of the ruins, where the ancient stone structure stood like a sentinel against the elements. Up close, Henri could see that what had appeared to be simple weathering from a distance was actually far more deliberate. The wind had carved strange patterns in the accumulated frost, but beneath the natural erosion were clear signs of human craftsmanship.

"The stonework here is far more sophisticated than it appears from a distance," Gabriel explained, raising his voice to be heard over the wind. "Someone took great care with this particular piece, even if the rest of the chapel was abandoned before completion."

Henri pulled off her gloves despite the brutal cold, knowing she would need the sensitivity of bare skin to properly examine whatever Gabriel had discovered. The frigid air immediately began to numb her fingers, but she ignored the discomfort as she knelt beside the altar.

"Show me what you have found," she said, already beginning to brush away the thick layer of moss and accumulated debris that had settled over the stone's surface.

Gabriel pointed to the base of the altar, where centuries of organic matter had created a thick carpet of decomposing vegetation. "There, along the foundation. I caught a glimpse of what looked like markings."

Henri began the painstaking process of clearing away the moss, working methodically despite her rapidly numbing fingers. The vegetation had rooted itself deeply into every crevice of the stone, requiring careful persistence to remove without damaging whatever lay beneath. As she worked, Gabriel positioned himself to block the worst of the wind, though the gusts still found ways to send icy needles through every gap in their clothing.

"There," Henri said suddenly, excitement overriding the discomfort as something began to emerge from beneath the organic matter. "These aren't natural formations. Someone carved these symbols into the stone."

As more of the moss came away under her persistent scraping, Henri could make out what was unmistakably a line of text etched into the altar's base. The letters were weathered but still clearly readable, executed in the formal style she recognized from medieval manuscripts.

"It is Latin," she breathed, her words forming white clouds in the frigid air. "*Ad hoc fidelis.*"

Gabriel crouched beside her, adding his efforts to the clearing process while she continued to trace the letters with increasingly unresponsive fingertips. "'Faithful to this,'" he translated, tight with concentration as he worked to expose more of the inscription.

Below the Latin text, Henri discovered another marking. A symbol that appeared to be a circle dissected by what looked like a crucifix, though the weathering and accumulated ice made it difficult to determine the exact design. The craftsmanship was precise despite its age, suggesting someone with considerable skill had taken great care in its creation.

"That symbol," Gabriel murmured, studying the marking as Henri brushed away the last of the obscuring debris. "I have seen something similar before, though I cannot quite place the context. It's familiar, but not quite identical to anything in my memory."

Henri continued her exploration of the inscription, now

working more by sight than touch as her fingers grew too cold to feel texture properly. But as she pressed along the length of the Latin text, searching for any other hidden elements, she made an unexpected discovery.

"Gabriel," she said urgently. "The letters! They are not carved into the altar itself. They are on a separate piece. I can feel the edges."

Gabriel immediately focused his attention on the area Henri indicated, adding his gloved hands to her exploration. Together, they began to trace what they now realized were the boundaries of a discreet stone element embedded within the altar's structure.

"There is a groove here," Gabriel confirmed with excitement. "Running beneath the entire inscription. This is not just decorative carving. It is a separate piece designed to be moved."

The announcement sent a thrill through Henri. Someone had gone to extraordinary lengths to conceal something within this abandoned altar, creating a hiding place so sophisticated that it had remained undiscovered for centuries.

Together, they worked at the edges. The centuries of debris and accumulated ice had created a natural seal that would require considerable effort to break, but the groove Gabriel had identified provided the leverage they needed.

"On the count of three," Gabriel said, positioning his hands for maximum advantage. "One … two … three."

They applied pressure simultaneously, and after a moment of resistance, the stone slab shifted slightly within its housing. Encouraged by this initial success, they continued working together, gradually loosening the ancient seal until the slab could be lifted free entirely.

"Careful now," Gabriel warned as they prepared to extract their prize. "Whatever is beneath this has been protected for centuries. We do not want to damage it through haste."

With infinite care, they lifted the moss-covered stone slab from its resting place beneath the altar. The piece was heavier than Henri had expected, requiring both of them to manage its weight safely in the wintry conditions.

"We need to turn it over," Gabriel said, his breath forming thick clouds in the frigid air. "Whatever message was meant to be hidden will be on the protected surface."

Together, they carefully maneuvered the heavy slab until they could examine its hidden face. What Henri saw there made her gasp with amazement, despite the numbing cold that was making coherent thought increasingly difficult. She fumbled to put her gloves back on.

Carved into the protected surface of the stone was an intricate design of breathtaking complexity. A spiraling circle of overlapping swords arranged in perfect geometric harmony. At the center of the spiral sat an elaborate heraldic crest, its details preserved with remarkable clarity thanks to centuries of protection from the elements. Each individual sword blade bore different markings that were unmistakably astrological symbols, rendered with the precision of a master craftsman.

"This is extraordinary," Gabriel murmured with awe as he studied the carved spiral. "The level of craftsmanship, the sophistication of the design … this represents many hours of skilled work by someone with access to the finest tools and materials."

Henri found herself enthralled by the intricacy of the carving. Each element of the design had been executed with meticulous attention to detail, from the flowing curves of the spiral arrangement to the precise rendering of each astrological symbol.

"Look at the central crest," she managed to say through

chattering teeth, pointing to the heart of the spiral with a finger she could barely feel. "Those are clearly the Pendragon arms, are they not? The dragon motif is unmistakable."

Gabriel nodded grimly. "Which confirms our suspicions about the Arthurian connection. But we are going to lose our fingers if we try to study this properly in these conditions." He looked up at the darkening sky, where heavy clouds promised even worse weather to come. "We need to document this thoroughly, but not here. We will carry this to the carriage and create a detailed record before we lose what little light remains."

The journey back to their carriage through the increasingly hostile weather was slow going, requiring careful navigation of ground that had become even more hazardous as the temperature continued to drop. By the time they reached the relative shelter of their conveyance, both were shivering uncontrollably and desperate for warmth.

"Get inside," Gabriel instructed Henri, taking the full weight of the stone and waiting for her to take her seat before heaving it onto the opposite bench.

Henri settled back with a weary sigh, grateful to escape the biting wind that had cut across the moor like a blade. Her cheeks were numb, her gloves damp from brushing sleet from her cloak, and her limbs ached from the uneven terrain. Across from her, Gabriel settled onto the bench seat, his hand resting on the slab next to him with the kind of care he might have afforded a fragile diplomatic dispatch. He called out to the coachman to return them to their inn.

They did not speak as the vehicle lurched into motion. The rattle of the wheels and the steady clop of hooves on the frozen road were accompaniment enough. Henri closed her eyes for a moment, letting the warmth of the enclosed space seep into her bones, while Gabriel leaned back, silent and thoughtful, one hand still resting atop the blanket-wrapped stone.

When they reached the inn, full dark had fallen and the scent of roasting meat wafted from the kitchens. The innkeeper showed them upstairs to a modest bedchamber with a low ceiling, a flickering fire in the grate, and a narrow table beneath the casement window. He promised to bring a tray of food along shortly, to Henri's relief.

Gabriel placed the stone on the table, unwrapping it with care while Henri pulled off her damp gloves and moved closer to the fire. The room was more comfortable than the carriage had been, though still carrying a draught that hinted at the age of the building.

"We will examine it now," Gabriel said quietly, already retrieving a roll of parchment, graphite sticks, and pencils from his portfolio. "While the details are fresh in our minds."

Henri joined him at the table, watching as he laid the parchment over the stone's surface and smoothed it flat with the side of his hand. Despite the chill in his fingers, his movements were precise.

He began to take the rubbing in slow, even strokes, working from the outer edge inward. Gradually, the shapes began to emerge. The spiral of swords, the fractured crown at the center, and the arcane markings they had only glimpsed in the failing light.

Henri watched in fascination as the image slowly emerged.

"The precision required for the original carving," Gabriel murmured, pausing to warm his fingers before continuing, "suggests a hand well-versed in both art and astronomy. This was not the work of a local mason following simple orders. Whoever did this knew exactly what they were recording."

Henri studied the developing rubbing. "Someone preserving something sacred. Hidden knowledge, perhaps.

This could be the work of Matteo di Bianchi himself. But why bury it beneath an abandoned altar in the middle of the Yorkshire moors?"

"Perhaps," Gabriel said, adding subtle shading to indicate the depth of the carved symbols, "we will understand once we decipher the message embedded within the design. But first, I need to ensure we have a complete record of every detail."

The documentation process took nearly two hours, with Gabriel working by the light of a small oil lamp. He captured not only the overall design but also the specific details of each astrological symbol, the precise angles of the sword arrangements, and the intricate elements of the central Pendragon crest.

Henri found herself impressed by Gabriel's approach, the way he systematically recorded each element of the carving without allowing excitement over their discovery to compromise the accuracy of his work. It was the kind of disciplined attention to detail that spoke to years of training in situations where precision could mean the difference between success and failure.

"There," Gabriel said finally, setting down his pencil and examining his completed sketch with critical eyes. "I believe I have captured all the essential elements. Now we can attempt to decipher what this remarkable piece is trying to tell us."

Gabriel stored his documentation materials and withdrew the Malory manuscript from its wrapping. The ancient text looked fragile and precious in the lamplight, its pages yellowed with age but still clearly legible. Henri watched with growing anticipation as Gabriel began the complex process of cross-referencing the symbols in his sketch with specific passages in the medieval manuscript.

The deciphering was painstaking work, requiring Gabriel to examine each individual element of the spiral design and match it with corresponding entries in the manuscript. Henri helped where she could, pointing out symbols that might have been overlooked and suggesting alternative interpretations when Gabriel was uncertain about a particular marking.

"This symbol here," Gabriel said, indicating one of the astrological markings with the tip of his pencil, "is Leo. And this arrangement of letters … if I am reading the pattern correctly …"

He continued working, occasionally muttering under his breath as he worked through particularly complex sections of the code. The room grew colder as the evening stretched on, but neither Henri nor Gabriel paid attention to the discomfort as they became increasingly absorbed in unraveling the ancient puzzle.

"I believe I have it," Gabriel announced finally, looking up from his work with satisfaction after nearly an hour of careful translation. "The complete message reads, 'The Lion's gate opens when the Silver Queen reigns in Arthur's sky. From cliff to sea, let the bloodline flow.'"

Henri felt a thrill of excitement as Gabriel spoke the deciphered words, immediately beginning to work through their possible meanings. "The Silver Queen! That must refer to the moon? Medieval and Renaissance texts often used such poetic language when referring to celestial bodies."

"Precisely my thinking," Gabriel agreed, setting down the manuscript and focusing his attention on Henri's interpretation. "And 'Arthur's sky' likely indicates a specific location associated with Arthurian legend, or perhaps a particular astronomical alignment that would have been significant to anyone familiar with the traditional stories."

Henri leaned forward to examine Gabriel's sketch of the spiral more closely, her mind working to connect the deciphered message with the visual elements of the design. "Look at how the swords are arranged within the spiral. The hilts all face inward toward the central Pendragon crest, but the blades point outward in different directions, almost like compass points."

Gabriel followed her observation with renewed interest, studying the arrangement with fresh eyes now that they had the deciphered message to guide their interpretation. "And this sword here ..." He pointed to one that appeared slightly longer than the others, its blade bearing what they could now identify as the astrological symbol for Leo. "It is angled distinctly southwest from the center of the design."

"Leo," Henri repeated thoughtfully, the connections beginning to form in her mind. "The lion. That connects directly to the 'Lion's gate' mentioned in our deciphered message?"

"Indeed it does," Gabriel confirmed, taking on the tone of growing certainty that Henri was learning to recognize. "In medieval and Renaissance symbolism, Leo represents strength, royal birth, and noble destiny. All qualities that would have been particularly significant to anyone claiming connection to Arthurian heritage."

Henri experienced a surge of understanding as the pieces began to fall into place. "So 'Lion's gate' is not referring to a physical structure at all. It is a metaphorical reference to Leo's domain, to the power and legitimacy associated with Arthur's royal bloodline."

"Exactly," Gabriel said, his excitement evident despite his attempt to maintain his usual measured demeanor. "And if the sword bearing Leo's symbol points southwest from our current position ..."

"Southwest would be Cornwall," Henri finished. "Tintagel, specifically. The legendary birthplace of King Arthur, according to most versions of the traditional stories."

Gabriel nodded slowly, though Henri caught a shadow of

concern crossing his features as the implications of their discovery became clear. "It appears our next destination has been decided for us. The question is whether we can reach Cornwall before others who might be following the same trail."

Henri felt a chill that went far deeper than the winter weather as she considered Gabriel's words. Their discovery was thrilling and represented a major step forward in understanding the ancient puzzle they had been following. But it also meant they might be drawing ever closer to whatever forces had threatened her at Danbury's estate.

"How long would it take us to reach Cornwall?" Henri asked.

Gabriel considered the question, clearly calculating distances and travel times in his head. "Under normal circumstances, perhaps four or five days of hard travel. But with winter conditions and the need to avoid main routes where we might be easily located ... it could take considerably longer."

It was a grim reminder of the assailant at Danbury's who had threatened her with the pistol. She only wished Gabriel would reveal anything he knew about it.

"Then we had better depart immediately," Henri said, hoping that their growing partnership would prove strong enough to face whatever awaited them in the legendary homeland of King Arthur.

# CHAPTER 17

*"Now I see well that such is our fate, and what is written must needs be."*

**Sir Thomas Malory, *Le Morte d'Arthur***

* * *

FEBRUARY 6, 1822

Henri had awakened to the most welcome sight she had seen in days back in Yorkshire. Pale sunlight streaming through the frost-covered windows of their inn, promising a reprieve from the brutal weather that had plagued their journey north. The improvement in conditions felt like a blessing from the heavens themselves, and she had found herself energized by both their remarkable discovery at the Fallen Chapel and the prospect of finally making good time toward their next destination.

Gabriel had seemed equally pleased by the change in

weather, his usual morning reserve giving way to something approaching actual conversation as they broke their fast and prepared for departure. For the first time since leaving London, Henri felt hopeful that their partnership might indeed be developing into more than mere necessity.

"If we leave within the hour, we can make excellent time," Gabriel had said, consulting his pocket watch with characteristic precision. "The roads should be passable now, and we can put considerable distance behind us before evening."

He had left with the coachman to return the stone piece to the fallen chapel, while Henri had packed their belongings with vigor, her mind already racing ahead to Cornwall and whatever secrets awaited them at Tintagel. As their carriage had pulled away from the inn with the morning sun casting long shadows across the Yorkshire landscape, she felt more optimistic about their prospects than she had since their wedding day.

The conversation during those first hours of travel had been the most open Henri had experienced with Gabriel since their night together in Calais. They had discussed the deciphered message at length, exploring various interpretations of its cryptic language and speculating about what they might encounter when they reached Arthur's legendary birthplace.

"The Lion's gate opens when the Silver Queen reigns in Arthur's sky," Gabriel had mused, his gaze fixed on the passing countryside. "If we are correct in assuming the Silver Queen represents the moon, then timing will be crucial to whatever we are meant to discover."

Henri had leaned forward with interest, grateful for any opportunity to engage Gabriel in substantive discussion. "You think the location itself changes depending on lunar conditions?"

"It is possible," Gabriel had replied thoughtfully. "In

Arthurian and Celtic mythology, caves and hidden places are often described as thresholds to other realms. Doorways that appear only when specific conditions are met. If there is a cave or passage at Tintagel that becomes accessible during the full moon, that could be the gate referenced in our clue."

The idea had sent a thrill of excitement through Henri. "And when will the next full moon occur?"

Gabriel had calculated quickly in his head. "If we maintain our current pace and do not encounter significant delays, we should arrive at Tintagel just as the moon reaches its fullest phase. The timing could hardly be more fortuitous."

Those early conversations had filled Henri with hope that their shared investigation was indeed fostering the kind of marriage she had envisioned. Gabriel was more relaxed away from the pressures of London society, more willing to share his knowledge and insights without the careful guardedness that had characterized so much of their earlier interactions.

But as the miles accumulated and the days passed in relentless travel, Henri began to notice subtle changes in Gabriel that gradually eroded her initial optimism.

By the time they reached the rugged coastline of Cornwall three days later, the easy companionship of their early travel had given way to a tension that Henri found increasingly difficult to ignore. Gabriel had grown progressively more distant with each passing day, retreating behind walls of polite reserve that grew higher the closer they came to their destination.

The physical demands of their journey were certainly part of the problem. They had traveled hard, stopping only when absolutely necessary and pushing their horses to the limits of endurance in their eagerness to reach Tintagel before the lunar phase changed. The long hours confined in the carriage, the uncomfortable nights at roadside inns, and the constant vigilance required to watch for potential pursuers had all taken their toll.

Henri suspected there was more to Gabriel's withdrawal than mere exhaustion. He had stopped making love to her entirely since before London, claiming fatigue whenever she attempted to initiate intimacy. While she understood that their travel was hardly conducive to romance, his complete avoidance of physical affection felt like a rejection that cut deeper than she cared to admit.

Even more troubling was his refusal to discuss anything beyond the immediate investigation. Whenever Henri attempted to broach the subject of their marriage, their eventual return to normal life, or what their future might bring once the mystery was solved, Gabriel would deflect with diplomatic skill that left her feeling more like a temporary travel companion than a wife.

The one bright spot in their deteriorating dynamic was their continued collaboration on deciphering the ancient puzzle. When focused on the intellectual challenge of unraveling the clues, Gabriel became animated and engaged, sharing his knowledge freely and building on Henri's insights with genuine enthusiasm. It was during these moments that Henri caught glimpses of the man she thought she had married, the partner she had hoped to spend her life beside.

But those moments were becoming increasingly rare as Gabriel withdrew further into himself with each mile that brought them closer to Tintagel.

The inn where they stopped as evening fell was an average establishment with few hardy travelers this late in winter. The innkeeper, a weathered man with the distinctive accent of the region, greeted them with polite curiosity about their business in such an isolated location during such an inhospitable time of the year.

"Tintagel Castle, you say?" The innkeeper glanced toward the window, where sea mist clung to the panes. "Aye, it draws folk who fancy the old legends. Arthur and Merlin, all that. But I will say there is not much up there in February that would not be better seen in spring."

Gabriel had deflected the man's curiosity, but Henri caught the way his jaw tightened at the innocent questions. Everything put Gabriel on edge lately, as though he were bracing himself for some unnamed catastrophe that only he could see approaching.

After a hurried meal that featured more silence than conversation, Gabriel announced his intention to visit the ruins immediately rather than waiting for morning. "The moon is full," he explained, though his tone suggested he was stating a fact rather than seeking Henri's agreement. "If our interpretation of the clue is correct, tonight may be our only opportunity to discover what we are meant to find."

Henri agreed readily, eager for any activity that might break the oppressive atmosphere that had settled between them. She wrapped herself in her thick cloak and followed Gabriel out into the cold Cornish night, hoping that their shared investigation might restore some measure of the *camaraderie* they had begun to develop.

The ruins of Tintagel Castle stretched over both the mainland and the rocky peninsula beyond, their dark silhouettes etched against the star-scattered sky. Two parts of the medieval structure were once linked by a bridge now long vanished, its remnants passing into memory. What remained were the ruins on either side, connected by steep stairways and a perilous narrow approach. Only the most resolute could navigate under the uncertain stars.

Gabriel carried a shuttered lantern that cast dancing shadows on the ancient stones as they made their way carefully through the mainland ruins first. The sound of waves crashing against the rocks far below provided a constant backdrop to their exploration, a reminder of the wild forces that had shaped this legendary landscape.

"According to our deciphered message, we must focus on the cliffside," Gabriel said as he consulted the sketch he had made of the spiral carving. "The clue speaks of 'from cliff to sea,' which suggests we are searching for something that joins the upper ruins to the water below."

Henri inclined her head, though her mind was not entirely upon the puzzle. They would need to cross to the island portion of the castle to reach the most formidable cliffs, and the narrow rocky path that remained would be daunting even in full daylight. The thought of attempting it under the present conditions made her pulse quicken with both dread and anticipation.

They began their search upon the mainland, studying the weathered stones of the outer walls for any trace of the symbolic markings they had seen in earlier clues, under the light of the full moon and Gabriel's lantern. When this yielded nothing, Gabriel took the lead across the perilous natural crossing to the island, where the most substantial ruins clung to the cliff top above the restless crash of the sea.

"Here," Henri called out after nearly an hour of careful examination along the western wall of the island ruins. "Gabriel, I think I have found it."

Gabriel hurried to her position, holding the lantern steady as Henri traced what appeared to be a faint carving in the stone. The etching was shallow and worn, barely visible even with direct illumination, but the design was unmistakably deliberate.

"A lion's head," Gabriel confirmed, his voice tight with excitement. "And below it … yes, that is the same symbol we found at the Fallen Chapel. The circle dissected by a crucifix."

Henri continued her examination of the area around the carving, running her hands over the cold stone in search of any other significant markings. "There is something else here," she said, her fingers detecting a narrow groove that originated from the lion's gaping mouth. "A crack or channel in the rock that leads downward."

Gabriel adjusted the lantern's position to follow the line Henri had discovered. The groove was indeed deliberate rather than natural, carved with the same precision as the lion's head motif. It descended from the symbolic carving in a serpentine path that gradually became obscured by centuries of accumulated moss and debris.

"From cliff to sea, let the bloodline flow," Henri quoted, her pulse quickening as she realized they were literally following the path described in their deciphered message. "This has to be what we are looking for."

They traced the carved channel as far as they could in the uncertain light, following its winding path along the outer wall until it disappeared entirely near the cliff's edge. The groove seemed to continue beyond the point where the castle's foundations met the natural rock, but the combination of shadows and rocks made it impossible to see where it might lead.

"We are missing something," Gabriel said, frustration evident as he held the lantern higher in an attempt to pierce the darkness. "The channel clearly continues, but we cannot see enough to follow it properly."

Henri studied the cliff face where their trail had vanished, her mind working through the implications of their clue. "Gabriel," she said slowly, an idea beginning to form. "What if the lantern light is actually working against us? What if whatever we are meant to see is only visible in natural moonlight?"

Gabriel hesitated, clearly reluctant to extinguish their

only source of illumination in such a precarious location. The cliff edge was daunting even with a light to guide them, and the sound of waves crashing on the rocks below served as a constant reminder of the dangers that surrounded them.

"It is worth trying," Henri pressed, her excitement overriding her caution. "The clue specifically mentions the Silver Queen. The moon. Perhaps we need to see this place as it was meant to be seen, without artificial light to interfere with whatever natural phenomenon we are supposed to observe."

After another moment of hesitation, Gabriel slowly closed the lantern's shutters, plunging them into what initially seemed like complete darkness. Henri felt a moment of disorientation as her eyes struggled to adjust, but gradually, the moonlight began to work its magic on the clifftop landscape.

The transformation was remarkable. What had appeared as merely weathered stone in the harsh glare of the lantern now revealed subtle variations in color and texture that were invisible under artificial illumination. The moon, nearly full and riding high in the clear winter sky, cast everything in silver and shadow with an almost ethereal beauty.

"There," Henri whispered, hardly daring to breathe as she pointed toward the cliff face. "Do you see it?"

A shimmer caught the moonlight on the damp rock face. Beneath it, a faint dark line appeared. Neither red nor brown, but something deeper, as if the rock itself had wept iron for centuries. The marking twisted and flowed like a serpent down the cliff's edge toward the sea, invisible earlier under the lantern's direct glare but now plain in the moon's silvered contrast.

Gabriel approached the dark groove, hushed with wonder as he traced its path with his eyes. "From cliff to sea," he murmured, the words of their deciphered message taking on new meaning as they watched the line descend toward the water.

"Let the bloodline flow," Henri completed in a whisper as the significance of their discovery settled over them. They had found it. The pathway described in their ancient clue, revealed only when viewed under the light of the Silver Queen.

The line, formed by iron oxide deposits or mineral-stained runoff in the stone, guided them to the beginning of a hidden path. Steep, moss-covered steps had been carved into the cliff face, so thoroughly concealed by centuries of overgrowth that they would have been invisible to anyone not following the exact trail prescribed by their deciphered message. The carved pathway descended toward the beach far below.

Henri felt a surge of triumph and excitement that momentarily overwhelmed all her concerns about Gabriel's recent distance. "We did it," she said, turning to face him with a smile that felt genuine for the first time in days. "We actually solved it. We found the pathway that has been hidden here for centuries, leading down to the sea."

Acting on impulse, Henri reached up to kiss Gabriel, her lips seeking his in a moment of shared celebration. For just an instant, she felt him respond, his body solid against hers in the cold moonlight. But then, abruptly, he pulled away, his hands coming up to create distance between them.

The rejection hit Henri hard, all her fears about their deteriorating relationship crystallizing in that single moment of withdrawal. "Gabriel?" she said uncertainly, searching his face for some explanation of his behavior.

But Gabriel had already turned his attention back to the hidden path, his expression closed and unreadable in the moonlight. "We should begin the descent," he said, carefully even. "We do not know how long these steps might be, and we need to discover what lies at the bottom before the moon sets."

Henri felt tears prick her eyes, though whether from hurt, frustration, or the cold wind that swept up from the sea, she could not be certain. The moment that should have represented the culmination of their partnership had instead highlighted everything that was wrong between them.

Still, she had little choice but to follow Gabriel as he began the descent down the moss-covered steps. The carved pathway was narrow and uneven, requiring careful placement of each foot to avoid the patches of slippery stone where centuries of sea spray had worn them smooth. Overgrowth only added to the challenge.

As they made their way down the hidden stairs toward whatever revelation awaited them at the bottom, Henri could not shake the feeling that they were descending toward more than just the solution to an ancient puzzle. Something fundamental was changing between them, and she feared that by the time they reached their destination, the fragile bond they had begun to forge might be lost forever.

The moonlight continued to illuminate their path, casting their shadows long and strange against the ancient stone. Below them, the sound of waves grew louder with each step, promising that their journey was far from over. Whatever secrets lay hidden at the bottom of this cliffside passage, Henri could only hope that discovering them might also provide some insight into the mystery of her husband's increasingly distant heart.

But as Gabriel continued his careful descent ahead of her, his attention focused entirely on the practical challenges of navigating the steep path, Henri could not escape the growing certainty that it was more than exhaustion or caution driving his withdrawal. There was a tension in his movements, a quality of anticipation or dread that suggested he knew more about things than he had shared with her.

The thought gnawed at Henri. If Gabriel was still keeping secrets from her at such a crucial moment, then perhaps their partnership had been an illusion all along. Perhaps she had been fooling herself about the possibility of true intimacy with a man who was incapable of letting anyone past his scrupulously constructed defenses.

As they descended deeper into the darkness toward whatever awaited them at the bottom of the hidden path, Henri clung to hope that the revelations to come might finally provide the answers she desperately needed. Not just about the ancient mystery they were pursuing, but about the enigmatic man who was now her husband and whether their marriage had any chance of surviving the secrets that surrounded him like shadows.

* * *

GABRIEL FELT the weight of his decision pressing down on him like the cold Cornish mist that had begun to rise from the sea.

*What have I done?*

The thought had been haunting him for days now, ever since they had left London and begun this increasingly perilous quest. What had started as a pursuit of answers about Horace's murder had transformed into something far more complex and dangerous, with Henri caught in the middle through no fault of her own except her unfortunate presence in Danbury's library that fateful morning.

Gabriel had been wrestling with guilt that grew heavier with each mile they traveled. Henri deserved to know why he had dragged her into this investigation, why solving this ancient mystery had become so crucial to him that he was willing to risk both their lives. The promise he had made to share his reasons hung between them like an unspoken debt, one that he found himself ever more reluctant to pay.

How could he explain Horace to her? How could he put into words what the gentle scholar had meant to a lonely boy who had been cast aside by his own family? The very thought of discussing his tutor brought back all the complicated emotions Gabriel had spent years suppressing. The grief, the loss, the desperate need for justice that drove him forward even when logic suggested retreat.

His grandfather's disdainful dismissal had been particularly cruel in recent dreams, the old viscount's cold scorn echoing through Gabriel's restless sleep. *"Weak, pathetic boy. Look at what your sentiment has brought you to. Endangering an innocent woman for the sake of a dead man who meant nothing to anyone of consequence."* Gabriel had awakened from such dreams with his heart racing and his clothes damp with perspiration, the familiar shame of childhood inadequacy washing over him anew.

*I should send her home,* Gabriel thought as he watched Henri examine the carved steps with scientific curiosity. *I should put her in the carriage and send her to Trenwith Abbey.* But he knew with crushing certainty that Henri would never agree to abandon their quest now, not when they were so close to uncovering whatever truth lay hidden in this ancient puzzle.

Gabriel stepped carefully onto the next of the moss-covered stones, narrow and uneven, and carved by hands that had valued concealment over safety. And the growing darkness made it difficult to judge distances accurately.

"Wait," Gabriel called softly to Henri, his voice tight with concern. "Let me go first. These steps are dangerous, and I want to go ahead to ensure the way is passable."

He could sense the protest forming on Henri's lips, but

Gabriel was already moving away from her, testing each step before committing his full weight. The thought of Henri tumbling down the cliff face made his stomach clench with a fear more profound than any he had experienced on any battlefield.

Every few steps, Gabriel paused to look back, waving Henri forward and then observing her progress with the intensity of a man whose entire world depended on her safety. Her movements were careful and deliberate, but he could see how the mist was making her task more difficult, how her skirts caught on the irregular stone edges, how her gloved hands struggled to find purchase on the slippery surfaces.

"Careful," Gabriel murmured each time Henri navigated a particularly tricky section, though he knew his warnings did little to address the fundamental peril of their situation. "Test each step before you trust it."

The descent felt like it took an eternity, though Gabriel knew it could not have been more than ten or fifteen minutes before they reached a narrow ledge that jutted out from the cliff face. Below them, the sea churned against the rocks with hypnotic violence, while ahead lay what appeared to be a crack in the cliff face—a dark hollow in the stone, wide enough to walk into, yet all but invisible, likely even from the deck of a passing boat.

Gabriel lifted his lantern higher, and the additional light revealed something that made his breath catch. There, carved into the stone at the entrance to the fissure, was an unmistakable marking. The circle and odd intersecting crucifix.

"This is it," Gabriel said quietly, though even as he spoke the words, a deeper uncertainty gnawed at him. They had followed the ancient clues successfully, deciphered the messages left by someone centuries ago, and now stood at what appeared to be their destination. But what did any of this have to do with Horace's murder? How could a Renaissance-era puzzle be connected to the death of a gentle Oxford scholar in modern times?

*Horace, old friend,* Gabriel thought with a mixture of affection and desperation, *what were you involved in that cost you your life?*

Standing on this windswept ledge in Cornwall, pursuing clues that predated Horace's birth by centuries, Gabriel felt more confused than ever. Yet he owed it to the man who had raised him, no matter how perplexing the trail might become.

Gabriel raised his lantern toward the cave entrance, noting how the tide had exposed what appeared to be a navigable passage into the hollow rock. But as they prepared to enter, the wind shifted suddenly, carrying with it a deep, resonant sound that echoed from the depths of the cave itself.

The noise sent a chill through Gabriel that was not caused by the cold sea air. Every instinct he possessed flared to life as he stepped closer to Henri, one hand reaching out to steady her on the narrow ledge. She pulled back, reluctant to accept his help.

"Do not be stubborn, Henri!" Gabriel said sharply with more authority than he had intended. "I need you to stay close to me and follow my lead exactly."

Gabriel positioned himself between Henri and the cave entrance, torn between his desperate need to uncover the truth about Horace's death and his growing certainty that he was leading his wife toward a danger neither of them fully understood. But they had come too far to retreat now, and the answers they sought lay somewhere in the darkness ahead, waiting to be discovered by those brave enough—or foolish enough—to pursue them.

* * *

GABRIEL'S sharp words thundered through her head, the harshness of his tone cutting through the excitement of their discovery and leaving her feeling raw and exposed.

*Stubborn.*

Was that truly what he thought of her? After everything they had shared, after all the ways she had proven herself as a capable partner in this investigation, did Gabriel see her as an obstinate woman who needed to be managed and controlled?

The hurt that washed over Henri was immediate and profound, made worse by the growing certainty that Gabriel's concern had less to do with genuine affection for her well-being and more to do with protecting his secrets. He needed her to solve this mystery, whatever personal agenda was driving his obsession with these ancient clues, and he could not afford to have her injured before their quest was complete.

*He does not care about me at all,* Henri thought with bitter clarity as Gabriel busied himself with adjusting the lantern's shielding. *I am simply a useful tool to him, someone to help him achieve whatever goal he has been pursuing from the beginning.*

The realization sent a chill through Henri. Several days into their marriage, Gabriel remained as distant and secretive as he had been when they were strangers. If anything, his walls had grown higher since their wedding, as though the legal bond between them had given him permission to retreat even further into his private world of guarded thoughts and undisclosed purposes.

Gabriel stepped into the cave first, holding the lantern ahead of him to illuminate their path. Henri followed reluctantly, her earlier enthusiasm for their discovery now overshadowed by the growing resentment that had been building inside her for days. The cave was larger than it had appeared from outside, with smooth walls that spoke to centuries of wind attrition and a floor of sand mixed with small stones that crunched softly beneath their feet.

"There," Gabriel said quietly, raising the lantern toward a section of the cave wall where the light revealed yet another carving. "Another marker, just as we expected."

Henri forced herself to focus on the discovery despite her emotional turmoil. The carving was indeed similar to the others they had found, featuring the image of a window, a woman and an organ depicted in one of the panes. Letters and numbers were etched beneath. Gabriel was already reaching into his coat for parchment and charcoal, moving with the efficiency that characterized all his professional endeavors.

"Hold the lantern steady," Gabriel instructed as he wiped the stone with a handkerchief to ensure it was dry before he began the careful process of creating a rubbing of the carved design. "I need to capture every detail."

Henri took the lantern without comment, though she found herself wondering if Gabriel would have spoken to a hired assistant with more warmth than he showed his own wife. As she watched him work, his complete absorption in the task serving to emphasize how little of his attention she commanded when something truly important required his focus, Henri felt her hurt crystallizing into something harder.

The rubbing process took some time, during which Gabriel maintained the same concentrated silence that had characterized so much of their recent travel. Henri found herself studying his profile in the lantern light, noting the tension around his eyes and the tight set of his jaw that suggested he was wrestling with thoughts he had no intention of sharing with her. Even here, in the midst of what should have been a moment of shared triumph, Gabriel remained locked away in his private world.

When he finally completed the rubbing and stored the parchment in his coat, Henri expected him to share his thoughts about what the new carving might reveal or how it connected to their previous discoveries. Instead, he simply took back the lantern and began examining the rest of the cave with the same thoroughness he had applied to their previous investigations.

"This does not appear to be a final destination," Gabriel observed after completing his survey of the cave's interior. "The carving likely points us toward our next location, assuming we can decipher its message properly."

Henri nodded her acknowledgment of his assessment, though she felt a stab of disappointment that even this professional exchange felt perfunctory and distant. Gabriel was already moving toward the cave entrance, clearly eager to return to safer ground where they could examine their new clue properly, and Henri had little choice but to follow.

The climb back up the steep steps proved even more challenging than the descent, as the continuing mist had made every surface increasingly slippery. Gabriel maintained his position behind her, occasionally offering terse warnings about particularly dangerous sections, but otherwise climbing in complete silence. Henri found his lack of communication deeply frustrating, especially when contrasted with the easy conversation they had enjoyed during the first day of their journey from Yorkshire.

*He is already planning his next move,* Henri thought as she navigated a particularly tricky section of the carved steps. *Calculating how to use this new information to advance whatever agenda brought him to Danbury's library in the first place. And I am nothing more than an assistant in his investigation.*

She was stunned at how much pain she was feeling. The

twist of her heart, the agony of being unwanted making the silence stretch between them as they climbed, broken only by the sound of waves crashing against the rocks below and the occasional warning about loose stones or slippery patches.

This was why she had vowed to never relinquish her independence. If only she had not been duped into falling for a set of kind hazel eyes and the glimmer of need she had witnessed shimmering in their depths. Gabriel was completely absorbed in his own thoughts, his attention focused far beyond their immediate surroundings, and Henri found herself wondering if she would ever be granted access to his thoughts.

*Uncle Reggie involved me in his Westminster dealings because he valued my insights,* Henri reflected with growing distress. *He made me feel that my contributions had genuine merit, that my intelligence and political instincts were assets worth cultivating. Gabriel, meanwhile, treats me like a particularly useful reference book. Consulted when needed, but otherwise ignored and forgotten.*

The comparison with her great-uncle's treatment was particularly hurtful because it highlighted what Henri had hoped to find in her marriage. Uncle Reggie had never made her feel like her gender was a limitation or that her perspectives were somehow inferior to those of his male colleagues. With Gabriel, Henri increasingly felt like she was being tolerated rather than truly welcomed as an equal partner.

By the time they reached the relative safety of the clifftop, Henri's pain had evolved into genuine anger. Gabriel's continued silence during their climb, his obvious preoccupation with matters he had no intention of sharing with her, and his apparent assumption that she would simply follow his lead without question or complaint had combined to create a resentment that felt alarmingly close to permanent.

As they stood once again among the ruins of Tintagel Castle, Henri found herself questioning not just Gabriel's treatment of her, but the entire decision to marry him in the first place. It had promised to be an adventure, an opportunity to forge a genuine partnership with a fascinatingly complex man, and to provide him the solace she had thought he needed. Now it felt like a trap she had walked into with her eyes wide open but her judgment fatally compromised by romantic notions that had no basis in reality.

Gabriel was already moving toward their carriage where their coachman waited, clearly eager to examine their new discovery in better light and comfort, but Henri remained rooted among the ancient stones, staring out at the moonlit sea and wondering if she had made the greatest mistake of her life in agreeing to become Lady Trenwith.

*Perhaps,* Henri thought with painful clarity, *some partnerships are doomed from the beginning, no matter how much one party might wish otherwise.*

# CHAPTER 18

*"He that doubteth is not firm of heart, and wheresoever he rideth or goeth, misadventure shall follow him."*

**Sir Thomas Malory, *Le Morte d'Arthur***

* * *

FEBRUARY 7, 1822

*Alaric Devayne pulled his worn coat tighter against the bitter coastal wind as he approached the fifth inn of the night, his hollow cheeks stung raw by the relentless coastal air. The obsessive pursuit that had driven him across the country was taking its toll. His gaunt frame had grown even thinner during the days of hard travel, and his sunken eyes burned with the fevered intensity of a man who had not allowed himself proper rest since Dover.*

*Engaging in conversation with the viscount's coachman in Yorkshire had been worthwhile. A few pints of ale and some well-*

*chosen questions about the quality of roads to various destinations had yielded the crucial intelligence. Cornwall. Tintagel, specifically, though the coachman was puzzled by his master's interest in such a remote location during the winter months.*

*Once they had departed, he struggled to keep pace with the grand carriage and its four matched horses, though at least he knew the direction to take.*

*Tintagel. Alaric had rolled the name over in his mind during the grueling ride south, trying to piece together what connection the legendary Cornish castle might have to the manuscript he had pursued with such determination. The place was famous for its Arthurian associations, that much he knew, but the specific connection to the Malory text remained frustratingly elusive.*

*Now, as he surveyed this latest inn from the shadows at the edge of the courtyard, Alaric felt the familiar surge of anticipation that had sustained him through months of investigation. The establishment was larger than the previous four he had checked, with a substantial carriage house that suggested it catered to travelers of means. If his quarry had indeed reached Tintagel, this would be exactly the sort of place they would choose for their accommodation.*

*The inn's courtyard was empty after midnight when Alaric ventured in, moving with the stealth that had served him well during his military campaigns. The carriage house stood separate from the main building, its large doors secured with a simple latch.*

*The interior was dark and smelled of leather, hay, and the lingering scent of well-maintained horses. Alaric moved between the vehicles stored there, running his hands along their surfaces and checking for the distinctive markings that would identify his target. The first three carriages appeared to belong to passing merchants or minor gentry, their modest appointments and provincial styling immediately distinguishing them from what he sought.*

*But the fourth vehicle made Alaric's pulse quicken with recog-*

*nition. Even in the dim moonlight filtering through the high windows, he could make out the elegant lines and superior craftsmanship that marked it as the property of someone with both wealth and taste. More importantly, he could see the coat of arms emblazoned on the door panel.*

*Finally.*

*Alaric circled the carriage slowly, confirming his identification and noting details that might prove useful later. The vehicle showed signs of hard travel, with mud splattered along its lower panels and dust coating its normally pristine surfaces.*

*The discovery filled Alaric with a satisfaction that went beyond mere professional accomplishment. For weeks, he had been pursuing a quarry that seemed always to stay one step ahead of him, possessing both the resources and the intelligence to make his task genuinely challenging. But now, at last, he had them within reach.*

*Alaric examined the carriage's interior through its windows, though the darkness made it impossible to determine whether the precious manuscript and sketch were stored within. More likely, such valuable items would be kept close, probably secured in their rooms at the inn itself. The thought of the ancient text being so near, yet still beyond his grasp, sent a familiar surge of frustrated desire through him.*

*He had come too far and sacrificed too much to allow proximity to substitute for possession. The manuscript represented more than just a valuable artifact to Alaric. In the right hands, the knowledge contained within those ancient pages could open doors that had remained closed to him throughout his life.*

*Satisfied that he had learned everything the carriage could tell him, Alaric slipped back out of the building and secured the latch behind him. The inn's main building showed several lighted windows, suggesting that not all the guests had retired for the night, but Alaric did not wish to enter and possibly encounter Lord Trenwith who would assuredly recognize him.*

*Instead, he made his way to the collection of outbuildings that surrounded the inn, searching for somewhere he could shelter for the remaining hours until dawn. He would need all his strength and mental clarity for whatever challenges the morning might bring.*

*Alaric eventually settled on a small storage shed that offered shelter from the wind while providing a clear view of both the inn's entrance and the carriage house. The space was cramped and uncomfortable, filled with the detritus of rural life, but it would serve his purposes adequately.*

*As he arranged his coat to provide some cushioning against the hard wooden floor, Alaric allowed himself a moment of genuine satisfaction. The manuscript that had eluded him for so long was now within a few hundred yards of where he lay. By tomorrow evening, if his planning proved sound, the ancient text would finally be in his possession.*

*The thought of success, so close he could almost taste it, helped Alaric ignore the discomfort of his makeshift shelter as he settled in to wait for morning. Soon, very soon, his long pursuit would reach its conclusion.*

By the time Gabriel and Henri returned to their inn, most of the lights in the local village were extinguished. Gabriel was acutely aware of Henri's rigid posture and the way she had avoided meeting his eyes whenever he had attempted to assist her over the more difficult terrain back at the castle.

Their room felt almost luxurious after the bitter cold of the clifftop, but the atmosphere between them remained as glacial as the winter night they had just escaped. Henri moved about the space with sharp, precise movements that spoke to barely contained anger, preparing for bed with an efficiency that suggested she wanted this evening to end as quickly as possible.

Gabriel watched her preparations with growing unease, recognizing the signs of the deep resentment he had somehow managed to seed. He wanted to bridge the gap that had opened between them, to explain his protective instincts and the fears that had driven his sharp words at the cave entrance. But the weight of his secrets, the complexity of emotions surrounding Horace's death and his own desperate need for answers, made such explanations feel impossible.

"Henri," Gabriel began tentatively as she settled into the bed with her back pointedly turned toward him.

"I am quite tired, Gabriel," Henri replied coolly with a finality that discouraged further conversation. "Perhaps we could discuss whatever matters you feel need addressing in the morning."

Gabriel stood uncertainly beside the bed, the parchment rubbing from the cave weighing heavily in his coat pocket. Henri's dismissal stung more than he cared to admit, but he recognized that pushing for conversation now would likely only deepen whatever damage had already been done.

Instead, Gabriel quietly retrieved the Malory manuscript from his traveling trunk and settled into the room's single chair with the ancient text and his collection of sketches and rubbings. If sleep was to elude him as it had for so many nights recently, he might as well use the time productively.

Further analysis of the rubbing revealed additional clues that pointed toward a specific location, though the manuscript's archaic language made precise translation challenging. Gabriel found references to "where the grim fell sings," which he assumed meant a location known for particular acoustic properties or perhaps wind patterns that created unusual sounds.

By the time Gabriel had completed his preliminary deciphering, dawn was breaking properly outside their window, and Henri was beginning to stir in the bed behind him. Gabriel gathered his materials and prepared to face what he suspected would be a difficult morning conversation.

The inn's dining room was sparsely populated when Gabriel and Henri descended for breakfast, with only a handful of other guests making use of the early morning meal service. Henri had dressed with her usual care, but Gabriel noted the way she maintained careful distance between them and avoided his attempts to engage her in casual conversation.

Gabriel ordered a substantial breakfast for both of them, knowing they would need their strength for whatever journey their latest discovery might require. Henri accepted the food with polite thanks but ate in silence, her attention focused entirely on her plate rather than on her husband.

"Henri," Gabriel said finally, unable to bear the continued tension any longer. "About last night—"

"There is no need to discuss it," Henri interrupted, modulating to remain private despite their public setting. "I understand your position quite clearly."

Gabriel felt a stab of frustration at her formal tone, but pressed forward with the information he needed to share. "I have been working on the cave rubbing. I believe I have made some progress in understanding what it is directing us toward."

Henri looked up from her breakfast with what Gabriel recognized as intellectual interest, though her personal warmth remained notably absent. "And what have you discovered?"

Gabriel noted her firm jaw and lack of affinity with a feeling of destiny closing in on him. He could only hope that solving this mystery would eventually provide an opportunity to address the damage his curtness had inadvertently caused to their fragile partnership. He needed to reopen discourse with her, coax out the lively Henri whom he had admired these past two years, but he was so damned tired.

Being married after a life of solitude was proving difficult for a man like him, and he prayed that when they reached Trenwith Abbey, when this quest was complete, he would find a way to make her happy.

* * *

Gabriel pulled out his sketch of the cave carving as he settled back into his seat, spreading it carefully on the table between them. The image showed a window with four glass panes, one of which depicted a reflected woman playing an organ while the others appeared shattered. Henri could see where water damage from their cave exploration had affected some of the delicate details, but the overall design remained clear.

"The trick to uncovering information," Gabriel said, consulting his notes while speaking, "is conversation."

"With whom?" Henri asked, despite her irritation with his continued air of aloof competence.

"Why, with everyone, of course!" Gabriel replied, his autocratic tone reminding her of his remonstration on the cliffside. Which made Henri want to shake him.

Gabriel retrieved the deciphered message he had worked out during his sleepless hours. "'She waits where the grim fell sings. Let thy hands match hers,'" he read aloud. "Combined with the image of the woman at the organ, it seems clear we are looking for a location that combines elevated terrain with some sort of musical connection."

Henri studied the sketch more carefully, noting how each glass pane contained fragments of music notation, though some had been damaged by the water dripping in the cave.

The woman's reflection in the single intact pane was rendered with remarkable detail, her hands positioned on what was clearly an organ keyboard.

"Gabriel," Henri said, her analytical curiosity overcoming her personal resentment, "why are you so eager to uncover these clues? What is driving this investigation beyond simple intellectual interest?"

The question hung in the air between them, and Henri watched Gabriel's entire demeanor change instantly. His easy confidence evaporated, replaced by the familiar mask of careful control that she had come to recognize as his defensive response to any inquiry about himself. His jaw tightened almost imperceptibly, and his attention became focused entirely on finishing his breakfast rather than continuing their conversation.

The silence stretched uncomfortably between them, and Henri felt her own anger beginning to build again. Here was yet another example of Gabriel's refusal to trust her with anything meaningful about himself, another reminder that despite their marriage and their shared adventures, she remained firmly locked out of his inner world.

"I am sorry," Henri said finally after the silence stretched too long, though the apology tasted bitter. "I did not mean to pry into matters you prefer to keep to yourself."

Gabriel looked up from his plate at her words, and Henri caught a glimpse of what might have been regret in his expression before his usual composure reasserted itself.

Henri found herself watching with reluctant fascination as Gabriel rose from their breakfast table and began what she was starting to recognize as his systematic approach to information-gathering. Despite her anger and hurt from the previous evening, she could not help but be impressed by the easy confidence with which he moved through the inn's common areas, engaging fellow travelers and staff with the same focused charm she had observed throughout their journey.

Gabriel approached the innkeeper first, striking up what appeared to be a casual conversation about local roads and weather conditions. Henri watched him laugh at something the older man said, radiating the kind of approachable warmth that made people want to share their knowledge with him. From there, Gabriel moved to a table of merchants who were breaking their own fast, seamlessly inserting himself into their discussion of travel conditions and local landmarks.

It was masterful, Henri had to admit, even as his skill reminded her painfully of how little of that charm he directed toward her recently. Within the space of twenty minutes, Gabriel had spoken with nearly every person in the common room, each conversation appearing entirely natural and unforced. When he finally returned to their table, Henri could see from his expression that his efforts had yielded useful information.

"Any success?" Henri asked, maintaining the sober tone she had adopted since their return from the cave.

"No one was familiar with a place called grim fell," Gabriel replied quietly. "However, there is another inn a few miles down the turnpike called The Grim Shepherd. This innkeeper suggested we might find more knowledgeable locals there."

Henri nodded her acceptance of this plan. For now, they had a task to see to.

The Grim Shepherd proved to be a smaller, rougher establishment that plainly catered to local farmers and laborers rather than traveling gentlefolk. Gabriel made it clear that he intended to conduct his inquiries alone.

"I will learn more without your feminine presence

distracting from my questioning," Gabriel informed her. "I am accustomed to working alone in such situations."

Henri felt the familiar sting of dismissal, made worse by Gabriel's casual assumption that her presence would somehow hinder rather than help their investigation. She settled herself in their carriage to wait, watching through the window as Gabriel disappeared into the inn's smoky interior, and found herself cataloging yet another slight to add to her growing collection of grievances.

*Feminine presence distracting from his questioning,* Henri thought bitterly. *As though my gender automatically renders me useless in any situation requiring discretion. Uncle Reggie never treated me as though my contributions were inherently less valuable because I happened to be born female.*

She was being overly sensitive, she knew it, but it did not stop the doubt that she would ever breach Gabriel's fortress.

He emerged from the inn soon after, his expression suggesting that his efforts had been more successful than his previous inquiries. Henri waited for him to settle back into the carriage before asking about his discoveries, though she maintained the impersonal tone that had become her default mode of communication with her husband.

"There is a manor house built on a cliff called Grimsfell Hall," Gabriel reported, consulting notes he had made during his conversations. "According to the locals, it is sometimes rented out during the summer months, but most people in the area prefer to avoid it."

"Why?" Henri asked, genuinely curious despite her personal frustrations.

"They believe it is haunted," Gabriel replied, his tone suggesting he found superstitions more amusing than concerning. "The hall is old. Built during the Tudor period, and the locals claim that one can sometimes hear organ music carried on the wind, even when the building is closed up."

Henri felt a surge of excitement that momentarily overrode her anger with him. "She waits where the grim fell sings. Let thy hands match hers," she quoted from their deciphered message. "Gabriel, this must be the place! The person who set the code would have been limited to words found in the Malory manuscript which is why they could not name the hall directly. If there is an organ at Grimsfell Hall, and the locals can hear it even when the building is supposedly empty ..."

"The connection does seem promising," Gabriel agreed, though Henri could already see his mind shifting to the practicalities of travel and lodging rather than sharing her delight in the discovery. "There is a solicitor who lets the property during the summer months. I hope he will be able to give us access."

Henri settled back in her seat as Gabriel departed to find the solicitor's office, but her excitement was tempered by the growing certainty that Gabriel would continue to treat her as a useful but ultimately dispensable assistant rather than a true partner in their investigation. Each success in solving the ancient puzzle only served to further highlight the fundamental failure of their burgeoning marriage.

*Will I never break through the walls he's constructed around his heart?*

Perhaps she overestimated her ability to draw him out, lured in by the vulnerability she had witnessed that first night they had made love. An openness that she had not perceived since their return to England.

# CHAPTER 19

*"Lo, fair lords, how falsehood is always to be dreaded."*

**Sir Thomas Malory, *Le Morte d'Arthur***

* * *

Henri spotted Gabriel returning to their carriage at The Grim Shepherd with the satisfied air of a man who had successfully completed a complex negotiation. She had spent the intervening hour alternating between studying their sketches and rubbings and watching the local patrons with the kind of anthropological interest that helped distract her from her growing catalog of marital grievances.

"Success," Gabriel announced as he settled back into their carriage, producing an ornate iron key from his coat pocket. "The hall's caretaker was surprisingly accommodating once I explained our interest in renting the property for the remainder of the winter season."

Henri examined the key with interest, noting its age and

elaborate craftsmanship. "He agreed to let us inspect the premises before committing to a lease?"

"Indeed. Apparently, Grimsfell Hall has remained empty for the past several months, and the owners are eager to secure tenants even during the off-season." Gabriel pocketed the key and signaled their driver to proceed. "The caretaker seemed particularly pleased by the prospect of winter occupancy, though he did feel obligated to warn us about the hall's ... atmospheric peculiarities."

Henri raised an eyebrow at Gabriel's phrasing. "You mean the ghostly organ music?"

"Among other things," Gabriel replied with the kind of dry understatement that suggested he placed little credence in local superstitions. "According to the caretaker, the hall has acquired quite a reputation for supernatural activity over the years. Previous tenants have reported strange sounds, cold drafts in closed rooms, and the occasional sighting of a woman in antique dress wandering the corridors."

"How conveniently dramatic," Henri observed, though she had to admit that such stories would certainly discourage casual curiosity about the property. "Did the caretaker mention anything specific about the organ?"

Gabriel consulted his notes from the conversation. "He confirmed that there is indeed an organ somewhere in the hall, though he seemed oddly vague about its exact location. When I pressed for details, he mentioned something about the old chapel but became quite evasive when I asked for more specific directions."

Henri found Gabriel's report intriguing despite her frustrations with him. The combination of local superstition and deliberately vague information suggested that Grimsfell Hall might indeed hold the secrets they were seeking, assuming they could overcome whatever obstacles had been placed in the way of discovery.

Their carriage wound along increasingly narrow roads that hugged the dramatic Cornish coastline, with the sound of crashing waves providing a constant reminder of their proximity to the sea. As they traveled, Henri began to understand why visitors might find Grimsfell Hall an unsettling place. The landscape itself had a wild, untamed quality that seemed to dwarf human attempts at domestication.

When the hall finally came into view, Henri felt her breath catch at the sheer dramatic impact of its setting. It was a substantial Tudor manor house built of weathered gray stone, its multiple chimneys and elaborate windows speaking to the wealth and ambition of its original builders. But what made the structure truly striking was its position on very nearly the edge of a prominent cliff, with endless views of the frothing sea stretching to the horizon.

The building seemed to grow directly from the rock itself, as though centuries of wind and weather had shaped both the natural cliff and the human construction into a single, integrated whole. Henri could see why the locals might attribute supernatural qualities to such a place. The hall was otherworldly, commanding its dramatic perch above the churning waters below.

"Grimsfell, indeed," Henri murmured as their carriage drew to a halt in the manor's courtyard.

The wind that swept up from the sea was unlike anything Henri had experienced in their previous travels, carrying with it the sound of waves crashing against the rocks far below and creating an eerie whistling effect as it passed through the hall's elaborate stonework system. Even from outside the building, Henri could hear the way the wind seemed to find every gap and crevice in the ancient structure, creating a symphony of haunting sounds that would indeed be unnerving to anyone not expecting them.

Gabriel helped Henri down and produced the caretaker's

key, leading the way to the hall's main entrance with his characteristic purposeful stride. The heavy wooden door did not creak in protest despite what must be years of disuse, opening to reveal an interior that was both grand and somehow melancholy in its abandonment. The caretaker must have been especially diligent to maintain the property so well despite it standing empty for most of the year.

"Impressive," Gabriel observed as they stepped into the main hall, their footsteps echoing in the vast space.

Henri had to agree. Notwithstanding its current lack of habitants, Grimsfell Hall retained the unmistakable marks of its Tudor origins. Carved oak paneling, tall, mullioned windows overlooking the sea, and a molded plaster ceiling overhead, beneath which heavy timbers likely bore the weight of centuries. The furnishings were draped in dust sheets, giving the rooms the hushed expectancy of a stage awaiting its actors.

Gabriel immediately pulled out their sketch of the cave carving, studying the image of the four-paned window with its depiction of a woman playing an organ. "According to this, we should be looking for a chapel or music room, probably somewhere that would have acoustic properties suitable for an organ installation."

Henri nodded her agreement, though she found herself wondering how they would search such a large and complex building systematically. "The caretaker mentioned an old chapel. Perhaps we should begin by trying to locate that specific room."

They spent the next hour exploring the hall's public rooms, each space offering fresh evidence of Tudor craftsmanship and architectural ambition. Ornate plaster ceilings, carved mantelpieces, and heavy oak doors spoke of a past both proud and prosperous. In one long gallery, intricate iron grilles vented the room, their rusting tracery emitting eerie echoes as the wind howled up from the cliffs below.

But despite their systematic search, there was no sign of the organ that the sketch so clearly implied should be hidden somewhere within the building.

"This is puzzling," Gabriel admitted as they completed their circuit of the ground floor. "The locals clearly know about an organ, the sketch depicts one quite specifically, and yet we have found no evidence of such an instrument anywhere in the obvious locations."

Henri studied their sketch again, paying particular attention to the architectural details visible in the Tudor window image. "Perhaps the organ is not in a conventional location. Tudor buildings often included hidden rooms or concealed spaces, especially if they were built during periods of religious or political uncertainty."

Gabriel's expression suggested that Henri's observation had given him a new direction to consider. "You are suggesting that the chapel itself might be hidden?"

"It is possible," Henri replied. "If Grimsfell Hall was built during the time of Henry the Eighth, when religious practices were subject to rapid and sometimes violent changes, the original builders might well have created concealed spaces for activities that could fall in and out of favor depending on the current monarch's preferences."

Gabriel looked around the main hall with renewed interest, clearly reassessing the architecture from this new perspective. "Then we need to search for evidence of hidden passages or concealed rooms. The organ, and whatever secrets it might hold, could be anywhere within these walls."

Henri felt a familiar surge of excitement at the intellectual challenge, even as she remained acutely aware of the emotional distance that continued to separate her from her husband. Whatever lay hidden within Grimsfell Hall, she was determined to help uncover it. If only to prove to herself that her contributions to their investigation had genuine value, regardless of Gabriel's apparent inability to appreciate her help in his mysterious quest.

After two more hours of fruitless searching through the manor's labyrinthine passages and chambers, Henri's earlier excitement had curdled into bitter disappointment. They had examined every room, every corridor, every obvious space where an organ might be housed, but found only gloomy chambers and dust-covered furniture. The water damage to their cave carving was beginning to seem like more than mere inconvenience. Perchance it had obscured crucial details that would have led them to their goal.

*Perhaps this is where our hunt finally ends,* Henri thought with crushing dejection. *Perhaps we have followed these ancient clues as far as they can take us, and the answers Signor di Bianchi seeks will remain forever out of reach.*

The possibility should have brought some measure of relief, given how her new marriage had deteriorated since leaving London. Instead, Henri found herself genuinely disappointed by the prospect of failure, not just because of the intellectual challenge the puzzle represented, but because solving it might have been the one thing that could have brought Gabriel back to her. The man who had seduced her with passion and promises in Calais, rather than this cold stranger who treated her like an unwelcome burden.

Gabriel, meanwhile, had become increasingly aloof as their search continued without success. The charming, attentive man who had swept her off her feet and convinced her to marry him seemed to have vanished entirely, replaced by this focused, monosyllabic investigator who barely acknowledged her presence unless her assistance was specifically required. Henri watched him move through the manor with his sketch, studying walls and architectural details with intense concentration while paying her no mind whatsoever.

*This is the man I married,* Henri realized with painful clarity. *Not the passionate lover from Calais, but this distant, secretive stranger who uses people for his own ends.*

When Gabriel headed toward what appeared to be a servants' staircase leading to the lower levels of the hall, Henri followed reluctantly, more out of habit than any genuine hope that they would find answers in the basement chambers. The narrow stone steps led to a network of service corridors and storage rooms that would have housed the army of servants required to maintain such a grand establishment.

Gabriel immediately began examining the walls with the same intense appraisal he had applied to the upper floors, running his hands along the stone surfaces and studying his sketch by lantern light. Henri watched him work for several minutes before her frustration finally overwhelmed her patience.

"Gabriel," she said, his name echoing in the confined space. "What exactly are you doing?"

"Looking," he replied without turning from his examination of a particular section of wall.

Henri's temper flared at his dismissive tone. "Looking for what, specifically?"

"Hidden spaces," Gabriel said, his attention still focused entirely on the stonework.

"And you expect to find them how?"

"Inconsistencies in the construction."

Henri stared at her husband's back, amazed by his ability to reduce their conversation to the absolute minimum number of words required to convey basic information. The man who had once spoken to her with such eloquence and wit now seemed incapable of stringing together a complete sentence in her presence.

"Gabriel," Henri said, taking on a sharp edge, "you promised you would tell me what this was all about once we solved the puzzle together."

"I said I might," Gabriel replied, finally turning to face her but offering no elaboration.

Henri's frustration rose like gunpowder that had been lit, and she grappled to find some semblance of self-control. Two weeks of disruption, days of mounting resentment, and hours of being treated like an unwelcome appendage to Gabriel's investigation had combined to create an explosive mixture that his casual dismissal had finally ignited.

"And I said I would give this marriage a try," Henri said, her voice rising despite her efforts to maintain composure. "And now I find myself thinking I might … not."

With that declaration, Henri turned on her heel and left the room, climbing the servants' stairs with angry stomping while her heart hammered against her ribs. She could hear Gabriel call her name behind her, but the sound only fueled her determination to put distance between herself and the man who had somehow managed to break her heart so thoroughly in such a short time.

Henri made her way through the manor's corridors blindly, her vision blurred by tears of anger and disappointment that she refused to let fall. She had been such a fool, allowing herself to believe that Gabriel's passion in Calais represented something real and lasting rather than merely a calculated strategy to secure her cooperation. She admitted to herself that she had stupidly fallen in love with a man who was fundamentally unobtainable, setting herself up for a life of dependence and heartbreak that would make her mother's widowhood seem pleasant by comparison.

*I should have listened to my instincts from the beginning,* Henri thought. *I should have recognized that a man who keeps so many secrets is incapable of the kind of honesty that real partnership requires. Romantic attachments make intelligent women act like fools.*

Henri had always prided herself on her independence, her ability to navigate the complex world of politics and society without needing masculine protection or guidance. Yet here she was, married to a man who treated her contributions as negligible and her presence as an inconvenience, trapped in a legal bond that she was beginning to suspect would prove far too constraining. She should have chosen passage to the Americas to start again over this doomed marriage.

*At least as a spinster, I had the respect of Uncle Reggie and his colleagues,* Henri reflected bitterly. *As Gabriel's wife, I am apparently an accessory to be deployed when needed and ignored when not.*

Henri had reached the main hall when she heard footsteps behind her, and for a moment her heart leaped with the hope that Gabriel had followed her, that perhaps her ultimatum had finally penetrated his self-absorbed focus and prompted him to address the fundamental problems in their relationship.

"Gabriel?" she called out, turning toward the sound.

But the figure that emerged from the shadows was not her husband. Henri found herself face-to-face with a gaunt, hollow-cheeked man whose pale eyes held a kind of fevered intensity that made her blood run cold. She recognized him immediately. The same man who had threatened her in Danbury's library, the menacing stranger willing to use violence to obtain the manuscript she had been examining.

Henri opened her mouth to scream, but the man moved with shocking speed, clamping a gloved hand over her mouth while his other arm wrapped around her waist with iron strength. Henri struggled desperately, trying to break free from his grip, but years of sedentary work as a secretary had not prepared her for combat against someone clearly experienced in violence.

"Quietly now, Miss Bigsby," the man whispered against her ear with the same cold menace she remembered from their first encounter. "Or rather, I should say Lady Trenwith, shouldn't I? Congratulations on your recent marriage, though I'm afraid the celebration may be rather short-lived."

Henri continued to fight against his hold, but the man was already dragging her toward what appeared to be a side entrance, moving in a determined manner that suggested he was accustomed to this sort of nefarious activity. Henri's mind raced with desperate thoughts of Gabriel somewhere in the basement chambers, completely unaware that the danger that had brought him into her life was now literally carrying her away from any hope of rescue.

*He will never even know what happened to me,* Henri realized with terrifying clarity as her captor maneuvered her through the doorway and into the bitter wind that swept across the clifftop. *He is so absorbed in his investigation that he probably will not notice I am gone until he needs me to discuss something.*

The irony was almost unbearable. After all her anger about Gabriel's failure to value her properly, Henri was about to disappear from his life entirely, taken by the very forces that had driven their quest from the beginning. As her captor dragged her away from Grimsfell Hall and toward whatever fate he had planned for her, Henri could only hope that Gabriel's guilt over losing her might finally prompt him to reveal the secrets that had remained locked in his heart throughout their brief, troubled marriage. Not to her, it would seem, but mayhap to some other future bride.

# CHAPTER 20

*"Wit you well, I loved you, and never other."*

**Sir Thomas Malory, *Le Morte d'Arthur***

* * *

Gabriel stood alone in the servants' corridor for several long minutes after Henri's footsteps had faded, staring at the spot where she had delivered her devastating ultimatum. The echo of her words reverberated in the confined space, each syllable cutting deeper than the last.

*"I find myself thinking I might ... not."*

For the first time in his adult life, Gabriel found himself completely paralyzed by emotion. The careful control that had defined his diplomatic career, the barriers he had constructed so meticulously over the years, crumbled in an instant as the full implications of Henri's declaration crashed over him like a winter storm.

*She is leaving me.*

A bolt of pure panic shot through his chest that was unlike anything he had experienced since childhood. All the rational arguments he might have marshaled about their marriage being a practical arrangement, about emotional attachments being dangerous liabilities, about the wisdom of maintaining professional distance—all of it evaporated in the face of one terrible truth.

*I am in love with Henri.*

Desperately, completely, irrevocably in love with the brilliant, stubborn, infuriating woman who had just walked out of his life because he had been too much of a coward to let her into his heart.

Gabriel sank against the stone wall, his legs suddenly unable to support him as waves of realization washed over him. Every moment of their journey together played through his memory with devastating clarity. Henri's excitement when they deciphered their first clue, her courage during their dangerous descent at Tintagel, her patient attempts to draw him out of his self-imposed isolation. She had been trying to build a real partnership, a genuine marriage, while he had been treating her like a colleague to be managed and controlled.

*My grandfather was wrong,* Gabriel thought with sudden, blazing clarity. *Uncle James was wrong. They shaped me into someone who cannot connect with another human being, someone so terrified of rejection that I reject others first.*

The old viscount's repulsion had haunted Gabriel's dreams for decades, those cutting words about weakness and unseemly emotion that had driven a five-year-old boy to lock away his heart and never let anyone close enough to hurt him again. But Henri had been different. Henri had seen past his fortified walls, had recognized the man behind them, and had been willing to fight for him.

And he had squandered it because he was too frightened

to take the chance that someone might actually care for him despite his flaws.

Gabriel forced himself to his feet, his mind racing with desperate plans. He had to find Henri, had to explain everything. He had to tell her that she was worth more to him than all the ancient mysteries in the world, that solving Horace's murder meant nothing if he lost her in the process.

Gabriel rushed through the manor's corridors, calling Henri's name and checking every room where she might have gone to calm herself after their argument. The main hall, the library, the morning room. All empty. As the minutes passed without any sign of her, Gabriel's panic began to transform into terror.

*Where could she have gone?*

Gabriel burst through the main entrance of Grimsfell Hall, his eyes scanning the courtyard for any sign of Henri's blue cloak or honey-brown hair. Their coachman looked up from tending the horses with mild surprise at Gabriel's obvious distress.

"M'lord? Something amiss?"

"My wife," Gabriel said breathlessly. "Have you seen Lady Trenwith leave the hall?"

The coachman shook his head with certainty. "No, m'lord. I've been here with the horses the whole while. Ain't seen her ladyship since the two of you went inside."

Gabriel felt his heart sink even further. If Henri had not left through the main entrance, where could she have gone? The hall was built on a cliff edge. Surely, she would not have attempted to leave on foot across such hostile terrain, especially not in her emotional state.

*Unless she is so desperate to get away from me that she is willing to risk anything.*

Gabriel raced back into the hall, his search now taking on a frantic quality as he checked rooms he had already examined, opened doors to chambers they had barely bothered to explore, called Henri's name until it echoed through the empty corridors. The silence that answered him was more terrifying than any response could have been.

It was only when Gabriel reached the ground-floor kitchen that he noticed something that made his blood run cold. The door leading to what appeared to be a service garden stood slightly ajar, and a cold draft was whistling through the gap. Gabriel knew with absolute certainty that he had not left that door open, and it was unlikely Henri would have ventured this way in such hostile weather.

Gabriel stepped through the doorway into what proved to be a well-maintained kitchen garden, one of the many areas around Grimsfell Hall that showed signs of ongoing care despite the building's empty solitude. But what he saw there made his worst fears crystallize into horrifying reality.

The neat rows of winter herbs had been trampled, plants uprooted and scattered across the gravel paths in patterns that spoke unmistakably of a struggle. Henri would never have caused such damage deliberately. She was too respectful of things, too careful in her movements to create such chaos accidentally.

*She has been taken.*

The realization hit Gabriel hard, driving all the air from his lungs and replacing it with a rage so pure and focused that it burned away every other thought. The mysterious forces that had been pursuing their manuscript had finally caught up with them. And Henri was paying the price for his failures.

Gabriel followed the trail of disturbance through the kitchen garden, his training in observation serving him well as he tracked the signs of passage across the uneven ground. Boot prints in the soft earth, broken plant stems, disturbed gravel. All pointing toward what appeared to be a second walled garden where the sound of voices carried on the wind.

Gabriel moved with the stealth he had learned during his most secretive missions, using the garden's layout to approach undetected. What he saw when he reached a position where he could observe the confrontation made his vision blur with fury.

Henri sat on a stone garden bench, her hands bound behind her back and her face pale but defiant. Standing over her was the same angular, sallow-skinned man who had threatened her in Danbury's library.

"I know you've learned something from that sketch," the blackguard was saying. "Tell me what you've discovered about the *Regis Aeterni*, and perhaps this unpleasantness can be concluded quickly."

Gabriel frowned in surprise. He had thought this man was of the *Regis Aeterni*. What had Horace written to him? The *Dominus*.

"I have told you already," Henri replied in a hoarse voice as if she had been screaming. She responded with magnificent stubbornness, steady despite her obvious fear. "We have not found anything of significance. The trail has gone cold."

Gabriel felt a surge of fierce pride at Henri's courage, even as his rage at her captor continued to build to blood-pounding levels. She was protecting their investigation even in the face of direct threat, showing the kind of loyalty and strength that he had been too blind to appreciate when it mattered most.

"Lady Trenwith," the man said with silky menace, "I'm afraid I don't believe you. Your husband has been far too persistent in his pursuit of this matter for it to have yielded nothing. Perhaps a little encouragement will improve your memory."

The man reached toward Henri with obvious malicious

intent, and Gabriel's famous diplomatic control finally shattered completely.

He had always been cool. Calm. Collected. Under every pressure. Some might say, emotionless.

But the sight of Henri being threatened by a scoundrel set off a primal rage, rising through his body like a tornado until he let out a barbaric growl, rushing forward to grab the villain by the scruff of his neck, causing him to release Henri in shock, and Gabriel slammed the fiend on the ground before grabbing him by the hair to thud his skull into the limestone rock. It was not the precision attack he had employed at Danbury's. It was blind fury until Gabriel felt Henri gripping his sleeve with her teeth and pulling back with all her strength to prevent a second slam, mumbling his muffled name.

Afraid he might hurt her, he relented, and the haze of red rage dissipated as he realized her attacker was moaning in dazed pain, but that she … she was well.

"Henri?" Gabriel gasped, hoarse from the primitive sounds that had torn from his throat during the attack.

Henri was staring at him with wide eyes, clearly shaken by the violence she had just witnessed. Gabriel had never let her see this side of him, the capacity for brutality that his prior military career had occasionally required. He feared she would be horrified by what he had just done, repulsed by the man he had revealed himself to be.

But instead of backing away, Henri leaned into him as Gabriel quickly untied her bonds, her body trembling with relief rather than revulsion.

"I thought …" Henri whispered against his chest. "I hoped you would come, but I was afraid …"

"I am here," Gabriel said fiercely, his arms coming around her with desperate possessiveness. "I am here, and I will never let anyone hurt you again. Henri, I need to tell you—"

"The manuscript," their attacker groaned from where he lay sprawled on the limestone, blood trickling from his scalp. "Where is the manuscript? I've come too far … sacrificed too much …"

Gabriel looked down at the man who had terrorized his wife, feeling that primal rage threatening to surface again. But Henri's presence in his arms reminded him that there were more important things than revenge. There would be time to deal with this threat properly once he had ensured Henri's safety and finally told her everything she deserved to know about why this investigation had mattered so much to him.

"Gabriel," Henri said quietly, searching his face with an intensity that made his heart race. "Before anything else happens, before we deal with … him … I need to know—"

Her question was interrupted by the sound of their attacker struggling to his feet, his pale eyes still burning with the fevered intensity. Gabriel moved to accost him before he could stand, quickly turning him over to plant a knee against the small of his back and grab hold of his wrists.

* * *

Henri followed Gabriel as he half-carried, half-dragged their dazed attacker back toward Grimsfell Hall, her mind still reeling from the violence she had just witnessed. She had seen glimpses of Gabriel's warrior instincts before, but nothing had prepared her for the primal fury that had erupted when he found her in danger. The controlled diplomat had vanished entirely, replaced by a man who would clearly kill to protect what he valued most.

*And apparently,* Henri thought with wonder, *what he values is me.*

Gabriel maneuvered their captive through the kitchen

door, depositing the man roughly on a wooden chair before binding his hands behind his back with his own cravat. Henri watched her husband work with growing admiration for his competence under pressure. Every movement was deliberate and controlled, suggesting considerable experience with such situations.

"Now then," Gabriel said once their prisoner was secured, his statement carrying the kind of cold authority that Henri imagined had served him well. "Perhaps you would care to explain why you have been pursuing us."

The gaunt man—Henri still did not know his name—looked up with pale eyes that burned with frustrated anger despite his obvious head injury. "You've no idea what you're interfering with," he said, his accent carrying traces of French that Henri had not noticed during their previous encounters.

"Then enlighten us," Gabriel replied coldly.

Henri pulled up another chair and settled herself where she could observe both men, fascinated by this glimpse into Gabriel's professional capabilities. She had seen him charm information from innkeepers and merchants, but this was different. This was interrogation, measured and menacing, by someone who clearly understood how to extract truth from unwilling subjects.

When the silence stretched on, Gabriel began to search around the kitchen. Eventually, he turned, holding a large butcher's knife, his expression so cold and purposeful it fairly took Henri's breath away. He stroked a gloved fingertip over the blade, his implication evident.

"My name is Alaric Devayne," the man said at last, his gaze fixed for several seconds on the gleaming blade. "I've spent the better part of two years pursuing references to something known as *Regis Aeterni*."

Gabriel's expression did not change, but Henri caught a

subtle shift in his posture that suggested the name meant something to him. "And what is your interest in this organization?"

Mr. Devayne's laugh was bitter and entirely without humor. "Organization? I'm not even certain it still exists. I found some old journals hidden away in a forgotten room at the Bodleian Library in Oxford. The ramblings of some long-dead scholar obsessed with Arthurian legends and a secret society who served the Eternal King."

Henri arched her brows. So this *Regis Aeterni*, Latin for Eternal King, was a reference to Arthur, then. Which explained their strange quest to old landmarks of his reign. The Bodleian Library was where any serious researcher would go to investigate medieval manuscripts and historical mysteries. If Alaric had been working there, he might well have encountered the same sources that had led Gabriel to his interest in the Malory manuscript.

"These journals," Gabriel asked carefully, "what did they tell you about *Regis Aeterni*?"

Henri realized that Gabriel did not seem surprised by the disclosure of the secret society, making her wonder just how much he already knew about this madness.

"Enough to know that they were supposedly the guardians of something infinitely valuable," Mr. Devayne replied, his fevered intensity returning as he spoke. "Something that has been hidden for centuries, waiting for the right person to claim it. The journals spoke of a powerful artifact, hidden away by this secret order until England has need of it again."

Henri exchanged a glance with Gabriel, recognizing the same mixture of skepticism and interest in his expression that she felt herself. King Arthur was the stuff of legend, but they had already followed a trail of very real clues to very real locations. Perhaps there was more truth to the old stories than either of them had initially believed.

"And you thought you could find this legendary artifact by pursuing the Malory manuscript?" Gabriel asked.

"The journals mentioned specific texts, specific clues that would lead to the hidden cache," Alaric said, desperation edging his reply. "Malory's work was supposed to be one of the keys. I've sacrificed everything! My position, my reputation, my future ... chasing this opportunity."

Henri found herself almost pitying the man, despite the terror he had caused her. There was a tragedy to his obsession, the way it had clearly consumed his life and driven him to increasingly desperate acts.

"You threatened my wife," Gabriel said, his tone growing colder. "Might you have done worse?"

Alaric's expression crumpled, and for the first time since Henri had encountered him, he looked genuinely remorseful rather than merely frustrated. "There was an old scholar in Oxford. Horace Pelham. He had access to a first edition of *Le Morte d'Arthur.*"

Henri saw Gabriel go very still, though his expression remained unchanged. The name clearly meant something to him, something important enough to cause such a reaction.

"I went to see him," Alaric continued, apparently unaware of Gabriel's response. "I thought I'd convince him to share his knowledge. But the old fool was stubborn, suspicious. He refused to discuss the book I was interested in, claimed he had never heard of *Regis Aeterni.*"

"So you killed him," Gabriel said with a deadly calm that made Henri's skin prickle with apprehension.

"It was an accident!" Alaric protested, his composure finally cracking completely. "I never intended for anyone to be hurt. I only wanted to search his study, to see what materials he might have hidden away. But he returned unexpectedly while I was there, and when he threatened to summon the authorities …"

Alaric trailed off, but Henri could fill in the rest of the story from Gabriel's expression. Whatever had happened in Horace Pelham's study, it had ended with an old scholar's death and this desperate man's flight into obsession.

"But you did not find what you needed in the book. Then you learned about the Danbury auction." Gabriel still spoke with that menacing calm.

"I thought it was providence," Alaric responded bitterly. "The very manuscript I needed, appearing at exactly the right moment. I was prepared to do whatever was necessary to obtain it."

Henri remembered the terror of that morning in Danbury's library, the way this man had been willing to use violence to get what he wanted. He had already killed before. She shuddered to think what might have happened if Gabriel had not arrived when he did.

Gabriel moved with fluid grace, to stare out the kitchen window at the darkening sky. Henri could see the tension in his shoulders, the way his hands clenched and unclenched as he processed what they had just learned.

"Gabriel," Henri said softly, recognizing that her husband needed a moment to regain his composure. "Should we send for the magistrate?"

Gabriel turned back to face her, and Henri was struck by the careful mask that had fallen over his features. The passionate man who had rescued her in the garden was gone, replaced once again by the controlled diplomat who revealed nothing of his inner thoughts.

"Yes," Gabriel said after a moment. "I will lock Alaric in the pantry and ask our coachman to return to town and bring back the proper authorities. Mr. Devayne will have much to answer for."

Once Mr. Devayne had been stowed in the windowless pantry, Gabriel moved toward the kitchen door, then paused and looked back at Henri. "Will you be all right here to stand guard for a few minutes? I need to give instructions to our coachman."

Henri nodded, though she felt a stab of disappointment at Gabriel's return to formal politeness. For a brief moment in the garden, she had glimpsed the man beneath. Now, faced with the revelation about this Horace Pelham's death, Gabriel was retreating behind his shields once again.

When he returned to the kitchen, he settled across from Henri. The silence between them stretched uncomfortably as her husband seemed to wrestle with thoughts he probably had no intention of sharing.

"Gabriel," Henri said finally, unable to bear the distance that had opened between them again. "Who was Horace Pelham to you?"

Gabriel's jaw tightened almost imperceptibly, but he did not answer immediately. Henri watched him struggle with the decision of whether to trust her with whatever painful truth lay behind his reaction to the old scholar's name.

"He was …" Gabriel began, then stopped, his habitual caution reasserting itself.

Henri felt her heart sink. Here they were again, with her on the verge of learning something meaningful only to watch him retreat into silence. She had hoped that her kidnapping, his dramatic rescue, might finally have broken through the walls he kept between them. But apparently, even the threat of losing her was not enough to overcome a lifetime of emotional barriers.

*Perhaps I was wrong to think he could change,* Henri thought with familiar disappointment. *Perhaps some people are simply incapable of the kind of openness that real marriage requires.*

But then Gabriel looked up and met her eyes directly, and

Henri saw something in his gaze that made her breath catch. Gone was the careful neutrality he usually maintained, replaced by a rawness that spoke to depths of feeling she had only glimpsed before.

"Henri," Gabriel said with a different quality than she had ever heard. "I need to tell you something, and I need you to understand that this is … it is difficult for me."

Henri nodded encouragingly, not daring to speak for fear of breaking whatever spell had prompted this moment of potential revelation.

"I am a private man," Gabriel continued, his words coming slowly as though each one required considerable effort. "I always have been. It has served me well in my career, allowed me to navigate dangerous situations without revealing information that could be used against me or against England."

He swallowed audibly, wetting his lips while she waited to hear what he needed to say.

"It is difficult …"

Gabriel's voice was raw, deep, and laced with reluctance, and he was clearly struggling with the words. Henri's breath froze in her lungs as she realized that she was about to hear from the inner man, the one who never spoke. This was not Gabriel's polished manners and practiced words. This was him attempting to talk from the hidden core he never revealed.

"To hope …"

He stopped again, and she wanted to coax him, but she was deathly afraid that if she interrupted him, she would never encounter another opportunity to learn what he was truly thinking. She did not dare move, did not breathe as she waited, not even daring to clench her fists in impatience. She held back every impulse as she strained to hear what he wished to say.

"That anyone like you … could …"

Henri steeled herself to keep her mouth shut. She fought against every character flaw she had ever possessed to remain silent.

*Let him finish his thought.*

Might she finally understand the complex puzzle that was her husband? Finally understand the man who hid in the shadows?

Gabriel exhaled heavily before speaking in a sudden rush as if a veritable dam were bursting.

"Love me in return."

And her heart shattered into a thousand shards as she finally comprehended the pain he disguised behind contrived charm and kind eyes. Something had broken her husband, had destroyed his self-confidence, but he was allowing her to see the wounded soul he was. Henri was awed by the trust he was placing in her, revealing his very heart, while daunted by the enormous responsibility of providing peace and support to a man who shouldered as much as he.

Until that moment she had not comprehended the full breadth of what it meant to be a partner, to be someone who helped lift the burden of another when it grew too heavy, but in that instant, she realized how much he needed her. Needed them. And it was as if she had been touched by grace itself to be offered such a vital role.

This was what marriage was about. This was what her twin had found with her husband. A true meeting of the minds. Of hearts. Solace from the troubles of life. Possibility of happiness, even in the face of danger.

Henri released a sob and rushed into his arms as he rose to receive her. "I do. I do love you, Gabriel! You are worthy and strong and so … so … so easy to love!"

Gabriel's arms came around her with desperate strength,

and Henri felt him trembling against her as years of barricaded emotions finally found release. She had seen Gabriel calm under pressure, charming in social situations, passionate in their intimate moments, but she had never seen him simply human, simply vulnerable, simply a man who needed to be loved despite his flaws.

"I have been such a fool," Gabriel whispered against her hair. "I nearly lost you because I was too afraid to trust that you might see something in me worth keeping."

"Never," Henri said fiercely, pulling back to look into his eyes. "You could never lose me, Gabriel. I fell in love with you in Calais, with your strength and your mystery and yes, even your stubborn refusal to let anyone close. I have been waiting for you to trust me with your heart ever since."

Gabriel cupped her face in his hands, his thumbs brushing away the tears that had spilled down her cheeks. "Then we have a lifetime to learn how to do this properly. To build something real together."

Henri smiled through her tears, feeling as though the ancient puzzle they had been solving was nothing compared to the mystery of Gabriel's heart that she was finally being permitted to unravel. "I want to spend the rest of my life discovering all the secrets of who you are."

As Gabriel leaned down to kiss her with a tenderness that spoke to new beginnings rather than desperate passion, Henri was overcome by happiness. This was their moment. They had found each other at last.

When their lips eventually parted, she rested her head against his chest and asked, "Will you tell me about Horace Pelham?"

# CHAPTER 21

*"With all joy of heart they loved together."*

**Sir Thomas Malory, *Le Morte d'Arthur***

* * *

FEBRUARY 10, 1822

Henri stirred slowly from the depths of sleep, her consciousness returning gradually like morning mist lifting from the shore. The now familiar weight of Gabriel's arm across her waist anchored her to wakefulness, though she kept her breathing deep and even, savoring these stolen moments before the demands of their day intruded upon the tender intimacy they had discovered.

The primary bedchamber at Grimsfell Hall caught the first pale light of dawn through tall casement windows, casting long shadows across the Persian carpet and mahogany furnishings. The room retained the grandeur of its origins while embracing more recent refinements. Brocade hangings, polished brass fixtures, and a marble fireplace, where the remains of last night's fire still glowed softly, decorated the space.

Gabriel's fingers traced lazy patterns along her shoulder, his touch light as a whisper but sending shivers of awareness through her entire being. His hand drifted lower with deliberate slowness, fingers splaying across her ribs before following the curve of her waist. Henri's breath caught as he explored just below her hipbone, his thumb drawing small circles that made her arch against him with unconscious need.

She turned in his arms, meeting his hazel eyes that held both tenderness and unmistakable hunger. The morning stubble along his jaw roughened his usually pristine appearance, making him look deliciously disheveled and entirely hers.

"Good morning," she murmured against his lips, her voice husky with sleep and want.

His response was wordless at first, expressed through the gentle pressure of his mouth on hers and the way his palms framed her face as if she were something precious and fragile. His kiss deepened gradually, his tongue tracing the seam of her lips until she opened for him with a soft sigh of surrender.

Yet Henri felt anything but fragile in his embrace. She felt powerful, alive with a fierce joy that made her bold enough to press her advantage. Her own palms began their exploration, trailing down the strong column of his throat to the broad expanse of his naked chest. She delighted in the way his muscles tensed beneath her caress, in the sharp intake of breath when her fingers found the sensitive hollow at the base of his throat.

"Henri," he groaned, her name like a prayer, his fingers tangling in her unbound hair as she pressed kisses along his collarbone.

Their lovemaking was different from the desperate passion of previous encounters. It was slower, deeper, filled with the luxury of time and privacy. Gabriel took his time worshipping her body with his palms and mouth, learning what made her gasp and what made her moan his name. When his lips found the sensitive spot where her neck met her shoulder, Henri felt herself melting beneath his attention, her body coming alive under his reverent caress.

She traced the old scar along his ribs, a reminder of dangers faced and survived, before her fingers moved lower to explore his hardening manhood, eliciting a response that made him grip the bed linens with white-knuckled intensity. The power she held over this controlled, careful man was intoxicating.

When Henri finally rose above him, her hair falling like a silk curtain around them both, Gabriel's palms settled on her hips with worshipful reverence. The pale morning light streaming through the casement windows painted his skin luminous, catching the flush that spread across his chest. She gloried in the way his breathing caught as she moved, in the way his grip tightened as if anchoring himself to earth.

"You are so beautiful," he whispered, his voice rough with emotion as his palms traced the curves of her body with infinite tenderness.

Henri leaned down to capture his lips in a kiss that spoke of possession and surrender in equal measure. The sensation of being joined with him, of moving together in perfect harmony, threatened to overwhelm her completely. She had never imagined such intimacy was possible. This complete fusion of body and spirit left no barriers between them.

Gabriel's palms guided her movements, his caress both

demanding and tender as they found their rhythm together. The ancient bed, solid as a ship and twice as old, bore witness to their joining without protest. Henri lost herself in the exquisite tension building between them, in the way Gabriel's gaze never left her face, in the breathless moments when the world narrowed to nothing but sensation and connection and the overwhelming rightness of being with him.

When release finally claimed them both, it was with an intensity that left Henri trembling over Gabriel's powerful form. They moved together through the waves of pleasure, each sensation magnified by their emotional connection. His palms stroked her back as she collapsed against him, her face buried in the curve of his neck as aftershocks rippled through her body.

When they finally stilled, breathing hard and limbs entwined, Henri pressed her face against Gabriel's shoulder and wished that they could stay like this forever. His arms tightened around her as if he loathed the thought of rising as much as she did, and she felt his lips press a soft kiss to the crown of her head.

"I love you," she whispered against his heated skin, the words escaping before she could stop them.

Gabriel's sharp intake of breath made her tense. They were still learning their way together, and he was still a private man endeavoring to share himself more openly. Then his palm cupped her face, tilting it up so he could meet her gaze.

"And I love you," he replied, his voice thick with emotion. "More than I ever thought possible."

An hour later, they made their way to the breakfast room where Mrs. Roskelly, the elderly housekeeper Gabriel had engaged along with the property, had laid out a proper morning meal. The woman was a treasure. She was discreet, efficient, and apparently untroubled by the unconventional arrangement of her temporary employers.

"The porridge is excellent," Henri observed, adding cream to her bowl while Gabriel examined correspondence that had arrived with the morning post. Alaric Devayne had long since been removed by the magistrate and his men days earlier, and she and Gabriel had settled in to the manor.

"Mrs. Roskelly mentioned she has been caring for Grimsfell for nigh on forty years," Gabriel replied, setting aside a letter from his contact at the Foreign Office. "Her words, not mine. She knows every stone of this place, which is fortunate now that I have rented the manor for the rest of the winter."

Henri paused, her spoon halfway to her mouth. "The entire winter?"

Gabriel's smile was slightly sheepish. "I thought we might need time to properly investigate. The clues in the rubbing point specifically to this location, and I suspected we would require more than a brief afternoon visit to uncover whatever secrets Matteo di Bianchi hid here."

"That must have cost a considerable sum."

"Worth every penny if it helps us solve the mystery." Gabriel spread butter on his toast with careful precision. "Besides, I find I rather enjoy waking up beside you in a proper bed instead of cramped inn rooms. This is time for ourselves before we take up the mantle at Trenwith Abbey."

Henri felt heat rise in her cheeks but could not suppress her smile. "You are terribly wicked, you know."

"Only when inspired by exceptional company. But we will have company soon, so our wickedness will be curtailed."

After breakfast, they retrieved the cave rubbing and Gabriel's measuring instruments from their room. The morning light streaming through the library's stained-glass windows cast jeweled patterns across the floor, and Henri found herself studying the way the colored light played across the ancient books and carved woodwork. They had searched multiple rooms over the past two days to possibly match the window in the clue to one in the manor, and had decided to re-examine this room of books with more patience this morning.

"The four-paned window," Gabriel said, consulting the detailed drawing he had made from the original. "Look at the proportions here. The width, the height, the way the central mullion divides the space."

Henri followed his gaze to the magnificent stained-glass window that dominated the library's east wall. The glass itself was newer than the Tudor frame, likely installed during recent renovations, but the underlying structure matched the rubbing with remarkable precision.

"It is the same window," she breathed. "But how could Matteo have known about renovations that would not happen for three centuries?"

Gabriel was already moving toward the built-in shelving that flanked the window, his measuring tape extended. "Perhaps he did not. Perhaps the window frame itself was the constant, and he counted on later inhabitants maintaining the basic structure."

"Or those inhabitants knew to maintain it," Henri mused.

He worked conscientiously, comparing his notes mapping out the manor to the physical reality of the room. Henri watched him with growing excitement as the pieces began to align.

"Here," Gabriel said suddenly, running his hands along the wooden backing of a particular shelf. "The proportions of the surrounding rooms suggest there should be more space behind this section, between here and the morning room beyond."

Henri joined him, studying the ornate carving that decorated the shelf's backing. Vines and flowers intertwined in typical Tudor fashion, but as her gaze adjusted to the patterns, she began to notice familiar shapes concealed within the design.

"Gabriel, observe here." Her finger traced a circular motif partially concealed by carved leaves. "It is the same circle we discovered at the altar stone."

Gabriel's breath caught as he followed her indication. The circle was there, subtle but unmistakable, and below it—

"The circle and crucifix," he said, but there was a note of uncertainty. "No, wait. Examine the proportions. The vertical element is too narrow, too tapered."

Henri leaned closer, studying the carving with fresh perspective. It was in the most pristine condition of all the carvings they had encountered and she could see Gabriel was right. What appeared at first glance to be a cross had something different about its lower portion. The vertical line did not end bluntly like a traditional crucifix but tapered to a distinct point.

"It is a sword," she declared. "The pommel and crossguard disguised as the top of a crucifix, but that is definitely a blade point below."

Gabriel nodded grimly. "And notice how much sharper the carving is here compared to the weathered stones we discovered at the altar and the castle. This was maintained far better."

He pressed down firmly on the wooden backing where the sword symbol was carved. For a moment, nothing happened. Then, with a hushed grinding sound of well-oiled mechanisms, the entire shelf section swung inward like a door.

Beyond lay shadows.

"The more we explore this strange house, the more it is

clear that the servants know more than they will speak of. This property shows signs of maintenance despite its shrouded state and has more servants ready to step in than I would expect for such a remote location."

Henri nodded. She had been thinking the same thing. The dust was minimal, local maids came in weekly under Mrs. Roskelly's supervision, and the housekeeper herself apparently worked here two or three days a week when it was not rented out. Full time when it was. But neither she nor the caretaker lived here. Keeping on so many servants for an empty building was exceptionally diligent for an absent master, not to mention a bit of an expensive undertaking. But their suspicions could not be confirmed one way or the other when the solicitor and servants all refrained from answering any questions about the ownership. They would have to pursue its secrets without assistance because its loyal retainers were friendly but unhelpful in this regard.

Gabriel retrieved an oil lamp from the library's reading table during Henri's examination of the concealed space. The flame cast dancing shadows as they stepped through the secret entrance, revealing a chamber unlike anything Henri had ever seen.

The walls on both sides were entirely covered with mirrors. They were not the silvered glass of modern manufacture, but older reflective surfaces that appeared to shimmer with their own radiance. The chamber stretched much farther than should have been possible given the manor's layout, and at the far end stood an imposing pipe organ, its ebony wood gleaming in the lamplight.

High overhead, thin shafts of daylight filtered down through what appeared to be concealed grillwork set into the walls near the ceiling. This was clever architecture that would be invisible from outside the manor during the day, providing just enough natural illumination to keep the chamber from complete shadow.

"It is a chapel of sorts," Henri whispered, her words echoing strangely in the elongated space. "Or was meant to be one."

Gabriel raised the lamp higher, studying the mirrored walls with fascination. "Observe how the reflections multiply infinitely. Every surface reflects every other surface. It creates the illusion of endless space."

As they proceeded deeper into the chamber, Henri noticed text carved into the stone along the base of one mirrored wall. Latin words, but arranged in a way that appeared wrong somehow.

"*snoitcelfeR fo llaH,*" she read aloud, frowning at the unfamiliar arrangement.

Gabriel held the lamp closer, then peered up at the mirror directly opposite. In the reflection, the reversed Latin text read normally.

"*Hall of Reflections,*" he translated. "Clever. The message only becomes comprehensible when viewed in the mirror."

They approached the organ with cautious reverence. The instrument was magnificent, easily the equal of anything Henri had encountered in London's finest churches. The wood showed no signs of age or neglect, and when she tentatively pressed one of the keys, the note that emerged was pure and clear, reverberating through the chamber.

"How is this possible?" Henri breathed, playing a simple scale. Each note rang true, as if the organ had been tuned yesterday rather than sitting concealed in a sealed chamber for decades or centuries.

Gabriel studied the arched stone ceiling overhead. "The acoustics are flawless. This chamber was designed specifically for music. And notice how dry the air is. There is some kind of ventilation system keeping moisture out."

Henri continued to explore the organ's range, marveling at the instrument's responsiveness. The sound appeared to transform the chamber, converting it from a mysterious concealed space into a sacred place.

"There must be more clues here," she said, her fingers stilling on the keys. "Matteo would not have led us to such an elaborate hiding place just to show us a secret chamber."

Gabriel nodded, raising his lamp to examine the mirrored walls more closely. "The sketch showed specific symbols around the organ. We need to discover what corresponds to those markings."

As if summoned by their words, the multiple reflections in the mirrors appeared to shift and dance, creating an almost hypnotic effect. Henri experienced the strangest sensation that they were being observed by countless versions of themselves, all searching for the same elusive truth.

The Hall of Reflections guarded its secrets closely, but Henri could sense they were on the verge of a breakthrough. Whatever Matteo di Bianchi had concealed here, they were finally close to uncovering it.

* * *

GABRIEL STUDIED the ancient organ keys beneath his fingertips, dappled with the patina of centuries and countless devoted palms. The Hall of Reflections had revealed its architectural secrets readily enough, but the true mystery remained as elusive as smoke. He glanced toward Henri, who knelt beside their spread collection of sketches and rubbings, her dark brow furrowed in concentration.

The lamplight caught the copper threads in her honey-brown hair as she traced the obscured portion of their cave carving copy with one delicate finger. Gabriel recognized the particular quality of her frustration from their journey together. It was the controlled frustration of a mind accustomed to solving complex puzzles through sheer determination.

"The water damage in the cave," Henri said finally with a note of defeat. "It is too extensive. We cannot make out what the notes are in the surrounding panes. Without that, we cannot follow the clue."

She looked up at him, and Gabriel saw both fierce determination and despair warring in her expression. "She waits where the grim fell sings. Let thy hands match hers. But how can we match what we cannot see?"

Her tone, the way hope and irritation intertwined, moved Gabriel more than he had anticipated. In his years of diplomatic service, he had learned to separate emotion from duty, to view setbacks as tactical problems requiring alternative approaches. But Henri's disappointment felt personal, as if her failure were somehow his own.

Without conscious thought, Gabriel crossed the chamber and drew her into his arms. The familiar weight of her against his chest, the way she instinctively leaned into his strength, arrowed affection straight into his heart. His mouth found hers in a kiss that spoke of comfort and shared purpose, of two minds working in perfect harmony toward a common goal.

When they parted, Gabriel tilted his head back to meet her gaze directly, his hands firm on her shoulders. Years of commanding men in the horror of battle had taught him the value of unshakable confidence, especially when facing seemingly insurmountable obstacles.

"Listen to me," he declared with the quiet authority he had learned to project during the most critical moments of negotiation. "We have solved every puzzle Matteo set before us precisely because we work together. Your eye for detail, my knowledge of codes, your intuitive leaps, my systematic approach. Together, we see what neither could alone."

Gabriel watched Henri's expression begin to shift, her disappointment giving way to hope. It struck him how much he had come to depend on that particular transformation. He treasured the moment when her eager mind seized upon a new possibility and began working at it with relentless focus.

"Each clue has led seamlessly to the next, has it not?" Gabriel continued. "The sketch to Roseberry Topping, the altar stone to the castle, the castle's symbols to this very chamber. Matteo was brilliant, but he was also practical. He would not have created a quest that could be derailed by a problem as common as water damage to ancient stone."

"You think there is another way?" Henri asked, though Gabriel could already see her mind beginning to work at the problem from new angles.

Gabriel pulled her closer, delighting in the way her smaller form fit against him, in the trust implicit in her willingness to be held and comforted. "I think that a man clever enough to encipher a three-hundred-year treasure hunt would have contingencies. The answer is here, in this chamber. We simply need to discover where he concealed it."

His certainty surprised him. Gabriel had learned through bitter experience not to make promises he could not keep, yet their partnership, the way they had successfully navigated each previous challenge, made him believe absolutely in their ability to solve this one as well.

As if drawn by the same magnetic force that had governed all their discoveries, they moved back toward the library, their attention focused on reaching their bedchamber with purposeful intent. Gabriel marveled at how natural it had become, this intertwining of intellectual challenge and physical desire as they ran up the stairs together. Once they reached the bedchamber down a long hall, their coupling was urgent, driven by the intoxicating combination of shared frustration and absolute faith in their partnership before they fell asleep in each other's arms.

Gabriel stirred first, his military experience making him sensitive to any sound that did not belong to the natural rhythms of Grimsfell Hall. The fire in the grate had burned low, casting only the faintest orange glow across the cool chamber. Beside him, Henri's breathing remained deep and even, her face peaceful in sleep.

Then he heard it again. The faint but unmistakable sound of organ music drifting through the halls.

Gabriel's body went still with the kind of absolute attention that had kept him alive through years of clandestine work. This must be the organ they had discovered in the Hall of Reflections. The sound came from deep within the very walls, harmonizing with the wintry winds that whistled over the Cornish cliffs with haunting persistence.

His hand found Henri's shoulder, giving her the gentlest shake that would bring her awake without startling her. "Henri," he whispered. "Wake up."

She came awake instantly.

"What is it?" she asked, alert despite having been pulled from deep sleep.

"Listen."

They lay perfectly still in the darkness, and Gabriel felt Henri's grip tighten on his arm as the melody became audible in the far distance. It was hauntingly beautiful, played with a skill that spoke of long practice and deep reverence. The music resounded from everywhere and nowhere, as if the very stones of Cornwall were singing.

"The grim fell sings," Henri breathed with wonder.

Gabriel nodded, reluctant to rise. "Shall we go see who it is?"

This adventure, he realized with a mixture of anticipation and satisfaction, was far from over.

Henri curled into his side with a contented smile, her naked body raising his interest, along with other parts of him. "It is late, and it is warm here in the bed. Let the grim fell keep its secrets for one more night."

# EPILOGUE

*"Much they marvelled, yet some were not pleased."*

**Sir Thomas Malory, *Le Morte d'Arthur***

* * *

FEBRUARY 15, 1822

The sound of the carriage wheels on the gravel drive announced their visitors before Mrs. Roskelly's knock on the library door. Henri glanced up from the sketches she and Gabriel had been studying in anticipation of their guests' arrival.

"Signor di Bianchi has arrived, milady," Mrs. Roskelly announced, her weathered features bright with curiosity. She likely had never encountered Italians before in such a remote part of England. "Along with two gentlemen companions. I have shown them to the morning room."

Henri exchanged a meaningful glance with Gabriel, who

was already rolling up their latest sketches. They had sent word to Signor di Bianchi several days prior, describing their discovery of the concealed chamber but deliberately omitting the more mystifying details until they could explain them in person.

"Excellent," Henri replied, smoothing her morning dress and ensuring her hair was properly pinned. "Please inform them we shall join them directly."

As they made their way through the corridors of Grimsfell Hall, Henri found herself both eager and apprehensive about Signor di Bianchi's reaction to their discoveries. The Italian art trader had invested so much hope in this quest, so much faith in the possibility that his ancestor's legacy would finally be revealed. She hoped their findings would not disappoint him.

Gabriel opened the morning room door, and Henri stepped through to find Signor di Bianchi rising from a chair beside the fireplace. His dark eyes held the same energy she remembered from their first meeting, though now tinged with barely contained excitement. Beside him stood two gentlemen she recognized immediately, both of the Scott family.

"Lady Trenwith," Signor di Bianchi said, advancing with outstretched hands and a warm smile. "How delighted I am to see you well. And Lord Trenwith, of course." He clasped Henri's fingers briefly before turning to Gabriel with high interest. "Your message spoke of extraordinary discoveries? I confess I have barely slept since receiving it."

"Signor di Bianchi, we are equally eager to share what we have uncovered thus far," Henri replied, returning his smile with genuine pleasure. She turned to greet her neighbors. Or rather, now that she was wed, her mother's neighbors. "And Mr. Angelo Scott, Mr. Nicholas Scott, what a surprise to find you here."

Angelo Scott stepped forward, brimming with youthful energy. "Lady Trenwith, Lord Trenwith, what a delight! We were with Lorenzo to help him in his search for you when you did not come back from the Danbury estate. He desired friends he could trust not to gossip while we endeavored to find you. When he learned you had uncovered something, he asked us to join him."

Nicholas Scott, leaning slightly on his walking stick, offered a nod of his head. Henri and he had known each other many years as neighbors but never conversed much. It was Nicholas's brother and her twin who had been inseparable.

"Miss Big—I mean, Lady Trenwith. I hope Cornwall is treating you well. Though I suspect it cannot be more challenging than my current company." He cast a pointed glance at Angelo, who was practically vibrating with enthusiasm beside him. Henri immediately understood the family dynamics. Angelo's zest contrasted sharply with Nicholas's more guarded manner, while both clearly respected Signor di Bianchi's pursuit on behalf of his family enough to accompany him on this journey.

"Angelo has time on his hands to assist," Signor di Bianchi explained, "and Nicholas brings a practical perspective that helps keep our endeavors grounded in reality."

"How flattering," Nicholas Scott remarked dryly. "I have been reduced to the voice of reason. Clearly, my reputation has suffered irreparable damage."

"Then you shall not be disappointed," Gabriel said with quiet confidence. "What we have discovered defies simple explanation. Perhaps it would be best if we showed you directly."

Signor di Bianchi's excitement was palpable as they led the small party through the manor toward the library. "I have dreamed of this moment for so many years," he confided to

Henri as they walked. "To finally see my ancestor's work, to understand what drove him to such elaborate secrecy. It will vindicate everything I have believed about his genius."

Henri smiled politely, but she was worried that Signor di Bianchi would not be as ecstatic with their finding once he saw it. She exchanged another glance with Gabriel, who appeared to share her concern about managing the Italian's expectations.

In the library, Gabriel demonstrated the mechanism that opened the concealed entrance, and Henri watched the visitors grow ever more inquisitive as the shelf swung inward to reveal the hidden chapel. Signor di Bianchi actually gasped aloud, his hands trembling slightly as he peered into the shadowed space beyond.

"Magnificent," he murmured, his professional composure giving way to genuine awe. "The engineering alone is extraordinary. My ancestor apprenticed with da Vinci himself, which was where he learned these engineering arts. To maintain such a secret for three centuries ..."

"The craftsmanship is remarkable," Nicholas added with grudging admiration, clearly appreciating the mechanical ingenuity despite his reserved manner.

"Wait until you see the chamber itself," Henri said, lighting an additional lamp to supplement Gabriel's illumination.

They proceeded through the entrance, and Henri heard Angelo's sharp intake of breath as the Hall of Reflections revealed itself in the lamplight. The mirrors caught and multiplied the flames, creating an almost supernatural effect that never failed to impress.

"*Madonna mia,*" Signor di Bianchi breathed, his Italian echoing strangely in the elongated space. "It is like stepping into another world entirely."

He moved immediately to examine the mirrors more

closely, assessing their age and construction. "These are not modern silvered glass," he announced after a moment. "The reflective quality suggests polished metal, possibly bronze or silver amalgam. Renaissance techniques, certainly."

"And the organ," Nicholas added, approaching the magnificent instrument with careful steps that accommodated his injured leg. "The craftsmanship is exquisite. This represents months, perhaps years of skilled work. Though I confess I am curious why anyone would go to such elaborate lengths to hide a musical instrument. Was Matteo di Bianchi perhaps lacking an ear for music and wished to spare his neighbors?"

Lorenzo di Bianchi, however, had grown strangely quiet. Henri watched him with increasing concern as he walked slowly about the chamber, inspecting the mirrors and examining every surface. His initial excitement gave way to disappointment.

"Signor di Bianchi?" Henri ventured after several minutes of silence. "What do you think of your ancestor's creation?"

He paused in his circuit of the chamber, his shoulders gradually slumping as the reality of what he was seeing settled upon him. When he finally turned to face them, his expression was morose.

"Please, all this formal talk. My friends call me Lorenzo."

"Is it not beautiful, Lorenzo?" Henri prompted, gesturing toward the infinite reflections and the masterful acoustics of the space.

Lorenzo shrugged, the gesture encompassing a lifetime of deflated dreams. "It is pretty and frivolous. Where is his mastery? His Sistine Chapel? His ode to the gods? Not a single brushstroke of his genius."

The words fell into the chamber like stones dropped into still water, creating ripples of uncomfortable silence. Henri felt her heart sink as she realized the depth of Lorenzo's disappointment. He had expected paintings, frescoes, artistic masterpieces that would establish his ancestor's reputation for posterity. Instead, they had uncovered an elaborate architectural puzzle, beautiful in its own right but devoid of the visual art that he sought.

Angelo Scott cleared his throat diplomatically, attempting to console his friend. "Perhaps there are other chambers, other discoveries yet to be made. This could merely be the beginning."

"Yes," Nicholas Scott added. "The complexity of this room suggests there might be additional layers to uncover. Perhaps the next chamber will contain nothing but elaborate coat hooks, and we can marvel at Matteo's genius for domestic organization."

But Lorenzo was already shaking his head, his disappointment too profound for such easy consolation or Nicholas's attempt at levity. Henri watched him with growing sympathy, understanding finally how much he had invested in this quest, how completely his expectations had been shaped by a lifetime of believing in his ancestor's artistic greatness.

The Hall of Reflections, magnificent though it was, reflected back only Lorenzo's broken dreams. Fortunately, there was, as Angelo Scott had suggested, more to be discovered if they could find a way to follow the damaged clue.

* * *

**Uncover the secrets of Grimsfell Hall when Angelo Scott chases midnight symphonies and learns that sometimes love grows in the darkest of places.**

# AFTERWORD

Henri's character draws inspiration from the remarkable Lady Hester Stanhope, who, in the early nineteenth century, served as private secretary to her uncle, Prime Minister William Pitt the Younger.

Intelligent, forthright, and unafraid to move in political and diplomatic circles dominated by men, Lady Hester proved herself an able administrator and a keen observer of human nature. Her work at the heart of government gave her access to the inner workings of power, while her wit and confidence allowed her to hold her own in conversations with influential statesmen of her day.

It is this blend of intellect, capability, and quiet audacity that I sought to capture in Henri's role as an indispensable aide and strategist.

Sir Thomas Malory remains one of history's most enigmatic literary figures. Depending on which side of the British aristocracy was describing him, Malory was either a profligate criminal or a political prisoner caught in the turbulent Wars of the Roses. What we know for certain is that he wrote *Le Morte d'Arthur* in Middle English while languishing in Newgate Prison, originally entitled *"The Hoole Book of Kyng Arthur and of His Noble Knyghtes of the Rounde Table."*

Before Malory's epic work, Arthurian legends were scattered across French, Welsh, and English sources. Malory unified these disparate tales into a single, continuous narrative of King Arthur's rise and fall before his own death at Newgate Prison in 1471. His masterpiece became the definitive English version of the Arthurian legend and inspired countless retellings, from Tennyson's poetry to modern fantasy novels.

One of his original handwritten manuscripts, the Winchester manuscript, is preserved in the British Library, offering scholars invaluable insight into his original intentions and the evolution of his work. I took some liberties with my ciphers from the manuscript, but they are based on the Winchester manuscript.

Roseberry Topping, that distinctive conical hill in North Yorkshire, has indeed been associated with Arthurian legend in local folklore. Its striking silhouette and ancient burial sites in the surrounding area have sparked tales of sleeping kings and buried treasures for centuries.

The Fallen Chapel mentioned in this story is fictional, though such forgotten religious sites dot the Yorkshire landscape. Many medieval chapels fell into ruin after the Dissolution of the Monasteries, leaving only mysterious foundations and local legends in their wake.

Tintagel Castle in Cornwall remains one of the most atmospheric Arthurian sites in Britain. Perched dramatically on the rugged Cornish coast, it has been associated with Arthur's conception and birth since Geoffrey of Monmouth's twelfth-century writings. The medieval castle ruins and the recently discovered sixth-century settlement beneath them continue to fuel speculation about the historical Arthur.

Merlin's Cave at Tintagel is very real, accessible at low tide beneath the castle headland. The natural sea cave has inspired centuries of legends about the great wizard, and visitors today can still experience the otherworldly atmosphere that sparked such enduring myths. The cave where Henri and Gabriel discover the carved clue is fashioned after such a cave but is fictional.

Grimsfell Hall is entirely fictional but inspired by the many Tudor and Jacobean houses scattered throughout Cornwall and Yorkshire. These ancient buildings, with their hidden passages, priest holes, and architectural mysteries, provided the perfect inspiration for a family determined to hide their secrets across the centuries.

The *Regis Aeterni*, a.k.a the Eternal King, conspiracy that threads through this series is my own invention, but it draws inspiration from the genuine secret societies, political networks, and scholarly circles that flourished during the turbulent centuries between the Renaissance and the Regency.

If you enjoyed this book, I would be truly grateful if you would consider leaving an honest review. It makes a world of difference in helping new readers discover the series.

And, if you are wondering what happens next, the hunt for Matteo's treasure trove of art continues at the mysterious manor house, where organ music sounds through the halls and there might be a ghost living in the walls. After all, someone must be playing those ivory keys that haunt the midnight hours.

***The Phantom Romance*** **will be the third book in the Inconvenient Ventures series, in which Angelo Scott is about to discover that sometimes the most beautiful mysteries are the ones that you find living in the dark.**

# ALSO BY NINA JARRETT

## INCONVENIENT BRIDES

**Five daring heroines. Five unexpected heroes. One scandalous series of love, redemption, and happily ever afters.**

In this sweeping Regency redemption arc, five flawed men seek forgiveness and love—with the help of five extraordinary women. Each story stands alone, but together they form a powerful tale of legacy, loyalty, and the courage to change.

Book 1: The Duke Wins a Bride

Book 2: To Redeem an Earl

Book 3: My Fair Bluestocking

Book 4: Sleepless in Saunton

Book 5: Caroline Saves the Blacksmith

## INCONVENIENT SCANDALS

**A tangled murder mystery to unravel one romance at a time.**

In the elegant world of *Inconvenient Brides*, five couples find love in the most unlikely places—while uncovering a mystery that could ruin them all. Each book delivers a satisfying, standalone Regency romance, but together they unravel a shocking murder that shakes the nobility. Only by the final page will the full truth come to light.

Book 1: Long Live the Baron

Book 2: Moonlight Encounter

Book 3: Lord Trafford's Folly

Book 4: The Trouble With Titles

Book 5: Lord of Intrigue

## INCONVENIENT VENTURES

**Five unlikely couples unlock a legendary secret.**

In the glittering world of *Inconvenient Brides*, five unexpected couples are swept into a thrilling race to unravel a centuries-old secret. From coded paintings to Arthurian relics, each courtship reveals another piece of a legendary puzzle—one with the power to shake the British Empire … or crown new heroes.

Book 1: The Courtship Trap

Book 2: The Hidden Lord

Book 3: The Phantom Romance

Book 4: The Rented Heart

Book 5: The Beloved Escapade

# ALSO BY ROGUE PRESS

Discover these Gothic Regency romances from Claire Karloff!

## MIDNIGHT BRIDES

**Regency Romance with Bite!**

Beneath the silk and satin of Regency England ... something stirs.

From Claire Karloff comes a brand-new collection of romantic tales where genteel drawing rooms hide ancient secrets, and true love must face the most chilling of curses. In this sweeping new series, intrepid heroines and haunted heroes collide in tales of mystery, longing, and redemption. Where the monsters are real, but so is the hope of a happy ending.

Duke Immortal

Earl Alpha

Viscount Unseen

## BRIDES & MONSTER HUNTERS

Coming soon ... **The Duke's War of the Realms**

Made in the USA
Middletown, DE
15 February 2026

28680155R00198